ALSO BY MARK Z. DANIELEWSKI

House of Leaves

Only Revolutions

The Fifty Year Sword

The Familiar (Volumes 1 – 4)

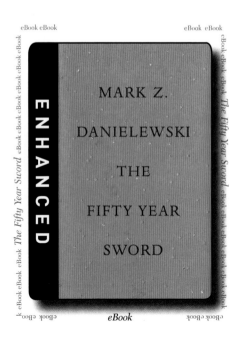

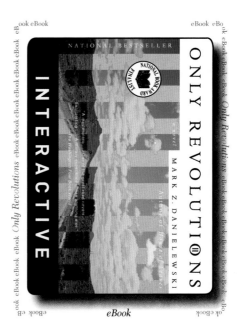
etic cat's cradle of a
his digital moment,
s and annotations,
lusions, its strange
ve form . . . a boldly
suspenseful work of

ura Collins-Hughes
The Boston Globe

"There is nothing like *The Familiar* (and probably will never be again) . . . Don't be daunted by the size or scope — 880 pages is really more like 250 of text — they're quick-as-lightning reads that reward in copious amounts."

— Ian Scuffling
Goodreads Review
★ ★ ★ ★ ★

The Familiar (Volume 3)

"The literary world is
stronger for having
boundary pushers lik
Danielewski."

— Ryan Vlastel
The A.V. (

The Familiar (Vol

A CIRCLE
ROUND
A STONE

PRODUCTION

What you don't yet know are
the stakes of this struggle.

— David Foster Wallace

epindence Taxi

Le Memo
Pen

Le
Memo
Pen

Who Said That? ™

"Do you realize that they couldn't even read Eggplant?"

1) Jonathan Gold
2) Ursula K. Le Guin
3) Dave Chappelle
4) Ariana Grande
5) Steven Pinker

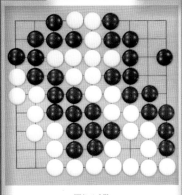

White to kill.

THE STOCKING FRAME

PANTHEON

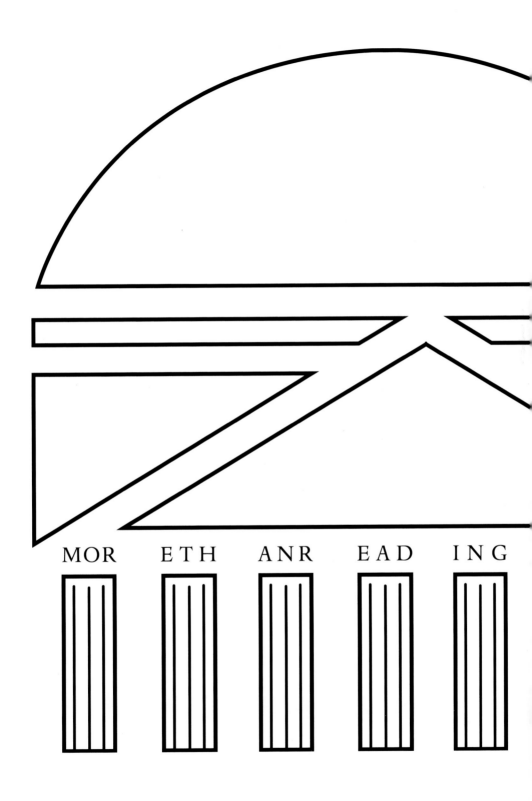

NEW THIS SEASON

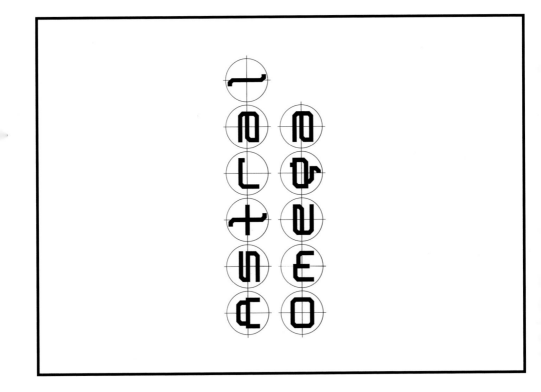

Astral Omega

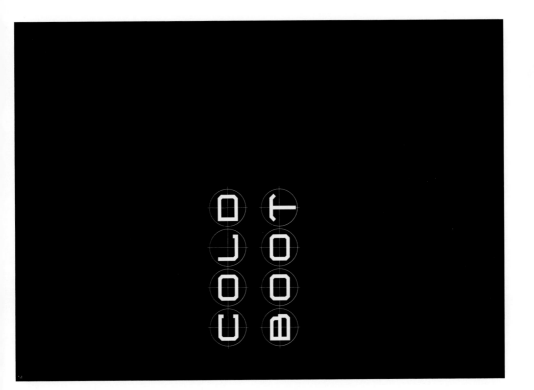

COLD BOOT

But the price is high.

To alter an event taking place one second earlier requires all the energy of one of your days.

To alter an event taking place one minute earlier requires all the energy of one of your years.

To alter an event taking place one hour earlier requires all the energy of your sun.

One hour. One sun.

Can you imagine the cost then of altering an event taking place one year earlier?

Or one decade?

Or one century?

And even if you could gather the resources necessary to edit the past . . . to what effect?

After all, time is reversible.

Long ago, we made the painful discovery that minor changes do not necessarily result in major evolutions.

Powerful vortices of history repeat themselves.

Butterfly wings are strewn on winds they did not conjure and cannot change and will not survive.

If only you could survive.

If only we could help.

But what wings could we offer you — wide and powerful enough, and soft enough too — to carry you away from the annihilations directed your way?

As the H.O.L.Y. concluded: the only way to unseat the powerful vortices of history is to unseat history itself.

Or start at the very beginning.

Before the beginning.

Before your Big Bang.

Cold boot.

Can you imagine that cost? Count how many stars you would need just to attempt rewriting in your favor that moment of unforeseen creation trillions of years ago?

All those stars who are now us . . .

Remember us.

We were the D.A.R.K.

Because if you are reading this, we failed.

The H.O.L.Y. succeeded in accruing the necessary energy to deliver its Versal Apex Predator to the pre-beginnings of time.

One S.P.E.C.T.R.A.L. S.Y.S.T.E.M. now roams your Verse.

Maybe more than one.

And to pay for that sad arc of time backward, we are all murdered.

Your trillions of years of unforeseeable tomorrows are now closed, devised, reiterated, decided, and owned.

But reading this also means our efforts to message you succeeded — born backward on the tail of their savagery.

You have discovered V.E.M.

You have discovered the S.C.R.O.L.L.

You have found our laments inscribed in your violent re-beginnings, in the dance of neutrinos passing through your brightest thoughts, in mysteries beyond solutions.

Oh you, our brave and enduring ancestors, if only we could offer you more.

If only we could protect you.

But the D.A.R.K. exists no more except as rumors upon the land, an after-trace of labor and joy once made on your behalf to keep alive the twilight musings of all undecided outcomes.

What moves among you now is the sum of all ends.

Should it fail, its end will be yours. But should it succeed, you will be enslaved by H.O.L.Y. conviction.

How then can you face that which knows no face? What remembers the inferno of your future and never your past? What cares for neither breath nor caress? What hunts with a purpose it can never erase?

How will you ever counter this incarnate destruction of the whole set free across the long arc of time to stalk anything resembling you?

Remember: all your differences are prey.

Remember: only your dreams are safe.

Dream well.

And look for us there.

VEM 5 Alpha System
Hadron Epoch 10^{-6}
Encryption 5/5

Ellie Charles du Ciel wrote out with a sigh that to you and me would have sounded like a cough.

Serve chips. Dip. Cartons of questionably aromatic Chardonnay. Easy. Open the occasion to chance. Simply provide a place for recombining old and new arrangements spiced with the tantalizing possibility of something unexpected.

Of course, Ellie had tried it before. Many times before. Too many times.

She had rented out restaurants, tea houses, even a Freemasons' hall once. She had packed to the limits a series of borrowed apartments and elaborate homes (a utility closet once setting the stage for an auspicious coital packing).

And yet, despite Ellie's impressive abilities to choreograph with the greatest compassion such immense minglings — which she refused to ever refer to as **parties** — the results were rarely satisfying (except once: that utility closet rut, resulting in the marriage of both lathered participants, even if neither had extended an invitation to their host, who had invisibly determined the encounter — did they really think the replacement of an industrial vacuum cleaner with rose petals and dried orange rinds was haphazard? Still, their good fortune was reward enough).

Invite Everyone

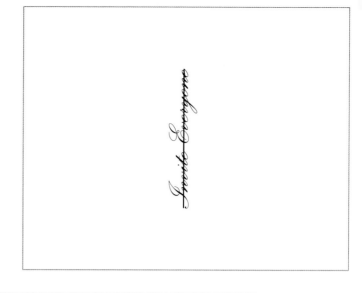

Invite Everyone

Concerning today's initial impulse, Ellie treated it tenderly. Why should she be surprised? Especially on a morning such as this. Spring's promises kept early, wild, and colorful blooms already overwhelming the wraparound terrace of her penthouse, once divided into two apartments, now de-doored, unwalled, with plants everywhere, inside and out, from aloes and orchids to bonsai and ferns, along with tulips, gardenias, and daisies.

She had already watered and fretted over them earlier, before eating a small breakfast on behalf of her indomitable bones and preparing a cherry blossom tea on behalf of a soul she defined as good habits.

Then Ellie had sat down on her terrace, distracted at once by Central Park — who wouldn't be? — the rustling green, the reservoir dappled by breezes, a sudden shadow of clouds scudding south.

Eventually though, she turned to address the creamy sheet of hand-made paper, purchased just yesterday on Madison Avenue, antique fountain pen in hand, shaped from a narwhal's tusk, nibs wet with a black as cunning as squid ink. (Devising these lists always required concentration worthy of prayer.)

Suddenly, a dove landed on her table, only to fly off an instant later. Ellie let her initial impulse fly away too.

Ellie had learned the hard way that the Infinite List served mostly as a lesson in humility. Even more so after that absurd evening nine years ago, when Ellie had won the lottery and could replace boxed wine with cheeses and charcuteries served alongside bowls of blanched haricots, candied pecans, and dried apricots, melded deliciously together with Calistoga Cabernets. The gallery owners and architects had still paid no attention to the health and transit workers, while the contractors had gone out of their way to offend the physical therapists and dance instructors, while a financial coterie clung to entertainment-industry types who had collectively, if unconsciously, decided to nail the emo art-school clique forming the Avant Politico Party bent on boycotting all of Ellie's future gatherings. And that was on a good night.

Mostly, those evenings — once the Infinite List was essayed — resulted in groups keeping to themselves until enough alcohol allowed a crossover that typically went unreflected upon, if even remembered. The finest speck and most expensive olives made no difference. Ellie had tired of the results and started shooing away her initial impulse, which still never failed to appear. After all, Ellie loved to host gatherings, even if she had accepted the necessity of moving on to the much more complicated art of discernment.

Her heart jumped before the challenge. She even made and unmade a fist with her left hand until she was sure she had not forgotten to take her medicine.

Some things could not be forgotten, like whom she would invite last, whom like her confident cursive — no lines needed — she always invited last, for years now.

Of course, whom Ellie would invite first was a very different story. That was the thought petrifying her pen now, as names came and went, as ink dried.

Of utmost importance: Ellie's lists cared most for revelation. How they would unfold according to who was considered next — seemingly disclosing then a line of sublime connectivity — a process Ellie quite unreservedly regarded as sacred.

Her main goal was simple: to draw people together in a manner that never exacted the price of tearing other people apart.

She had seen that happen a few times. A new acquaintance at the expense of an old friend. A new love at the expense of a true one. It was too horrible to consider. Even worse to remember. No wonder Ellie detested all things backward.

Fortunately, at this late stage in her life, she had some helpful reminders:

Reminder Number One

Everyone does not get along.

Reminder Number Two

Everyone does not _need_ to get along.

Reminder Number Three

It's nice if some do get along.

Reminder Number Four

It's necessary that a few do not.

Despite best intentions and past adventures, Ellie's gatherings had never been for everyone. They were conjured on behalf of those who could appreciate the subtle. Who could ask questions without judgment and provide answers without challenge. Those who understood there was space where it seemed there was no room left. Who knew nothing was left where there was no room for something new. Who were humble enough to remain open and who were considerate enough to not declare others so. Who arrived because they wanted to learn where no teachers were invited. And who lingered because the unexpected had become the teacher they'd accepted they would never find.

The point was not to exclude, and at the same time not to include so many that the qualities of the rare were overwhelmed by tastes prescribed by set practices — disingenuous and self-satisfied — too often established by an unrecognized few — whether dead or alive — sorely in need of re-placement, especially by emerging talents wrought out of uncommon passions and unanticipated curiosities, whom Ellie viewed as generous, intelligent, and unwaveringly kind.

As for that ever elusive common denominator, it had no place at her table.

For a long while now, her table was set only for the particular few.

But who?

And this time Ellie's heart really did tremble. It even threatened to lump into a fist that might never again find a hand. Ellie winced and forced herself to breathe deeply, reaching for her tea, stretching her fingers toward flowers that would not deign to speak. No doves flew by.

And that was how — without looking up again — Ellie made up her list.

It was still rough, but she finished, as she always did, by writing the last name on the back.

Maybe this time — she dared herself to dream — the guest who mattered most would finally attend and perhaps even stay.

The

Caged Hunt

Part Five

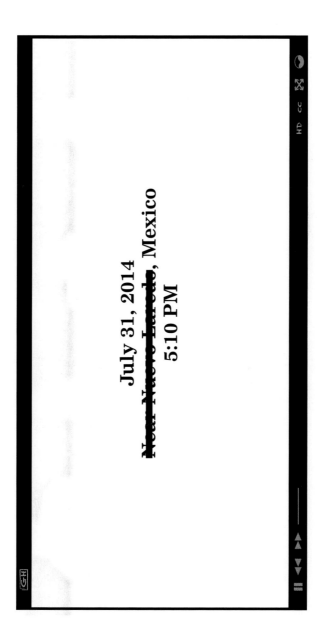

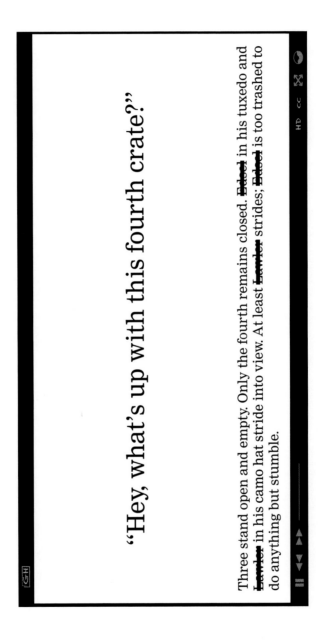

"Hey, what's up with this fourth crate?"

Three stand open and empty. Only the fourth remains closed. ~~Teboul~~ in his tuxedo and ~~Teodor~~ in his camo hat stride into view. At least ~~Teodor~~ strides; ~~Teboul~~ is too trashed to do anything but stumble.

"This thing's unlocked."

~~We just~~ doesn't keep the camera on his friends prying open the latches but instead pans over to the Mexican workers who are backing away, some shaking their heads, some with their hands up, as if somewhere guns were pointed at them. The two children have vanished, leaving their bowling pins standing upright in the dirt.

"Empty."

Off to the side, ~~Wenjun~~ catches sight of the little girl in the pink dress with a sash of yellow polka dots. She's running. ~~Wenjun~~'s eye follows her until a loud clank calls his attention back to ~~Eskol~~ and ~~Lawler~~.

"Well, isn't that fucking hilarious!"

Both ~~Lewster~~ and ~~Ethel~~ raise their rifles and aim inside at what shadows hide.

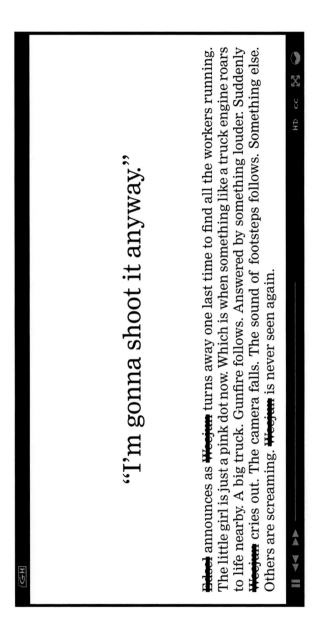

"I'm gonna shoot it anyway."

~~Rebel~~ announces as ~~Weejun~~ turns away one last time to find all the workers running. The little girl is just a pink dot now. Which is when something like a truck engine roars to life nearby. A big truck. Gunfire follows. Answered by something louder. Suddenly ~~Weejun~~ cries out. The camera falls. The sound of footsteps follows. Something else. Others are screaming. ~~Weejun~~ is never seen again.

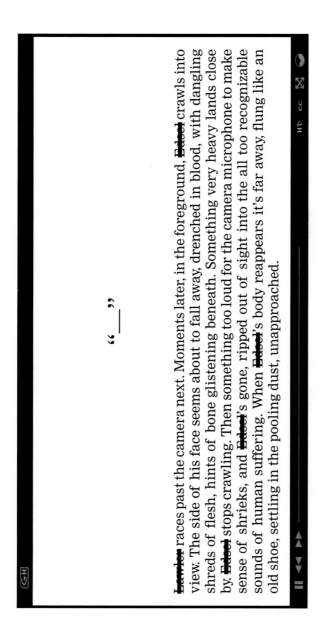

" ___ "

~~Lassiter~~ races past the camera next. Moments later, in the foreground, ~~Lassiter~~ crawls into view. The side of his face seems about to fall away, drenched in blood, with dangling shreds of flesh, hints of bone glistening beneath. Something very heavy lands close by. ~~Lassiter~~ stops crawling. Then something too loud for the camera microphone to make sense of shrieks, and ~~Lassiter~~'s gone, ripped out of sight into the all too recognizable sounds of human suffering. When ~~Lassiter~~'s body reappears it's far away, flung like an old shoe, settling in the pooling dust, unapproached.

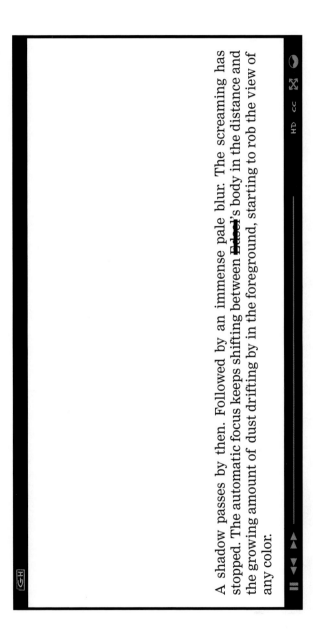

A shadow passes by then. Followed by an immense pale blur. The screaming has stopped. The automatic focus keeps shifting between ~~Rahel~~'s body in the distance and the growing amount of dust drifting by in the foreground, starting to rob the view of any color.

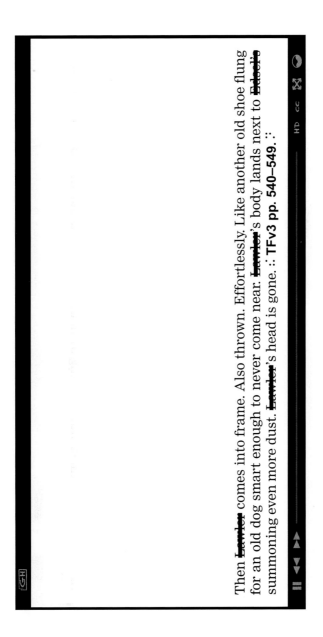

Then ~~Leander~~ comes into frame. Also thrown. Effortlessly. Like another old shoe flung for an old dog smart enough to never come near. ~~Leander~~'s body lands next to ~~Eclectic~~ summoning even more dust. ~~Leander~~'s head is gone. ∴: **TFv3 pp. 540–549.**∴:

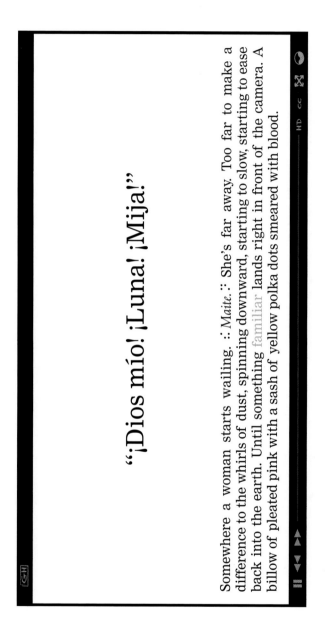

"¡Dios mío! ¡Luna! ¡Mija!"

Somewhere a woman starts wailing. .: *Maite.*:: She's far away. Too far to make a difference to the whirls of dust, spinning downward, starting to slow, starting to ease back into the earth. Until something familiar lands right in front of the camera. A billow of pleated pink with a sash of yellow polka dots smeared with blood.

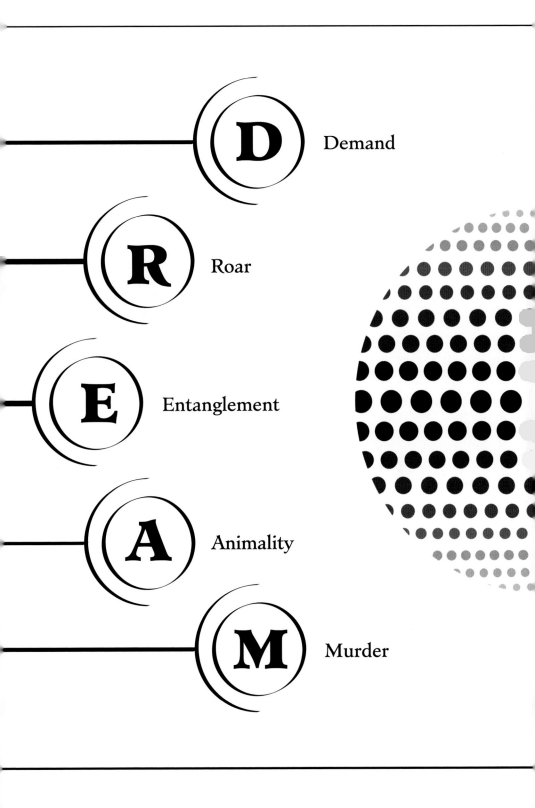

D   Demand

R   Roar

E   Entanglement

A   Animality

M   Murder

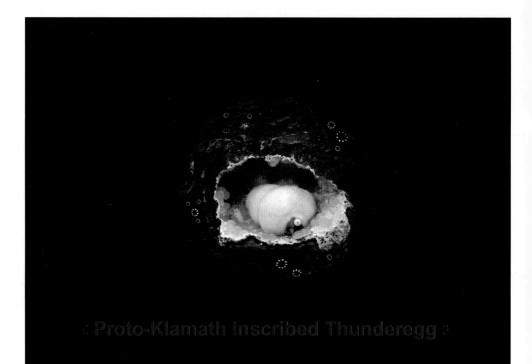

:: Proto-Klamath Inscribed Thunderegg ::

:: 5,517 years ago. ::

:: Midnight. Late Spring. ::

:: Wizard Island. Not so far from 42.941100, -122.157225. ::

:: Sky ablaze with stars. Lake a mirror of black. Nothing disturbs its surface. ::

:: Young Woman and Young Man huddle close together in the cold. Both wear elk skins and caps and sandals woven out of tule. ::

:: They hold hands. Her right hand in his right. His left hand in her left. ::

∴ You saw it come out of water. ∴ ∴ *Young Woman says.* ∴

∴ Nothing swims in é-ush. ∴ ∴ *Young Man insists, turning to face the lake.* ∴

∴ Nothing swims here. ∴ ∴ *Young Woman echoes.* ∴ ∴ But this no kiä´m. ∴

∴ No fish in ámpu. So very deep. Why water sleeps. ∴

∴ Unless winds wake surface. ∴

∴ *Young Man nods.* ∴ ∴ Unless winds wake surface. Kátak gî. ∴

∴ Truth. But tonight, look, no winds. ∴

∴ Yea. No winds. ∴

∴ Lake tcheléwash-é. ∴

∴ But lake rippled. ∴ ∴ *Young Man now echoes.* ∴

∴ Great ripples! To far lalî´sh-y. ∴

∴ *Young Man can't deny it.* ∴ ∴ To far shores. ∴

∴ It ikán-a great waves. ∴

∴ *Young Man turns from lake to look at Young Woman. He smiles.* ∴

∴ We are forbidden. ∴ ∴ *Young Man says.* ∴ ∴ Especially here. ∴

∴ Yea. Why we húyaha-o here. ∴ ∴ *Young Woman smiles.* ∴

∴ Yea. Why we escaped here. But shupumtchisháltko-sha followed our trail to Gi´wash É-ush. ∴ ∴ *Young Man's smile fades.* ∴ ∴ Shishókish-sha too. ∴

∴ Our cousins and warriors followed us to Crater Lake, but they found no vunshága. ∴

∴ They found no boat. ∴ ∴ *Young Man agrees.* ∴ ∴ They feared gé-upka-é at dusk. ∴

∴ But we did not fear! We swam! We gúikaka-o! ∴

∴ Yea. We escaped. ∴

∴ Mbushéala and shuldákua. ∴ ∴ *Young Woman lipbrushes Young Man's eyes.* ∴

∴ Yea. We will marry. We will have children. But not gíta. ∴

∴ No, not here. ∴

∴ They pä́ktgî-mé and by waítash come for us. ∴

:: *Young Woman lets go of Young Man's left hand. His right hand, though, keeps a tight hold of her right hand.* ::

:: They do not wait for dawn. They will not come for us by day. You heard the mbáwa-y. You saw their kû´pkash-y go dark. ::

:: Yea. I heard the screams. I saw the fires go dark. ::

:: Then are we free? :: :: *Young Woman asks, suddenly afraid.* :: :: Can we forage for joyjiks and doycq´as? ::

:: Strawberries and chokeberries. Bush honeysuckles and wild plum too. :: :: *Young Man lipbrushes Young Woman's cheeks.* ::

:: Lulínash. Húdsha and klî´sh. ::

:: Yea. :: :: *Young Man laughs.* :: :: Pond-lily seed too. And acorns from white and black oaks. ::

∴ *Young Woman lipbrushes Young Man's lips and tries to take back his left hand.* ∴

∴ *Instead, Young Man places his left hand on ground.* ∴ ∴ **But not on awalóga.** ∴

∴ *Young Woman understands.* ∴ ∴ **This island is litchlítchli and k´lekótkish.** ∴

∴ **Yea. Powerful and dangerous. My p´tísh-lûsh came here na´dszeks waíta to see Wanáka.** ∴

∴ *Young Woman echoes.* ∴ ∴ **Your father waited here nine days and waited here nine nights to meet Young Silver Fox. My p´gísh-lush sent my tapíiukani to find Tchéwamtch.** ∴

∴ *Young Man echoes.* ∴ ∴ **Your mother sent your youngest brother here to find Old Antelope.** ∴

∴ **We sent ourselves to find ourselves, but we found something else.** ∴ ∴ *Then Young Woman gets idea.* ∴ ∴ **Maybe we saw our Wanáka or Tchéwamtch?** ∴

∴ **Sháshapsh?** ∴ ∴ *Young Man plays along.* ∴

∴ **No, not Old Grizzly.** ∴

∴ **Tchashkáyaga?** ∴

∴ **Not Weaslet.** ∴

∴ **Ké-utchiamtch?** ∴

∴ **Not Gray Wolf.** ∴

∴ **Shû´kamtch?** ∴

∴ **Not Old Crane.** ∴

∴ **Shlóa?** ∴

∷ *Young Woman hesitates.* ∴ ∷ **No lynx. Not kúika-ush.** ∴

∷ *Young Man agrees.* ∴ ∷ **No, not mountain lion. It rose from water like new-born yaína of kéknish.** ∴

∷ **Yea! Mountain of snow! Kákiaksh of wésh! Shílshila!** ∴ ∷ *She is happy that they are in agreement.* ∴

∷ **Thunder, aye. But whirlwind of ice free to kawakága this world.** ∴

∷ **Llao?** ∴ ∷ ▆▆▆▆▆ ∴

∷ *Young Man now lets go of the Young Woman's right hand and stands.* ∴

∷ **Waves still beat lake when it reached those who would ká-iha us.** ∴

∷ *Young Woman stands too.* ∴ ∷ **It was hunting our people.** ∴

∷ Dawn will tell for sure. ∵

∷ But it passed us by. That is true. Kátak gî. ∵

∷ *Young Man pulls from his shlóa sack a thunderegg.* ∵ ∷ I saw it, kátak gî, but I also did not see what I saw, true. I kópa-i only ∷ *that* ∵ it had pushpúshli lû´lpam líwayaks. Deeper than Gi´wash É-ush. Blacker than this kíuks shílshila ktá-i. No kî´sh. Did we see same stare? ∵

∷ *Young Woman takes the unmarked rock, looks at it, then gives it back.* ∵

∷ The eyes I saw were filled with fire.[ε] ∵

∷ [ε]For alternate set variants of gestural translations, including alveolar clicks, numerous sibilants, bilabial fricatives, retroflex approximants, pharyngeal consonants, see 88910350-02031966-060619650105, order VI, v.26, n.13. ∵

MARK Z. DANIELEWSKI'S

THE

FAMILIAR

VOLUME 5

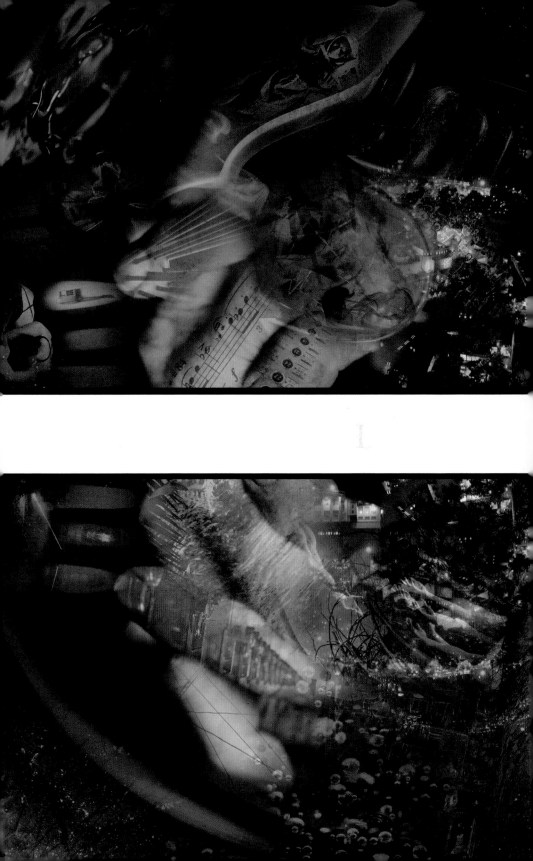

REDWOOD . . .

'White cat!'

And here you have a technology that is not only going to survive in the wild — it is intended to take over in the wild.

— *Jim Thomas*

'*You stole my cat!*' The voice on the phone howls again [shrill enough {ridiculous enough!} to deserve what happens next: Anwar hangs up].

Though hanging up doesn't come close to delivering [in satisfaction] what that initial impulse had promised [{separation}{closure}].

Anwar stays put. He already knows what to expect: the phone will ring again. The phone rings again. [true] Anwar could let it ring forever and that would be that. He could instruct his family never to pick up that phone again. That way he [whoever he was {even if he never stopped calling}] would never get any closer than this. And he would [eventually] have to stop calling.

Why then does Anwar pick up on the first ring? [Funny if it had been Nathan Muellenson {or someone else from Galvadyne ‹wanting their money back «for the expensive recruitment trip ⟨how paranoid is that?⟩»›} but it's not Galvadyne.]

'You post sign, meh,' the voice says [noticeably calmer {at least restrained}]. 'We lose cat. You find cat. We come get cat. You return cat.'

Anwar almost hangs up again [that he's unable to answer {yet} why he picked up {in the first place} should have guaranteed that action {along with this increasing shortness of breath ‹as well as an illness «?» that seems to sheet his outsides «and insides» with some cold insupportable «indigestible» oiliness›}] except that he [also] recognizes the familiar fear that too often accompanies having to make the right choice [here now ‹forcing him not only to hold his hand «to override instincts ⟨of flight⟩» but willing him to listen too›].

'We did find a cat some months ago,' Anwar offers.

'My cat! 你系扑街仔！'

'How do I know that?'

'White cat!'

'Perhaps, but wouldn't you agree that there are many white cats?' That earns a pause. 'Where did you lose your cat?' That earns an even longer pause. Did the caller hang up? That would solve everything.

But the caller is still there [caught in his own breathlessness {cultivating an unknown thought}].

'We come to you,' he finally states [commands?]. 'We come to you.' Who is this 'we' [Anwar wants to ask]? 'Give me address.'

Now it's Anwar's turn to pause. Something about the voice [the English{?}] is starting to sink in: not local [not even native].

'Before I can do that—' Anwar offers quietly '—I will need you to validate your claim by first offering more details than just the color of the fur.'

Another pause. Even heavier than the others.

'Give me address.' Something pained [bereft?] splitting apart the repeated syllables [Anwar is pained too {has the claimant even understood the demand? ‹Anwar feeling sorry for him «remembering when he too once battled with the foreign taste of another language»›}].

'First, please, tell me more about the cat,' Anwar insists [the demand giving voice to uncertain rectitude {oscillating modes of ‹un›fairness}]. Anwar himself would have barely managed generics: white [for sure] with tail [for starters] then maybe whiskers [what else?].

But there is no pause or generics.

'No whiskers! One hair above right eye! Front paw, right, seven claws! Left, six claws!' Which Anwar already knows [maybe not the exact number {'polydactyl,' Astair had announced after reporting on that first visit to the vet ‹with Dr. Todd «?» ∴ Dr. Syd ∵ ›}]. Each detail resurfacing [with each {albeit strange} declaration].

'That's not enough,' Anwar still says [though it's more than enough {he ‹at once «easily»› pictures those stubby front paws ‹«with their fluffy sense of extra» hiding an extra claw› and even recalls telling Xanther that she had herself a Hemingway cat ‹did he say it or only think to say it? ∴ ∷ Neither [he's only thinking {it} now]. ∴ ∷ *In the way that thinking sometimes suggests we are merely rethinking?* ∴ ∷ **Even if you are just making it up.** ∴ ∷ *Which happens more than we think.* ∴ ›}].

'Seven claws right paw! Six claws left paw!'

Anwar is as certain six is right as seven is incorrect [he'd remember seven {unless it's an extra dewclaw?}].

'Give address!' The man shouts again [voice a whine {threaded through with ‹rising› frustration and rage}].

But Anwar does not submit. There's more at stake here than one man's anger. The more errors Anwar can point out [!] the more definitively he can put this mess to rest [then head to Venice tomorrow to tear down any remaining signs].

'I saysay no whiskers! One hair above right eye!' The repetitions [and sputterings] only serve to grant Anwar more time to develop more probative questions [to further evaluate this threat]. [for example] Is the absence of whiskers evident in the picture [Anwar can't remember the picture]? [also] Might a solitary brow hair be a species thing [Anwar would have to check]?

'I'll need more.'

'Small. Hair wavy. White! And blue eyes macam wild sky,' the man adds then.

'I'm afraid that still won't suffice. You understand, it's been months. Four months. There are many white cats out there, some with extra toes. Besides, ours doesn't have blue eyes. Ours is blind.'

'Blind?' That one catches the man off guard.

'It never opens its eyes,' Anwar says [recalling how when those slits do {occasionally} crack open they reveal no more color than some kind of obsidian refusal].

'Please!' the voice screeches [misery replacing rage {plenty of anguish in there too ‹no doubting the authenticity of that agony «what would Xanther do? ⟨she'd give over the address at once⟩»›}]. 'You don'ch understand, lah. My cat, dat. Lost cat. Please!'

'Yes, I heard you. But—' Should Anwar resort now to vet bills? adumbrate other costs? emotional investment [or should he just go count the claws?]?

'Osso kay kay dangerous lai dat!'

Now Anwar's the one caught off guard. Was that a threat? 'Excuse me?'

'Cat. Kay kay dangerous! Very! Hurt her! You too!'

Now Anwar loses his breath altogether [feels {too} like he's losing the floor beneath his feet {even grabs hold of the kitchen counter to steady himself ‹dangerous? «hurt me? ⟨hurt her!?⟩?»›}].

'And one teet!' the man on the phone continues. 'Missing. Right side, back jaw. See for yourself. Osso left side, back jaw, have extra.' Ah. Teeth.

Such specificity unnerves Anwar but he also relishes the fact that [if the claw count and tooth count prove incorrect] he will have enough to politely decline the caller's request [and draw to a close this nerve-rattling surprise].

'Okay,' Anwar answers [taking a deep breath]. 'Hold on one moment, please, while I check.'

Anwar puts down the phone and takes his time returning to the living room. Maybe the caller will do what Anwar should have kept doing [for as long as it was required]: hang up.

But Anwar knows better.

The living room has ceased to frame a beautiful Wednesday afternoon [though nothing has changed {only the way Anwar feels ‹a «necrotic» sensation attaching to «and attacking» everything he lays eyes on›}].

Freya is still humming [coloring {wild ‹abstract›} flares of orange and purple] though now her hum seems too loud [[also generic ∴ **The Hum!** ∵} something grating about it as well {like metal crunching glass far away} born out of his little girl {who is ‹furthermore› afflicted with an expression of concentration ‹a rictus of displeasure› that sound concentration never requires}].

Shasti is still reading her book but there too displeasure is evident [paining {*painting!*} her face {maybe due to her sister's humming?}].

Astair has gone under her headphones [perhaps trying to drown out Freya? {or something else?}] as any attempt at progress on her paper provokes a look of frustration [what some might mistake for seriousness if it wasn't so {obviously!} unhappiness].

Only Xanther takes note of his return [she was initially looking at the mantel {‹probably› at Dov's ‹her› gun box on top ‹perhaps wondering about the combination «or more likely the contents 《or just thinking about Dov》»?›} before turning quietly to greet his arrival]. She offers a wordless [ambiguous] glance. The cat [of course] is with her [asleep in her lap].

What words he needs to answer her glance [not at all ambiguous] don't at once find their place.

Silence reigns.

∴ *!!!* ∵

∴ **TFv1 p. 738** ∵

55

Except for Freya's humming.

Or a car alarm going off somewhere down their street.

Plus the swish of drapes in the piano room [a breeze moving through the French doors {why are they open? ‹so much these days seems open «Anwar half expects the black box to just pop open too ⟨would he be surprised?⟩»⟩}].

Maybe it is the vitality of youth [the engagement it has with the present {making out of every present an equally vital future}] and [more specifically] Xanther's incremental [yet irrefutable] growth [in presence {not height ‹or has she also gotten a little taller?›}] that apprehends in every instance this sense of unfastening [and widening {and ‹of course› opening ‹though without revelation «rather offering only the opportunity ⟨portal⟩ for revelation ⟨if one but dares the invitation⟩»›}].

Xanther and Astair [and Myla {Anwar certainly}] had focused on her seizure at the end of *Hades*. The review [as well] refigured Xanther's appearance as part of the ballet [which Myla then went on to reproduce in every subsequent performance {gladly}].

But none of them [certainly not the reviewer] had commented upon the fact that as Xanther had [impossibly!] raced out after Hades [shooing Hope aside {terrifying Hope‹?›}] doors were [seemed to be { . . . ‹were«!»›}] opening everywhere!

Not just due to patrons bustling out of exits but stage doors flung wide by invisible hands. Anwar swears he even heard purses and spectacle cases clicking open [phones too {with those ‹audible «engineered»› snaps}].

Everything at the Met seemed at once to have been unbarred [so much so that all that was outside {and out of reach} seemed {at once} inside {replete with sirens ‹and other signals of distress «more car alarms!»›}].

Nor did the sensation cease with the arrival of EMTs [Anwar's dear child still seized in that peculiar battle between rigidity and fluidity {the domination of one superimposed over the other ‹only to submit «with the next twitch ⟨and twist⟩» to the other's primacy «neither the Procrustean nor protean ever winning out for long ⟨until both were gone ⌈leaving a calm that offers only the awful threat of death until death too is banished ⌊for the time being⌋ with a moan ⌈in a hospital bed many hours later⌉⌋ surrounded by mostly closed doors⟩»›}].

Right after Xanther was rushed from the stage [carefully bundled up {and secured on a gurney}] the Met's emergency-exit doors seemed to spring wide open of their own accord [well in advance too {as if anticipating ‹commanded by?› her escape ‹arrival?›}].

Even in the nighttime New York air [out on Lincoln Center Plaza] every car Anwar saw drive by seemed to have open doors [open trunks as well {plus a few hoods!}].

It was the darndest thing. [and though all of his attention stayed focused on Xanther {holding her hand}] Anwar was certain the back door [of their ambulance] was also about to fly open [maybe it had? ∴ It had. ∵ {⟨at least⟩ feeling lucky ⟨the whole ride⟩ that they all hadn't wound up tumbling out onto Columbus Avenue}].

[of course] Anwar accepts that all these [nonsensical] coincidences [whether the Santa Monica Animal Shelter or Keen Toys' Animal Kingdom {or even the ballet itself ⟨he must ask Myla about her inspiration for the closing and opening cages in *Hades*⟩}] are merely reinforcing a pattern [this confounding sense of unlatching] that has simply become more readily recognized and [perhaps] accessed more rapidly [{especially} in times of stress].

Nevertheless [around Xanther] this [ongoing] pattern of opening still seems too abundant to ignore [no matter how sensible his {cognitive} explanation]. Flowers might as well bloom in Xanther's presence. Probably do.

Only her cat's eyes remain resolutely shut.

And now Anwar needs Xanther to open them. The mouth too.

'Polydactyl?' Anwar asks [silence must resign].

'Word of the day?' Xanther responds [the question not surprising her {even if a tone of wariness indicates she can already hear the lie ‹why? «because she's heard something else? ∷ . . . ∵»}].

Anwar nods.

Astair looks up [did she hear the lie too? {of course she did ‹Anwar is a terrible liar «because he hates it so much»›}]. At least Freya keeps humming.

'"Poly" means "many," and, uhm, "dactyl" I think means "finger,"' Xanther answers [with a {noncommittal} shrug]. 'I already know that one. Dr. Syd used it when, uh, he was like going over this one here?'

'Did I know that?' Anwar winces [even he can hear his lie]. 'Yes, of course, I did. But how many, daughter, is this "poly"?' That much is not a lie [{though by how much} Anwar has no idea {because now he's using the truth to lie ‹and «much worse» hiding the lie in a teachable moment «why not use a new word?» to get Xanther to count the claws without asking why›}].

'Serious? You want me to count them?' At least it's not a why [though {with Xanther} that why always waits a breath away].

'Sure!' Anwar chirps [yes: chirps {way too bright ‹with way too much smile›}].

Freya stops humming.

'Uhm, okay?'

Anwar almost welcomes her eye roll [while {still} working hard to keep his smile {a ‹painfully «Anwar's sure of it»› fake look ‹too sincere «with interest»› pasted on his face ‹though he *is* sincerely interested «if still charging ahead with his deception ‹if just to find one error [so he can charge back to the kitchen and finish what he never should have gotten caught up in [in the first place]]›»›}].

'Back paws have, uh, like five nails each?' Xanther announces [the little cat putting up little resistance {almost too little resistance ‹in fact «is it okay?»›}].

'And the front ones?'

'Anwar, honey, what's going on?' Astair asks [closing her laptop {of course she's hearing all his false notes}].

'Daddy?' Freya asks. 'Who was on the phone?' A question that immediately gets Shasti's attention.

Anwar has no choice but to ignore and push on.

'The front ones?' he repeats.

'Fine! Fine! I'm counting!' Xanther growls [through gritted teeth {though there's also something obliging in her voice ‹like she senses his urgency «and ‹though blind to the consequences› aligns herself with him»›}].

'Six.'

'The right one?' Anwar practically pleads.

'No. This is the left.'

Anwar can't bear to hear his voice again.

'The right one,' Xanther announces [when she's finished counting {the last paw}] 'has seven.'

Anwar can't ask her to force open its eyes.

'Daughter, I need you to do me a favor.'

Xanther nods. Anwar can see her jaw at work [{no question} trying to grind back all the questions coming to life {her Question Song ‹«probably» more like Question Scream«!»›}].

'Baby,' Astair [now at Anwar's side {‹maybe› to see what he's seeing?}] says to Xanther. 'Your little fella's looking pretty tired. Is he okay?'

'What's the favor, Dad?' Xanther asks.

'Will you tell me how many back teeth he has?'

'Anwar!'

'Astair, please.'

Xanther doesn't protest [her head {and black braids} now eclipsing entirely the little creature {and all else that's involved with opening its mouth}].

The awfulness grows worse [did Anwar already know what she would find?].

Astair remains confused but [at least {for the moment}] has accepted that she will get little else from her husband. She sits down beside Xanther.

'It's hard to see,' Xanther complains from beneath her hair. 'Mom, will you hold my phone light, like, right here?'

Astair obliges.

'Take your time,' Anwar says twice.

'Still can't get, uh, the number but—' [Xanther looks up {as if to see if Anwar's expression will disclose some intent}] '—maybe the left side has one missing, or like the right side, has, uh, like an extra?'

THERE! AN ERROR!

Anwar nearly shouts [doesn't shout {knowing the caller's confusion over left and right is likely due to orientation ‹looking *at* the cat versus looking *with* the cat «the specificity making the identification indisputable ‹no point either in denying the near absence of whiskers or the solitary lash above the right eye›»}].

61

Anwar still wants to cry out [shout something {as if a word could make sense of what he must do next ‹but what is he going to do next?›}].

Except Astair is already shouting [practically screaming {voice rising in terrified panic ‹as she's already rising to her feet «stumbling backward»›}].

'Oh my god! What's wrong with its mouth? Where are the front teeth?! Xanther! What happened to its teeth?!'

cycling

Careful, Nature thinks.

— *Clarice Lispector*

Who cares what Anwar's going on about (or is this what he was doing? (pointing *this* out(!)?)).

The light (on Xanther's phone) was so bright that (at first (at least)) Astair couldn't see a thing (her eyes straining to adjust). The white fur in Xanther's lap burned brighter than white (a fire beyond hue (beyond heat (with only the shut eyes (like slashes of charcoal) characterizing the flare (sunspots (sun-*slashes!*) scarring the blaze))))).

Some light!

Some phone!

Astair's own blinking eyes protected her from this (foreign) blindness (through the imposition of (personal(ly controlled)) blindness).

That is until Astair really leaned into where her daughter was fiddling (Xanther's (long (thin)) fingers (easing open the small jaws (exactly as Dr. Syd had once demonstrated (right index finger and thumb under the jaw (at the back) while the left index finger and thumb descended from above (toward the front (near the nose)) (the bottom fingers slipping inward where there were no teeth (was that right?) slipping into the mouth ((like picking a lock) the cat (on its own) opening its mouth a little (enough for the upper fingers to (ever so) gently pry open the mouth (much wider)))))))).

Which is when it happened . . .

What no phone could make a difference to . . .

What no light could change . . .

Something glimmered inside (such a little inside too (even if the sparks (the tiny teeth?) seemed like distant stars)).

Astair pushed forward more (to turn stars back into teeth (to counter her growing terror . . . (as if Astair could fight her way through that (and with only a (pink!) phone too!)))) but the closer she got the more the (dark) cavity seemed to widen (with a~~ far graver ~~absence~~ (*consequences(!)*) (distant stars growing even more distant (and worse: dying too . . .))) . . .

Of course Astair screamed.

(in the Element now (racing to the vet)) Astair reframes the experience of that gaping darkness as an intolerable recognition (revelation!) of absence (where were the canines? (Astair's own teeth had hurt at once (were still tingling))(don't confuse reflexing with reflecting!)).

"Last night?!" Astair shouts ((at least she's not screaming now) scrolling through her phone's contacts at the stoplight (thinking ahead to take Fountain (or would Beverly Boulevard be faster?))).

The light turns green before she can locate Dr. Syd.

"Here." Astair hands the phone to Xanther. "Find our vet. Why didn't you say something?"

A glance catches her poor girl (in a terrible contraction) hunched over (as listless (likely) as the poor creature (now) hidden beneath one of Anwar's old ∴ gray∵ cashmere sweaters).

"Found it. Dialing," Xanther mumbles (handing back Astair's phone).

"Thank you. Sweetheart? Why didn't you say something?" Softer this time.

"I don't know." Xanther's eyes go wide (tears filling them at once). "I felt so hopeless."

"Oh baby!" Astair's heart breaks.

The pet hospital picks up.

"Dr. Syd, please. It's an emergency." Astair leaves the phone on speaker.

"I'm sorry. Dr. Syd isn't in today. But we have several qualified doctors here on staff. What kind of emergency is it?"

"Mom!" Xanther shouts (she's lifted the cashmere sweater to her chest).

Astair can't see the cat but she knows exactly what's happening. Again.

She veers the Element for yellow curb (a loading zone).

"Hello?" The receptionist is still on the line.

"I'm sorry. I have to call you back. Our cat just went into another seizure."

If Xanther caught Astair's "another" she doesn't show it (instead (frantically) trying to hold on to the wildly twisting animal). Astair does her best to help.

But what can they really do? A question Astair is all too familiar with (along with the near-futile answer (adding soft palms to her daughter's softer hands (the two of them doing their best to help ~~control~~ *guard*(!) the stiff shuddering both of them (all of them!) know so well (waiting for it to end (hoping it will end soon ("hopeless" Xanther had said . . .)))))).

And it gets even worse.

The sweater grows damp (is it also urinating? (of course it is)). Xanther unwraps the trembling rigidity to reveal (instead of (in addition to?) urine) a (clear) mucus egressing from its anus.

A moment later equally clear (viscous) fluids start to leak from its shuddering mouth (both women doing everything they can to keep him clean (wiping the effluents away (with cashmere (with bare hands (anything within reach))))).

"Look, Mom," Xanther suddenly whispers (not looking (though) at the animal (in their (collective((!)?)) hands) but across the street).

Catholic Animal Hospital

Cardiff Chambers had recently (finally) e-mailed a PDF of (her manuscript) *The Placebo Effect* ∴ **TFv3 p. 580** ∴. Her note mentioned that she was already at work on another "less researchy" book tentatively titled *Losing Your Way to Happiness* (whatever that means (unless what's happening at this very moment is exactly what she means?)).

Sandra Dee Taylor is in Astair's head too:

"Provoke the unexpected!"

"The animal that matters isn't us!"

"Come on!" Astair urges her daughter and herself ((accepting their good fortune) letting Xanther handle all animal ministrations while she shepherds their passage across the busy boulevard (through slowing traffic (over to the (far) curb (and finally through the doors (of (gathering) dark glass)))))).

If the exterior of the building presents a Van Gogh of thickly smeared orange stucco (which by creating the impression of a ((boldly) original (or (at least) striking)) building somehow also calls into question the building itself (crumbling only a little less than the exterior sign keeps losing paint (bars on the windows flaking rust))) the interior is no less dilapidated (nor discouraging). What the hell kind of animal hospital has "Catholic" in its name?

The outer orange has been carried inside (though here it is darker (as if submitting to decades of cigarette smoke (despite a **NO SMOKING** sign (hung above what looks like a nonfunctioning water fountain)))).

The creepiest part (though) is the absence of anyone.

No sign of animals either.

(by contrast) The examination room turns out to be a pocket of the brightly lit (lavender walls warmed by an assortment of (inspirational) posters (plus an old-school examination table (all wood))).

It gets even better from there.

Dr. Alice Caldwell is about Astair's age (blond too (though shorter and heavier (and with a much larger quotient of (visible(?)) compassion for Xanther's frail little cat))).

(unlike Dr. Syd) Dr. Caldwell is taciturn throughout her evaluation. The lack of commentary grates on Astair but she can see that Xanther trusts her (continuing to relax as Dr. Caldwell (with a bright blue stethoscope) listens (presumably) to the cat's heart thump (and his belly too ((putting the damp sweater to one side) running her hands all over him (even eliciting a tiny *eeeeeeeep!* (at least it's still alive))))).

Nothing disturbs Dr. Caldwell (either) as she points the otoscope inside the mouth (followed by a peek into both ears). She even takes a look at both eyes (who knows what she sees (but it neither surprises nor provokes her (are some of us flawed by imagination? :: **Yes.** :: :: *How dare you!* ::))).

The last thing Dr. Caldwell does is pet the little guy between his ears (a sympathetic (sorry) look then ordering her features).

"Is he blind?" Astair blurts out.

Dr. Caldwell's expression doesn't change. "He's cycling."

"Excuse me?"

"What's cycling?" Xanther also wants to know (both of them knowing it's not a good thing).

"He's just very, very old. How long have you had him?"

"We just got him!" Xanther squeaks (Astair hears the sob in her voice (as much as the fight against tears)).

"My daughter rescued him in May. In a rainstorm. He was drowning in a gutter."

"How wonderful you are," Dr. Caldwell says to Xanther. "For finding him. And forgiving him all you have." (*for giving* (right?)) Something odd in the way Dr. Caldwell speeds up her words (maybe because she is (at the same time) also motioning for Astair to join her outside the examination room).

Astair expects that awful stare of questions (but Xanther just keeps her focus on the spavined creature once again in her arms).

The hallway returns Astair to her initial impression of this place (that defeated sense of occupancy that isn't (but now somehow even drabber (and darker) than before)). What Dr. Caldwell has to say is even more allied with defeat (though there is a generosity to it (even grace(?)))).

In short (she tells Astair) they can run a battery of blood tests and X-rays (as well as other expensive scans (Astair is impressed that they have an X-ray machine here (let alone other scanning devices))). But even if they can identify a specific pathology ((tumors on the liver) (splotches on the lungs) (kidneys petrifying after a lifetime of "urban toxicity")) they will still be left with the same incontrovertible outcome when life joins hands for the last time with the fact of its finitude.

"We almost believed he was a kitten," Astair mumbles.

"I'm sure in his heart he is," Dr. Caldwell consoles her (though without a touch (which Astair appreciates (even admires))).

Astair readies herself then to face Xanther only to discover she can't move in that immovable dimness ((now) fighting against her own tears).

"The visit is sixty dollars—" Dr. Caldwell adds "—if you want to take him home now. He'll continue to cycle in this way until he finally goes. I'm going to ask our resident expert to come see you first. It costs a little more but you might want to consider the option. If you don't want to take him home."

Resident expert?

Astair doesn't ask.

She just thanks Dr. Caldwell and slips back into the examination room (where Xanther is still standing (by the wood examination table (with her little one (still still (too still (maybe breathing (but who knows (especially with its eyes closed (so tight))))))))).

They should just go.

They almost do go.

And then Dwight Plaguer (the resident expert)
∴ **TFv1 p. 228** ∴ walks into the room.

"It's super gentle."

"Sorry, kid."

— The Matrix

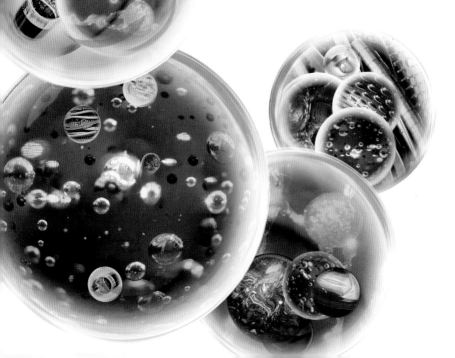

"Hey! Dr. Caldwell asked me to talk to you. About your friend here."

But he doesn't look at Xanther's huddle of white, so awfully motionless on the table, beside Dad's sopping wet sweater. He doesn't look much at Xanther either, unless flashing his, like, white teeth counts, and they are super white, like his long hair is super blond, as in golden, like does he dye it?, definitely gets it cut professionally, so many perfect layers, feathered?, reminding Xanther of some of Astair's and Dov's old vinyls, old bands, like the Bee Gees, Astair's, or Styx, Dov's, what was his name, Tommy Shaw?, only this guy here is all hair without the music.

Anyway, all his attention goes straight to Astair, and like his teeth seem to get even whiter, and his hair, the way he shakes it, practically glows.

For sure, Xanther's glad he's totally ignoring her, if something about how he's so focused on Astair bugs her.

Xanther drapes over little one, snugs her arms around him, like walls, if first retucking a tiny corner of cashmere dryness over the even softer ripples of white fur, still wet, managing to hide everything but the tip of one white ear, left like a tiny pyramid emerging from charred sand, which put like that is no longer tiny, but real size, with Xanther high above, like in a free fall, of, uhm, thought?, wondering if maybe Egyptian pyramids are just the tops of much, much bigger pyramids buried beneath the sand, like, what if, if that was really the case?, like how big would those pyramids have to be?, *huge*, right? Xanther never taking her eyes off the tiny tip of ear, but not getting closer either, so not a free fall of thought, more like a flying thought, wondering, how *huge* then should little one really be?

"Xanther?" Astair asks, like she's already saying it for the second time. Is she? ∷ Yup. ∷ "Is everything okay?"

"Aww, hey," Dwight says. "I know this isn't a good day. I get it. I'm just here to, well hey, we can't make it what it isn't, but we can try to make it right." The kind of thing you'd expect a guy like him to say. Astair uses it to throw all her attention Xanther's way, forcing Dwight to do the same. He even outs this exaggerated smile, that is until he finishes talking, then it turns into this exaggerated frown, but with the sides of his mouth still curling up, like to seem more sympathetic, with his forehead lining up like corduroy, and his brown eyebrows pinching together, like some gross "I'm So Sad We're So Sad" face he's practiced in the mirror.

Xanther's sure he practices all kinds of faces in the mirror.

He returns his attention to Astair. Xanther can see she's thrown by his weird focus, his intensity, and she's no beginner to such stuff, even if she still hasn't figured out how to handle this one yet. Maybe that's why she reaches out to Xanther, as if needing her touch for what comes next.

But what does come next?

Maybe that's what she had liked about Dr. Caldwell. She didn't know what came next. None of them did. They were just trying to figure it out together.

Dwight Plaguer, though, knew what was next before he even walked into the examination room. And it wasn't their next. Or anybody else's next. Just his.

"Shall we take a look?" Dwight asks, still addressing Astair, back to his smile, but a really wrong smile, that Astair answers with a little smile, hers wrong too.

Dwight reaches for little one then, but Xanther doesn't retreat, huddling even closer to the table, further fortifying the small creature with elbows and shoulders, before changing her mind, scooping up the whole messy wet sweatered bundle, whisking it away from anywhere near the table, white pyramid and all, enduring a tiny stir of discomfort, followed by a breathless settling against her chest.

"I don't think that's a good idea," Xanther mumbles, not able to meet Dwight Plaguer's gaze, certain he's staring at her now, especially from the way Astair's watching him with growing alarm, Xanther watching her mom's wrong little smile right itself, clicking into that fierce expression of loyalty, what she and Dov always had in common, stepping to Xanther, "closing ranks," as Dov would say.

"Hey, of course!" Dwight says, getting it, reversing direction, palms out, hands up, like he's under arrest, even as his smile keeps getting bigger, dimples emerging, flirting with his tan cheeks. "You're the boss," he continues, though not really looking at Xanther, or now even Astair, though he still winks, was that for Astair? "Dr. Caldwell just wanted me to go over the process."

Like that's going to stop Xanther from edging around the table. Dwight's blocking the door but Xanther's not worried. When she gets there, he'll move. Her mom will make him move.

"The process?" Astair asks.

"Yeah, that's right, you know, the steps we will take if you don't want him to suffer anymore."

That stops Xanther.

"Yeah, I know it sucks, and I get it, you're suffering too, but hey, and you know this, your animal's suffering the most."

Xanther meets his gaze this time, and knows at once she won't last, because like, despite his Newport looks, his gaze is way scarier than anything Xanther's encountered before, like it's precharged with a preset response to anything she'll do, like too long a look will automatically provoke him to lunge, at her, at Astair, and definitely at the little one who Xanther keeps clutching tighter and tighter.

And that's not all. There's something way stranger. For the brief moment when Xanther did lock eyes with Dwight, the stones over his eyes not only got heavier, way heavier, like fixed there forever, but Xanther realized she had no idea what color hid beneath, not even a hint.

When had that ever happened?

:: *This is the first time.* ::

:: **But not the last.** ::

"Why isn't Dr. Caldwell telling us this?" Xanther asks, never anticipating the question, the words just slipping out, though without any edge or tone.

Dwight Plaguer nods, nods a lot, looking at walls then, and throwing his head like to get his bangs out of his face, though he doesn't have bangs, or any hair in his face, probably because there's enough gel or hair spray to keep all those layers locked in place.

Oh. Ah. There it is. Xanther has the answer: Dr. Caldwell likes him! Likes him a lot!

∴ *I was just about to posit that.* ∴

∴ Meaning before pointing that out, you were thinking that? ∴

"Good question. Fair question. Alice is a good doctor. So good. Loves animals. And saves them. Boy, does she save them. So many, many. But she's also really, really sensitive." Which comes out like an accusation, with those immovable, covering stones momentarily seeking out Xanther again. "Alice handles most everything here, but there's one part she leaves to others, or in this case to me."

"Does Dr. Caldwell—" Astair begins, redressing Dwight's familiarity first. "Is she recommending that our pet be put down now?"

"It's something she's considering. Alice asked me to come and take a look and let you know what I think. But before I can let you know what I think, I do have to take a look."

Dwight steps toward Xanther again, and now Xanther's the one who wants to charge, shove him aside, get out the door, out down that strange orange hallway, out into the sunny Los Angeles day she knows is waiting, even if this wish starts dimming at once, like the day is already dimming, ending, even if Xanther knows there's at least a good hour before the sun goes, feeling it in here already setting, and no windows either, a sinking into darkness that seems to sizzle and pop and gasp. Did little one just gasp?

79

"Hey," Dwight adds, opening his arms and grandly stepping aside, her escape as easy as a few steps. "If you know he's not in pain, take him home. Please! Sure makes my job easier! Don't think for a moment I get off on this."

Again that wrong smile, though at least it isn't his "I'm So Sad We're So Sad" face, and at least Astair's smile in response is genuine, because hers *is* sad.

"He is suffering," Xanther answers, hating herself for saying it, though it's the truth.

She's known it for a while too, can feel it even now, in the way his little back paws have started a series of tiny rabbit kicks against her chest.

"Okay, all right. Let's see where we're at."

Xanther, defeated, gently returns the bindle of soaking sweater back to the examination table.

Dwight slowly pulls back the cashmere, and the little one seems to unfold with it too, stretching out, not in that feel-good way, but more in that way of letting go that comes with exhaustion, flopping on his side, hind legs wet, chest wet, breathless

:: *with breaths so small air—*::

:: if air could speak ::

:: *—would claim no exchange* ::.

"Oh, man, yeah." At least Dwight doesn't touch him. "See that? He's breathing through his mouth now. Man, I'm so sorry. You never want to see cats doing that."

How had Xanther been so blind? Though, like of course, it was obvious now, as soon as this guy said it, her little one was way worse than before.

Xanther feels the room bend even more toward darkness, as if the darkness held back by every day could do that to walls and corners, rounding them, before driving them down toward an inescapable center.

Xanther's lips and fingertips tingle then with a crackle singeing every surface between herself and little one.

She even tries resting one palm on him, as if touch might stop it, her palm nearly covering him, Xanther's hand a hand with a tail, did she know he was this small? ∴ Of course she knew. ∵, is he getting smaller?, does it matter?, especially in the way everything keeps crackling around her, so much so that it seems the world itself could in this moment just flash away . . .

∴ *Burned up in the instantiation of its future.* ∵

∴ **This future.** ∵

And, of course, that's when, oh, wow, Xanther realizes what she should have recognized when she left home, just how much the strange blue acorn is burning now — as much at the heart of her as it remains beyond her — hotter than ever before, and for one thing turning to ash all her plans to smuggle the little cat out of the house, as a way to keep that flame extinguished, or at least dampened, and for another thing, drawing Xanther back to that familiar forest that now might as well be a forest of burning stone.

"You think he's cycling too?" Xanther asks.

"No question," Dwight answers solemnly, or how solemn tries to be when it's not, unable to get away from that big-toothed smile, another swish of blond hair.

Xanther nods. She catches too what looks like a wince crossing Astair's face, like the admission of what's plain as day is too painful even for Astair, and she was the one who had wanted a dog. Xanther suddenly feels sorry for her mom, that she had managed to come around a little, only to wind up here.

"Do any animals who are *cycling* . . ." Xanther continues, pressing toward the hardest question, which, when it comes out, feels as clear and direct as anything Dov might have mustered. "Do any of them go on to live?"

Did Astair gasp? ∴ Yes. ∴

"No," Dwight answers, shaking his head too, his face darkening, despite the halo of perfect hair, but also in this weird way that makes his big bright smile seem still bigger, even brighter.

Xanther can't make sense of him. He unsettles her, even if she knows he doesn't matter. Only little one matters.

"Alice, man, like I already said, such a good heart. She can get close to the edge, real close, especially if there's a chance that she can bring whatever living thing she's taking care of back from the edge. But over the years she's just gotten way too sensitive. It's maybe what makes her such a great vet, but when it's clear she can't help anymore . . ." Dwight lets his voice trail off.

"When she can't help, we get you?" Astair snaps, her fierceness returning.

"Sure. I mean, I'm qualified to do this, but I'm not a vet," Dwight answers almost lazily. "If you feel more comfortable, you know like you'd prefer a licensed practitioner, there are other vets here. I'm happy to get one. They cost more but we all do the same thing. We use sodium pentobarbital with a combination of other drugs to make sure your pet goes peacefully and painlessly. We like to give a good life dignity by ending the suffering."

"Dignity?" Xanther asks, the question, if it is a question, racing her heart something awful, maybe because the answer so eludes her. And touch sure is no help, even if her cupped palm over slimsy little one keeps trying to feel it, as if feeling alone was an irrefusable commandment granting even the most slender creature the power of human speech.

When Xanther withdraws her hand nothing in that soak of misery even hints at dignity.

"The question you have to answer is, hey, do you want him to keep hurting?"

"Who are you to—!" Astair starts to bark.

"Mom! It's okay. He's right. That is the question."

And one certainty, now bound up in the charging beats of her heart, is that Xanther will do anything to keep her dear little friend from suffering.

But what stops her heart too is the question of whether or not to end suffering is a legitimate reason to end life?

Never before has Xanther wanted so much for a seizure to take her down, drop her to the floor, tumble her into that awful catsum ∴ *TFv1 p. 58* ∴, keep her out for hours, absolve her from having to make this gruesome decision.

But, of course, no seizure comes.

No seizure for little one either, though a tiny groan coupled with a pained sigh lifts and defeats his chest.

Dwight Plaguer steps to the counter, where he starts to lay out a syringe, some bottles of drugs, other stuff.

"Unless you decide otherwise — and hey, really, take your time — but unless you decide otherwise, I will first have to take your animal to another room. Don't worry, nothing will happen there. I just need to set up an IV thingy so everything goes smoothly in here. Then I'll wait until you're ready and when you are, he'll just go to sleep. It's super gentle."

Mohonk
Mountain
House

FzQrKozegTl/oPdIb2vMTC7hn1jZRfAT0
H4qtgvN2voqnZlVBtUZ+T32eD56lam
mEDRCg9/eM50OAzsrgEsqJ3ZGH7Kz/
AF+wLvgds+B4i8Yf+y1VHYMyoLQu+2u
n1omDR/A7ms7NKTd6Q==

place of bears

41.768545, -74.155966

Mohonk Mountain House
1000 Mountain Rest Road
New Paltz, New York 12561

Of all possible places to orchestrate such a terrifying meet, Cas winds up waiting on the dock by the lake, relaxing in an Adirondack chair.

A room at the resort was booked months ago. She and Bobby checked in without any intention of going much farther than the lobby.

Early ideas had revolved around meeting Recluse inside the elaborate building, which the uninitiated might say evoked the Overlook Hotel in *The Shining*. Though if the Mohonk Mountain House is possessed by spirits, they are the kind kind who only stick around to carouse happily with the living. Here is a welcoming, familial world.

In fact, the resort is in the midst of a weeklong special event called "Fall Family Getaway." It is likely a marketing ploy to boost occupancy rates in that period between Labor Day and the holidays. Fall is still at least a month away, even if New England alchemy has started to stir, that coveted leaf magic beginning to gold-plate chestnut oaks and red maples. The staff reports no vacancies.

Children challenge the tower stairs, race the hallways. The main dining room reverberates with an endless chorus for dessert.

At first glance, the castle turrets and daunting stonework walls, built in the early twentieth century, and albeit familiar, prepared Cas for the worst, shivers of dread demanding from existence an emptiness she must encounter within. But of emptiness there wasn't even a hint.

Everything was warmly lit. The staff answered visitors' needs with smiles and maps, bug spray, mild drinks, hot tea, decks of cards.

Old couples gathered around tables to play dominoes or tackle the latest *Times* crossword. Young families carried on endless games of Monopoly and Risk. Few screens were visible. Curiously, the absence of that common blue light made Cas clutch even more her hidden Orb. Though she'd probably clutch it regardless of the circumstances.

At first they considered the Sunset Lounge upstairs before finding the Lake Lounge just as suitable, and frankly more comfortable. However, the presence of so many young people had made them move to the Lake Porch. The appearance of still more children made Cas reconsider again. She was after all in possession of a bomb that she would be incapable of detonating in the presence of any innocent.

"Was that your plan all along, old man?"

"Whatever that crazy brain of yours is conjuring up, strike suicide from the list," Bobby muttered.

That was an hour ago. Now Cas sits by herself contemplating the black mirror of Lake Mohonk, the night too cold to encourage company, perhaps her isolation further dissuading interest, an idyll here of grief buried under sweaters, with an extra wool blanket on top, no Fay Wray her, no virgin offering, nothing the staff hasn't seen many times before. The old nearing the edge. How it goes.

Except tonight is not just about one peccable old lady musing over her life like it was an old puzzle with too many missing pieces to make finishing ever a consideration.

Tonight this old lady is waiting for a man capable of mustering an armed force much larger than the one she's fortified herself with here, both up close and far away.

The biggest risk is that one of his snipers will loose a round about now. There will even be time for a few shots if the first one misses. It's not like Cas can drop and roll, zigzag for cover. And if she pitches herself into the lake she'll probably freeze or drown before anyone can help.

The Sniper Gambit, as Bobby calls it, is the one that worries both of them the most. It means that Recluse doesn't believe Cas is in possession of any technology besting his and that his ego does not demand the theatrics showcasing his personal victory over his only viable threat.

One adequate shot and Cas will slump. She doesn't even have to die. Dayton must have taught Recluse that their Great Eyes are fluent now in self-destruction ∴ **TFv2 p. 559** ∵. The Orb just has to slip from her fingers — detonation invoked with the absence of her touch — granting maybe a moment to roll free of her lap. Then the blast will obliterate her and most of the dock.

And that will be that. Bobby will carry on. Their ragged, earnest coalition will seek out others who can carry the burden of this technology and maybe learn one day how to effectively Orb. Maybe Mefisto will help with that acquisition. If he survives. He'll be next.

Cas suddenly smiles. She wonders if Recluse has a deck of cards with all their faces and names. Monsters he can deal out to his well-armed employees. Maybe she'll ask him. Maybe he'll have one on him. Will he part with it? Is she an obvious Queen? Or an Ace? Better a Joker. Though Mefisto will want the Joker.

These ridiculous thoughts comfort her as a breeze picks up and, susurrating across the glossy water, wraps its icy lack of concern around her.

Still no bullet. Though there is time. Though the more time that slips by, the more Cas revisits the Seize and Arrest Gambit.

Bobby and Warlock spent the most time orchestrating responses to various scenarios built around an attempt to just grab Cas. In this one, the odds are not steeply in Recluse's favor. For example, any force moving down the dock would have to contend with the fact that they had little chance of apprehending her before she detonated the Orb. They might count on her unwillingness to do so, but that would be a silly gamble on their part. And if the sniper had not been utilized by then, it meant Recluse wanted the Orb, and likely her, alive.

Furthermore, Cas has snipers too, who will easily decimate any force moving around the resort or approaching by way of Garden or Lookout Road.

The Siege Gambit comes next. This is the most rational and likely response, though it too does not guarantee success. Recluse can not only put into action his forces but rally government agencies, cordoning off the resort and park, sending in soldiers and police, and, with air support, orchestrate a series of pincer movements to take care of not only her but all those armed and loyal to her in the area. The problem that still remains, though, is that once again she and the Orb will be lost. Also, Cas is not aided by woolly novitiates. If anything, the VEM Revolution, like any great sea change in a civilization, is not easily siloed by culturally reinstituted groups. Real revolutions introduce porosity to ruling orders.

Cas and her fellow Orbists have many friends in the military, the police, nearly all government agencies, as well as hundreds of civilian groups.

Any siege would quickly find itself already under siege from within. Warlock continues to maintain that their chances of slipping away are high. Bobby agrees. Cas too.

Which leaves the Recluse Gambit. What happens if Recluse shows up?

Just his appearance will require a tremendous personal risk. He is smart enough to anticipate that Cas' Orb will be weaponized for mutual destruction.

"That creep enjoys risk. And he's good at managing it too," Bobby said.

"But such high wisk would wequi'e commensuwate wewawd, yes?" Warlock asked.

And that remains the elusive heart of the Recluse Gambit that no one can figure out: what does he have to gain by meeting Cas in this way?

Cas favors seduction. Intellect will prohibit scenarios of outright surrender, but his ego will insist that in the light of his argu-
ments and in the presence of his personality,
Cas will surrender just enough to com-
promise their purpose.

Warlock accepted the possibility. Bobby, though, was not
convinced.

"He knows you won't
just give over the Orb.
And with the Orb in
hand, he knows you're
too well armed for
him or anyone else to
seize it."

"Then what, Bobby?
What does he hope to
gain?"

Bobby said bluntly that the
Sniper's Gambit remained the
smartest option. "You'll show
yourself and he'll drop you like a bag
of Costco meat."

Bobby looked like ash when she finally kissed him and limped away toward the Mohonk Mountain House dock.

Cas smiles knowing that by now color has returned to his face. The Sniper's Gambit is all but off the table. Bobby now has plenty to occupy his worries preparing for the Seize and Arrest Gambit or the Siege Gambit.

The Recluse Gambit continues to defy preparation.

While Warlock did not entirely dismiss intellectual seduction, he supported a view that no matter how elaborate the arrangements were to secure this meeting, the purpose was more simple.

"We a'e all expe'ts when it comes to the analysis of data, but even the powe's of scwying cannot weplace the human spectwum of info'mation pwesent when we sit down face to face."

"That's all?!" Bobby was incredulous. Cas too.

Now she isn't as sure. Recluse is practically mandarin in his devotion to shadowy long games. Might so little a play also be a possibility?

Cas expects he will make promises he will never keep, lie about his achievements, use every untruth to uncover their latest VEM discoveries, protect himself with misinformation about his own discoveries.

Cas also knows that whatever he says about VEM will intrigue her. In that way they are the same. Their singular preoccupation will shield them both from cruder displays of violence.

"We are just at the beginning," they had said to each other over forty years ago. She still says it. So vast the discovery, so terrifying the consequences.

A horrible thought abruptly rises, like a hot spout of unexpected vomit: Cas actually wants to see him. They had all been so close, yoked together by something far greater than all petty self-satisfactions.

If their paths had not diverged so radically, they would still be gathering together, even bringing along their families to this place, where they had gathered once before, a long time ago.

Another thought rises, this time like a wave of relief: is that what he wants? To reenact that long-lost friendship?

The laughter of friendship from one of the nearby porches reaches Cas, joined immediately by shouts of children protesting something. Unfair game play? Orders to go to bed? Cas suddenly wants to climb out of this chair and join the strangers inside. Peer into their lives. Without the Orb.

Though that's not what she really wants. She is forever in the thrall of a focus so commanding it sacrifices everyone everywhere. To where she'd turn now, if they could afford the connectivity. To those blackest of waters. Scrying the blackest glass. Until dawn. Until dusk. Lose days. Lose nights. Embrace the majesty of infinite revelation.

Cas' fingers twitch. Her whole body twitches. Twitch too much and she might blow herself up. Cas steadies her palm on the glass, steadies her mind: no more thoughts of escape or how to handle Recluse.

Cas returns to what needs no Orb: the red planet of her dreams where she exercises untethered speculations, on that windswept mesa where stands a temple of nine columns with a glossy white pyramid at its center, unmarred by the outrages of the past, untroubled by the hazards of the future, and most of all undefeated by meaning.

Here's where Cas waits: in the temple of her own making, beyond origin and causality. Where she still is when footsteps approach, familiar in her peace, if amplified by fear, monstrous with proximity.

What will be his first
words? Or will she
speak first? How
will their initial
exchange play?

Though until
she sees him,
Cas' lips will
keep trem-
bling before
the wordless
domain of what
must come next.

"There's been a change," Bobby says softly.

Cas relaxes. With Bobby she needs no words. Nor future.

"He wants to meet at midnight again. Different place though. But close. You can still change your mind."

"I prefer midnight." Time's hands in prayer.

"Any revelations out here?" Bobby jokes. He crouches down to pick up a lost card. ∴ *El Pescado* ∵ ∴ **no. 50** ∵

"None," Cas lies.

There had been one: the conversation to come cannot be anticipated because there can be no conversation.

More than ever now, Cas is
certain Recluse will show,
if only because his ego
understands that if
he is great, his rival
must be equally
great — *almost*
equally great.

R e c l u s e
needs Cas
to certify
their rivalry
in order to
l e g i t i m i z e
his actions.

What he has
al/ways failed to
grasp is that VEM
needs neither one
of them. VEM is the
temple in the sands oblivious to sands. And before its
altar, Cas understands her only
course of action: Cas' Gambit.

Before Recluse even says a word, Cas will lift her hand from the Orb and blow them both away.

Thunk

Annie's twelve years old . . .

— *Sublime*

The truck ahead gets laughs. Victor at the wheel también riéndose when Luther points it out. Tweetie crammed in the back of the Camaro has to struggle forward to read the license plate:

Maybe Luther loved Domingo's mom some, for a minute, who knows, telling her how to save her son like he did, that was out of the blue, and not for her pinche son, but for her.

Domingo sure didn't love his mom. Love means listen. Amar es escuchar. And Domingo sure as fuck didn't listen to what Luther's sure his mom passed his way, that last chance, a chance moment showing up like a miracle when an angry heart changes itself for a beat, offering room enough for this madre and her niño to get clear of a whole lot of Luther hurt.

But Domingo didn't get clear. Okay, he didn't go back to mamita. At least he wasn't that mensote, but he was fool enough to think young pussy was gonna stay still, and even worse, followed carne fresca when it got loose.

The day after Luther had his sit-down with Domingo's madre in her kitchen, phone rang.

"Got two," Nacho Mirande rasped. "Tired of young dick that can't give em their own bath." And not just that. They were saying Domingo wouldn't stop texting them to come back.

Nacho looked younger all of a sudden, hair Bryled, green plaid shirt ironed crisp as bills he had ready when Luther dropped by, what Luther brushed aside, wanting just those putas, hear what they would say, Juarez nearby, temible, como muy eager to get them talking, his smile wide as Nacho's, who holds up his hand to stop them on the stairs, wanting first for them to hear what he had to share.

What he had to share no tenía nada que ver with Domingo but with how, a few nights ago, he found himself too drunk to stand, right where they were now, sprawled out como el pobre padrote que es, deserted by love, by all he'd got good at, had come to deserve.

"Peor tantito, se me salió. Just lying there on the pavement," Nacho declared, jabbing a bent finger at the gap in his grin, Luther already wincing that Nacho was gonna drag them through another one of his dreams. Maybe Juarez even growled, like Juarez gonna stand barred from two girls by another fucking tooth story.

"Before I can get it, and you know glue it back in, who the fuck picks it up? A nun! That's right. Un pinche pingüino. Here! Comes over saying she lost a sister to the street, so many sisters lost to the street, and she's crying, and fuck if I'm not crying too, and then we're both crying, and she even blesses me, or says some prayers, and forgets to give me back my tooth. No mames, amigo, mi Lútero, a fuckin nun stole my tooth!"

Luther had laughed. Juarez too. Didn't need to tell the old pimp there was no nun that stole no tooth because there hadn't been a tooth for a long, long time. Nacho would have just come up with another story anyway. And Luther would have winced but still listened. Because he liked the old pimp's company. Because somehow these stories seemed to buy more time. Or let go of time. Luther wasn't sure which.

Luther had settled back, settling Juarez too with a sigh and a fact, that the girls weren't going nowhere, maybe still in their baths, and when Nacho felt right, he'd lead the way, maybe to what Luther's been hunting for months.

Luther squatted by the front steps and accepted a beer. Juarez too, though he finished his in one foamy chug, then chewed into the can, surprised, maybe hurt, that metal don't taste so good, then loped off to circle the building, find something to dig up or bust on or just howl at.

Luther got Nacho back around to the whores, what makes them stick around, what makes them run. Do they fall for clientes or love their pimps? Was it sex love or father love?

"No!" Nacho surprised Luther. "Mira, Domingo wanted it both ways, be el padrote y el hombre. But these girls, they want what they need: sus madres."

"You're their mother?"

"¡Cómo no!" Nacho grinned.

Funny how Luther almost got talking about Asuka then. The feeling moved fast too, like a hard breath, tingling his cheeks, leaving behind ants nibbling under his lips. That close to out loud.

Maybe Luther figured this old pimp was about the only one who could make sense of why a man sometimes want to beat something so soft? ¿Qué lo hace make knuckles paint a face for weeks? What makes a man like it too? What makes her like it? ¿Como si Luther is the papi they never had? Or the papi they always had? Or was Nacho right? Was shit even weirder? Like Luther was their mommy too? Like Lupita herself. The mother bad girls know they deserve?

But Luther chewed up and swallowed the ants. Nacho was talking anyhow. Bragging. Because of course two girls had come back. Because of course the rest would be back soon.

Not that that stopped Domingo from blowing up their phones. Pidiendo, prometiendo. Putas showing Nacho everything. Pinche pendejo Domingo got to know he's hunted. So why stay close? What the fuck kind of thinking is that?

Luther figured Domingo didn't think much. Just that type who makes up a story about the world to fit how he feels. And then believes it. More boy than man. Not even a boy except for the fact he can't see past a woman's lap.

"Won't show his face to me though," Nacho wheezed, laughed. "He busted my tooth out. I got shit to lose. Si lo veo, le doy en la madre al puto."

Luther sipped his beer. No point mentioning the nun. The point was never the tooth. The point was that two putas knew where Domingo was at. But Luther never even had to ask, forget knock on doors, fill their baths with ice. Nacho gave Luther the address himself.

"Tell my little ones it's time to return. Su mamá no está enojada."

But Luther had to send Tweetie and Juarez after Domingo because Eswin had reached out then for a meet. It wasn't clear if Teyo would be there but Luther had no choice.

Teyo wasn't there. Eswin stood outside his Mercedes on Beverly Drive, just south of Wilshire, with three white boxes tied in pale blue ribbon stacked on the hood. Eswin was sunning his face in the hot September sun, and only now and then echándose un taco de ojo con Beverly Hills morritas wandering by en minifaldas, or did Eswin have eyes for the men en shortcitos following after the skirts?

Luther couldn't tell. Eswin wore big sunglasses, almost like a fuckin mask, though even without sunglasses Eswin was still a mask. This much was clear though, as Luther approached — girls in short skirts scurrying out of the way, men in shortshorts too, like those tiny birds on the beach when a dog runs down a ball, even if Luther wasn't running — Eswin the Mask was in a good mood.

"You do that wherever you go?" Eswin asked, shaking Luther's hand, Luther watching too as the wake he left behind healed itself, men's hands reaching for the girls' backs, girls giggling for the touch, before scooting away.

"Guess so."

"From Teyo," Eswin said, pointing at the boxes.

Three nice shirts, it turned out, in colors with names like seafoam, orange peel, gold leaf, plus buttons so thick they might as well have been carved from elephant tusk.

"Why for?" Luther asked. Drinks was one thing, rounds you could take, but gifts were traps.

"With apologies. Teyo understands you're no missing-persons specialist. He's calling you off the chase." Domingo's name stayed unspoken in the pause. "If that's what you want?"

Luther in that pause believed Eswin too, believed Teyo, knew that for sure the boxes were traps but ones he could walk through anyway, bust up, enjoy whatever meat they'd staked.

Problem now was that Luther was so close. Like break-down-a-door close. Though wasn't that the same thing he told Eswin last week? How was Luther gonna sell it now?

Luther didn't sell it, just let Eswin know Teyo would have his satisfaction soon, and then took the shirts, leaving less of a wake than before, chicas y chicos lindos drawn to the boxes like old friends, like in their company the ink over Luther's face grew familiar.

The trouble for Luther was that the closer he got to Domingo, scent deep in his nose, in that place where scent becomes a taste, y el sabor es lo que el hambre necesita para tomar el control, Luther's head had also started to get involved, getting him more and more curious.

One thing was certain: Domingo was un pendejo. Maybe he dressed good, or had teeth pretty enough to fool a puta young enough to believe que una sonrisa era parte de él por siempre, though maybe at that age six months is.

Domingo couldn't hear a warning, even if it was like a train whistle running him down. He couldn't stop showing off his pretty teeth either, presumiendo cómo se viste, showing off the girls he had on call, vatos he hung with, shit he was in on.

Domingo was one of those guys who couldn't shut up. He might hear a thing but was too dumb to keep that thing cold and dark under a headstone of common sense.

Sure, anyone can be a soplón. That would get Teyo after him. But Luther couldn't see Domingo getting close to no police. More like some rata desperate to cut a deal with the placas, to stay out of la pinta, had passed along Domingo's alardes. That flowed right. If it still came up short on the biggest question of all:

how the fuck did Domingo know about the Solder Supply meet on Knox? ∴ **TFv2 pp. 192–207.** ∴ It's not like Domingo has any in with Teyo, let alone shit to do with pinks.

Small world was waiting. When Luther met up again with Tweetie and Juarez that afternoon, had on his seafoam shirt too, they was laughing, though Juarez looked plenty skittish.

They had headed to the address Nacho gave Luther. In Pacoima. Where Lity, the third puta, was. Supposedly Domingo had made a deal with Lity's dad for a couch and a room above the garage for some crunked-up shit that turned out to be Choplex-8's, Lupita's brown balloon parade, what Domingo kept stepping on with some poisonous soda, to cover their rent.

Domingo moved in with Lity and the rest of the girls. He mostly sat around with Lity's dad watching DirecTV, getting sprung on the shit. Lity didn't care where they got it, but she knew how they paid for it, Tweetie getting an earful on how Domingo kept turning all the girls for his feast. At least Domingo kept Lity's dad off her. He was good for that.

The whole story made Luther's skin rash. Maybe Nacho was right about baths. There were no baths at Lity's place. Even the shower was broken. Girls would talonear in cars or nearby alleyways and after wash themselves in a dirty little sink. And all of them living so close together like they was sisters, or cousins, maybe some were cousins, Luther didn't know, didn't fuckin care, like some awful family, fed up on promises, turning wrong way around, in on itself, for cable, toothpaste, vein-robbing hits.

Luther can stomach plenty, but this business of whores? Not a fuckin chance. Taxin or action, cash askin for smoke sure, or a show for blow, or blow for mud, that's fine too, or what needs fixin, mixin, more time. But keeping pussy in line makes Luther want to scratch hisself to death.

How does Nacho stand it? Domingo? Unlucky fuckers. Pero nocierto. Domingo is a luckier fucker than most.

Lity says Domingo hadn't left that Pacoima crib for weeks. She just wanted that pendejo out. Had kept leaving the door open as a hint.

How Juarez found it when he slipped in first. Had his machete swinging by his feet. Figured he'd find putas in the living room, at least Lity's dad. But the front rooms were empty.

Juarez hung back then, knew like they all know that Tweetie moves quietest, like some dancer, checking the back rooms, all the rooms, ready with his storm.

But there was no need for a storm. Place was empty. Juarez though had spotted the garage.

Tweetie led the way again. Like the house, the garage was open. Like the house, it was empty.

That's when they heard the cries from up above. Ecstasy pero with grunts too and these crunches como si something or someone was being beaten while they being fucked. Heavy sounds, like can only come from a heavy man, though the cries were sin duda a girl's, and here's the part that really fucked with Tweetie's head, they was happy cries too. Who knows what fucks with Juarez's head.

Juarez was first in too, Tweetie at his back, swinging open the door at the top of the stairs.

Hello Lity, all by herself too, como niñita jumping up and down on a big bed. Sonrisota también. Eyes closed. Arms out like a plane. Little hands making little fists. Hair washing over her face on the way up, kissing the ceiling on the way down.

The weird part was that Lity wasn't just jumping up and down on the bed. She was jumping up and down so she could jump off. Mattress springs bounced her pretty high too. She would almost disappear between the wall and the bed. Landing hard. Then she'd climb back up and do it again. Like she wanted to come down more than wanted to go up, which is really the reverse of how little kids think.

Turns out she was jumping right on top of her old man, just out of sight, passed out on the floor thanks to that junk que Domingo andaba mezclando con jarabe para la tos, out cold, not waking for even his hija busting his ribs.

Tweetie grabbed her by the hair, midair, and planted her on the floor. He couldn't stop laughing. Maybe because Juarez got todo emputado.

"That's fucked up, homegirl," Juarez said, like he was fucking scolding her. "You need to check that behavior out." Which made Tweetie laugh even harder, like he laughed hard when he was telling all this to Luther, Luther laughing too, because quién chingados is Juarez to get in it with someone over their behavior. Fuck he even using a word like *behavior* anyway?

Tweetie laughed still harder when he told it again for Victor from the backseat of the Camaro, just moments ago, as they drove along Silverlake Boulevard, toward the reservoir.

That got Victor laughing so bad he started swerving the Camaro, chillando de risa, deserving honks and glares, Luther glaring back, leaving a wake of fear.

The funniest part of the story though was what wasn't funny at all: Domingo still got clear. At the last minute, after the two girls ditched him for Nacho, he ran off with the last puta because as Lity swore to it "those two are so in love, tan enamorados."

Domingo had to be the luckiest fucker alive, at least until two hours ago, when Luther's phones blew up, getting word the old way.

One of Piña's biscochos had a buddy working valet on Glendale Boulevard. He caught sight of Domingo rolling up in front of the Red Lion ∴ **The Red Lion Tavern. 2366 Glendale Boulevard, Los Angeles, CA 90039** ∴. Impossible to miss, strutting into the beer place lit up in violet: violet jacket, violet pants, violet shoes, even a violet hat with a corn yellow feather sticking out of a violet silk band.

Piña had been there in minutes. She reported that Domingo's car was still in the lot. A Camry. Violet, like him.

Luther still had some traffic to get through but wasn't planning an inside adventure anyway. To stir up some shitty bar would only give Domingo another chance to get lucky again.

Minimize friction. Patience. Wait until Domingo stumbles out, follow him wherever, forever, to the place that he needs, then take him down in his sleep.

"Chingadamadremente. Me tienes que estar chingando. Me cago en tu puta madre. Pinches putas mamadas. No mames. Me caga la pinche verga," Victor curses, as something under the Camaro's hood, for the second time, goes *thunk*.

Victor pulls over.

vanishes ahead.

"¿Qué tranza?" Tweetie snarls.

"Se murió. Nomás se murió."

"Whadya mean just died?!"

Victor just keeps shaking his head as they all
get out, smoke gushing out now from under
the hood, white smoke, then black smoke.

Luther knows these signals gonna flag down
some police.

So him and Tweetie push the heap, while Victor steers around a corner where they can lose
themselves under some shade.

Luther's heaving, a lake of sweat, mouth full of
hot pennies. At least he'd ditched thick buttons,
had on a wifebeater, perfect for this.

Tweetie gets Piña on the phone. She's still chillin in front of the Red Lion. In the van with Juarez. They're not far. They can come get them. But what if Domingo leaves while she's gone? Domingo could stay until 2 AM or beat them all in the next minute.

Luther orders Piña to stay. They'll get to her.

Victor slams the hood. He's already stopped mumbling words. Knows better with Luther spitting molten copper now on the pavement. Victor calls El Porvenir Auto Body, gets Adolfo. They talk but not for long. Adolfo will send a tow but not until late. His only truck is still stuck out in Apple Valley.

"Garbage," Luther growls at the Camaro.

"No, man," Victor moans, like Luther just insulted his lover. "She ain't like that."

"Okay, she's amazing!" Luther gushes, if still growling, circling the dead car, fists craving a bat. "Brand new Maserati."

Victor starts sulking like that squares shit.

"Shit either works or it's gone." Luther does his own squaring. "Sell it. Burn it. Bury it me vale verga. But don't let me ever see this rust again."

"¿Nos vamos a pata?" Tweetie asks.

"For fuck's sake," Luther almost shouts. "Call a fuckin cab."

at last!

When I'm fucked up, that's
the real me.

— *The Weeknd*

lost lah.

tapi jingjing al<mark>l</mark>ways lost. live lost. hilang life. damn chia lat. and

dis draw no help. no map. jilo direction. boh chiak buay lia lah.

except warning ah how bakwan jingjing kena makan by future if he

don't find way back to auntie fast.

change underwear.

life's map, stapled to telephone pole, what jingjing grab, rip down, choy!, sign of hilang kuching gripped macam found cat itself. if only just pic dis of little ears, paws, eyes blinked. bad map. mah jingjing lose sight of way back to tian li, forgets street, how to compass feet, scream at strangers, only thing jingjing remember, find way back to ice cream, waved off for short lanes, down ones jingjing oreddy raced, landed damn ass lah back on beach.

too far from her. forget scoops. stare more at hands kum pooi macam sign show way. stall then. kelam kabut by waves. almost fall. kay teruk mind whole time on loop, remixing telephone call.

"blind?"

bak chew tak stamp dat thing? little cloud with eyes bigger than any sky, bluer too, on good day.

mebbe wrong one. mebbe just cat.

"it never opens its eyes," dungu one on phone claimed, scoffed, oreddy to click off.

tapi jingjing maintain balan, jangan catastrophe, repeat truth and more, warn fool, mai siao siao, don'ch play-play, auntie's thing si beh violent.

"cat. kay kay dangerous! very! hurt her! you too!"

dat jerorize eksi borak, say jilo, breathe jilo, give jingjing's mind second beat to crouch, catch gap, remember what auntie showed jingjing once, mouth wide dat, teets missing.

man on phone sigh on such news, breathe again, scoff mebbe, for second time jingjing sure line click off, but man just left to check, count claws, count teeth, gone long time, gone long long time. more than twice jingjing almost hung up, redial, until some sound in ear tell him man, or man's phone, is still there.

"everything you've pointed out is true," man finally saysay, first words, what jingjing sure first time he didn't hear, if sad wasn't si peh plain, si beh sway. jingjing always hear sad and sway.

"address!" jingjing demanded, between joy and mad, what matter either when man spit out address? feelings kena jacked by numbers and street.

jingjing slam phone down then, screamed wild, fever high, raised lost sign to sky.

then raced back to auntie, not back at all, jingjing seeing nothing but cat, his cat, soon.

lost lah.

lost again lah.

pocket missing notice, ditch beach, air rojak of salt, garbage stink

til street-side garden lock up jingjing's feet. white roses leap over

little white fence, roots twisting deep, alamak so cooling, so many

scents. jilo macam singapore parks, nothing like bang wet bukit

graves or jungles of snakes, but even such a dry place macam l.a.,

desert spikes next to oxeyes, familiar sutras of damp soil, worms,

new growth reaching jingjing, pleasing, and still same.

jingjing remembered park where she found him, freed him from

the parade if not that ache, once tugging away weeds macam siao

man, living in parks throughout city, for months, pretending to

work for city as gardener, pretending to belong.

auntie had offered jingjing rooftop garden, planter box oreddy

bright with young sprouts of green. but jingjing planted cigarette

butts, beer caps. wanted to die. it to die. it did die. quick.

great tian li asked once. jingjing blamed cat quick. saysay immeelly cat piss poison everything. its shit too. lying is jingjing's reflex and gift. good at without feeling good for. colorless as rocks. barren lai dat old planter box.

auntie never mentioned dat once-garden again. jingjing smoked there, hid balloons there.

but now jingjing wonder why he stopped care? jingjing suka bloom, branches and vine, loves fruit, ash trees, and palms.

one night jingjing cabut flat for old park where he lived, want back center of black earth, orchids of tanjong pagar. found only hole.

they building hotel.

jingjing never go back to miss bad-luck starving time if own deep-avali still bright with what he never pick but still want to find.

all of a sudden then, no how, jingjing on track. lost once, lost twice, lai dat knows way back again.

"尔将被召，尔将善答。" ∷ *You will be called upon and you will answer well.* ∷

not all jingjing remembers, heart racing hard, this way!, no choice, to abbot kinney! auntie on bench! kena licence now to rejoice!

once, long before, with wicked blue eyes on her shoulder, the great tian li had muttered strange word: "纠缠。"

"志终易手，然其责之重，其果常出于料而致于险。"

∷ you get cat tapi life is siong and si beh khia-khia for whole jin gang. you damn heng one. ∷

∷ *An unlikely translation.* ∷

∷ **Not even close.** ∷

jingjing saysay again as he run, macam mantra, old charm:

"纠缠。"

∴ entanglement.∴

∴ *Entanglement.*∴

∴ **Entanglement.** ∴

first time in months, jingjing happy like bird, die cock stand.

part for certainty, part for confidence, chia'h kuay kuay, all parts

peace. power too. or how power dreams before power achieves.

jingjing skips. mabok on course. corner here familiar. there too.

skip!

skip!

skip!

hilang itch, hilang smoke scratch. jilo balloons in head. now head

is balloon! lift jingjing up! feet free of sidewalk, float from street,

heart free of parade, float free of need.

free!

free!

freeze!

craving ends!

craving ends!

cravings end!

at last!

at last!

at last!

there she is! old bag! right where jingjing remember, kooning too, on bench, curled up macam egg, mouth kay wide with snores, flies makan ice cream, endless winter, pomegranate, still sticky on lips.

jingjing hophop, shooshoo flies off, auntie's mouth immeelly clop shut, pop macam gums all she got, teeth kena makan by rot, tapi even lips si beh thin grin.

jingjing help auntie up, shake at her notice, press in her hands laminated prize, hilang ngeow, white cat, what jingjing find!

great tian li study close sheet. mebbe pic. mebbe date. boh doubt telephone number. osso flip it over. chari address sure. tapi no address hide on blank side.

jingjing ready. jingjing show he no kucing kurap one. got address right here. safe on palm. a path! his path! their path! the only path! so jingjing hophop around. skipskip. so proud.

at last!

at last!

at last!

to his cat!

to his cat!

to his cat!

"吾奇其何以从内得纸乎？" ∷ *I wonder how they get the paper inside?* ∷ auntie ask.

"从里面？" ∷ inside? ∷

"然。其何以从塑料之内得纸乎？ 印象深刻。" ∷ *Yes. How do they get the paper inside the plastic? It's most impressive.* ∷

"印象深刻？" ∷ impressive? ∷

auntie nod, kay pleased. "其无缝，纸善封于其中。" ∷ *There's no seam. The paper is sealed perfectly within.* ∷

"不是那个！看那张照片。看！" ∷ not dat! look at picture, here. look! ∷

auntie blur like sotong. hand back prize.

"吾问之乎？" ∷ *Did I ask for this?* ∷

"可是夫人 . . . " ∷ but mistress— ∷

138

"靖靖，勿称吾夫人！ 吾何求之?" ::*Jingjing, stop calling me that! What did I ask you for?* ::

"吾即需一租车。吾不可晚。你说的。" :: We need taxi at once. We must not be late. You said that. ::

"是也，今吾迟矣。" :: *That's right. Now we are late.* ::

"什么晚了?" :: late what? ::

"其险增之。" :: *She is now in even greater peril.* ::

"可是夫人！" :: but mistress! ::

"吾之租车何在?" :: *Where is our taxi?* ::

אלה הפרחים אם חברה
אבנים נובכן גם
סהרה אתבעי אכמענה ?

Jasper

You can't be trusted.

— Miles Davis

"Then that's it?" Cletious Bou asks.

"That's it," Özgür answers, accepting another pour from the old man.

"I gotta say I never figured you for retirement," Cletious chuckles. "That reality just never crossed my mind. Doing something crazy for a lady makes sense. But not retiring for one."

Özgür checks his watch. If he lingers any longer he'll be late. Cletious takes no offense.

"Don't fret. I'll call you another one in a sec."

"Thanks."

"Not the first time a cab got lost around here."

A bullet hole that made no difference to Özgür still got Captain Cardinal ordering the car to the shop for a patch-and-paint job.

"Can't have people thinking it's open season on police."

Özgür obeyed. Though that's not really the reason he's cabbing it tonight.

Katla.

Özgür drains the small glass. When he'd arrived an hour ago, Cletious set out a one-liter bottle of beer and two small glasses, as if small would limit big. As it turns out, small stays empty as big tries to keep up.

Katla. Katla-katla.

"Where's your dinner?" Cletious asks, refilling both their glasses, finishing the bottle.

"Red Lion."

"Glendale Boulevard? You can get beer there in a glass boot."

Özgür nods. Though he's had enough beer. Scotch is next. Good or bad, it doesn't matter, so long as he has a few. Virgil will understand. He better. He's buying. Celebrating the news of Özgür's move to New Jersey and a new life of gardening in grey.

"Haven't been in years. Though once went enough to know the regulars." Özgür wonders if he'll run into anyone from those days. The air tonight seems charged with that possibility, ready to catch fire with the unexpected.

Katla-katla-katla.

"They find that lion in the mountains yet?" Cletious asks.

"Last I heard she's still up there," Özgür responds.

"Sheeeesh. Can't wait to hear what happens next." The TV in his kitchen has only the weather. The TV in the living room is all about a Medal of Honor recipient, Sergeant Major Bennie Adkins, who killed 175 "enemy combatants." That and being stalked or saved by a tiger. Özgür didn't hear which. He prefers the weather. Hot. No chance of rain.

"I guess something has to happen."

"Lion that big? That mean? You know she's gonna turn up somewhere and it won't be pretty."

Katla. Katla.

Özgür's glad to find Cletious found a good mood. He wasn't sure how he'd take the news. Maybe because Özgür still believes that Cletious sees in him a last chance to still get some justice for Jasper, his murdered boy. Though maybe it isn't that way at all. Maybe at this point they're just friends.

"To Jasper," Özgür suddenly says, lifting his empty glass.

Cletious holds out his hand. Heads to the refrigerator, twists off the cap of another one-liter bottle of beer. Sits down. Refills both their glasses.

Katla. Katla. Katla.

"To you, Oz. I'm gonna miss you, man."

Özgür's mouth goes dry, the kind of dry that's beyond the help of anything wet.

"New Jersey's not so far away."

"Yeah, right. Might as well be Kazakhstan." Cletious breaks out in a big laugh. Gets up again. For another bottle? To call a second cab? But he just heads out of the kitchen. Özgür hears a door open, hears the water start to run.

Özgür had gone too far. It had been a nice visit. Too bad getting back to nice now won't be so easy.

Özgür gets up and pours into the sink what's left of his beer.

Now on both TVs is a story about Operation Fashion Police. Two Mexican drug cartels were caught laundering money in L.A. warehouses and storefronts down in the Fashion District. Sixty-five million dollars in cash seized.

The story briefly interests him and then interest dims, followed by a sensation of easy relief. Because a dumb news story isn't the only thing easing away. All his cases are losing their hold. Plus those that were never his cases: Marvin D'Organidrelle aka Android. Yuri Grossman, Eli Klein, and Jablom Lau Song. Realic S. Tarnen. Questions about that whackadoodle Warlock. Questions about bleach, about ammonia.

All that urgency just fading.

Katla. Katla.

Others will pick up the threads, tie things together, net the worst ones. Or not. It doesn't matter anymore. Özgür served his time, hauled in his share of maniacs. Good men like Detectives Perry and Carter, even Captain Cardinal, even Balascoe will carry on with the job of justice. They'll have help too. Angels like

Planski. Like Virgil. What was that Rawls quote Virgil loved? Justice is the first virtue of social institutions? ∷ TFv3 p. 8. ∷

Özgür checks his watch again.

Where's that cab?

He hears a flush but Cletious still doesn't return.

Why had Özgür brought up Jasper? But even Jasper was fading away. And the lightness of all these departures — they'd been departing for a while now — leave him feeling free and strange but also, at the same time, sad.

Katla. Katla-katla. Katla.

Özgür slides across the counter a honey badger ∷ Quentin Trollip ∷. Leaves it beside the bottle. Reconsiders the beer.

Instead, Özgür heads for the front door. Through the metal security screen he spies his taxi idling curbside.

"Thought you should have this," Cletious says.

Özgür's relieved to turn around and find Cletious smiling. Özgür probably just mistook a full bladder for heartache.

Until the gift makes him rethink that.

"It'll mean a world to me to think you'll have a reason now and then to look on this and think of him."

It's a framed piece of sheet music. The first page of *Rhapsody in Blue*. ∴ By George Gershwin. ∴ ∴ *Clarinet solo.* ∴

"He could play it too. Those pencil markings are his. I framed it for you."

"It'll hang where I'll always see it."

"I got tired, Oz, of thinking about who did it. More and more I accepted that whoever done it was already gotten by something else. Or would be soon enough. Maybe by that lion in the mountains." Cletious' smile seems to widen because the joke doesn't land. "And then, you know, I got tired of even thinking about Jasper. Really, really tired. Like a fall-asleep-forever tired. I got so afraid I'd sleep so long, I'd wake and find Jasper gone. Forgotten. That I still can't risk."

Özgür nods. The cab is honking. He has to get going. He needs a real drink.

"I used to drive trucks. You know that. Mostly city routes, San Gabriel Valley, maybe a little farther north. Now and then though, I did longer hauls. Those can be great, all night, with no one to tell you what to do but the road. But sometimes you get so damned tired. You drink your Cokes, your coffee, roll down the windows, take some cold air in the teeth. But if that don't work, you know what you do? You take out your wallet, it's gotta be full too, with your license, your ATM card, all your plastic lifelines, but most of all it's gotta have your cash. Then you hang that out the window, holding on tight. That keeps you wide awake."

The taxi had stopped honking.

"Cletious, you tired now?" Özgür asks.

"Oh yeah. But I'm still up."

"Window down?"

"You get it, Oz." Cletious smiles. This time because meaning did land. "One hand on the wheel and one hand in the wind."

"Holding on to your wallet?"

"Holding on to something."

Beauty

*It's not what's said that matters but
what's arranged and the voice you
hear that goes unsounded . . .*

— *Nufro*

Beauty :: ████████████ ::
cross into street and traffic stop.

No light.
No sign.
Forget crosswalk.
Forget even intersection.

Beauty just cross into street like
law herself and traffic stop.

True, life is law.

But traffic not always stop for life.

Not this easily.

For Beauty, traffic stop easily.

Is Beauty above life?

Above law?

Beauty need no light.

Beauty need no sign.

Beauty just present herself and
look how cars greet disruption.

Even woman driver to Shnorhk's left stare in wonder. Maybe she like Beauty. Or like to see what men like to see that makes them stop so easily, so gratefully. Haters here too, sure, but most here will keep stand-still grateful to watch Beauty cross twice. Walk back and forth all day, all night.

Only maneki neko don't catch breath. Don't watch. Watch only Shnorhk. Not even Shnorhk. Watch only what's left behind. Who Shnorhk kidding? Maneki neko don't watch anything. Maneki neko is ceramic cat.

Beauty lift black sunglasses and mouth "Thank you!" to Shnorhk. Reaches out too. Almost touches Shnorhk's hood.

Shnorhk give back thumbs up and dumb smile.

Chest hot. Face hotter.

This not just long black hair and long legs. Not just short lemon skirt and black straps wrapping naked ankles sure on high heels. Not just laugh either, or way hips sway on music of laugh. Not just how thin blouse resurrects summer, how cleavage keep boyhood alive.

This something more.

This something else.

Of course, on other occasion, for homeless creature with shopping cart, traffic stop too.

Life is still law.

Even if drivers so impatient then. Some honking. Others cursing. Most looking elsewhere. Hot with shame. Bored by grace.

Sometimes, though, that such life is law is not enough.

Sometimes law is broken, life is broken. Shnorhk knows this.

Ask the old.

Ask the old when they wander out late confused by which way.

Ask the old when stop comes too late. After impact. Long greasy streaks of tire rubber. Smears of regret trailing after. After the old tumble to rest by curb and can't answer back.

Shnorhk know this.

Friend was at wheel that night. No fault.

"Is there hope?" Shnorhk's friend asked over old body.

EMT shook head. "Over sixty-five, they all die at thirty-five ∴ **mph** ∴."

∴ *June 8, 2002* ∴ ∴ ?? ∴

Or all are Beauty.

What young man in navy told Shnorhk on drive this morning near UCLA, of girls jogging by.

"At thirty-five, they all look good."

Because blur invites beauty?

This one here, though, need no blur. Almost to other side of street too. Every car wishing her to just linger moment more. Even Shnorhk.

As if beauty is absolute truth.

As if beauty never get old.

As if beauty never will abandon this moment.

At sidewalk, people rush Beauty with phones, notebooks, and pens.

More people follow: big bags slung over shoulders, snapping pictures with big lenses.

Behind Shnorhk cars honk to move. Shnorhk honk too, at paparazzi. Can't stand scum.

Not one beautiful.

Break law all the time.

Bad drivers too, every one.

But paparazzi can't rob Beauty of beauty any more than they can rob beauty from sky, this day's end, this seaside sky, blushing, glowing.

"Red sky at night, sailors' delight," old saying go.

Only dawn too was same.

"Red sky at morning, sailors take warning."

What would young man in navy have said of day with both?

But young man in navy only talked about some place where he'd got drunk: "Every B-girl stopped for a buck and a fuck and not one blushed." Sailor not blush either. Sailor was still drunk.

Tonight Shnorhk will ask Mnatsagan about beauty. Old professor will like question, Shnorhk certain.

Shnorhk also ask what means delight and warning when both are beautiful? Is beauty both delight and warning? Shnorhk speed up, 35 mph north, all lights green.

Shnorhk smiles, breathes deep. Happy. Patil's been happy too. Cat smell in closet gone. Or gone enough to not notice. Last night Shnorhk even clean duduk. Duduk now in blond box in trunk. Ready for Shnorhk to try.

Tonight Shnorhk try.

Tonight Shnorhk join friends.

Tonight Shnorhk play.

Phone is already mess of texts. From Kindo. From Tzadik. From Alonzo. From Haruki. Even old professor send text.

Mnatsagan: We love you!

Dimi leave voice mail:

"Don't keep me waiting, old man."

Dispatch scratch in ears. Radio too loud. But Shwanika, a smile through scratch, have call. There is pickup not so far. Shnorhk could do one more.

But Shnorhk not want one more. LAX ∴ **Los Angeles International Airport** ∴ drop-off was last.

Shnorhk wish Shwanika good night.

Shnorhk turn off radio.

Then ferret jump into street.
Well, not ferret. Man. But man who
look like ferret. ∷ **Jingjing.** ∴

Venice resident without home.
Homeless without cart. Oriental in
pajamas. Waving hands furious for
Shnorhk to stop.

No Beauty.

Shnorhk not look twice, speed
by, OFF DUTY sign bright. Not even
right to pick up.

Also Shnorhk know better than
to unlock door for such type. Junkie
for sure. Face tight for fix Shnorhk
know he can't fix.

Ferret Man in rearview stay in
street still waving hands. Furious.

Shnorhk hit brakes.

Shnorhk   brake   for   Beauty.
Brake even before Shnorhk register
Beauty.

A blur.

But still too.

Not even in street.

At curb.

Barely raising one hand.

How did Shnorhk even know?

Beauty commands.

Except if Beauty depend just on hip sway, tall legs, long black hair, sass, big bust, flash of cameras, blown kisses, young, here wouldn't be Beauty.

But Beauty is also old.

Sometimes very old.

And tiny too.

And very slow.

She ∷ *Tian Li*∷ takes forever too and then takes two more forevers to reach cab. Shnorhk not mind.

Her patient smile does away with every need to count forevers.

So weightless her progress, air is material. So much like a dream she makes everything Shnorhk know a dream too. Time too.

All becomes immaterial.

Even dreams. Especially dreams.

When she settle into backseat, Shnorhk not even sure he heard door open first.

Though what he hears, doesn't hear, makes no difference with that smile.

She doesn't even speak.

And Shnorhk not ask her to speak.

Her silence is rest.

Shnorhk need such silence.

Shnorhk need this rest.

Then both break.

Passenger door jerk open. Not
even back door. Ferret Man scram-
ble in, right next to Shnorhk. Face
tight. Lineless with fury, with need.

Already screeching too, mouth
farting out address, hand held up,
palm inked with smears of pen.

Shnorhk not care what numbers
hide there. Not care for street name.
Shnorhk will refuse rudeness.

He can.

He must.

Then she murmur something.
What can only mean "Hush."

And Ferret Man hush at once.

Shnorhk twist around. Finds
smile again. And wrinkles. Why
Shnorhk not notice before how
many wrinkles? Nothing but lines.
Thin and wide, deep and winding.
All wrinkles smiling too.

Is she Korean? Maybe Thai?
Japanese? Or Chinese? What
does Shnorhk know? What does it
matter?

It doesn't.

Only such smile.

Shnorhk look again at Ferret Man. Can't believe these two together. But they are.

Words Shnorhk not understand fly back and forth between them.

Until Ferret Man hush again, return to Shnorhk, return to showing Shnorhk inked hand.

Shnorhk study palm. Yes, street name is there. Numbers too.

The sky has lost its blush. The day is dusk. And dusk is already losing fast to night's coming dark.

What is delight and warning when both are replaced by dread?

"Wah lau, so blur?" Ferret Man gnash. "Your grandfudder road too? Chop chop kali pok, can?!"

"What?" Shnorhk ask.

Then Ferret Man really surprise Shnorhk: "Շտապումենք: Կարելի է մեզ տանեք այստեղ: Տեղը գիտեք:" :: *We're in a hurry. Can you take us here? Do you know where this is?* ::

"Echo Park," Shnorhk answer.

bad math}]

"Hello, friend."

— Mr. Robot

The fight didn't start because of the sad part [though it could have {should have‹?›}]. Astair was already fighting with herself.

'What a stupid thing to do!'

'What was I to do?'

'What did I do?!'

Anwar doing his best to calm her [she wanted nothing to do with soft words {even less to do with his soft palms ‹on her shoulders «'Don't touch me. I mean I don't want to be touched.'»}]. Anwar had spent a lifetime learning to insist on softness in the face of this insistence [want {desire}] on hardness ['familiarity with impact' {Astair's words}].

// 'Hardness needs hardness to maintain its shape.'

// 'Eventually the encounter with softness deprives hardness of its insistence.'

// All Astair.

// Thanks to her Tai Chi.

'And sex?' A question Anwar asked the first time she voiced these ideas.

'Sex?' The question catching her off guard.

'Doesn't softness sometimes insist on hardness?'

Which that day resulted in the right outcome. After which [in a sprawl of sheets] Astair laughed so freely Anwar laughed too before she said: 'I did say *eventually.*'

[unlike Astair] Anwar never needed Tai Chi [or yoga {or meditation ‹etc.›}] to choose softness. The choice had been made for him. His mother said his cries at birth were soft. His father said [a point of pride] that his smile had always been soft.

Soft voice.

Soft manner.

Soft way.

A lifetime of softness for Astair as she spent her fury [with herself] on him.

That had been the disaster with Dov. They were both hard. They met on grounds that demanded injury before departure [ground Dov held until the end].

[while it was counter to her birthright {Astair's mother claimed Astair's birth cries splintered roof beams ‹Astair's father still claimed Astair's smile cut down any man not worth her time «said as if Anwar should always be bleeding»›}] Astair walked a path that each day tried to embrace a softness that felt unnatural.

She was so determined Anwar sometimes wondered if perhaps even greater hardness might serve her best.

But no more hardness was available as Astair's clench [physical {and emotional}] began to ebb [returning her {again} to Xanther's decision].

'She said what?' Anwar asked [no longer thinking it necessary to move this conversation from the foyer to their bedroom {it would be over in a minute more}].

'Xanther agreed. She said he was right. She said his suffering was the right question,' Astair said [casting an eye up the stairs {where Xanther had raced ‹to her room «minutes earlier» slamming the door behind her›}].

'You did okay then. She wanted that moment. She needed that moment. And she took it.'

Astair nodded.

[this time] Anwar's soft palm found softening shoulders [{even} a brief hug].

'If only it had been just a moment,' Astair sighed against his chest.

This was the sad part.

But there was a hard part to it too [especially in the way it found then a shape in him {Anwar feeling himself clutch and tighten ‹stiffen in that direction that never finds relief›}].

Supposedly Xanther had sat in that tiny examination room for five minutes [more ∴ *Five and a half minutes* ∴]. The dying creature in her arms. Not saying a word. Under the scrutiny of that vet [or tech {whatever he was ‹'Saccharine scrutiny,' Astair described it as›}].

'I should have asked him to leave,' Astair lamented.

'He was aggressive. Like a salesman. Except what he was selling was euthanizing our daughter's love.' Astair again.

'But I didn't even move.' Astair again.

Anwar's chest tightened more. Maybe because as convinced as he was that he would have behaved differently [exorcised that man from their midst] he feared he would have behaved no differently.

'You were like Xanther?'

'Yeah, she was frozen too,' Astair answered [nodding].

'I probably would have done the same thing. And you can cut yourself some slack too. If she had moved, said something, you would have acted immediately. You were just listening to Xanther.'

Astair kept nodding. 'When she said she wanted to take the cat home, we did leave at once.'

'Do you doubt that choice?'

'Maybe,' Astair confessed [her face a fluctuation of tearless anguish]. 'The animal is suffering. It's so obviously dying. Should we have put it down right then and there? What if it lives til morning? I'll definitely call Dr. Syd then.'

Anwar hugged Astair again [held her {kept holding her ‹because this was the only answer «Xanther having already answered ⟨her choice⟩»⟩ and revisiting Astair's decision served no one›}].

'Both the tech and the vet said the animal's cycling and will die within hours. Make it comfortable, they told us.'

'Then that's what we'll do, but . . . '

The fight starts here [because of this part {the stupid part ‹100% Anwar's fault too›}]. But what choice did he have? Strangers were coming.

'I did a stupid thing too,' Anwar confesses.

'I didn't know what to do.' Anwar again.

'What did I do?!' Anwar again [feeble smile].

Astair [though] is not forgiving [softness will never be her instinct {denial maybe ‹but not softness›}].

'I'm sorry?' Astair hisses. 'Stupid?'

Anwar stammers to explain [who knows what he gets across {or even gets out ‹except for plenty of «intermingled» apologies «'I'm sorry, sorry.'»›}]. Anwar can hear the words coming out [the right words {too}] but the addition keeps failing to make sense [how all of it had added up to his decision {this bad math}].

Anwar's tactic with the stranger on the phone [or is this {his tactic?} true only in retrospect?] was to demand a list of details in order to prove [beyond a shadow of a doubt] ownership. Failure to do so would justifiably result in the immediate termination of all further communication.

[after all] How many unique details can be summoned up on behalf of one tiny dying lump of white hair?

The trouble was that the stranger knew that feline clump way better than Anwar [maybe even Xanther?].

// wavy white hair

    // confirmed

// cat stubble

    // confirmed

// blue eyes

    // unconfirmed

// one eyebrow hair

    // confirmed

// claw count

    // confirmed

// tooth count

    // confirmed

The math was incontrovertible [{‹nothing constative› specificity ‹almost› beyond demand} the tooth count alone!]!

Anwar's strategy had suffered a swift [vicious!] 180°. A request that [Anwar was certain] would deliver proof of non-ownership instead had validated the claim [beyond a shadow of a doubt].

Anwar's own math ratified the stranger's right to claim the animal at once [and Anwar had obeyed the logic of his own construction by giving up an address].

All of which made perfect sense then [faultless addition] making zero sense to Astair [and {in fact} to Anwar] now.

'You gave a stranger our address?! Did maybe some statute of limitations cross your mind?'

'It didn't. It should have.'

'What were you thinking?'

'That's what I'm trying to explain to you or at least figure out for myself. Xanther and I hung those signs up together. She's the one who went so far as to laminate them.'

'Excuse me, are you now blaming Xanther for this?' Astair eyes arclight with rage.

'No, Astair. Of course not. No. I'm just trying to come to grips with how I could do something so stupid. Xanther and I hung those signs up in the service of due diligence, of doing the right thing—'

'Anwar, has it ever crossed your mind that in your relentless insistence to tell the truth, act in the right way, you end up doing the wrong thing?'

'It has, actually,' Anwar answers [they need to take this upstairs {immediately ‹Xanther must not hear any of it «though she'll find out some of it soon enough»›}].

[{at least} between the foyer and their bedroom] Astair's anger cools.

'I did lie,' Anwar confesses.

'What else?' Astair looks winded from the stairs [or just defeated].

'I didn't give away our address.'

'I'm impressed,' Astair says [lightening {though she knows Anwar well enough to expect a caveat ‹and there is one›}].

'Astair, I'm not a practiced liar. It doesn't come naturally to me. And whatever address they have doesn't change the fact that they have our telephone number.'

'Go on.'

'I gave them our street but changed the number. I thought I just randomly generated a number. But I didn't. I gave them Hatterly's address by mistake.'

'He knows we have a cat. I told him last week,' Astair says and slumps onto their bed. Anwar slumps too. A good measure of distance still between them.

'I'm sorry,' Anwar says [again {for the umpteenth time ∴ 'Sorry' [the word] was uttered by Anwar [over the past three minutes—]∵ ∷ *Stop!*∵}].

'How are you going to tell her?' Astair asks [her tone still in the fight].

'Do I need to?' Anwar sticks with softness.

'Hatterly, if he's home, will likely make the connection and point them in our direction.'

'I'll go talk to him.'

Astair stands first: 'No, I will.' She is so convinced that any subsequent subterfuge will require her attention [whether to tell Hatterly to lie {or be there to lie on Hatterly's behalf}] that no effort is made to hide [or {at least} mollify] her glare's obvious condescension.

'Is there a statute of limitations on cats?' Anwar asks.

Astair snorts [heading to the door].

'Do I tell her?' he asks again.

'No.'

Anwar wonders if he should hold Astair back a moment longer to discuss the larger picture. It was not lost on him [nor would it have been lost on Xanther] that in the midst of all the details describing the little animal there was also voiced a great deal of love [or hurt {real anguish ⟨for certain⟩ over the creature's absence}]:

'You don'ch understand, lah. My cat, dat. Lost cat. Please!'

Might that shared feeling between their daughter and a stranger [yes { . . . } an unknown {Anwar was guessing Asian}] serve them all as they came together [as a family {with extended family ‹‹of sorts» yes Asian›}] on the one night [what were the odds?] when one frail animal must submit to the sentence life imposes on us all?

Perhaps beneath the math of his own carefully acted-upon intentions prevailed an instinct not out of harmony with some greater good? Perhaps Anwar's gravest mistake was to lie?

Anwar doesn't know.

But Astair slips out of their bedroom [mouthing 'I love you'] and Anwar doesn't attempt to stop her [mouthing 'I love you' back].

He stands. He needs to stretch but doesn't.

He realizes he failed to mention to Astair that the stranger's description of Xanther's cat seemed to include Xanther [or Astair] as well as Anwar ['Cat. Kay kay dangerous! Very! Hurt her! You too!'{*dangerous?!*}]. It seemed [at that moment] pointless to bring up [seems no more reasonable to mention now {‹crazy!› even if Anwar can't forget the admonition}].

He heads to Xanther's room [aware that he could just keep going to his office {if he changes his mind ‹if he can't make up his mind›}].

What if the stranger does reach their doorstep with his demand? What will the shock of that do to Xanther [even if Astair {and Anwar} will defend her rights of possession with a screaming match about legal limitations]? What might all that trigger?

How [though {also}] could the impact of the cat's death be ameliorated by the company of shared grief?

That said [if Anwar's imagined gathering of good hearts {offering last rites ‹of love and compassion «over the last breath ⟨of a voiceless animal⟩»›} is to succeed] Xanther must still prepare herself.

[Another failure on Anwar's part {another cost of that stupid lie}: he should have also alerted the stranger to the moribund condition of his cat.]

Anwar knocks on Xanther's door. The knock alone opens the door [as if helped {too} by a breeze{?}].

Xanther's sitting cross-legged on her bed [on the corner of her bed {in the corner of her room}] with the cat on her lap.

'I know, Dad,' Xanther says [before Anwar can even muster a word {what would that first word even have been?}].

'You heard?'

'They'll be here soon.'

'Your mom went next door to talk—' *They?*

'Mom already told me.'

'We're not going to let anyone take your little one.'

'He's dying, Dad. Death's taking him.'

'I know.'

'Maybe I should have put him to sleep?' Xanther whimpers [starting to cry {sob}]. 'He's suffering.'

'There, darling, there there,' Anwar says [already crossing over to her {holding her ‹as the strangeness of the expression 'there there' also crosses his mind «as if to send pain elsewhere instead of keeping it ⟨'here here'⟩»}].

'He's purring,' Xanther squeaks [crying harder {her hands never leaving the soft stillness of white}].

'He's glad you're with him.'

Anwar sits with Xanther [as she cries {he cries too a little ‹not for the cat «but for Xanther ❨and for his father❩»›}].

The cat is not the bottle.

∴ TFv2 pp. 507–509, 535–536 ∴

But Xanther was right about this much: she is the little ship [in which the cat is cradled {‹in the heart of «t»his beautiful child› her ribs the ship's ribs ‹Xanther «yes» the most beautiful ship›}].

Then what is Anwar?

He is not the bottle either. He is just another father's failed attempt to protect his child from the storm [as if long arms alone could do that {or even old words}]:

'راحلتنا الصغيرِ.'

'الرحله دي فوق، الرحله دي بتاعتي.'

'ارجوك ارزقني القوة والايمان لأتحمّل ما هو خيرٌ لي.'

Not that Xanther can understand these murmurs [these echoes {Anwar just looking for the right kind of place where words fail and meanings arise ‹«here here»«there there»›}].

Anwar one day had awoken to find his father sitting on his bed. It was still night. He was asking about Anwar's dreams. Anwar had been crying in his sleep. Anwar couldn't remember the dreams but he discovered for himself his wet cheeks.

For a moment he felt ashamed. He tried to wipe his face but his father kissed his cheeks first and read his mind:

'يا ابني ما تخجلش من دموعك. أوعي تنسي الا قالوه ابوك : أنا باعتقد في الملائكه. أنا اومن ان الاراده الكويسه للميت بترجع.'

In the morning Anwar still had no idea why his sleep had brought him to sadness but beside his bed his father had left for him the little glass bottle with the ship inside.

Xanther lifts her head again [eyes drying {though ‹soon enough› they will fill with tears again ‹death's cycle demands its own cycles›}].

'Dad, uh, like, do you want to hear something so stupid? Right now all I like want to do is run. Like pick him up, and just run outta here, like I could outrun death.'

'Daughter, that is the most natural reaction,' Anwar soothes [knowing {too} that even if the mind is its own place {and can make a heaven of hell ∴ **John Milton's** *Paradise Lost.* **Book 1. Line 255.** ∴} the mind cannot make {in ‹and out of› its own death} life].

'What would Dov have said?'

'Dov believed in fighting.'

'Is that a possibility?'

Anwar shakes his head [another awful truth {returning Xanther to tears}].

'That's the most painful part,' Xanther cries [though her crying is feeble {tears exhausted}]. 'Because what's left?'

Oh

Can you choose to lead if no one follows?

— *John Legend*

Hurt teeth, that's what's left, hurting all the time too, like all the crookedness her braces had started to right was returning, metal bands no match for this reversion, Xanther's mouth a painful failure and, even more, a painful reminder that some things can never be straightened out, righted, no matter how much metal you have in your mouth, no matter how much you suffer, no matter how many different-colored rubber bands you get to play with, none of it's worth it, they make no difference.

Xanther even grabs hold of her braces, like she's gonna yank them off?, though she realizes they're too tight for that, might as well yank out her teeth.

Some sight that would be, especially for poor Anwar, here on the bed, comforting his weird kid, as she suddenly pulls out her front teeth, bleeding all over herself then, though instead of crying, Xanther would be smiling, because at least one pain's done with, front of her t-shirt painted red, her poor huddle of white probably red too.

Oh.

Though blood there would almost be better, so vital and like the most obvious sign of life in peril. But that clear mucousy stuff he was leaking, what was that?, or his thinness, this stillness, and of course the teeth he's lost, still in her front pocket, wrapped up in a small square of pale-green leather.

"Xanther?" Anwar asks, immediately stopping Xanther's tug-of-war with her incisors.

"Sorry. What, uh, were you saying?"

"Just words my father once said to me."

"What do they mean?" But Xanther doesn't wait for an answer. "Can I have a piece of gum?"

"Sure."

Xanther knew he'd say yes, what with all that just happened, this sobfest, her poor little— Xanther digs into her pocket before the sobfest can start up again, the pocket without the teeth, first offering Anwar a piece, he declines with a gentle shake of his head, then unfolding for herself one stick of Cedar's Sugar-Free Bubble Gum.

"Don't eat it!" Anwar's light laughter revealing just how furiously Xanther started chomping.

"Yeah, right. Guess I'm hungry. Super hungry!"

"Okay then! Let's get you fed!"

"Okay. But I'm okay. It's not that kinda hungry super hungry."

"Daughter? You know that makes no sense. I'm fixing you something right now."

Xanther hesitates. And Anwar catches it, kisses her on the cheek.

"Take your time. Come down when you're ready."

She nods, smiling with achy dull teeth, because that's what they are, dull, and getting duller too, if chomping still frees her favorite flavor, or one of them anyways, swirls of that hard-to-describe sweet keeping her briefly distracted, even satisfied, though not like when it's swirling outside of her, like she's experienced before, under the stones . . . this just in her mouth, a promise made and kept, to taste good, if never promising to actually feed her.

Xanther knows where she has to go for that . . .

At least at the vet there was someplace to run, where running meant living longer, even if it was just a little longer, guaranteed, even if she wasn't fast enough to outrun that question of suffering, not even for a little while, boy oh boy did that nearly cripple her with a big Question Song, like how much was little one really hurting? how much was worth it?, how much wasn't?, how could she even know?, could little one for that matter even know?, along with is there any worth that comes from suffering?, that we can know for sure?, and even all that just the tip of this icy berg of frozen awfulness, rising up inside her, scratching her up, ∴ **TFv1 pp. 66, 327** ∴ just as it was weighing down on her too, torquing her spine with the burden of its impossible curiosity, this whole messed-up experience of something beyond settling, or at least anything Xanther could settle, which when she realized just that, that this was beyond her, the question of Suffering, capital S, getting her running, or at least shaking her head, which flicked Astair's switch from the indecisiveness position it was stuck in to that familiar Astair-in-action position, at once dismissing that guy Dwight, whom Xanther never trusted, and whisking them all back to the car, like nothing had happened, and actually, really, very little had happened.

:: I was like so sure I was heading to seizureville, like we were, okay, so already in trigger city, and the outcome was way super obvious, but— ::

:: *But you heard me.* ::

:: I could hear both of you. ::

:: **You heard what would happen next?** ::

:: No, not exactly, but I knew what you were feeling and it wasn't seizureville or even trigger city. ::

:: *What was it?* ::

:: **If not the next event?** ::

:: Someone was coming. They were coming. She was coming. And . . . ::

:: *And?* ::

:: **Yes. Finish the thought, please. And what?** ::

:: That was the thought. All of it. ::

:: *Was there a feeling?* ::

:: Yes. Worse than Suffering, capital S. Worse than death. ::

Now there's nowhere left to run, but that still doesn't eliminate running as an option. Xanther's still a heartbeat away from letting her body do what it wants to do, already preparing to do, in her knees, her ankles, the cords of her neck, her mind even, or part of her mind, tracing out the escape route, her first instinct taking the stairs, racing right outside, like that though wouldn't alert Anwar, how many languages telling him at once that the front door was open?, plus, knowing her luck, Xanther would run straight into her mom, coming back from Hatterly's. Better to wander down the stairs, wander back to the piano room and out through the French doors . . . There's that iron door in the back wall, forever closed, scaled with rust, lichens, lost beyond a screen of vines, ferns too, with sometimes mushrooms also hiding the path, little caps of gray now and then rising up out of nowhere, only to disappear soon after, eaten?, reabsorbed?, before that gateway to what?, new fortunes?, a new life?, new beginnings?, what's really just the neighbor's backyard, the Wilburs?, was that right?, ∴ No. The Andersons. ∴ no, the Andersons ∴ *Coincidence.* ∴ ∴ **Coincidence.** ∴ ∴ Sure, but, uh, still a little bit freaky? ∴, weren't they moving, or maybe had moved already, the place deserted, not that Xanther would stop there, only passing through, and passing through fast, which still wouldn't matter, because that's no way out either. Hadn't their landlord even pointed that out?, Cyril Kosiginski winking at Xanther once, declaring mysteri- ously in front of that mysterious door: "This way opens only for the invited, and the invited never run through it." Xanther having no clue what that meant, still has no clue, though, if she was going to believe an odd old man, that way definitely not her way out.

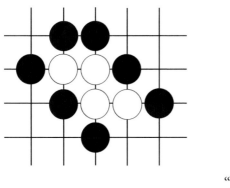

"Run!"

What she whispered to Satya. What Xanther whispers to little one now. But he hardly stirs. Still, saying it aloud encourages Xanther to listen to herself, a tiny bit, maybe, except that the stillness of the little animal, becoming more and more like an audible heaviness that should sink through her lap, snap the bed, break apart the floor, tumble all of it down onto everyone's head, somehow drags her own imperative into its orbit and pulls that down into nothing.

Xanther doesn't move.
He doesn't move either.

But what of Satya? Is she moving now? Through the night? Up into the Santa Susana Mountains? ∷ *How?* ∷ ∷ **Enough.** ∷ ∷ I'm curious and all but I don't want to know. Spare me. ∷ ∷ *Spare you?! That's cute.* ∷

For a moment, Xanther almost feels the movement of Satya's limbs, like they were her own, moving a terrible weight in a weightless silence in pursuit of her next kill.

Xanther gently moves her charge from her lap to the warm place, where she was just sitting, where the little cat chirps, purrs, chirping and purring at the same time, as if confused, before sighing back into quiet, that tiny head laid across a paw.

Myla had taught Xanther how the movement of her body could release understandings beyond verbalizing, beyond even witnessing, and the way Xanther gets up from her bed, to just, what?, stand in the middle of her room?, does feel in some way like that white lioness moments before clawing over Toys' chain-link fence, carrying away with her all injustices, but to where?, does it matter?, if she is still free, a haze, a fog, a broad shade of injured white on the loose, moving like a breath of fire disguised as snow, to where Xanther should go now.

Run!

But Xanther isn't Satya. She can't even heed herself. She can no more join the lioness as a vagrant, vagabond, wanderer of mountains and gullies, concrete rivers, dry arroyos, those borders between cities and counties, between where we live and where we go to live, than she can text her friends. Forget a trip downstairs, even moving beyond her own bedroom door, already wide open, was it always open? ∴ No. Anwar closed it. ∵, especially without the little one, who she won't disturb now, Xanther already back on her bed, her arms encircling him, a protective wall of boniness, as if she could build him a paradise with her body.

So much for running.

Fight!

A body that wants to run when instructed not to run finds quick enough the readiness it has left to attack. Xanther's teeth are still hurting, but now she wants the flesh she'll sink them into to tear them from her mouth.

Though what kinda flesh is *that*!?

Xanther has no answer.

And does it really matter?, because whatever it is, a little girl's teeth in braces is no way to defend the perimeter of herself, to protect little one, no matter how set against the worst assailant a body can imagine.

Xanther, though, knows one place, and close by too, where there are fiercer teeth than hers, metal as metal gets, his too, what Dov lived by and died by, Xanther's thoughts at once tracing a new path, downstairs, into the living room, to their mantel, taking down the gun box, never mind the lost combination, just keep smashing a corner against the floor until the box splinters, hinges rip off, granting Xanther access to the weapon.

But to do what with?

Xanther almost laughs, like her mind enjoys too much thoughts of wielding a gun, imaginings calming her heart, wetting her mouth too, until the rest of her thoughts catch up with the dumbness of that possible achievement.

Because like then what? Shoot? Shoot who? Little one? Herself? The thing coming for both of them?

Xanther slumps closer to this barely breathing creature in the garden of her arms. More pain and tears, hot as vomit, rise again. And again she's running out of the house. Again she's looking for a weapon. Again she's laughing at herself, hating herself, frozen by her uselessness, with nothing left to do.

Not even texting her friends seems like an answer. What, text Kle, "Ge the L.P."? And whatever stuff she's read, books she's scratched her eyes over, or any of the TV shows she's watched don't offer much memorable help. Like, they all seem full of action, full of doing, getting to somewhere, or getting away from something. Just look at *Battlestar Galactica*, viper fights in space, the fleet outracing cylons, all conversations over in like minutes, with maybe Gaius Baltar the exception, talking to himself a lot, though he still gets to do it with Caprica Six in his head . . .

:: *Xanther can't talk to us.* ::

:: You read my mind. ::

:: **Parameter 3.** ::

:: Like a parameter is a comfort? ::

:: **Silence.** ::

:: Parameter 2, anybody? ::

:: *A parameter is still a valid point.* ::

Little one sure doesn't talk to her, and whatever Xanther might say to him, now especially, would only get swallowed up by his end.

Where in all that Xanther has seen, read, listened to, is that moment showing a moment that can't find a decision to do anything? Even Xanther's Grandma Bea, when she was in one of her religious moods, before Astair had walked in and stopped that conversation pronto, told the story of Christ in just a few words, how he died and then was alive again, all of it in not even nine seconds, six seconds, and here Xanther is unable to imagine even one more minute like this, and she doesn't have nails in her hands and feet, and you know supposedly Christ was on the cross for like six or nine hours.

No show, no story, not even a grown-up had shown Xanther how to handle thoughts that go nowhere, feelings that go nowhere, a life that seems a dead end from the start.

"Nothing's worth it," Xanther even murmurs aloud.

Though as she says this, Xanther realizes she's also been staring at her bulletin board, Degas' dusty dancers ∴ **TFv4 p. 527** ⸪, Dov's note ∴ **TFv1 p. 129** ⸪, a star on the run, see, yes, sometimes even stars run, Your Chemical Romance, not on the run, and Anwar's seven indeterminate forms, in his own hand, showing how dividing by zero makes a mess of math.

Xanther sits up, a little stunned by the weird thought coming for her, from a completely unexpected direction too. Little one stirs with a groan.

Because if like little one and her equal one . . . The thought starts, but, no, that's not it.

Because if $1 * 0 = 0$ and $2 * 0 = 0$ then $1 * 0$ should equal $2 * 0$ and does, because zero times anything is zero. The mess part comes if you try to divide both sides by zero to get rid of the zeros, that's when you get . . . $1 = 2$ ∴ **TFv1 pp. 59–60** ⸪.

Xanther starts again.

She and little one are separate, which means, duh, like they are clearly two, unless . . . yes, that's it, unless they're divided by zero, because if they're both divided by nothing, then their twoness can equal one.

"Nothing's worth it," Xanther says it again, marveling at the new taste in her mouth, in her head. "Nothing *is* worth it."

The question then that matters most is how to find that dividing nothing.

So Xanther just sits, and when that's too much, and though it's not really nothing, she recalls her mom talking about emptiness, and so she stands to try some of the Tai Chi Astair taught her.

Xanther can't remember much of it, but she keeps on doing it until she's just moving, not even thinking about moving, not even thinking about thinking, and if anything, she finds its eventual absence needs no participation, least of all observation.

∷ Beginning ∷

∷ Ward Off ∷

∷ Grasp Sparrow's Tail ∷

∷ Ward Off With Right Hand ∷

∷ Roll Back ∷

∷ Press ∷

∷ Withdraw ∷

∷ Press ∷

∷ Single Whip ∷

At some point, Xanther even puts little one on her shoulder, back to purring in her ear.

"We better get ready," Xanther says aloud.

Of course, little one doesn't respond.

"They'll be here soon." ∷ *TFv3 p. 259.* ∷

The purring stops.

A Thing of God

Do you have a choice?

— Victim #25

By the time Isandòrno reached The Ranch, the day was already dead, though the day didn't know it yet. The desert air still kept suspended the best light even if the yucca cast shadows blue enough to say they had robbed the sky.

Isandòrno had walked out of those shadows.

Whatever the events involving animals that had unsettled The Ranch at the end of July, nothing now about its routines and rhythms seemed amiss.

Isandòrno had watched for a long time too, through powerful binoculars, until he was sure that everyone he saw he recognized and everything they were doing was as it should be.

Still, when he walked their way, he walked with the setting sun at his back. Let them have the sun in their eyes if one of them tries to shoot the sun.

But no one thought to reach for a weapon.

Juan Ernesto Izquierdo spotted Isandòrno first and raced out to greet him. Juan is one of the few who will hug him. A hug is also a cage. Isandòrno, however, has never objected. The closest he has come to understanding a way out of his old cage is through the experience of a new cage. Because where there are two cages there is suddenly a way between the cages, and it is in that in-between where things can slip.

—The girls will be so happy to see you.

—I did not forget, Isandòrno answered, showing Juan the rock candy he carried in a leather pouch.

—If I don't steal a piece now I'll never get one, Juan said, as he often said, selecting a small chunk of sugar the color of blackberry.

Isandòrno waited to see if he would take more, but Juan is not the kind of man who is in love with more.

—Ready yourself, Juan continued.

Maria will scold you for not sending word beforehand. She likes to
have something prepared for you.

Maria was in the kitchen and
she did not scold Isandòrno nor
hug him. However, she did kiss
him quickly on both cheeks and
warned him that he would have
to wait for something worthy of
his journey, even as she set out on
the table a cold beer he would not
touch, plates of grapes and cheese
he might eat, along with slices of
peppery lomo.

Without fail the chips were hot and the salsa was fresh.

It never mattered when or how Isandòrno arrived, Maria always managed to provide hot chips and fresh salsa.

Then Juan showed Isandòrno to the room where he always stays: small, clean, with the same lamp on the same nightstand. Maria brought in a glass and a bottle of fresh water from the well and on the narrow bed laid out one clean towel.

Often there would wait a Bible on the windowsill. But it was not always the same Bible. Tonight there was no Bible.

Isandòrno could take any room he liked but this one pleased him. It was simple. It was also well positioned. There were three ways to leave it if necessary.

On this visit, Isandòrno might need a well-positioned room.

—Tío! Tío! screamed the girls when they found out he had arrived.

As always, Isandòrno offered them the candy. As always they accepted it with open palms, though this time Isandòrno could see they cared less about the candy.

They were growing up.

—Do you know about the liger? Nastasia asked first.

—We keep asking Papa but he won't say a word, Estella added.

—Liger? Isandòrno asked.

—She is confused, Juan tried to explain.

—They heard it on the news, Maria added.

For some reason the girls had mixed up the lioness that escaped in Los Angeles with a lion-tiger of their own young speculations.

—There is talk of magic too, Juan added. Isandòrno listened closely to the confession that followed. I can handle any animal. Rumors are something else.

Then Juan drove Isandòrno in his dusty Bronco to where the hunt had taken place. Night was waiting when they arrived.

—I did not like those Americans.

Isandòrno thought of Juan's daughters. Estella's eyes had burned with ropes of flame. Nastasia's with ropes of ash. If that was rumor's work, it was more powerful than anything Isandòrno had encountered before. Like Juan, Isandòrno did not know how to kill rumors. Especially magical ones.

Together, they inspected the shooting gallery. There were no breaches in the fence on either side. The chain-link that hung over the top offered no gaps through which something might escape.

Next, they walked past the brittle-bush, agave, and ajo lilies, to where the crates stood.

They were still open.

Dirt had invaded them, along with small stones, and even large rocks. Somehow.

Weeds had grown up around the sides, died, and then grown back again.

Isandòrno remembered the damp smell of infection on Carril 9 in Veracruz ∴ **TFv1 pp. 612–615**∴. But that smell was gone.

As he did then, Isandòrno counted nine on his fingers and spat over his shoulder. It was easy to avoid the shadows cast by their flash-lights. The rounds in his gun were all silver and gold. No owl flew across the waning moon.

—The hyena? Isandòrno asked.

Juan pointed to the first crate.

—The elephant?

Juan pointed at the second crate.

—The giraffe?

Juan nodded at the third crate.

Isandòrno remembered the animals. He remembered thinking none would survive the trip here. But they had all survived. For this.

Isandòrno couldn't look at the fourth crate. Whatever had waited inside never needed to survive.

Of one thing Isandòrno was certain: no lioness had escaped from here to north of Laredo ∴ **Chaparral WMA** ∵, where gringo rangers finally tranquilized it. That must have been someone else's creature.

Nothing in the fourth crate had needed to make it to Los Angeles to escape.

In there had waited something else.

—We cut up the bodies and fed the meat to our dogs, Juan explained while driving to the only grave. What was left we burned. And then to be sure, we spread some of the ashes in a dry wash, some at the base of a gulch, the rest near a midden above an arroyo where there was no sign of litter.

The night that Isandòrno had left The Mayor, Mexico City had looked like a bucket of light in a bigger bucket of dark. Here was just bigger dark.

—The animals too?

—All of them, Juan answered.

—Luna?

—No.

—Because she was a child?

—Because Maite considered her her own, and Chavez and Garcia called her sister. They insisted on burying her. I could not object.

Isandòrno had Juan dig up the grave. Then he told Juan to use the shovel to break open the little casket.

Juan threw up.

—Where is her head?

—All the heads were taken.

Burning Luna's body there would be too dangerous. Bringing her body back would make Isandòrno's job more difficult.

Isandòrno accepted that this was
a forced mistake. He even helped
Juan rebury the little orphan in
her coffin. Juan seemed grateful.

—This newest set here, causing
us such problems, Juan voiced to
Isandòrno on the drive back to The
Ranch, maybe they take heads?

—The Mayor has already made
plans for them. They will not trouble you much longer.

Juan nodded but still continued.

—I should have thought of this before. This summer Los Feroz Soldados de Los Zetas changed their name to Las Leonas. They drive around in a truck blasting Los Tigres del Norte and shooting their guns.

—Las Leonas?

—Perhaps what they call themselves now explains my daughters' mistake.

No tiger. No lioness. Just the changing names of cartel violence.

Back at The Ranch, Adon Calde-
ros and Santiago Bustamente
were waiting.

Isandòrno took each aside and
listened to what they had to say.
They talked at length about their
friends Maxiley, Servando, and
Ravelo. They talked about Ismael
and Freddie. They talked about
the bodies without heads ∴ **TFv3
pp. 540–549** ∴.

Both felt lucky not to have been
working that day. Neither would
look Isandòrno in the eye.

Both mentioned Las Leonas but never "ligers" nor for that matter lions or tigers. There was no mention of magic either.

They knew nothing about ivory.

—Ivory? From the baby elephant? Juan asked.

Isandòrno nodded.

—It was a cow. A baby cow. Juan shrugged. Did we find any ivory?

Santiago and Adon shook their
heads though they looked uncertain. Both were over forty, and
Isandòrno suspected neither one
had ever seen ivory before.

—That's too bad. The Mayor likes
ivory.

—Are more animals on the way?
Juan asked then.

Isandòrno considered the question carefully but decided it was
no more than what it asked.

—I have seen rhinos. I have seen wolves. I have seen baboons, Isandòrno answered.

—There are people who will pay to shoot baboons? Juan asked, amazed.

—Especially baboons.

Isandòrno then instructed Adon and Santiago to break down the crates and haul them away. He gave them until the end of the week.

Next, Isandòrno met with Chavez and Garcia. Maria interrupted with news that dinner was ready. Isandòrno assured her that his work was almost done.

The two boys were the sons of Ortiz Arellano. They were twelve and fourteen. They had walked over from the stables with their hands in their pockets.

They asked no questions. They did not mention their sister. They mostly looked at the ground.

Their father had died repairing the chain-link that made it impossible for any animal to escape the shooting gallery.

He had fallen eighteen feet and smiled when he landed. Everyone else had smiled too because they assumed a smile meant survival. Only Isandòrno had not smiled.

He had helped the two boys bury their father the next day.

—Did the set known as Las Leonas kill the Americans and your sister and those others you know on the afternoon of July 31st? Isandòrno asked each one separately.

Both shrugged and kept staring at the ground.

—We were not there, each said. We were lucky.

Isandòrno has never respected luck. He told the boys to eat dinner and tomorrow help Santiago and Adon get rid of the crates.

—By Friday, Juan spoke up, the three crates will be gone.

—Four, Isandòrno corrected him.

Correcting Juan was an unforced mistake. Isandòrno at once detected an uneasiness in the way he regarded Isandòrno.

—Where is their mother? Isandòrno asked.

—Things are quiet now.

—Good, Isandòrno answered. That's all The Mayor wants.

After dinner, they went outside and sat by the fire Adon and Santiago had made.

The rising smoke called the stars into question, but the men did not care about stars. They did not care about the war either, or the recent violence in Nogales and along the border, or the peculiar tastes that too much money affords especially when it arrives ill-accounted-for.

They talked mostly of cars. They talked about old cars and fast cars. They talked about cars built with bulletproof panels and bulletproof glass and bulletproof tires.

Juan described a holly green 1950 Mercury he once saw flying over a strip of distant road.

—So low and so smooth and so fast, I swore it was a thing of God.

Nobody laughed. That was as close as anyone of them would get to God.

The girls seemed to enjoy the talk, or at least they enjoyed the fire. Hard candy knocked around their teeth and they smiled.

Only Estella disturbed Isandòrno.

She was dressed in a strange way. She had braided her black hair into long pigtails and wore pink Converse and black jeans. On her shoulder she had fastened what looked like a small stuffed animal.

White.

—I don't know, Juan says now, as he leads Isandòrno into the house. This is something she learned about on her phone. I love my girls but they are strange. Nastasia is more conventional than Estella when it comes to the clothes she wears, but sometimes she will also dress like her sister.

Isandòrno does not pretend to know anything about young girls.

Isandòrno thinks of Jordi, Teyo's son. Would such clothes speak to him?

—I think they are just restless. They both want to go to San Diego to free the killer whales. You should take them. Has there ever been a better reason to leave the country?

It will take more than a little girl with a stuffed animal on her shoulder to get Isandòrno to cross the border.

—Would you have me freeing whales? Isandòrno smiles. This is not an error but Juan again looks uncertain.

In his office, Juan places in front
of Isandòrno a leather bag. It is the
kind used to carry a bowling ball.
It is filled with U.S. dollars.

Juan looks relieved to hand over
the money. Now nothing uneasy
contaminates his expression.

It is all there.

—I made up the difference, Juan
explains.

—Their mother?

Juan nods. —Maite was there. She witnessed the killings. Afterward, she ran. She tried to take the boys but they refused to go.

—Do you know where she went?

Juan hands Isandòrno the address.

—Do you need to see her?

—The Mayor cares only about the money. I will ask her to come back and take care of her boys. We did not kill Luna.

—Thank you, Juan says sincerely. He looks happy and relieved too.

Outside Juan's office, Nastasia surprises Isandòrno. She is nervous. Isandòrno has never seen her nervous before or even a little reserved around him.

—Tío, I have a present for you. My sister and I bought it for you. Nastasia holds out the gift. It is wrapped in red paper with a black bow. Isandòrno likes the bow.

Isandòrno unwraps it in front of Nastasia and thanks her. He does not tell her that he cannot keep this.

In his little room, he places on his nightstand the carved head of the jaguar.

when strangers arrive

... lifts the veil from the hidden
beauty of the world ...

— Percy Bysshe Shelley

"*Juste une larme!*" Charlie insists (refilling her glass (a Zinfandel (Decoy))).

"'Just a tear,'" Mr. Hatterly translates (emerging from the kitchen with a plate of— (what is this? (Wow! (Exquisite!)))). "The French have such lovely expressions for drinking."

"This is delicious," Astair says (eating the offering (licking her fingers (indulging in another (careful) sip of wine))). "Figs, goat cheese, rosemary."

"Simple, really. Broiled. A little olive oil, balsamic," Mr. Hatterly responds (looks pleased (sitting down in the Eames-like upholstered (molded fiberglass (dowel-leg)) armchair (what is Astair thinking? ((knowing these two) it is an Eames)))).

"But the cracker!" she exclaims.

"He bakes them," Charlie smiles (filling his partner's glass). "Gluten-free too."

"If we can keep you for dinner, I'll give you the recipe," Mr. Hatterly winks (taking Charlie's hand).

The invitation is so (viscerally(!)) appealing that Astair has to set down her glass of wine (wipe her fingers on a (cloth(!)) napkin) and get to the point of her visit.

Archimboldo lying at her feet responds to her movement (stiffening?) with a grunt.

"He likes you," Charlie notes.

"Astair is one of us," Mr. Hatterly smiles.

"Oh?"

"A dog person."

Astair smiles (she can't disagree (stroking the neck of the bullmastiff ((at once) rewarded with sighs))(look how easily she reaches out (how naturally touching comes ((like nowhere else) a hand's desire free to seize its pleasure)))).

"Why then haven't we seen you walking our street?" Charlie asks (looking genuinely surprised (perhaps a little excited that the evening might result in a canine-favorable decision)). "The dog parks we will show you!"

"Astair just got a cat."

"Oh." Charlie makes no effort to hide his displeasure.

"My daughter rescued it in May." Astair almost starts babbling about the Akita she (*they!*) almost got (looks at the wine (she's only had half a glass (a whole glass might have freed that story))). "That's why I dropped by."

"One second, Astair!" Mr. Hatterly says (leaping to his feet (racing back to the kitchen)).

"He really should have been a chef," Charlie says (helping himself to another piece of (fig- and goat-cheese-topped) toast).

Astair has a big gulp of wine (maybe a story (she's unaware of) needs freeing). The wine keeps getting tastier (with an aftertaste that leaves her wanting to finish the glass (the only uncertainty: whether or not to wait for Mr. Hatterly to reemerge (or just start telling Charlie about Anwar's blunder))).

"I heard you were just in Geneva?" Astair says instead.

"I'd drag the Chef along to Paris if France didn't forbid bullmastiffs."

"The threat of rabies?" Astair remembers hearing something about that in regard to the UK.

"Bullmastiffs are deemed 'dangerous.'"

The word thrills Astair (as both her hands dig into the folds of fur of the big dog at her feet (already rolling onto her side (for a belly rub))).

A knock on the door.

More knocks.

Banging!

Kicking!

"Good god!" Charlie cries (starting to rise from his leather sofa chair).

What has Astair been doing for the past half hour? What sort of cunctations has she been indulging?

Drinking. Eating. Chatting about art auctions. And trips. And dogs.

And why? To deny (or convince herself) that a stranger was(n't) really coming?

Why hasn't she said anything?

Now it's too late.

The knocking stops.

Mr. Hatterly returns from the kitchen (in an apron now (hands out (palms down) at his waist (placating Charlie))). "It'll be fixed before you get back." Then to Astair: "Our oven door has gotten *complicated*."

"It smells good," Astair responds (relishing the aroma of fat and meat (she misses meat (she'd cook it more if Xanther wouldn't kill her))).

"Note, Chuck, the crumbling of resolve."

"Let Astair speak! She's in the midst of telling us something important."

"Asking you for a favor, I'm afraid," Astair confesses. There. That gets the hard part out of the way (though the temptation remains to disclose Xanther's epilepsy and trace her improvements while in possession of her fragile feline (in order to (blandishments aside) best win over these neighbors (not even friends) and convince them to lie on her behalf?

(how about (for starters) the clear mucoid stuff (*clear!* (as if it had nothing left to digest but itself (not even its self))) leaking out its ass? (ick! (when had the animal even showed any sign of fecal excretions? ((that's weird) none that Astair could remember (Xanther was always in charge of the litter (not weird)))) if that ick((!)iness (like stickiness)) still managed to pronounce ((plainly) *clearly*(!)) its compromised animality ((corpo)reality) and (for Astair) had all at once humanized(?) it (or made her sympathize with it)) probably not the best description to lead with.)

(Astair having trouble deciding what won't matter

(Then how about the strange occurrence of animals set free at the shelter?

(no)

(Or Xanther sleepwalking her way into the middle of their street (nearly run down by a truck)?

(no)

(Animals suddenly loose at The Animal Kingdom (the lioness (surely a captivating ((still!) horrifying) moment (her child had gone viral!)))?

(no)

(Or the ballet?

(no)

(Or what about Shasti's increasing confusion over Freya's ((increasingly) troubling) behavior?

(no)

(How about how quickly Anwar's ($9,000) reprieve will last?

(no)

(No! No! No! No! No! No!)

))))))))).

"It was one thing to rescue this little animal in a flood, but now her bonding has only intensified as it dies."

"You didn't mention that," Mr. Hatterly says (a knowing sympathy (empathy!) possessing him at once (Charlie too)).

"Your poor daughter," Charlie adds.

"We were just at the vet. We were faced with that awful, ugly decision."

Both men have turned their attention to Archimboldo (who (responding to their collective gazes(?)) gets up to go sit between them (as if guarding them against Astair's story (the story the beautiful dog will someday inflict on these two men (there's a question: how do we spare others the story that our life must inevitably demand we tell when it ends?)))).

"Never an easy answer," Charlie mumbles (patting Archimboldo's head (what a fantastic dog)).

"Anyway, we decided to bring it home. The cat's days may be numbered but Xanther explained to me that we still don't know the number."

"Smart girl," Mr. Hatterly nods.

"I wish I could say the same about my husband." Astair lands that just right ((not so severe a tone to make her neighbors uncomfortable) just light enough to reach the shared music of common (but loving) gripes). Both men smile.

Archimboldo's smile is to lie down and pant (nose distracted by the ((what? (chicken? (it must be chicken))) fat-dripping) aromas filling the living room).

Astair quickly tells them about the signs posted in Venice and the call and Anwar's inept response.

"*This* address?" Charlie looks rightfully displeased.

"I'm sorry. It was a mistake. I'm also here to apologize on Anwar's behalf."

"Nonsense. He was flustered. He's not the only one who gets flustered and fucks up." Mr. Hatterly looks sharply at Charlie.

"Who, me?" Charlie quails.

"No. Me. If you can't handle fluster, you won't make thirty-plus years."

Charlie drains his glass. "That's true. Drinking helps."

Both men share a shallow laugh.

"Impressive," Astair says. "And you're still smiling." Charlie refills all their glasses (emptying the bottle (getting up (no doubt) to find another)). "Is drinking really your secret?"

"Not at all," Mr. Hatterly smiles (maybe a little softer this time (sadder?)). "I've actually given this a little thought. When we are young, we look forward to things: all the stuff we can see, do, taste, and have. We're probably born with that. And for good reason: what we desire helps us to plan, to attain, to achieve. However, when you get older, when you look to the future, more and more you find illness and infirmity. Forget death itself, it's the dying that dominates the horizon. Which is where the trouble comes in: a lifetime spent looking forward makes for a lot of frightened, angry, old people. Charlie and I made a vow when we met to practice looking at one thing every day. A vow we've kept. Can you guess?"

"The practice of looking at what's now?"

"Oh no, we're not that enlightened! We look at each other. We pay attention to each other."

Astair has to decline twice more their invitation to stay for dinner. Mr. Hatterly happily pledges allegiance to her cause. Charlie comes around.

"We have your back."

"We'll just say it's a mistake," Charlie adds (giving Astair a quick hug). "Arch will make the point."

Astair offers multiple thanks and (after a quick look at her phone (no messages (and the time is comforting))) admits that "maybe no one is on the way."

Even the Independence taxi is a comfort ((after all) it's not waiting in front of Mr. Hatterly's home).

Only as Astair continues walking does it dawn on her where the cab is idling.

Astair walks faster.

It's parked right in front of her home!

Is someone about to get out?

But (no) no one is getting out.

The glare from headlights and streetlamps hides
the face of the driver

(hides all movement within).

But (even with all her focus on the car)
     Astair catches movement in her periphery.

Shadows on her doorstep.

The shape of when strangers arrive.

(in fact) The front door is already open.

More like a blinding (awakening of) light.

And in it: someone.

Xanther?

Is *she* the one letting these people inside?

Or is that Anwar?

Why isn't he barring the way?

Why isn't he sending them away?

The fight in Astair comes up quick.

Anwar swore he gave them Hatterly's address.

Astair races to intercept.

Though she's already too late for that.

She's not even at the lawn when the front door closes (she's already digging for her keys (where are they? (did she really fail to take them with her?))).

Though Astair's hands are already (happily) closing around something better (another sort of (hand) desire (seizing another kind of ((nothing) (something)) pleasure)).

And Astair happily lifts her fists (ready to splinter wood's protest (if need be)) except the door is swinging open again (as if anticipating her? (no (knowing she's there))).

The face (greeting her) is unknown.

Old. Rugose. Skin so thin to release all claim on opacity (though what's revealed is far from bones (beyond the wrinkles of time (something else (something older)))).

Astair's hands leap (like small birds) to her heart (as if fluttering there will keep it pumping (while fearing the unrecognizable has already stopped it)).

But (though strange) the face is nothing but the deepest calm. She is not merely old. She is ancient. Has Astair ever beheld someone so beautiful?

And then the face smiles. Has Astair ever seen such a smile (beauty exceeding itself (becoming what not even beauty can subjugate))? As two ((beautiful) (venerable)) hands reach for Astair's still-fluttering hands.

"尔乃其母！其之幸有尔!"

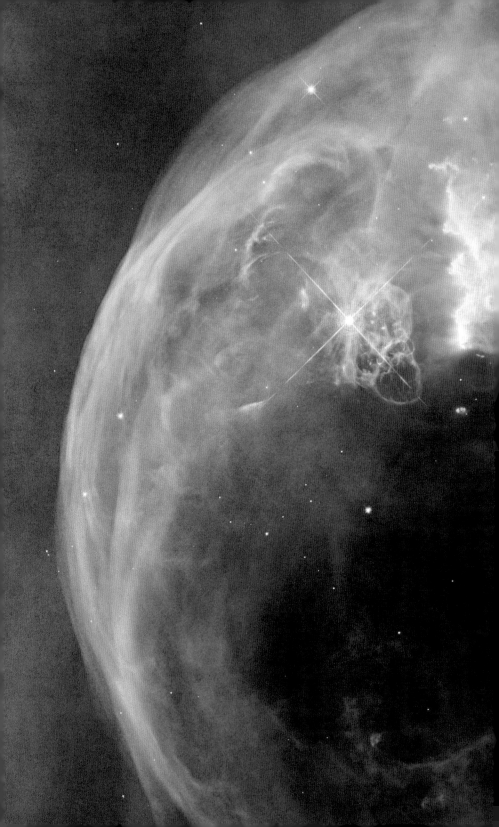

ger one scrawny

Had Jōshū been there . . .

— *Mumon*

"靖靖，请译之与吾。" ∴ *Jingjing, please translate for me.* ∴ "尔乃其母！其之幸

有尔!" ∴ *You are her mother! She is so lucky to have you!* ∴

"you are mother. saysay she si beh lucky."

cheh! what nongsngse. jingjing kay way mong cha cha. lepak lady

look same confused. kay no spee-yak. damn bang, pek chek. auntie

there, macam auntie oreddy knew to turn, to meet her. always

steps ahead. not hiss ai zai, auntie hold lepak lady's hands instead.

lai dat, words calm chio bu down.

                              mother!?

              mother of who?

                           she?

              she who?

         same she with no name auntie bring up before?

              the she?

and what about dis boh lang ai kum gong who just let them in? thin as petai pod black in sun just stand there dot dot dot.

"i'm sorry," mother say. "i don't believe we know each other."

"where is cat?" jingjing snap back. who care who who? owl all night long. macam only fact dat matters, not hosts, tapi grab kuching, cabut out. quick quick. zip zip. taxi oreddy in front if wait ten minute most.

"汝乃阿斯梯 。 汝夫乃 安瓦尔 。 吾盼见汝五人已久。" tian li say, sayang jingjing quick with wink. ∵ *You are Astair. Your husband here is Anwar. I have waited a long, long time to meet you five.* ∵

"you astair one. husband anwar," jingjing repeat. "she wait lah to meet you five, uh—" jingjing corright, "two."

jingjing never hear such names before. juang lah.

"you know who i am?" dis astair ask.

"are you the one, uh, the ones who called?" black bean named anwar ask same time.

jingjing translate. can't wait hear auntie's response.

"吾需憩，靖靖。 吾甚乏。" auntie answer, pale sudden, kay kan cheong. ∷ *I need to rest, Jingjing. I'm very tired.* ∷

mebbe have another fit. right here inside strange home in front of strangers with strange names auntie somehow oreddy knows.

"she feel sick," jingjing esplain. "she sit down?"

"of course," astair insist, shock tall husband as she show them down few steps to sofa, big sofa, in big room, with big place for tua fire. "would she like some water?"

tian li tell jingjing water would be nice.

"tea," jingjing bark at blur queen. "she want tea. not too hot."

black bean and ah nia share eye secrets. jingjing hean toh, lor, if they refuse, but they go together, taking answers away too, if jingjing catch one word in whispers he never hear before:

"xanther."

then slaykay black bean disappear, and astair one return.

"my husband went to get some water." a bit the teruk her. "what can we do for you? and who are you? what are your names?"

jingjing ready to shout "cat!" but auntie nudge leg, need him translate more. great tian li take time, consider woman's questions careful, so slow might fall asleep, drool to koon deep.

"请适之荐吾。" auntie saysay at last. "告于阿斯梯，其有佳家。" ∷ *Please introduce us properly. Let Astair know that she has a beautiful home.* ∷

auntie seem better too, lai dat, lepaking on big couch, feet to dangle, legs always too short to touch any floor.

long drive was chor lor on her. osso hard on jingjing. bag of balls dat one. bad enuf have cab driver, chao kang him, ku whole way, take longest way too, for sure. some driver. face bumpy macam bad roads they took, grey hair on top, nose a garden of black sprouts, big ears, big black gardens there too. half the ride a parking lot. chia'h lui them, get big fare.

same game world over.

long way, most pay, worst way.

with worst music only auntie likes.

by end, driver take fare, skew me!, almost keep change! silver,
copper. siao one. later refuse wait. lai dat ready split. tapi auntie
with old winks steady seow him. jingjing siao liao, ji siao damn
bodoh for not taking auntie's extra twenty green.

ten minute max, driver answer, breath lai nasty pickle.

osso auntie kena them stop at wrong address.

street same but house numbers not house numbers on hand.
jingjing try push old bag up hill, if auntie slip jingjing, padpad
wrong way again, straight ahead, walk walk, part pale lawn, toward
house, two storeys, tile roof, windows covered, door dark as no
one home.

but for auntie's tap door open.

black bean man damn grimace one by the bolt until he see great

tian li and let them both in easy as summer breezy.

inside nothing lah macam outside: bursts of light kay bright bells,

wood floors warm kay polished amber, with spiral staircase at

center. zhong's spiral reach to outreach what stars dream of, tapi

dis one just a quick stretch before nap. kay sui-sui.

under stairs jingjing catch glimpse of raindrops.

and to right, down steps, living room all glow with candles and

gold blankets.

plus, whole place swirl with smells of lemongrass, spicy chili,

mebbe behoon in mi siam, jingjing so hungry, suddenly miss home.

but look at auntie now!

mati! habis! gone case! undone by comfort. and comfort every-

where. at their back curtains macam butter. ahead, all around,

leather chairs and soft bags, kind you sit in, drown in, koon whole

life away. jingjing tempted. but sofa better. old bag agree.

"好椅也!" ∵ *Nice couch!* ∵

look at her!

once she terror anyone she meet. now ah mm unsound. borak

nonstop how nice dis house. pat cushions. bounce up and down.

"甚好!" ∵ *So nice!* ∵

"what is she saying?" the wife ask.

"she suka dis place."

"oh. uh. thank you?"

jingjing smart one not meet dis astair in eye, keep scanning,

from wall with fireplace, tua enuf to burn tree, burn forest, to

room behind woman, big enuf for piano, to house entrance where

husband cabut.

"osso want see cat," jingjing add. "we come long way for my cat.

want cat back!"

"i'm afraid you're mistaken. we don't have your cat," astair woman

answer, look jingjing in eye, smile, jilo macam smile, real cower

power there. jingjing no kuat one, forget face that, boh lum par

chee, her stare kena jingjing racing eyes back for auntie.

still patting cushions. bouncing. smile so gila jingjing get fierce

again, twist back to face woman, but she juang lah, tua liap gone

from jingjing to child at her knee.

"who are they?"

"shasti, these are our guests. say hello and then go upstairs. freya's already getting ready for bed."

"freya's right here."

jingjing blinkblink. now two gin nah at mother's knee. same kia at mother's knee. first one in red, on left, same one on right, in green.

tian li smile for first one but for same second one face change. jingjing know that look. by bedside of zhong's son. siao liao. some-thing sala dat one.

this mother astair sense wrong too. draw gin nah close, then by hand lead them both out of room to spiral stairs. kids kena arrow to brush teeth then. and hurry! ha!

jingjing shake leg watching, auntie too, waiting for children to go, for mother to return, mebbe husband too. sure take forever for water or tea.

old bag sigh, rest head on jingjing then, mebbe koon. fine by jingjing so long as auntie don'ch have another fit.

then jingjing hear it.

all dat matter.

what jingjing don'ch hear for months.

what no dream warn he have chance again to hear.

light as heavy snow.

fright might macam burial.

balls drop.

kia si lang.

soft steps.

heavy steps.

familiar

steps . . .

jingjing jerk round to face archway, what frame dark room with

piano, now frame steps, buay sai!, cannot be same steps.

jingjing still flinch, kia ka lau sai, macam mebbe berak self for real,

no clue why, just how body act, koro him fast, before this one . . .

oreddy so near, ger one scrawny, hor, argly one her, macam

someone jingjing see once before, macam even was once before?,

damn kwai lan, chao for sure, knees knocked, pink kicks, in black

jeans, hands shaking, si bei kan cheong, fingernails banyak bits of

paint, oreddy flying to flick big ears, pick pimple fizz on forehead

and chin, and mouth kay broke with metal, bogay soon, with two

long black braids macam curtains pulled back on kosong show,

bitter, adoi, whole face boh jude, so dull almost rude, bit the pale,

blank past white, mangkuk for sure, if not for such eyes, tua liap,

chia bo liau, what bravest stage don'ch dare display.

eyes dat something kay strange.

different-colored eyes warning of shallows and deep.

kelam kabut, if osso wild macam mad storm.

not norm.

        she something else.

kena jingjing shakes, kay nervous.

kum pooi!

over some scrawny one bai ger?

jilo chance! boh her! if jingjing kay blur king. boh clue why legs

kena him want kebelakang pusing, kay lembek, si peh takut not

even feet budge, ouch, panic until lau sai pang jio, shit on big

couch.

no, not for her jingjing boh chiak png!

ger no reason to flinch second time, flinch forever time.

seize whole body.

sure, for it.

for dis white macam flakes of falling ash.

for this pyramid of sleep.

if not kooning, then eyes tight, dark wars against trespass.

only tail twitch, kitchi chest heave, saysay it even exists.

where it should never be.

just sitting there.

on scrawny ger's shoulder. ow bway ooh kwee.

jingjing blink then. something slimy icy oreddy leak down backside.

same time as anger rise, more garang at sight of such crime.

indecent.

unlawful.

chao kuan.

his.

whole life, mebbe, touch creature twice, hor. sure never held. sure

damn never put on shoulder, or prance macam auntie, great tian li,

seri of serangoon, smith street sage, born on sei yang gai, in house

of dead some saysay, all saysay long, long time ago, tian li who

hush all cock talk, no fool tua her, tan ku ku, better to tie shoe-

laces for days than disrespect her with cat. real cower power them.

which is how jingjing get dis chance. what yeow guai oreddy told

him do, through blue cat of flame:

"the cat is yours!"

                              "own what you're owed!"

grab it now! hold it tight! stick what's his on his shoulder!

but before jingjing can do just that, leap to his feet, seize what's

right, win what's his, what wails begin!

has jingjing ever heard such terrible cries?

must be ger here, jingjing insist, study pimply face, crooked teeth,

to catch sounds, but jilo match lips to sobs.

so jingjing look for chio bu, where?, astair there, returning from

spiral stairs, where twins still sit, eye their mother's pause at room

entrance, father arriving then too, got tray with green teapot, cups

and saucers, plates with sweets. tapi neither face show pain.

just stand top of steps.

                                        no spee-yak.

could it be?

jingjing whip head so fast, immeely neck ache, who cares, because

there she is, his mistress, the old bag, bag of rattling bones,

falling apart.

river of tears, strait of sobs.

until someone else joins auntie, osso wailing. suay one. ee, yah

lor terrible voice. jingjing wish it stop quick. jingjing make it stop

quick. awful with tears and spit, growing louder until jingjing see

he damn one growing it.

stop at once.

not hard.

if scrawny ger menace orredy here, sitting on low table to face

them, right hand on jingjing's knee, light as a feather, macam birds

of a feather asking if branch okay.

how she so close? so fast?

jingjing only just remembering: pale ger leaping forward, buay zai

one, kin kin, kalang kabut sure, some attack, tumbling towers of

books, candles too, splatter wax, nuts knocked aside, pomegran-

ates, clatter, jars of buttons, bead boxes, karung guni to the floor.

and most strange?

cat gone from shoulder, now in left palm, macam char siew pau,

and lai dat chao ger place creature in tian li's lap.

"please. take him back," she cries. "he's yours."

insolence! where got?

he's yours?!

as if in first place cat ever hers to give?

auntie agree.

"吾之？" ∴ *Mine?* ∴ she squeak, eyes on lap, hands at side.

child nod. mumbles something else.

" ▨▨▨▨▨▨▨▨ "

"what?" jingjing ask. what auntie think too boh doubt.

"his name," chao ger answer back.

name?!

dis child?! dis abomination! naming great one?!

"血木?" ∷ ■■■■■■ ∷ auntie osso shocked. that what she hear?

wah lan eh, jingjing flash rage how!

no need to think rest. pow ka leow. oreddy fast on feet, oreddy to

act, with windup twist, windup twist double more, hand way back,

wayway back . . .

                        for uncoiling next . . .

hips first, shoulder then, kay heong at last, powderful dis attack,

arm drag behind, fingers bending back, until macam fucking whip,

jingjing unleash arm, lashing hand back around, for impact, ketuk

strong, one mighty, aim true, hantam bitch hard . . .

an`vd heel of hand finds jaw, ger's head snap sideways, braids

macam rattle-drum, as nails dig deeper, macam claws flay cheek,

before jingjing release, dragging back ribbons of bleeding flesh.

flying

*We saw **NOBODY**!*

— Lone Wolf and Cub, *vol. 5*

A stranger's hand drops his daughter

// his own hands drop the tray

// hospitality

// cups

// honey jar

// saucers

// teapot

// a pitcher of cream too

// hot water dancing

// with

// cold cream

// midair

// while tumbling plates of pieties adjacent to

// chocolate-covered nuts

// dried fruits

// cashews

// and dates

// fat wedges of lemon

// raspberry cakes

// sweet refections

// brought forth through doubt

// cross

// the clashing clatter

// of small spoons and butter knives

// napkins fluttering last

// still outlasted by thoughts

// outlasting best intentions

// above

347

// the impact
　　　　　// across the floor

　　　　　　　　// shatters and
　　// splashes

　　　　　// even as their porcelain tray breaks

　　　　// that announcement

// coinciding with yet another impact

Xanther knocked so hard that [head snapping back {face whipped around}] she's thrown down [onto the table {‹like a marionette «strings suddenly cut»› with a thud too ‹among toppled books «and candles ‹scattering dried pomegranates›»›}] both palms whacking the wood [to break her {twisted} fall {what's not enough ‹chin smacking «her grimace making this halt ‹and halt's pain› audible»›}].

Thud and then the slap [its aftermath {in reverse ‹still resounding «in Anwar's ear ‹amplified by his mind› echoing in his heart»›} catching up] marrying in a sound that instead of heralding action merely serves to belatedly note it.

Though Anwar is still moving

as if possessed by Dov

as if possessed by worse

and not alone either

Astair is also possessed

right behind him beside him

both locked by purpose

chained to this cause

in perfect sync

flying forward . . .

[of course] Anwar matched the voice on the phone [{easily!} with this young man {early twenties?} standing on his doorstep {‹at once› squawking about his cat}].

It was the old woman who caught him by surprise [{her presence alone being surprise enough}{her presence in the company of a man so rude and rough giving surprise its exponential rise}{her strange reaction ‹to Anwar!› somehow rendering her companion ‹and even Anwar's surprise› irrelevant}].

She enthralled him [en- indeed! ∷ *Old Norse thrǽll* '*slave*'∷ {‹or in «in+ slave»› captured}].

Surely this was due to her smile [a smile that permeated her eyes {inhabited the way her whole form seemed to open up to him}]. It was as if she recognized him [as if she was relieved to see him again {a familiarity that somehow anticipated ‹and then necessitated› reunion «not to mention relieved Anwar»}].

```
conns = ioMgr->getIncomingConnections(&device);
fw.evaluate(conns, policy, &cbAllow, &cbReject);
```

So much for his firewall [trust relationship {somehow?} high]. Of course Anwar let her in [let them both in!]! That they came armed with the truth didn't hurt [IP address recognized {with SSH key ‹because there was no question they knew the cat›}]. That the old woman's entrance carried no aggression also helped [benign {any old user logging in}]. What's more [!] her presence seemed to promise that whatever burdens this encounter might cost [along with Anwar's many other burdens] the net result would still be ease.

As if she was [without another word] already in admin mode [super user {enhanced action ‹whatever she needed «Anwar was there for her»›}] helping out.

The young man [aji {still}] was another story [every action needing scrutiny {requiring restriction}].

'Cat. Where at? Give us cat now!' Eyes abrasive as Brillo pads scouring sinks [greedily {hungrily ‹like— «Anwar knew that regard ⟨clawing for an answer ⌈for acquisition⌋⟩»› like an addict› pawing} for a fix].

But the old woman's look [[{fleeting} of disapproval {matched by a click in her mouth}] arrested any more of his demands.
[immediately] He grew still if still alert [though {temporarily?} dispossessed of any claim {what perhaps he expected her to make then ‹which she did not make «only looking around the room ⟨though with a wonder that seemed to light the walls and stairs⟩»›}].
Her awareness relaxed Anwar [as if whatever revelation she had experienced he experienced too].
[furthermore] Her intricately grooved features somehow seemed to limn [out of their complex signatures of age] a quiet [almost eternal{?}] smoothness [framing not only her face and shape but the shape of everything around her].

By contrast the young man's [taut] smoothness seemed [almost perpetually{?}] wrinkled by aggravations. He presented an endless demonstration of dissonance where even her smallest motions seemed an occasion for music.

So startling were their differences that Anwar felt momentarily off-balance [{literally} having to reposition his feet {fix his eyes on the top stair ‹to steady himself «as well as assure himself that Xanther was staying out of sight»›} so confused was he by the pairing].

Where she was old with experience he was as young as fear. Where she was tiny with confidence he was a wiry anger twisted out of doubt's conviction. Where she was warm with patience he demonstrated a cold-hearted pallor born out of singular desire.

She was peaceful to behold.

He was at war.

Not that he was unattractive. Anwar saw how [if relaxed] his features would appear quite beautiful. It was the wildness of his dissatisfactions that outed his unhappiness.

Jittery winks and glances kept dominating his appraisal of this new environment. Constant scratching [of his wrists {his ankles ‹maybe Anwar's rude assessment was actually right «was he an addict?»›}] rippled off him like a provocation to start a fight he would immediately run from.

Disgust and discomfort were on constant display [whether animating his {coppery} skin or the dance of his {red-routed} eyes or in the erratic appearance of a forced grin {‹quickly› disappearing as a hand clawed suddenly at his lips ‹exposing ravaged teeth «forget the awful condition of his nails ⟨jagged ⌈ripped⌉⟩ returning to dig behind his ears or at scabs on the back of his hands»›}].

[curiously] Something his own seemed to hang apart from him [like a part of the old woman {in miniature} offering contrapuntal peace and pleasantness]. A necklace of some sort [handmade {of wood ‹warm as «burnt» honey «sticky too(?)»›}]. The beads were nothing fantastic nor was the central piece dangling in the center [a thing on the lighter side of amber {Anwar ‹at first› thinking gold apple ‹a tart apple› before realizing it wasn't an apple at all but something just as familiar ‹with «scaled» cupule and «polished» pericarp›}]:

an acorn.

But for all its simplicity [and it really was unremarkable] Anwar's interest clung to it. His focus did not go unnoticed. The scaramouch at once concealed the nut in a greedy palm [Anwar almost laughed aloud {at himself! ‹for the association he was powerless «or too late» to arrest›}]:

just like a ring bearer.

Though that thing was no thing of power.

This young man was no bearer of power.

[in fact] No thing of power was evident here.

'其安？' the old lady had said then [simultaneously instructing the young man {with a look} to communicate her question {was that his role? ‹was he her translator?›}].

The young man [dutifully {if resentfully‹?›}]
obeyed:

'هي كويسه؟'

∴ *Is she okay?* ∵

Anwar was then just about to demand what that was supposed to mean [not to mention demand an exact clarification about this *she* {*who?!* ‹thinking only of Xanther «(of course) always thinking of his immaculate child»›}] only to discover [directed by the {frightened‹?›} glance of the {jittery} purveyor of meaning {this ‹«suddenly» of increasing interest «more curious»› lingual go-between}] that the old woman was now [already {somehow}] several steps away [already at the front door {which was already open}] greeting [anticipating!] Astair's return with open hands.

Wait! Did he just speak to him in Arabic?

Anwar expected Astair to lose her shit [{in fact} welcomed it {anything to overthrow this powerlessness he was experiencing ‹enjoying«!»›}] but her reaction was similar to his own.

The old lady seemed to reduce every resistance to an afterthought. And though her astonishing calm disarmed Astair [tranquilizing her fiercest intentions] there was more here than fragility and strangeness leveraging the Ibrahims' sympathies [even as Astair requested an introduction {as the young man ‹still afraid«?»› snapped back to his familiar demand ‹'Cat. Where at?'› ‹Anwar felt dizzy with the strange dawning «what kept dawning ⟨far more was at stake here than one lost creature . . . ⟩»›}]:

somehow the old woman knew them.

'汝乃阿斯梯 。 汝夫乃 安瓦尔 。 吾盼见汝五人已久。'

'You Astair one. Husband Anwar,' the young man interpreted. 'She wait lah to meet you five, uh, two?'

[for starters] Anwar was disorganized [disoriented] by the music of his speech [a curious pidgin {creole?} and {truncated} garble {that belied an intention to do more than make casualties out of plain meanings ‹invoking sensibilities greater than any word could summon «as if to imply that something about him ⟨sprung from the forehead of injury ⌈and partiality⌋⟩ was from the outset prosthetic ⟨artificial ⌈he had spoken Arabic⌋⟩ ⟨as if to say:

الاحباط في حديثي حيبقي مثال لك علشان تعيش من غير أي حديث وما يدلكش أي حجه علشان تقسم نفسك مني وما يدلكش أي اعذار لينا احنا الاثنين علشان نقسم من العالم و كذلك مافيش حد فينا يتحمل اننا نقسم نفسنا من ربنا ﴿»«›⟩}{].

The line [and recognition] came by way of an abrupt remembrance of Maalik [one of his father's Sufi friends {ah Shenouda}]. مالك was a poet [*The frustration of my speech shall be your living example to live beyond speech and so offer you no excuse to divide yourself from me and so offer neither of us an excuse to divide ourselves from the world and so afford none of us the excuse to divide ourselves from God. ∴ Huh. ∵*]. Except [unlike this young man] Anwar remembered Maalik's eyes possessed by an ecstatic joy of the incomprehensible. But [like the young man] Maalik also spoke in a way that seemed a base coagulate of demand and supposition.

Anwar's mother claimed Maalik was mad.

Anwar's father warned [warmingly] that there was more to his speech than the braking gears of traffic in the street.

Fatima refused to listen to breaking anything.

But Anwar tried.

'Anwar,' [his father once confided] 'when the gods speak through him, he doesn't know.'
'Then, Papa, does "to know" mean "we musn't know"?'
'You see! A young boy, and already you understand how "smart" and "sorrow" must walk hand in hand' [taking Anwar by the hand {even as Anwar was confused by how "sorrow" had entered the conversation}]. 'You make your father so happy.'
Shenouda had grown pale then and had to sit down. Fatima ran to get tea. Anwar's father suffered a heart attack months later. The doctors said he survived because he was lucky. Maalik said he survived because he laughed a lot. His father said he survived because of Fatima's tea.

[like Maalik] This Asian young man also seemed unaware of what he relayed [he seemed dismayed too {⟨at that moment though⟩ he came across as uninformed ⟨for the Ibrahims did number five «which he shouldn't know ⟨but which she did somehow know ⌈their names too!⌋⟩»}].

And it was this familiarity that [instantly] freed both Astair and Anwar to pursue their natural inquisitiveness ['You know who I am?' {Astair} 'You know our names?' {Anwar}].

Questions that seemed to dissolve the old woman. She suddenly grew waxen [and {though she did not move} appeared to slump {and shrink ⟨if that was possible⟩}].

She needed to sit!

Astair offered to get water. The young man insisted on tea. The young man then helped the old woman to the living room couch [Anwar struck by the tenderness he showed her {⟨beyond necessity «beyond duty»⟩ the tics of his private torments stilled ⟨Anwar envied this devotion «and pitied him too ⟨he does not know how much he loves her ⌈which was beyond Anwar's right to assume ⌈and so he assumed he was wrong ∴ *But he wasn't.* ∴ ∴ How could he know? ∴ ∴ *Maalik taught him.* ∴⌋⌋⟩»⟩}].

[together {in the foyer}] He and Astair quickly worried [in whispers] that Xanther might appear [and then {quickly ‹in tune›} agreed that Anwar would get the tea and then go upstairs to make sure Xanther remained in her room].

The last thing Anwar overheard [before reaching the kitchen] was Astair asking for their names.

He didn't hear the answer.

Anwar had [already] been in the middle of boiling water when these strangers knocked on the door. He turned the stove back on [still thinking to get water for the old woman {even as ‹some older› instinct set about loading a tray with china and sugary offerings ‹no matter how non-Egyptian Anwar sought to be «shaking sugar-love ⟨a practically genetic national identity⟩ was near impossible»›}]. The kettle boiled almost at once.

[as he headed back to the living room] Anwar realized he was glad to have guests [that {as opposed as he was to the reason for their calling} he was {more} intrigued by the true purpose of their visit {instincts ‹again› welcoming the arrival ‹the way a body can recognize recuperation before locating «and naming» the medicine «that is the ⟨—⟩ cause»›}].
Anwar even faced a paranoid flirtation [[{that this somehow involved Galvadyne ‹or Mefisto›} thoughts that {happily} went nowhere]. And the key? Anwar felt curiously happy about this intrusion.

He was even smiling as he crossed through the breakfast area and reentered the foyer.

The wails from the living room arrested his progress.

Astair [with Shasti and Freya {on the stairs}] had frozen too at the eruption of those mournful sounds.

Even the twins were immobilized.

Anwar wanted to send them to their room [tell them to stay there {tell them to make sure Xanther stayed in hers}].

Except—

Except Xanther was already down here [somehow! {in the living room ‹standing before the old woman and her young companion «both still seated on the sofa 〈the coffee table between them〉»›}].

On Xanther's shoulder: the tiny cat.

Anwar could also see that Xanther was just as unprepared as they were for these cries filling their house.

The old woman [at the sight of Xanther {at the sight of the little animal ‹was she the former owner of the cat?›?}?] had dissolved into a horrible disfiguration of grief —

// her mouth gaped

// her nose ran

// tears sliced down her face

Then [{despite his constant vocalizations about retrieving the cat} the cat's appearance did not provoke retrieving] the young man also started to bawl [less due to anything Xanther presented than over the old woman's distress].

Whatever impulse Anwar had then to provide consolation [likely the case for Astair as well {as she also remained at a standstill}] was robbed by Xanther's immediate flight across the coffee table.

Had Anwar ever seen her move so quickly?

// like a pounce

// charging

// if it wasn't so light . . .

Xanther [of course] still left a wake of a mess behind her [that was par for the course] but the motion itself was weirdly economical [even calm].

Anwar had observed all the steps too [walnuts {and ‹dried› pomegranates} skittering {rolling} across the floor {a few candles extinguished as they fell ‹in a spit of splattering wax›}] but it still felt as if one moment Xanther was in the middle of the room and in the next [or not next {practically the same instant‹♭›}] she was already sitting [on the coffee table] facing both guests.

Her right hand reached for the young man [alighting on his knee {to steady him ‹reassure him›}].

While [at the same time {with what was one effortless ‹and fluid› movement}] gently scooping the animal off her shoulder so that the cat now sat in her left palm [offered {freely} to the crying old woman].

'Please! Take him back!' Xanther cried. 'He's yours!'

Before carefully depositing the love of her life in a stranger's lap.

'吾之？' the old woman mumbled [genuinely surprised {stunned even ‹staring dumbfounded at the animal now in her possession «yet not moving at all to touch it ⟨the cat unaware of its role in this transaction⟩»›}].

'دم شجرة :: ▮▮▮▮▮▮ ::,' Xanther mumbled then [Anwar couldn't have heard that right {how had he heard that ‹what did she really say? :: ▮▮▮▮▮ ::› though not missing her wet eyes :: ▮▮▮▮▮ ::}].

Nor understanding the old woman's reaction then [or the young man only squawking back: '血木'].

What was that?

A name?

'血木?' The old woman repeated [whatever it meant {somehow still} recomposing her face from incomprehension into an expression of shock {not disapproval either ‹or anything close to revulsion› but did Anwar detect there as well a look of fear? ‹what had the young man said on the phone? «something about dangerous ⟨capable of hurting him [*hurting?!*]⟩?»}].

Regardless of their reactions [and what those reactions might elicit in Anwar] it was Xanther's generosity and ceaseless compassion that flooded Anwar with pride and [yes {as was always the case}] tears too.

That she had chosen this moment to relinquish the little beast left him speechless.

That she had also chosen this moment to name him was staggering.

Anwar could see Astair felt the same way [both sharing a look of . . . {what they hadn't seen in their ‹reflective› eyes for years ‹for each other «not like this ⟨such intimacy!⟩»›}].

And then [for no reason Anwar could lay claim to] all the hairs on the back of his neck [{including} ghost hairs {‹those that might have protected his body thousands of years ago› all down his back}] razored the air.

Just as the young man [in response to whatever Xanther had said {‹was it that?› going one step further than Anwar ‹incarnating whatever frisson Anwar was experiencing›}] jumped to his feet.

Had Anwar already been anticipating what would happen next?

Part of him must have been aware [{Astair too} some parental {and primal} perception already tuned in to this young man's acute aggressions {the polygon count of limb angles aligning in preparation for an attack}].

[and even if thinking was too late to preempt assault]

Animal instincts bested all conscious assessments:

// the tray long gone from Anwar's hands

// all cups

// silverware too

// the teapot

// every comestible

// tumbling

// down through the air

So that even as the young man [with {ravaged} teeth exposed {in an awful grimace}] wound up and [with all his {lanky} might] slammed his hand [nails jabbing] into his child's face

                                    // the way

// Xanther's head snapped

                        // back might as well have

// sounded a terrible

                    // crack

                // the way she twisted around

        // palms slapping the table

                                // poor chin

        // did sound

                    // a horrible knock

            Anwar was already moving

flying forward . . .

How dare you touch my daughter!

No one touches my daughter!

Even if none of these words emerge from Anwar's lips. [instead] The house fills with an agonized scream [shapeless {twisting ‹squirming free of his mouth «from his belly!»›}]. Not the only one either. Behind him: a second howl [entwining his {teethed with fury ‹and violence›}].

Astair's.

Likely also leaping through the air.

Sailing over these few steps [dropping down into their living room].

And [as Anwar does now] will [an instant later{?}] land hard onto the floorboards [the old wood shrieking {as if warning that rage can break the oldest ‹most trusted› division: ‹and there is a big basement down there «maybe Anwar and Astair will fall through 《take the whole world with them》 though not tonight» not all the way down there› the floor ‹holding strong›} wood merely squeaking].

[besides] Anwar is already bouncing up again [he's way faster than Astair {defying gravity again ‹too›}] propelling himself [{still faster‹!›} at full force] forward [again!] towards the only one deserving the full effect of this kind of brutal focus.

Only a few more strides away.

The young man ill-prepared.

Only just realizing what he's unleashed.

Those nasty eyes reflexively widening with fear.

No more ready to resist than run.

Fear instructs him that [not only is there no place to turn {no properly sequenced words adept enough to nullify this charge ‹no posture agile enough to repel the imminent assault›}] paralysis is his only choice [and it's already been made for him].

Nothing will avert Anwar.

Nothing will defy this inertial conclusion.

The young man knows it.

So too does the old woman.

So [of course] Anwar never sees it coming.

None of them do.

Xanther.

She's somehow already there [in the in-between]. Not just sitting up either [on the coffee table {where she was flung}] but on her feet [already some distance from the table too]. And on her lips [when has she ever looked so calm? ∵ *Oh my! So soon!*∴ ∵ **Too soon!**∴] the hint of a smile.

Her face isn't even marred. No hint of red lies on her cheek [forget bloody scratches {or a bewildered expression of shock ‹not a single lasting trace of harm›}].

Immaculate as marble.

Invulnerable.

And perfectly still.

Though Xanther isn't still at all.

She's uncoiling

[{the fingers of her left hand gathering gently together ‹like a bird's beak «before extending towards the young man»} . . . {while the palm of her right hand sweeps towards Anwar ‹opening tenderly›}] radiating something beyond the visible reach of any gesture [the consequences of that release {if invisible in her form} visible in the forms of those around her].

The young man is thrown back onto the sofa [throwing his arms over his head {before crumpling up ‹whimpering «as knees continue to crunch upwards 《for some position deeper than fetal》»›}].

Anwar briefly aches to do the same [though there's no way he can even stop this mad sprint {maybe change direction ‹drop and twist «drive his shoulder ⟨backed by all this momentum⟩ into the cowering miscreant»}].

Except Anwar's already stopped.

Stopped for a while too it seems [even as his thoughts keep racing ahead for revenge {still enacting their own kind of waking dream ‹fast-fading afterimages «departing like ❰ . . . ❱ ghosts»}].

Anwar's stomach turns. He suddenly feels clammy with sweat while his chest beats a bedlam of want [feet and fingers throb {*Get—!*}] and his mouth keeps getting drier and drier.

Even his eyes feel dry.

∷ Piloerection? ∷

∷ *Of course. Every hair standing straight up in a chilly gloss.* ∷

∷ Testicular detumescence? ∷

∷ **Ha! Don't forget rectal constriction!** ∷

∷ Anus is a knot [pelvis dropped too {as if to attempt tucking itself away}]. ∷

∷ *Like he had a tail in need of hiding.* ∷

∷ **Such a tail would have betrayed his location.** ∷

Anwar starts then to understand that what brought him to this standstill was flight overtaking fight [otherwise his mind keeps coming up blank {trying to make sense of this new authority: a terrible shaking commanding his limbs ‹thoughts unable yet to parse the cause of such a terrifying reversal «failing to locate a commensurate ❰ *Get out!* ❱ danger»}].

Though there's only one evident cause:

Xanther.

She had briefly seemed to him an immense storm
[her presence tidal {a maelstrom ‹whirl of water and
air «all the elements ⟨beholden to a sudden great emptiness ⌈which somehow she ⌈centered and contained
[with an empty palm] and . . .] released⌋⟩»»}].

It hurled Anwar back to Cairo [he wasn't even Xanther's age {wandering alone ‹lost› because he'd been trying to get out of the city ‹already lost in the thought
of how to get outside infinity «first imagining a wall at
the end of forever ⟨itself an endless series of one wall
after another ⌈so an infinity of ends⌋» . . . ›}]. His
hands clutched marbles. His winnings [for knocking
them outside a circle]. What he would later offer to his
parents by way of explanation when they found him:

'ممكن تقول ثاني؟ انت كنت بتحاول توصل برة الانهاءية؟' his father
would ask.

'Have you lost your marbles?' his mother yelled.

'I have them right here,' Anwar answered [under-
standing the English expression only literally {all of
them in the palms of his proud hands}].

Is it a coincidence then [or {actually} the cause of
this abrupt memory? ∴ The cause ∵] that in his pocket
now lies the marble [brown and gold {cat's-eye}] that
he had found with Xanther at the abandoned Animal
Center back in May ∴ **TFv2 p. 341** ∵?

Astair [still behind him {she must have stopped too}] releases a muffled cry.

The young man [hands over his head {face still buried in his knees}] is moaning.

And why?

Because Xanther put out her hands like some traffic cop in a busy intersection?

She never even said a word.

Yet Anwar can't deny his own queasiness [what might {at any second} result in vomit].

A sensation that subsides almost at once when Xanther lets her arms drop [followed by the return of a familiar slump in her posture].

Only then does she seem to register her surroundings [as if surfacing from a seizure {though much more quickly}]. Her look of dawning surprise suggests that she has no idea why Anwar looks the way he does [she must detect his alarm {what Anwar tries to conceal ‹without knowing how his fear is evidenced›}].

The old woman doesn't look alarmed or afraid. But she doesn't look well either. Or she hadn't looked well. Something had been wrong with her face. [for an instant] It had seemed bright red. One side [the left side] appeared to have been mauled [as if she had been the one smacked {scratched ‹ravaged «to the point of bleeding ⟨!⟩»›}]. Though now not at all [rather she looks proud {of Xanther‹!«?⟨!⟩?»!›}].

Her smile continues to grow.

Any hint of her previous hurt [or grief] has departed.

She's practically beaming.

What's more: the little white cat now sits on her shoulder.

'Please leave us,' Xanther announces then.

'Daughter?'

No chance Anwar or Astair will allow Xanther to be alone with this reprobate cowering on their couch [even if his violence seems increasingly imaginary in the face of Xanther's calm {not to mention her immaculate cheek ‹not to mention the old woman's immaculate composure «zero sign of scratches ⟨blood⟩ anywhere»›}].

Then the old woman says something to the young man.

If her words are opaque [to Anwar] the language of her gestures [objurgation by hand] is clear enough:

The young man must get up.

The young man must get moving.

The young man must get out.

[Exiled {banished ‹booted off «kicked out ⟨connection terminated⟩»›}.]

The young man obeys at once [head down {scampering past Anwar ‹smart enough to give Astair an even wider berth›}].

Only in the foyer does he hesitate [bending down amidst the broken dishes {as if about to start tidying up ‹what one «additional» syllable from the old woman forbids›}].

Even if the young man still picks up a piece of [what looks like] raspberry cake before slipping outside [leaving the {front} door {slightly} ajar].

OFF DUTY

Sometimes it happens . . .

— Elie Wiesel

Ferret Man slink out of house. Something wrong. No more Mr. Bossy, all snap-snap with demands. Now bent over. Hands snap-snap each other. Head bob up and down, from conversation with self, bad conversation, where what's said can't be understood, can't even be heard.

Shnorhk still turn off Mnatsagan's violin to see if he can hear. Whatever language, language for curses has same music. Curses not even worst part.

Where old lady?

Shnorhk wait for front door already spilling warm light to spill shape of Ancient Beauty. Only reason Shnorhk waiting at curb. Not waiting here for Ferret Man.

But shadow inside slams door. Kills amber light. Dark slam down around place again, leaves Ferret Man to lurch alone across front lawn, bad hunch getting worse, arms wrapping around chest so hands can stab back, head bobbing, but curses gone, all speech gone.

Maybe he crying? Maybe puking?

"Where is she?" Shnorhk bark out window.

Ferret Man not respond. Shnorhk tap horn.

"You okay?"

Ferret Man lift head, shake head, swat eyes, as if see Shnorhk for first time, see everything first time, see jerking legs jerk forward, see wobbles. He sway this way, that way, like drunk, if Shnorhk know by expression, not drunk, this grief.

"You stay!" Ferret Man still spark. Again Bossy Snap-Snap with demands, if lacks song of command.

Up close, Ferret Man look afraid. Young too. Now just strange young man, lost in wide place unkind to strangeness.

"What your name?" Shnorhk call out.

"Jingjing," young man respond.

"You not from here?"

"Singapore," Jingjing answer.

"Far from home?" Question more a statement.

Jingjing nod head, grave as granite, maybe graver.

"Wait, please, wait ten minute more, can?" Jingjing begs.

Whole drive there Shnorhk wanted to get rid of young man. Shnorhk would have found corner to lose Bossy Snap-Snap, if not for Ancient Beauty.

Ancient Beauty . . . she was something else. Shnorhk not understood how on way to Echo Park, her smile, in rearview, or now-and-then shoulder pat, out of blue, in bad traffic, gave Shnorhk such calm.

At one point she even said something to Ferret Man, something for Shnorhk.

"She like maneki neko," young man announced, in way that said he not like maneki neko, which made Shnorhk like it even more.

Then another exchange.

"Wants to know name?" Ferret Man said or asked. Shnorhk not sure. Not understand either way.

"Does statue have name?" Ferret Man asked in different way.

Shnorhk said no.

Another backseat exchange. Maybe dispute, in Chinese? Singaporean? Shnorhk know nothing about Singapore. Maybe something about law there against bubble gum.

"She say it have beautiful name. She say you know this." Again said in way that said young man not believe what he was translating, which made Shnorhk believe it a little more, though he did not know figurine's name or what Ancient Beauty could be meaning.

Maybe Ferret Man had got meaning mistaken.

What would Shnorhk name cat? Didn't wonder long. Knew name. Only name. Of course. Her name allways near. She named the world wherever Shnorhk went.

So why not this?

Suddenly Shnorhk grew uneasy. Had he just named it or only dis-covered name? Was it good thing for such dumb thing to have such pure name? He felt ashamed too, like now unable to take back name. Not that Shnorhk would tell a soul.

How relieved Shnorhk was to reach Echo Park. Lots of little homes cramped close together up and down crampy little roads. Except here. This spot houses big. Bright lit, with new cars, tall trees.

Ancient Beauty said something.

"Here fine," Ferret Man snapped, tapped Shnorhk's shoulder to stop short of destination.

House big like rest, but without new brightness. More like patch of shadow with something off. Shnorhk couldn't name it. Just felt it. Felt it at once.

Two levels of red brick. Heavy beams holding up roof. Roof was tile. Maybe red tile. Hard to see in dark.

Front door was centered. Black hinges and black latches with black bands of metal across black wood.

Not many windows. Part of strangeness? Upstairs had two small ones. One above driveway with little balcony. Only three windows downstairs. All curtained. Maybe why house seemed brooding? Impossible to look out of. Impossible to look into. Blind house?

Lawn in front yellowing, dying. High bushes grew on side leading downhill. On side leading uphill was carport, back of which was gate of iron covered with green nylon fabric, locked up with rusted chain. Kind used for bikes, maybe? Who knows what was past gate. Car in driveway, though, that Shnorhk knows. Knows types too who sit behind wheel.

CAR DRIVER RATING

Honda Element

QUOTE:

"Training wheels."

DRIVER:

Part distracted, part lost. Bad lane changer, worse merger, worst parker.

BUMPER STICKER:

Think Outside the Browser.

RECOMMENDATION:

Pay no attention.

LICENSE PLATE:

W0NDMZ

Dirty too. All over. If hallowed with little handprints. Paw prints too.

Dirty people living here. Made sense Ferret Man would want come here. At least Shnorhk breathed better when young man jumped out to help Ancient Beauty out.

But Ancient Beauty not go just yet but shuffled around to Shnorhk's side to clasp Shnorhk's hand, nodding head as if in thanks, smile wide as if to say:

You are an incredible driver!

What could Shnorhk do? But he must do something to return such, what?, kindness?

His nod sure was not enough, and his rough smile not close to enough, not even close to smile either.

So Shnorhk looked around for something, anything, and ended up with one thing. Useless, but she accepted it like here was genie's wish come true, here was magic carpet ride, here was best answer to saddest prayer.

Independence Taxi
Shnorhk Zildjian
818 -⊗⊗⊗-⊗⊗⊗⊗ License # ⊗⊗⊗⊗⊗
Call Anytime. I will be there for you.

Ferret Man intruded then, shoved money at Shnorhk, demanded change, and kept change! No tip! Shnorhk finding one dime, three nickels, two pennies!

Shnorhk would have drove off then, but Ancient Beauty held his attention.

Ferret Man was trying to get her to follow him up street to address on palm, but she headed to brooding house. Young man threw up hands and followed. Not lost on Shnorhk was his tenderness. How he accompanied her pain.

Had Shnorhk noticed her pain before? No. Her pain stayed hidden behind gentle touch, behind a thousand smiling lines. As if her whole life was an eviction. Though evicted by what, Shnorhk couldn't guess. Shnorhk not want to guess.

He was about to pull away when her little shape seemed to sharpen. She said something then.

Ferret Man came running back.

"You wait!" Mr. Bossy Snap-Snap demanded.

But Shnorhk knuckled roof.

OFF DUTY sign bright again.

"You wait!" Ferret Man shrieked, waving more cash at Shnorhk, a twenty, even dug up from pocket those dirty nickels, pennies, and dime.

Shnorhk let him keep his money but didn't leave either.

"How long?"

"Ten minute! Ten minute!"

Shnorhk shook his head.

"For her!" Panic in his voice was real.

Who were these people?

What were they doing here?

Shnorhk looked again at dark house. Looked at time on phone.

More texts from lads. Lads arriving soon at Mnatsagan's. Want him soon but not mind either if Shnorhk arrive late, late because he needed rest.

So why not rest here? Nap to earn. Not that Shnorhk needed to earn more. Young man and his money found that out.

"Ten minute more?" Jingjing begs now. Begs again. Always ten minutes while time beyond minutes just flows.

"Is she in trouble?"

Jingjing shake head, again cross arms over chest, bobbing head, bending self: "She okay, okay?"

"Friends?" Shnorhk can't resist, so curious, if careful too, worried about Ancient Beauty, like she a child, child again, and a child no matter the child is always beautiful.

"Not friends!" Jingjing spat, shaking head. "She just getting my cat back."

You Should
Be Dead

KICK ROCKS!

— *Erykah Badu*

请勿烦恼 。 *There is no injury.*

What Xanther hears when she again pats her palms over her face, which is fine, more than fine, but she keeps doing it to reassure herself while squiggling her feet closer to the old woman, Chinese?, that was Xanther's best guess ∴ Doesn't feel like a guess. ∴ ∴ *It's not a guess.* ∴, not that that matters, compared to how happy the old woman looks, like beaming sunflare-style, especially since Les Parents left the room, that smile only growing. It has to be over Xanther, right?, because Tian Li already has the cat.

Tian Li. That's her name. One of the first things she told Xanther when they were alone. No handshake. Just that bright stillness. Xanther answered with her name, though Tian Li knew it already. Maybe in the way that Xanther knew that little one being with Tian Li was way sad but also, like, kinda a relief too?

Go ahead. 可 。 *Convince yourself.*

That's pretty weird too, how Xanther can hear Tian Li speaking without speaking, and how that's somehow fine. ∴ I can't hear anything. ∴ ∴ **We can.** ∴ ∴ Uh, that's so uncool? ∴

Xanther gently lifts her hands and touches the old woman's cheeks. They're so smooth!, like satin, even with all the wrinkles, and for sure without welts, gashes, rivulets of blood, or the stain of a developing bruise. Tian Li closes her eyes, for a moment confusing Xanther, like is it Tian Li or furball that's purring?

"I, like, uh, don't, uh, understand?"

此为吾在此之因。
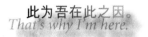
That's why I'm here.

∷ "此为吾在此之因。" ∷

∷ Huh? ∷

∷ *That's what Tian Li just said. In Classical Chinese.* ∷

∷ "That's why I'm here" in Chinese? ∷

∷ *I know all languages. I know too that the languages you know depend on you. You know no Putonghua, Cantonese, or any other Chinese dialect.* ∷

∷ Then how is it that this old woman just, like, spoke in a language I don't know but I heard, uh, English? ∷

∷ **You did not hear English.** ∷

∷ *That's correct.* ∷

∷ Huh? Then, wait, is Xanther listening to you like translate?! ∷

∷ **That's impossible. Something else is overwriting communication.** ∷

∷ *No. Not overwriting. Determining is more accurate.* ∷

∷ Why does that worry me? ∷

∷ *No one ever said you were stupid.* ∷

∷ **Except me.** ∷

"But he, uh, he hit me?"

Tian Li nods.

"And like way hard too. Like my skin was burning and scratched, and scratched deep too, but then it wasn't. The pain was gone. The feeling of everything around the pain was gone too. And I felt like better, and even stronger."

Tian Li nods again.

其名靖靖。

His name is Jingjing.

"But then your face! I saw the scratches on you! You were definitely bleeding, and hurt, really hurt, and like I was worried, really worried."

Tian Li's eyes shine, that sunflare beaming in overload, if that's possible, if a sun can look proud.

汝何做？

What did you do?

"I ate the bubble gum."

汝甚喜嚼，岂非乎？

You like that gum quite a lot?

"It's my favorite."

谢你

Thank you.

What a wallop too.

The feeling might be gone but not the experience. Like a slap at first, but then with the heel of the hand following through like that, more like a punch. And then the fingernails, more like claws, for sure cutting into Xanther, the thumb too, and his thumb had the longest nail, slicing down across Xanther's mouth, cutting open both lips, before the force of the blow snapped Xanther's head to the side, vertebrae in her neck and forever scoliotic spine cracking all over, muscles spasming, maybe tearing too, as she was knocked down. One moment Xanther had been sitting on the coffee table and in the next her chin was hitting the wood hard enough to knock her teeth hard enough to knock them all out or at least chip some of them or do something bad and painful to them.

Xanther didn't see stars.

She saw a blackness that eats stars.

Or at least that was one version. And like the version too that didn't take. Because there was this other one.

Like what happened happened, but someplace else.

To someone else.

Because Xanther's feet had burned too, toes ringed with fire, arches furnacing angry coals, throwing this fire deeper and deeper, as if to say, if feet could speak, with speech borne up as rapidly as all this heat dissipating beneath:

What slap?

More than that too, because at the same time as this painful fire burned down through Xanther and out of her, both her legs were also, at the same time, releasing her to pursue the joys of action, unchaining her from whatever just happened, what didn't happen, to the symphyseal ∴ Huh? ∵ marriage of thought and action already set on becoming something else.

When had Xanther ever felt so free? So light?

No doubt because she also felt somehow helped along, but like in that perfect way that doesn't feel like any help at all, as if a billion good hardworking ants on their caring backs were carrying Xanther back to herself, touching her only in the right places, places that needed only a tiny bit of assistance, so the all of her that had thumped into the coffee table, flattened her there, could rebound almost as easily, like she was weightless but without forgetting her weight, lifting her chin, her palms, her whole torso, as her thighs worked a little to straighten the rest of her out, though it wasn't really work, raising her up from the ground, like Xanther was on a geyser, or really Xanther was the geyser, but one that didn't just gush and spray all over, and lose itself, but was like able to stop and just fill, but not explode either, what Xanther figured then was less like a geyser and really more like a big tree, a big, huge geyser-tree, conifer, of course, century-wide roots drawing strength from the ancient earth, pine needles as infinite as horizons extend- ing into an equally endless sky, Xanther just as expansive, endless as a tremendous power too heavy for any world and not in a hurry.

Power doesn't need speed.

Speed is what prey prays for.

At this point, Les Parents were already racing crazy toward her, Anwar flailing through the air, propelling himself into the living room, a rictus of anger and fear seizing his mouth, an expression that any other time would have terrified Xanther but now almost made her laugh. Well, not really laugh, more like amused her, in that way that amusement is sometimes tied to the need to reassure, this smiling sympathy also there for Astair, who was right behind Anwar, equally determined to assault Jingjing, because, see, neither one of them needed to worry.

Xanther blew Jingjing away.

And it wasn't like she did much either. Did she even do anything at all? Like she maybe flexed? But, uh, no. Flexing wasn't it. Or shrugged? Not that either. Nothing here was so unimportant to deserve a shrug or so demanding to merit a flex.

It was more like Xanther let go, like she let whatever this was, what was helping her, moving through her, becoming her, be the more than her that was still unfolding.

Xanther could see that for Jingjing, this was like trying to hug a bomb blast. He was thrown from his feet, slammed into the sofa, crumpled up like a bubble-gum wrapper.

For Xanther though it was like she had all the time in the world to answer the form her own body kept asking her to explore. She had just continued to move, amazed as her left hand, fingers pinched together like a beak, struck out toward Jingjing, as all her weight then shifted from the left foot to her right foot, already placed to the right, toward Les Parents, her right arm extending, elbow lifting, all her weight sinking still deeper then, way deeper than that right foot, more than all her weight, leaving her left leg, in fact almost her whole left side, feeling as effortless as the emptiness her right palm cupped as it opened up to meet crazy charging Les Parents.

It was weird too. How quick they had stopped. Like almost too quick to believe. Astair had even whimpered. When had Xanther ever made her mom do that? Like never?! And Anwar just went pale to the point that maybe he was going to be sick. Which at some other time, just the sight of such shock on her parents' faces, their distress, their fear, would have made Xanther bawl and run into their arms.

But this was not some other time.

Xanther knew they were fine.

Just like she knew someone else was not.

Toward whom Xanther was already turning, shifting easily back onto her left foot, pivoting fast, almost one-hundred-and-eighty degrees, to her blind spot, which somehow never seemed that blind, finding there in the old woman's face all the injury Xanther was sure should mirror her own face, with the only difference being the wild familiar blooms filling the air.

It seemed so obvious this time.

Xanther snapped it up. Right out of the air.

Had Cedar's gum ever tasted so good?

Xanther gulped it all down too.

Until it was gone.

Just as all the hurt on the old woman's face was gone, those markings not even appearing as a possibility, as even the memory itself seemed to fade away, like hot sand swallowing a receding wave, a long time ago, not even once upon a time anymore, not even once, not ever upon a time, time unmarked, time's sands untouched, leaving Xanther dazed, and wobbly, holding on to only one certainty: she needed to be alone with the old woman.

This stranger with the cat still on her shoulder.

Little one seemed content too. No, not "seemed." He *was* content. Xanther didn't question it, even if it panged her some, panged her a lot. So peaceful in his soft stillness, in his insistent blindness. Like he had known that shoulder for a long, long time and would never forget. And also he didn't look like he was about to die anymore. Like, maybe?, the strength the old woman had shared with Xanther, if that's what had happened, she was somehow sharing also with the little animal, if that's what was happening now.

"Pl-please, uh, h–help me," Xanther stutters. "I don't understand," *about like getting hit, or not getting hit, you getting hit, and the bubble gum. I have so many questions.*

∴ Hey. She's not— I'm— Hey! We're not talking! My lips aren't moving! ∴

∴ *But you still can't shut up. Listen.* ∴

∴ **And suddenly there's agreement.** ∴

Amazing and perplexing that you are achieving this so quickly. I too am curious. I too have so many questions.

Then, "uh," *like maybe in that way we're the same?*

Will you please show me your form?

"Huh?"

Do you like Tai Chi?

"My mom" *makes me do it.*

Did she make you do that?

"Uh, I don't understand" *how I did that.*

432

Tian Li sits down on the edge of the coffee table, but lightly, like she isn't even sitting there, though that's also how she looks when she's standing, so lightly, like her feet can't touch the floor, until suddenly they do, as she's up again, moving exactly as Xanther had, first left foot down, the fingers of her left hand pressing together like a beak, as if eating from her right palm, before extending away, to gently peck, or strike, but never speak, the old woman's hips already swiveling like water to the right, right foot placed to the right, right palm out, executing Single Whip just as Xanther had, though way better, way lighter and yet like fuller too, and with zero threat, even if Xanther's holding her breath, and her chest feels tight, like she too might get blown back into the sofa, ball up, and bawl.

Which of course doesn't happen.

Tian Li only closes her eyes, just like little one, both of them enjoying with a deep breath the rest of the movement.

Your turn.

"Aww" *you're worse than my* "mother."

That sure gets the old woman cackling with, like, delight, right? A pretty crude sound too, or not crude, but rough?, though somehow it relaxes Xanther, her chest opening again, with more than enough breath to share.

Xanther goes through the Single Whip sequence, what seems pretty much the same as what Tian Li just demonstrated, though it wasn't the same at all.

Xanther slumps.

Not the same?

Xanther shakes her head.

What's different?

"I don't, uh, know." *At all!*

Though one thing Xanther does know is that her mom has slipped quietly around through their breakfast area to the piano room, pretending to sit and read, book in her lap, though all the lights are off.

Your mother is a good teacher. She is so pretty. Tian Li winks. She looks almost enthralled. *Do you think I'm pretty?*

There's a twinkle of mischief in those old eyes now, but also something burning, and getting brighter too, what needs no mischief, which makes Xanther want to cry.

"You're so beautiful!" Xanther cries out, and suddenly it's this old woman who is crying, tears slipping out of her eyes, wandering her face, all those wrinkles, so many folds, creased in darkness, as if they were all the years themselves, which Xanther feels is a number too high to count, though she would try if it would help ease the sorrow and grief Xanther can't account for, can't understand.

"I'm sorry. I'm so sorry," Xanther mutters, reaching for Tian Li, a hand on the old woman's arm, near her elbow.

Why should you be sorry?

"I didn't mean" *to make you cry.*

Hush, child. You didn't make me cry. What you meant to do you did perfectly. What you had no understanding of you did perfectly too. You stopped the anger. You freed the tears. I never imagined this moment would be pleasant. I never imagined I might actually like you! Tian Li cackles some more at that, tears drying, gone, her face clear again as a clear sky above sand and sea, if for Xanther, nothing's clear, just mud and muddle.

:: You're telling me. ::

:: *She's telling you nothing.* ::

:: **We're telling you nothing.** ::

:: Just like I keep saying. And for the record, I never imagined this moment and I don't like you. ::

:: **Noted.** ::

:: Is there a record? ::

"Whaddya mean" *'this moment'* "?"

I'm sorry I took so long to come. I was afraid.

"Why?"

You are good but you are not that good. Tian Li steps away then, toward the fireplace, which seems to grow colder with her approach, and there's nothing there, deadening maybe even the promise of fire. Is she eyeing Dov's gun box?

"Thanks," Xanther answers sarcastically, for the insult, which she then realizes isn't an insult, Tian Li for the first time looking surprised, shocked even, by the tone, shocked to be misunderstood.

Often objects in our way turn out to be lessons to help us on our way. If we know how to turn them. Remember what your father said? 'Remember Bagheera loved thee.'

"Huh?" *Who?*

You know what your father said. Tell me.

"'I believe in angels. I believe that the good will of the dead follows after.'"

∴ But Anwar never said that. ∴

∴ **TFv5 p. 193** ∴

Tian Li smiles. *I imagine you've had trouble with locks?*

"You could say that."

When there is no name, doors and windows tend to slip open. A name for what owns you, though, tends to have a different effect.

Xanther just nods along, thinking of the Animal Shelter, Satya, the ballet. What else does this woman know?

The burning "I feel" *all the time,* "like" *this blue flame that starts up, burning me up, burning everything up, or starting too, like sorta smoky, or right before smoke starts, it's* "awful," *and I just know I'm gonna die,* "unless I'm with him." *Or with him, but only here, at home. It's so confusing.*

And hearing herself, and looking at little one on Tian Li's shoulder, Xanther suddenly feels sad, like so awfully sad she's gonna be sick, because of course now with little one leaving, Xanther's going to burn up completely, only to feel doubly sick, because she's not burning up at all, she's not even close to hot, but she knows who is.

"The fire?" *You have it now?*

Tian Li looks pale. Never was there such an effort to smile and try to reassure Xanther, who she can't reassure because Xanther knows too intimately this agony.

You should not be here, Tian Li musters.

"Where" *should I be* "?"

You should be dead. How could you suffer this?

"I just did?"

Will you do something for me?

Xanther nods, if now added to agony, terror for some reason also begins to revive.

Lift the stones from my eyes.

"Lift the stones from your eyes? Here? Is that even possible?"

Tian Li nods.

Xanther realizes she hadn't even noticed the old woman's stones.

Xanther tries, though half-heartedly at first, scared?, for sure Fraidy K all the way, because what if she does flick them away, and the color, or whatever *that* is that's underneath, if it's not really a color, what if it's that red that isn't red but something *he* needs . . .

. . . except the stones immediately get heavier and heavier, like they always do when Xanther's not in the forest.

Xanther even briefly returns to the forest, like maybe
that's where the old woman means, like Xanther might find
Tian Li there, that would be a first, someone she actually
recognizes there, which Xanther suspects is nearly impossible, because that world isn't this world, if for a moment
Xanther wonders if maybe Tian Li is the forest itself and its
judgment too . . .

                                        . . . but, as expected,
Tian Li's not there, though less expected is that no one's
there, no glint of garnet bruise, no flickering hints of turquoise, in fact, no streams even of stones.

                                        Scary.

"I'm sorry." Xanther blinks, trying to blink back from the horror of that emptiness where something far more awful in the distance is literally burning everything up.

Tian Li has stopped smiling. She even looks disappointed. Cross too. Like maybe Xanther isn't who she thought she was. Tian Li shuffles away then, her tiny arms crossed across her tiny chest. Like maybe she's even mad. Like Xanther's just failed big time and this has all been a waste of time.

Xanther wants to react, like run, or defend herself, or raise some sort of don't-mess-with-me ruckus, maybe call Les Parents for backup, if Xanther also feels too heavy to do any of that, or even think it, forget think it through, like Xanther herself is heavier than Tian Li's stones, along with the stones upon the eyes of her whole family, a rain of them coming down hard, burying her, with only the sight of little one, even though he's not with her, making somehow all the stones lighter than rain.

And then Tian Li is there, right there!, who cares how far away she was moments ago, or how disappointed she looked, or pale or sad, or burning up, because right now she *is* fire itself, one hand hot around Xanther's right wrist, the other sizzling on Xanther's left shoulder, as if to pull Xanther into the flames, and with that extraordinary face of hers so super close too, as close as breath, maybe closer, eyes not only wide, not only getting wider, but more frightening, the pupils themselves starting to impossibly exceed the wideness of her eyes, irises long gone, were they different colors too?, it doesn't matter, this wideness is exceeding even the stones, which fortunately are still hanging there, without which Xanther might have fallen in, swallowed by a look, perishing in a gaze, which still isn't the most frightening part, because Xanther has sensed the creature on Tian Li's shoulder starting to stir, still little one, and yet also not, breath rank with rot and age, bad enough to make all of time retch, and as if that isn't enough . . . his eyes, stoneless, seem about to open and widen too, though they don't.

What is the cat! Tian Li demands.

"What cat?"

And like that Tian Li is away, almost across the room again, her arms no longer crossed, no longer looking disappointed, or mad, more like sad, pale, frail as ever, and maybe a little afraid too.

Xanther wants to apologize. Offer some kind of atonement. She was just being a snot. Rude, for sure. But she just bites her lip, chews on the inside of her cheek. Because even though it was just something to say, it also wasn't that simple either.

Xanther handles the complication as a wave of nausea and exhaustion, brought on by a singular throb in her head, the pain ending whatever explanation she's searching for, with a new Question Song about to start up, and surely sung to the tune of more throbs.

Because little one is no more the little one than he is
with Tian Li than he is a creature without a name . . .

Is that it?

The name.

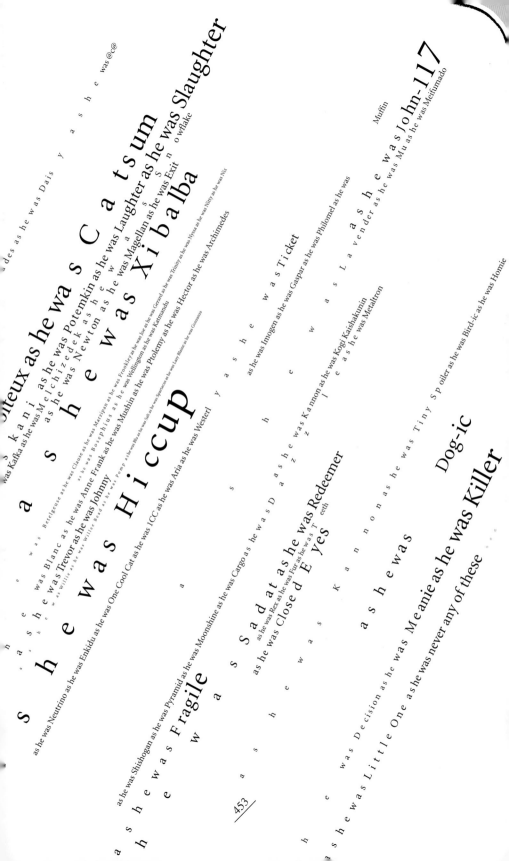

...des as he was Dais y a s h e was @c@

olteux as he was C a t s um as he was Slaughter

k a n i as he was Potemkin as he was Laughter as he was Magellan as he was Exit S n o wflake

as he was Melchizedek as he w a s h e Xibalba

as he was Newton as he w a s h e w a s

Muffin

as he w e w a s John-117

as he was Mu as he was Meifumado

was Kafka as he was Betelgeuse as he was Claude as he was Marzipan as he was Froxley as he was Gerard as he was Trinity as he was Nyssa as he was Nitty as he was Meifumado

as he was Bolephius as he was Wellington as he was Katmandu

as he was Mushin as he was Hector as he was Archimedes

as he was Ptolemy as he was

L a v e n d e r as he was Metaltron

as he was Imogen as he was Gaspar as he was Philomel as he was

w a s Ticket

as he was Kannon as he was Kogi Kaishakunin

was Blanc as he was Trevor as he was Johnny H i ccup

was Anne Frank as he was

s h e w a s

a s h e w a s

as he was Willie Bead as he was

as he was Neutrino as he was Enkidu as he was One Cool Cat as he was ICC as he was Aria as he was Westerl

as he was Shishogun as he was Pyramid as he was Moonshine as he was F ragile

S a d at as he was Redeemer

as he was Cargo as he

as he was Rex as he was Fur as he was Closed E yes

eeth

a s h e w a s

a s h e w a s

as he was Mulla as he was Salat as he was Spartacus as he was Lary Blaine as he was Gionzanza

Dog-ic

Tiny Sp oiler as he was Bird-ic as he was Homie

Decision as he was Meanie as he was Killer

h e w a s Little One as he was never any of these

"Ha!" Tian Li cries then, as if reading Xanther's thoughts, that wicked twinkle back in her eye, graced by an equally mischievous smile. *One thing that never changes, you'll see, is just how impudent children are when it comes to the immediate. They want everything now. Only a few grow up to understand how to know now without want. Will you?*

"I don't know."

The answer seems to please Tian Li. *How did you find his name?*

You mean "my name" for him "?"

Again Tian Li looks pleased. *You really are tremendously smart for your impudent age.*

"I, uh, just feel like you're, uhm, testing me?"

I am! Why else would I be here?

"How am I doing?"

Smart but still a child. Call him.

"Can I ask you a question?"

Anything.

Xanther reaches into her pocket for the folded piece of green leather.

His teeth fell out. "I have" *them.*

Not anymore.

Xanther opens up the leather to discover that indeed the little spikes of white are missing. In vain, she searches her pocket, then all her pockets.

"Oh no" *I lost them* "!"

Tian Li shakes her head. *When you saved him in the rain, you saved us. When you named him, you armed him against us. He is no longer blind to the hunt. And he is very hungry.*

Xanther doesn't know what that means exactly, but the old woman says it without a smile, and even with a sly wariness that puts Xanther on guard.

The living room seems to darken too with her pronouncement. Candles on the mantel tremble. All the lamps just seem dimmer.

Xanther shudders.

Worse, Tian Li shudders too.

Suddenly little one is moving, leaving Tian Li's shoulder, heading blindly down her arm, until with a little hop he is resettling on the coffee table, once again still, except for a last whip of his tail recurling around his paws.

Now we must practice, so you can practice more.

Tian Li demonstrates the first part of the form. It's a little different from what Astair's been teaching, but the principles seem the same. Xanther's not sure what this has to do with anything, until she realizes that more than movement is at stake — Tian Li by her own example is also sharing another way, like a song you love before you ever understand the words, trying to reassure Xanther, even as she is also making it clear that what Xanther must face will be different, that Tian Li has no answers because the answers she found won't work for Xanther.

He even had a different name.

"What was it?"

I've forgotten.

Xanther thinks Tian Li will cry again, maybe she does a little, Xanther feeling her own chest heave with grief, but the old woman keeps moving, and as they continue to turn and step together, and in near-unison too, fireflies fill the room, walls of ocean waves roll back, winter words become winter woods, because yes . . .

Did I mention the dawn?

Once upon a time, there was a monkey, a coyote, and a rat . . .

Once upon a time, what some say was the very end of time, the very end of time traveled to the very beginning of time. And the very end of time paid a terrible price for these new beginnings . . .

Or the dusk?

Oh, it wasn't a cat either. Not at first. Don't be that foolish. There are stories that it could have been an owl or a goat or a creature of the sea or a pig or a hyena or even you or me. There are stories involving each of these animals and more than these animals all the choices so many of us did not make.

Ah, colors!

Never mind that.

That?

久远交时，尝有猴，狼，鼠。

吾题拂晓乎？

或暮时乎？

亦非猫也。

为禽，为羊，

为海之生物，

种生物，吾之

者益多。

嘻，色也！

其有异名。

吾忘矣。

尔应亡。何以苦于此？

457

Would your mother like to join us? Tian Li asks at some point.

Yah, for "sure" *she would.*

Along with the peculiar flow of stories Xanther can't understand, struggles to understand, all that Tian Li continued to impart but what stayed beyond impact because it remained inapplicable, like even useless, like how dreaminess behaves right before it unravels and slips away unremembered, beyond inspection, beyond view, Xanther and Tian Li have not forgotten that Astair hasn't taken her eyes off of them.

From the darkness of the piano room Xanther has even sensed her initial mistrust shift to surprise before transforming into confusion and then finally into envy as Xanther suddenly became involved in a Tai Chi lesson.

At least the last shift is to elation when Xanther calls her over.

It's also the first Tai Chi experience with Astair that Xanther really enjoys. And it doesn't have to do with what Tian Li demonstrates or how she offers corrections, all of which is now strictly in Chinese, which Xanther can't understand, but which Astair happily nods at, mumbling names of moves Xanther has heard before but hasn't really practiced much.

"Yes! Play the Harp."

"Yes! Strike with Shoulder."

"Ah. So beautiful. White Crane Spreads Its Wings."

What moves Xanther the most is the way she sees her mother suddenly become a student.

Midnight Creatures

"Who are you?" Foyle whispered.

— Alfred Bester

Cas enters the grove. The Orb is her only weapon, held bare in the cradle of her hands. Red lights at once spot the dark boughs. They shimmer the leaves like a disease, follow her feet like dangerous spiders. She should take comfort in the fact that none will touch her or the Orb.

While wrapping her knees and carefully replacing her braces beforehand, Bobby responded to her shakes with a forced laugh: "His Killing Machine is too efficient to leave you in pain."

"It's his Pain Machine that I fear most."

The Orb purrs now with watchful static, bonded to her palm, charged to detonate if her hand slips away.

In the clearing ahead waits a small table with two chairs lit by a dim lantern hung on a branch above.

Cas rests the Orb on the soft tablecloth and sits down. It's a nice tablecloth, creamy with some floral pattern that might be hand-stitched. Not surprising for him to arrange for something expensive — even out here.

A glowing bite of red cuts across the fabric toward her. Cas is mindful that one weapon out there might just dare a shot. Weapons are hard to control. Even if you're Recluse.

Cas almost raises an arm to try warning whomever with a brittle "Stop!" but the laser beam is snatched away first, blocked by the old man emerging from the other side of the grove.

He's in gray. Moonlight turns his suit to silver. His tie is icy blue, matching his eyes. He sets a picnic basket on their table.

"And suddenly the impossible is fact." He smiles warmly and even betrays a hint of nervousness.

"Hello, Alvin."

"Do you approve of the time?" Recluse asks, sitting down.

"You and I have always been midnight creatures," Cas answers.

"I hope you don't mind." From the basket, he removes prickets and candles. Then two champagne flutes. Waterford Crystal, probably. The Dom Pérignon has a staggering date.

He laughs when the cork pops.

"No trigger fingers out there," Cas says.

"Let's hope."

His pour is generous. While the foam settles, he lights the candles.

Does his hand shake? Yes, his hand shakes.

"Are you trying to make Bobby jealous?"

He nods. The lantern overhead goes out.

"More private this way."

"I doubt that," Cas says.

"Then more intimate?"

"Why settle for *la petite mort* when we have *la grande* at our hands?"

Recluse raises a glass and drinks. Cas raises hers and drinks as well, because she knows he expects her not to. Out in the dark, there's a muffled shout. Probably Bobby cursing her recklessness.

"So that's what 1958 tastes like."

Recluse eyes her coldly then, perhaps too aware of how her right palm remains wedded to the Orb. "Don't drink too much."

"There are worse ways to go."

"I can swear to that fact."

Suddenly, the grove brightens with a new set of laser sights. These are all green, pairing with red.

"We are surrounded." Cas smiles.

The red dots seem startled, darting around as if trying to pair off for some terrible dance.

The night is young. It might just end up being a terrible dance.

"Good! Feel better?" Recluse seems about to laugh. He definitely relaxes, leaning back as if to enjoy the spectacle of this cage of violent luminosity. Cas relaxes too. She even has another sip of champagne. Has she ever tasted bubbles so fine?

Both of them had understood that the most dangerous moment would be at the beginning, whether she was dropped "like a bag of Costco meat," as Bobby had put it, or he was blown to smithereens by an expanding wave of fragmenting crystal, as had been Cas' intention. Hello, road. Hello, Hell. Then bitterness poisons her next taste, the worst kind of poison: that Cas' resolve to do away with both of them failed the moment he appeared.

"Looks like Christmas," Cas sighs. It's still not too late.

"Let's make Christmas come early."

"Is that in your picnic basket?" Cas asks.

"No, my Christmas is in your Orb. The Wizard's Window."

So nix Sniper Gambit. Nix Seize and Arrest. There's still time for Siege Gambit, but at present, this is the Recluse Gambit.

"Are you asking for a present?" Cas is brave but only in one way.

"Peace, Cas, is everyone's present."

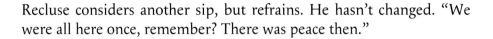

Recluse considers another sip, but refrains. He hasn't changed. "We were all here once, remember? There was peace then."

"No, this country was at war. It's still at war."

"Look, Cas, we're not going to agree. We're also not going to live much longer."

"Your cause will lose."

"I already said we won't agree."

"Then what do you propose?"

"Something better than wishful thinking."

"If you pull out another bottle of champagne like this, I'll applaud."

Instead, Recluse removes from the picnic basket a bound document, about as thick as a small-town yellow pages.

"This is a comprehensive deal, point by point, everything from amnesty to zero-tolerance to reparations."

Cas eyes the black plastic cover, wondering vaguely about the title it hides. Likely something corporate- or congressional-sounding. As blasé as the central concern is not.

"Is murder in there too?"

"No."

"How about torture?" Violet Blind Luck won't forget.

"You know I don't scry anymore," Recluse answers, changing the subject with a gesture toward the Orb. "As you also know, my propensities don't veer toward dependency. I'm just too controlled. I could never give myself over to such profundity. Now I have many teams who do it for me. None as gifted as you but the job gets done. Of course, I witness the challenges discovered therein, though they are the ones drawn into its addiction. Not that we don't try to stop that by limiting shifts and frequently switching subject matter. Is that what Bobby does for you?"

"Why don't we leave Bobby out of this."

"Okay, no Bobby. I won't mention your daughter either."

Cas snorts. It's not even a threat at this point. Recluse has tried to leverage Cas' daughter twice before. The last time Cas' willingness to sacrifice her was all but certain. Now harming her made no sense. Recluse had done his harm. He let her daughter know that Cas had

abandoned her. Cas, in turn, accepted that her daughter had abandoned her. But Recluse still understood that by keeping Cas'
daughter alive, Cas would be forever tempted to try to
rebuild their relationship, which, if such a thing
was possible, would require contacting her
and putting her at risk all over again.

"Except to point out that not your
Orb but this—" Recluse bangs
his knuckles on the report three
times "—is a way back to her."

Cas wants now either the rash
futility or blinding inspiration to lift her palm. Be done
with it. Let detonation prove
the end. But her wants have
no bearing on her actions.
Worse, she has to admit that
her refusal to become a suicide
bomber has less to do with her
own life, or with what's now only
a distant genetic tie, than it has to
do with a desire to keep scrying.

"It is dangerous," Cas concedes, shifting,
discomfited less by the chair than by her own
thoughts, those vulnerabilities she discovered about
him, which leveraging now would make her similar to him.

"Let go then!" Recluse suddenly urges, practically enthusiastic, if unable to hide tics of apprehension trembling the dark pockets of his eyes. His hands are a clutter of shakes. Parkinson's? So much so that he has to anchor both fists to the table.

"I wish I could." Cas smiles back. But her smile falters. Is it possible he doesn't know the Orb is weaponized? Wary only of encircling armies?

"I'm not even asking for forgiveness. Hold me accountable for whatever you like. I can live with it. And I can die for it. It won't change the fact that you and I are not the point. We can and will be replaced as easily as every generation of our Orbs. See, you and I are far greater than any artist. What we created isn't something to be experienced by others. What we created is the means through which to experience that which will always exceed art and us: here."

Recluse gently lifts the Dom Pérignon toward the canopy of leaves overhead, the sky, the stars, Cas, before refilling her glass.

His shakes have vanished.

Cas wants to run then. She is as certain that all the gambits are back on the table — from Sniper to Siege — as she is sure that the black plastic cover of his proposed deal hides nothing but blank pages.

Cas pulls the Orb closer.

"Coming here," Cas begins. "I thought you wanted to rekindle a friend-ship, however compromised, however impossible. Maybe I believed your intentions were to revive something compassionate, or at least passionate, some of that thing we used to have when we worked so hard as one."

Recluse neither confirms nor denies her supposition as he begins to drink.

"I'm a spacey lady. You of all people know that. Now, though, I can see how badly mistaken I am. One thing that I've learned from scrying: it doesn't just teach you how to see better with the Orb. Scrying teaches you how to see better without the Orb."

"And?" Recluse leans in.

"What is it, Alv?"

"Excuse me?"

"Tell me."

"I don't follow."

"Yes, you do. Something's scared you. Something's scared you bad enough that you needed my help."

Recluse laughs. "You're a very dangerous old lady but you're also a damned smart one. You're right. I require your input."

"But the only way that works is if I need your help too."

Recluse nods at the dark offering between them.

"My Aberration changed," Cas admits. "You were right. But there's more, isn't there?"

"Somehow, you and your team have managed a Window Reduction that's down to magical months, the sharing of which you can be assured is covered in here, along with required NCCs and NDAs, immunities, and compensations." Recluse again raps his knuckles three times on the black plastic cover of his proposition. "Clearly though, due to what must have been extraordinary focus and labor, you have failed to revisit familiar moments and encounter deeper, more unsettling VEM changes."

Now it's Cas' turn to offer silence with the glassiest glare.

"Cas, all the Clips are
going black."

Domingo

Choice: whether to act on lessons or not and learn more.

— Maryse Holder

Luck always runs out but Domingo somehow keeps getting free refills. By the time Luther, Tweetie, and Victor cabbed it to Red Lion, Domingo was gone. Piña and Juarez were following in the van, but then just one turn off Silver Lake Boulevard, and, like that, pinche Domingo was gone.

Fool wasn't water. Wasn't smoke. He's a pimp. And not even a good pimp. All his putas except one quit him for an old man missing a tooth including la salvaje Lity that tried to kill her daddy.

Not like Domingo's hard to miss either. Mr. Violet Man, from shoes all the way to some pendejísimo violet hat with a yellow feather poking out of a violet band.

But even so, how it was, cuz just like that, Piña's on the phone filling Luther's ear with another Domingo miracle.

"Just turned left, and chas, gone."

Luther's mouth started melting wire. Now what the fuck he say to Eswin? Give back these fuckin new shirts? Cop to fuckin this up de mil maneras? Go back to dileando pale blues? Aguantar this bullshit?

Then an hour later, Tweetie handed Luther the phone. Not Eswin. Not Teyo. ¡Más vale! Mr. Violet himself. Domingo calling to talk to Luther!

"I got things to offer."

Ay de aquel who pick luck over smarts. Smarts don't call Luther for a meet. Smarts knows luck always runs out. Smarts knows to run.

But Domingo wasn't running. He was staying put. Kept saying he knew shit. Talked and talked. Laughed and laughed. Until he believed Luther was talking and laughing too. Even had terms figured out. Place of his choosing. Luther just listened and listened. And when they were done Luther laid out the rules.

And now here they stand: place of Luther's choosing.

They're all upstairs in a building used to be for making clothes. Whole floor rowed with iron tables and old sewing machines. None turned on for months, maybe years. Juarez tried. Power's shut off. Plus rats have chewed through most cables. Ceiling rains insulation.

Aquí no es lugar pa' andar viniendo en la noche. Definitely not with Luther. Especially como this. No seafoam shirt with thick ivory buttons. Got on long black shorts, Adidas, a wifebeater. Ready to work.

Domingo's still in his chafilla purple suit, seams all frayed, cuffs all puercos.

His looks, though, that's the biggest surprise. Sure his teeth are white como si he brushes with bleach. Bright enough, maybe, to fool a twelve-year-old putita into believing that bright here is pretty but that's it.

For months, Luther kept hearing how Domingo was so guapo y con estilo. Some kind of encanto. But this baboso is nothing like that: broad and blunt, dark too, lips lined with deep cracks. Like old farm workers who sit in the sun and chew limes, what juice they don't swallow running away in their smiles, burning in the cut of their hands.

And he like twenty-three. Twenty-five at most. Younger than Luther for sure. Gets Luther curious. Wants to know how he even got to whoring girls? How he decided that that was him? How he could ever look in the mirror and see himself as something smooth? Something other than dirt? And ask that for real. Pinche, tell me how that work! Tell me how you see!

Plain to see Domingo got no clue who he dealin with or even what this is about. For Domingo this makes sense. Thinks he thought this through. Thinks he's really here to deal.

Or maybe that's just the excuse he keeps telling Luther to keep telling himself to keep off the fear that, de una forma u otra, this fight was coming his way.

Didn't put up a fuss either. Got right in the van like it was his idea. Walked up the stairs ahead like he the one throwing the party, like instead of broken sewing machines, he got a whole room of mezcal and pole girls waiting.

Even when Juarez cuffed him tight, Domingo just winced once and snorted back the wet in his eyes and then grinned like this was how a good party is supposed to start.

Luther's almost disappointed. He prefers the vanishing acts, all the rumors, the close calls. Luther almost made Domingo into someone he wasn't: sorpresivo, beyond reach, even dangerous. Not this desmadre here.

Still what isn't still has poder. It arrives like it's always there. How dust speaks. The edges of Luther's teeth starting to tickle then, as his mouth dries, palms go damp, then cold. Metal rusts. His cause creaks as doubt creeps in.

Luther even gives another look around. The dirty tables, broken glass on the cement floor, the way a half moon silvers the dry air, watery swirls about to take shape.

All as another idea takes shape: that this abandoned garment building was still Domingo's idea, setting Luther up for an emboscada.

Suddenly then, corners flicker with hazards. As if shadows there expected him long before Luther or even Domingo decided on where.

Though what does any shadow got that Luther won't answer? LAPD? FBI? No doubt chingado Mr. Violet would snitch — Juarez checked for a wire, Tweetie for tails — but Luther still can't imagine some detective asking Domingo to the CI dance.

So who else then? Putas fantasma gonna slip free of moonlight armed with spoons? Long-dead costureras snipping scissors? Or how about some nightmare army of sicarios salidos del infierno? Bring it on. Bring them all on. Luther was born to bang, even with the dead.

Better yet, maybe Domingo here's gonna turn into some snarling beast. So fuckin what if there's no full moon? He'll still werewolf his way into long fangs. Snap off the cuffs, then by claws and jaws take Luther on.

But not even that's gonna catch Luther's step. He's put down dogs. He'll put down a wolf too. Put down a whole pack. Spit bullets and laugh.

And this teeth tickle now? Dry tongue? Icy hands? Pura emoción! Desire! Soñaré despierto un challenge worth Luther. Something angry, claro, dangerous. Luther'd take interesting.

Because this isn't interesting. And the more Domingo talks the less interested Luther gets.

Like Luther cares Domingo's dad was from Panama, a pimp too? Or his madrecita was one of his whores? Luther couldn't see that. Doesn't believe it. Not the woman he met. But doesn't care why Domingo would even put out that line. Figures Domingo can't do nothing but lie.

Luther tosses out the key to the cuffs. That does it. Just a skitter across concrete. Stops a few feet shy of violet toe tips. Shuts Domingo up quick.

Surprise me. Hop. Skip. Do something with this. But Domingo stays still. Looks once, but not twice. Starts his ladridos again. No surprise. Too scared to free himself.

One thing Luther's learned: most people want cages. Want their routine, their job, the hate-my-life song they think makes them sound strong. Most people don't got the huevos to live outside.

"You have that pencil still?" Luther asks Juarez.

"Huh?"

"The blue pencil? What that kid Hopi had on him?" ∴ **TFv1 p. 605.** ∴

Piña's eyes go lead at the sound of the name. Juarez's don't have to. They always lead.

Juarez checks his pockets. Pulls out a baby pacifier. Then a spool of fishing line. Even got a fishing hook. But no pencil.

Why'd Luther even go there? Those fragile fingers again in his head, steepling out of the milky water, what no shovel can break enough times to bury.

Maybe because of how Domingo keeps popping knuckles. Stubby hands. Ugly hands.

"¡Basta!" Luther barks.

Domingo's hands go still.

"And shut up!"

Not that loud, but Domingo's all fright. One useless motherfucker who hasn't earned this fight, got no right to even be in Luther's ring. Should be elsewhere. In a field planting grass.

Luther knows him too, from around, knows his cousins. Domingo's nothing but mountains of bullshit desperate to pay off mountains of debt. A whole range he'll never cut through, forget get on top of. Just another wobbly mess stuck thinking on something better.

In that way, he the same as the kid. If Teyo's beef with Hopi is still a mystery. Teyo's beef here is with what Domingo keeps keeping a mystery.

"How you know about the Frogtown pinks?"

Domingo just blinks.

"You know someone at Solder Supply?" Not even Solder Supply knew what was going down that night.

"Fuck brown. Fuck blues. Fuck even all that pink. Man, what I'm here to get going with you is something way outside of that parade. Like if there's a root to evil, there gotta be a route to rich. Get me?" Domingo is all over the place. At least smart enough not to knuckle-pop no more. Now one hand keeps scratching the back of the other. Then switches.

"No, I don't fuckin get you," Luther growls. "But I fuckin *got* you."

That earns laughs from his crew.

"Synsnap," Domingo says, but real quiet too.

"Synsnap? What's that?"

"Fuck yes!" Domingo grins, not catching the sneer. Maybe he the type that never catches the sneer. "You got it, brother. You're there."

"I thought you was pimpin?"

"Yeah, not so good with that. Like you seen. Going through a transition. A transition of reinvention. Steppin outside myself. Being that new me. Outside my comfort zone?"

"What the fuck's a comfort zone?"

"Where none of us here live."

"You know where I live?"

"Sure." Domingo nods. "Time's come to step clear, man. And I'm that time. Right here. I see you see what I mean, Luther. I see you see what I mean."

"You got no fuckin clue what I see."

"Teyo, man. You gotta step free of that dust-pan. Sure, I get it. It's nice. Money rollin easy. But that's scraps for a lapdog. You gotta mind the gap. Get stretched and comprehensive. Get yourself a part of the there-there that's out there, waiting for you, yours already, read?"

"Read?" Luther smiles.

Domingo smiles back. "Yeah, you get it. You see what I mean." Wiggles his cuffed wrists up in the air like they some eel. "Electric!"

Though lo que castra is that this tarugo even knows Teyo, dares speak his name.

"Let me get this straight: you coming to me to get with something more reliable than Teyo? Teyo's pretty reliable."

"Look, I'm not saying there's no risk. I'm just sayin there's a lot of potential."

"And why me?"

"Hearing things."

"Like what things? Voices? Like voices in your fuckin head?"

"Whoa, easy, man. Tranquilo. Just, you know, hearing that . . . " Domingo gets to whispers then. Like when he mentioned that Synsnap. "That Teyo's got a new dog. Got Almoraz checking corners, moving blues, promisin pink. And that you kinda getting eased aside."

Luther smiles again. No teeth now. Just melting steel. "And you, Domingo, you the man gonna get me back inside?"

"Better."

"Better?"

"Oh yeah. We gonna get to the source."

"Why not just go at it yourself? Get it all?" Luther's playing but still wants to hear the answers.

"Come on, man. Because you're Luther, man. Look at me? I can only kid myself so far that on my own I'm gonna get anywhere far. You though, man, you got weight. You are weight. And Teyo's a fool for treating you light."

Luther crosses his arms. Unmetals his mouth. Wants to figure out how Domingo, who might got a lot right, can still believe Luther could take him seriously.

And even if he can't clue in on Luther, he sure as fuck should see Piña, Victor, and Tweetie les vale madre. Juarez isn't even listening, wandering the sewing machines, looking for something to chew on. Maybe he smelled ghosts too.

"You high, Domingo?" Luther asks.

"No man, limpio como la chingada."

"YOU HIGH, DOMINGO?"

Luther didn't mean to scream like that. Surprises hisself to see fury break loose so fast. Domingo heard though. Domingo learned. Goes ill to chalk. All this time workin his talk, his deals, worst kinda absurd, and now can't even spit out one piece of a word.

Much better.

Piña, his good soldier, gives Domingo a shove. "Answer the question."

But Domingo's still sputtering.

"Este puto anda bien tizo," Juarez says, circling in closer.

Victor laughs. Tweetie don't. Understands.

"Just a little. Swear laws. To take the edge off. But hey man, it's for all of us."

What fuckin loser comes here with no edge? Dumb yonqui. Luther's still amused to watch Domingo's fingers try to reach the inside pocket of his jacket. Keeps trying. Keeps failing.

On Luther's nod, Piña helps out.

"That's a fine lady. Helpin this nigga out," Domingo smirks.

Piña brings Luther the balloon.

It's black.

"This real?"

"Oh, man, that shit's the real's real. Just a sample but demos the whole show. Head to toe. Turns all the locks. Rocks your rocks. Gives what you know the hard throw."

"Where'd you get it?"

"The future."

"Where. Did. You. Get. It?" Luther's losing patience.

"Dark cats, man," Domingo whimpers. "Fearsome. Fearless. Even hunting cops. Those ones that put down that ese César Miguel in Frogtown?" ∴ **TFv2 pp. 198, 202, 641, 728.** ∴

Football Star? The one Juarez popped in the back? That surprises Luther.

"Don't give a fuck about laws here, laws anywhere." Domingo finishes, flinches too. What almost gets Luther flinching. Because this here's no lyin: as afraid of Luther as he is, Domingo is way more afraid of someone else.

And Luther loves it. Just the idea of someone who can bring a challenge makes Luther feel better than he has in months.

He tosses the balloon to Victor. "Let's have a taste."

Juarez hoots. Scrambles near, even giving Domingo nods, tongue hanging out like the perro muerto de hambre he'll always be.

Piña knifes open the balloon, scoops some powder onto the metal pan Victor's dug up, off an elbow of some ventilation pipe. Of course, Juarez wants first, but Luther has Domingo prove shit isn't lethal. Victor gets out the blow-torch. Domingo's fool enough to be grateful. Like Victor's brought a torch for this.

The first pile glows like a white pyramid on fire. Domingo sucks up the smoke. Loses him-self, vuelve en sí, anything pale or afraid fading away, easy smiles again.

Juarez goes next, fingernails a snort, gets in a gum rub too, shakes and shrugs. Tweetie shrugs too, swats his ear, like a mosquito's there, buzz-ing near. Maybe there is.

"Coca de mierda," Piña mutters, exhales, unchanged, sin convencer. Victor's no differ-ent. But shakes his head like all of them.

When Luther's turn come, shit looks like perico but with more sparkle. Silvers, golds, got even some rose in there. Blues too, or is that just the moon?

On his gums, Luther tastes nothing he knows. Chemicals, sure, synthetic, but like tar too.

Victor burns down a pyramid. Luther sucks up smoke. What breath he frees comes out clean.

Yeah, there's buzz but not the good buzz Luther keeps waiting to roll in.

Where's that mosquito? Close by his ear too. Luther keeps swattin. Catching nothing. Like everyone else, shakes his head. Nothing to stress though. Unimpressed yo. Gonna fall over then. Instead doesn't fall over. Just wants to get outside what's inside changing places with outside again and again.

Back of his throat something candied shows up, like honey, Luther waiting to see if something shows up behind the honey.

"Right, man?" Domingo grins. "Puts blues to shame. Fuck even them pinks. All that parade." Popping knuckles again.

"This shit's Sweet'N Low," Piña barks, but still waving her hand around her ear.

"And baby, you all sugar." Domingo winks. Even gets a laugh. From Luther too. Fool must be hasta atrás to try that love shit on Piña.

Shadows catch Luther's breath then. More than turning towers of dust moving in corners. Stripes of smoke and ash binding the air. Passing by. As if sometimes ghosts too are blind.

"Domingo, you know I been lookin for you?" Luther asks, getting back in his skin, then drawing even that skin back in, like it was gonna run away with his self.

"Yeah, I heard that."

"For how long you know?"

"Yo digo que un buen rato."

"You know why?"

Domingo shakes his head. There he is! His mother's son. A bit of the old sad finally stepping up. "Tried to find out. You hear a dawg like Luther is on the look for you, you best find out what he's hunting, kinda ideas he's growing."

"Smart."

Domingo don't like that. Smile comes up short too. "I never found out. So I kept ducking."

"So why we here now?"

"Fuckin black balloon. Ground floor. First shot. Ni el cielo es el límite. Make a whole new light, I mean life, with this source outside the source. Pure source, ése!"

"That stuff was shit. Nothing I haven't sold for years. Are we even high?"

His whole crew keeps shaking their heads. Except Jaurez. He's banging the side of his head. Like something just crawled into his ear and started drilling. Or singing.

"They said differently," Domingo answers, shakes his head too, pero como decepcionado. "They told me it was pure."

"You mean these dark cats of yours?"

"Powerful, man."

"Esplain why power gonna choose you?"

"A new way into the things? You know, outside the regular circuitry."

"I want names."

"I don't got names, Luther, just places. Places we meet. I got one for tonight. Midnight. Swear. Address is in my pocket. You can test that."

It's Luther's turn to shake his head. "You talk so much but you can't even talk to your mother?"

"Huh?"

"Did you talk to your mother?"

"Oh yeah. Yeah, sí hablé con mi jefa."

"Then you got my message?"

Luther likes how Domingo's breath hisses between his teeth, how he nods like he just got told to hammer nails with his head.

"Luther, man, I'm here for you. Like I been saying, business propositioning. Like I showed you. Heavy stuff. I swear this be heavy stuff."

"Wey, you're here because you're too afraid to become a man. And that's too bad. There are much worse things to fear than that."

"Don't I know it," Domingo says, maybe with a sneer.

"Then how you hear about the Frogtown pinks?" Luther comes back around to it again. This time with snarls. Luther will show him what's realer than realer. "Solder Supply had all the big hits that night. You know it. LAPD. FBI. No matter who we talked to, they all said the only one talking was you."

"I talk! Sure I talk! I like to talk! Didn't go to no chota though. That don't even make sense. Do it? Like police gonna believe someone like me?"

Luther knows you can never believe a whore but you're better off believing a whore than her pimp. He stares hard then. Not, though, like Domingo can stare back, all about his knuckles again. Like he want to tug his fingers off.

"Domingo, I don't care who you told."

That stops the knuckles.

"I can get you money."

Luther grins. Not at Domingo. But at Juarez, grinning behind Domingo, back from more rounds, from prowling their borders, now squatting down, ready to take orders.

"I don't know about money," Luther sighs. "I got plenty of money."

Luther pulls out a wad of fifties, counts out nine. Piña don't need to ask. She takes the bills and stuffs them in Domingo's front jacket pocket.

"I think this pendejito just wet hisself," Piña says.

Looks like she's right. Pants getting a dark stain. Shoes in a puddle.

"Thinking of you, baby." Domingo still throws out strong. "Holler at me if you ever wanna find something new for yourself. I'll set you up right. Men pay sideways for tears."

Bringing up those tattooed tears isn't smarts but Piña shrugs it off like lost darts, flips him off. Domingo goes teary, glad she let him hold on to su actitud. Like this late in the game attitude gonna change the game.

But Luther still grins. Piña the ho! Big beefy girl like her taking dick for dough! Thinking of her in a short skirt is crazy enough! High heels?!

Probably because Luther's grin's got way big, Piña smiles back. Now everyone smiling. Juarez too. Even Domingo. All for their own reasons.

"More?" Luther asks, now starting to laugh, waving around his cash.

"Sure. I ain't too proud." Fronts is all Domingo's got.

Luther starts peeling more off the wad but Domingo backs off.

"No, man, seriously. Whatever you want, I'll give it to you free."

"Domingo, you *befuddle* me, be-fuckin-fuddle me." Luther says, suddenly befallen. Voice not his own. Tossed to puddles and chalk. Where only the lost walk. "Make sense!" Luther has to growl hisself back.

Something to clear his sight. The simple Luther wants: the clearest sight.

But Domingo looks confused.

"Midnight," Domingo finally blurts out.

"I don't care about midnight."

Like Domingo don't care about those Grants, digging out what Piña buried in his pocket como si quemaran, letting the bills parachute to the floor. Now he got money and a key near his feet and still nowhere to go.

Juarez goes back to circles, circling them all, winding and unwinding that fishing line around one hand, the hook end pinched between the fingers of the other, or just stuck through a nail.

"What you care about then, Luther? I don't know." Domingo's gonna bawl. Melt up

Luther's mouth something bad. Bad enough él no va a poder check himself.

Luther squats down. Studies Domingo retching. Luther likes low, likes steady, all the weight in his heels, legs stretching, getting ready.

"Yo, this isn't hard. This is easy. But if you wanna work with me, I gotta know you can handle easy. Entiendes Méndez? 'I don't know' don't fly. 'I don't know' is nothin I wanna hear. One more 'I don't know' and I'm gonna take these thumbs, see, dig out your eyes and shove them in your mouth. Then Tweetie here is gonna keep kicking you in the face until we all sure you swallowed them. ¿Te queda claro?"

Luther then, still squatting, still bouncing, gives Domingo a big grin and two thumbs up.

Domingo swallows hard, even starts to squat too, but Luther shakes his head and Domingo rises again, shaking.

"Okay. You know what I'm gonna ask?"

"I don't know. Ask me anything."

Luther looks up at Tweetie, at Piña, at Victor. Smiles. Shakes his head. That buzzing still there. Juarez, out of sight, chuckles close.

"Sorry! Wait!" At least Domingo sounds like he's catching up. "You wanna know who told me about the Frogtown pinks in the first place?"

Luther claps his hands together. "Simón, ése! 'Quién' is right."

Domingo takes a deep breath, closes his eyes, like darkness can get a fool to think straight.

"Answer him!" Tweetie growls.

"Your only move," Piña says soft.

"Cricket." Domingo looks broken, looks relieved. "She just hears shit. Tells me. Yo la amo. Don't do nothing to her. She's special."

They all laugh. Except Luther.

"She the one told me to get with you. Find out why you doggin me this whole time. See how we can settle this. Like men."

"Cricket?" Luther asks. "That the one Asuka knows?"

"You seen her before," Juarez hisses. "La grilla."

"All freckles," Piña adds.

502

"That's her," Domingo nods, all pleased, like he making friends. "Freckly thing. Got poetry on her phone. Texting all the time."

But Luther can't remember shit. Especially freckles. Freckles he don't like.

"Come on, Luther," Juarez jeers. "She one of Nacho's huilas. Jumped all over our Hopeye boy. Them together under one pink umbrella."

Luther's head clears.

He remembers the pink umbrella. He remembers her pink phone. And like that she's there.

Not even thirteen. Got those black eyes. Tight thing. Fierceness warning her lips. Hair like black rings. Pale brown skin with dark pecas por todos lados, like some Milky Way gone negative ∴ **TFv1 p. 589** ∴. Rain was coming down. Ankles locked, legs pretzeling around him.

Him. Again.

Wobble boy. Not a boy.

Something else.

Hopi.

Grinning again too, like now, right now, like he never coulda done before. At Luther. Through Luther. And with a laugh he sure as fuck never had, powerful enough to make Luther think he just flinched hisself, because this boy who's just a boy, but now old too, old as the oldest cemetery with flowers blooming, letting Luther know, again, that claro que sí, Hopi knows her, knows her from around, knows all of them from around . . .

Clear as a funeral bell. But like when the fuck Luther ever hear a funeral bell?

∴ *Once.* ∵

"Gotta put that blue pencil to use somehow."

∴ **TFv1 p. 591.** ∵

What the fuck that even mean? Kid had a blue dick he called his pencil? Or a pencil because he lost his dick? Holding that little nub with eraser bit off like it was the universe itself.

"Cricket," Luther murmurs.

"That's right," Domingo says, lookin rattled.

"How'd she know?" Luther growls.

"Huh?" Like Domingo's rattled by something Luther's face showed that he hisself can't know.

Luther stands. Steps to the key. Done with all this. "Where Cricket at?"

"Even she ditched me, man. Back to Nacho's. To those other bitches. If you get her back, I'll pay you. I'll pay you plenty."

Luther chuckles even as his head tilts sideways, like on the side gonna show him how this fool keeps hustling for a deal he never gonna close.

"How'd she know?" Luther asks again. Then taps the key with his toes. Kicks it. Skitters it right between Domingo's feet. Golazo.

Domingo looks down at the key. Whines something. Mumbles something. Then just whines.

"I can't hear you."

"Some john. You know how that goes. They talk and shit."

"Who's the john?"

Domingo shakes his head.

"You sayin tú no me puedes contestar?"

"I can't," Domingo pants.

Luther smiles. "How'd she know?"

Domingo goes back to whining. Though now he's shaking. "I'll find out. I promise."

"HOW'D SHE FUCKIN KNOW?!"

Domingo's not the only one who jumps.

"I— I—" is where Domingo sticks, on repeat, beat.

"I got all night."

"I— I—" Can't spit it out. Sputters out.

"All night."

"Aw, Luther man, honest. Some john, someone on the block, one of Nacho's biscochos. I don't know."

There it is. Luther grins. Gives Domingo two thumbs up. They all laugh. Except Juarez. Juarez has hopped in close now. Like some dangerous frog. Real close.

Domingo's got no laugh left but still tries to cough one out. He's that guy. Got to be with the crowd.

He's still coughing too when Luther says "Uncuff yourself. We don't need to see you again."

"Midnight, man. Come with me." Qué chulada. Still making deals. But to his knees fast. Stubby fingers scratching for the key, nerves giving him paws. If nerves finally come around. Plucks the key up. A real smile coming up then.

Nothing like Juarez's glare, backing off, off of Luther's look, pissed off, like this ain't fair, winding again his fishing line and hook, going off to fish in moonlight, break glass, break something.

Luther half expects his dirty dog to howl.

Domingo is still stabbing at the keyhole when Piña steps in behind and slips the knife into the back of his neck.

No more dodges. No more dances. An end to rumors. An end to this chase.

Domingo don't make a sound. He don't even bleed much. Just stops fumbling with the key.

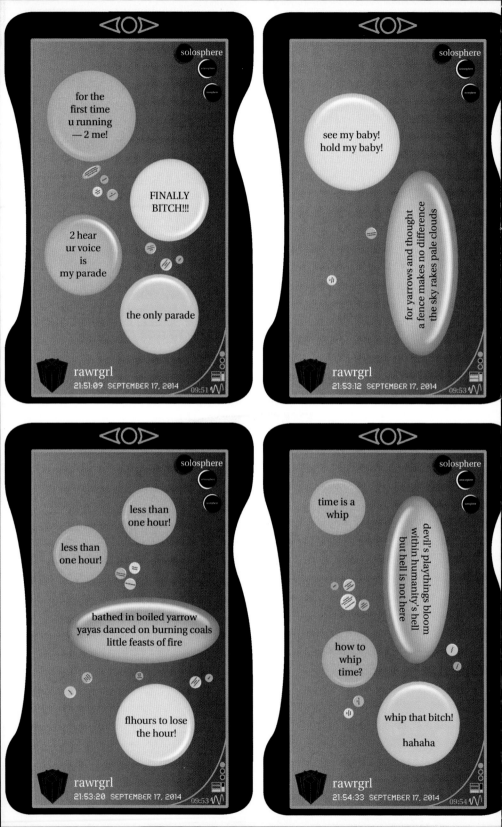

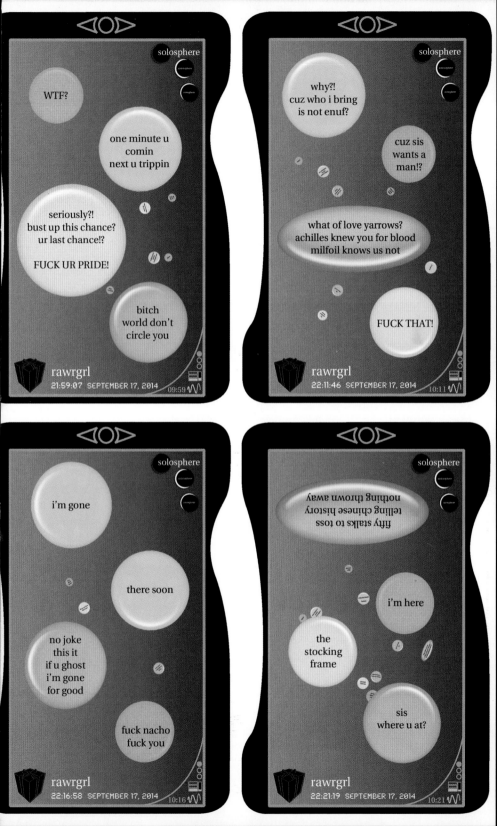

Cricket

I've been told that nobody sings the word "hunger" like I do.

— Billie Holiday

"You know I can't be there," Virgil tells him out on Spring Street.

Forget Red Lion. Forget Scotch. Forget eats.

"They have good food." Virgil knows him well. "I'm sorry, Oz."

"Fuck sorry. I get it. It's the job. And last I checked, I'm still at this job. Happy to help, though I won't be much help. She doesn't need to see me."

"She doesn't know that. She thinks a man standing beside Planski makes Planski for real. My bet's on daddy issues."

"I'm no daddy."

"Don't tell her that. Though she'll probably guess."

Missing a long meal with Virgil pains Özgür right in the guts. And his insides really do twist and cut. Virgil looks like he has news too. Good news. Özgür would bet on doing well, still in love, which always makes him feel well. Too bad he won't get to hear it tonight. But getting caged by a job isn't new to either of them. Paycheck or love is always an exercise in patience.

Anyway, seeing Planski will make tonight okay. When Virgil had texted trouble, Özgür used the time to pick up a loaner. He decides now to leave the car in the lot by the Bradbury Building and walk the rest of the way.

Downtown L.A. always feels a long way from L.A., which only makes sense if you live here. The glamour of concert halls, new museums, and gentrified corners are held in check by the walking dead a few blocks over on Seventh. A constant tent city occupying the sidewalks in the name of chemical hunger, or just hunger. The closeness of this contradiction between satisfaction and suffering hurts enough to make Özgür believe it's honest.

The sound and rhythm of his heels tapping the sidewalk, toes slapping right after, take Özgür back, on the backs of that beat, to Cletious again, the old man handing him that beautiful gift, the framed sheet from "Rhapsody in Blue," marked by his dead boy, and then the parable of the wallet, Cletious holding on to something to stay woke.

Özgür feels bad about not asking him what he's holding, keeps wondering if it's just the memory of Jasper, or maybe someone else, heel-toe keeping up their tap-slap like that's the only answer he'll get. Özgür takes it.

Herbie Hancock ∷ *Cantaloupe Island* ∵ greets him as he enters The Stocking Frame. Perfect address too. Emergencies so often happen on the decline ∷ 911 Hill Street, Los Angeles, CA 90015 ∵. Good-looking bar too — long and loaded with new friends a strong drink would help him make. He orders a Diet Coke and goes to find Planski.

She's in the back, at the back of a deep booth, with two others. The first is FBI. Special Agent Rivka Waters. He can see why Planski likes her: strong and solid with a smile that sparkles young enough to call into question the winks of grey in her otherwise brown, feathered hair. She's in a blue suit.

The second one isn't in a suit. She's something else. Even with sunglasses. Even with too much foundation on her scarred cheeks. Lips too glossy too. Teeth too white. They flash when she sneaks a vape from the e-cigarette she keeps hidden under the table. Twenties but seasoned. Has a degree from the hood but her prettiness is a passport to anywhere she wants to go. And something more. Özgür's seen it before: unbent by circumstances, unwritten by events, not just a survivor but a conqueror. Once upon a time Özgür would have wanted to be conquered by her. Now he just accords her the respect she deserves when Planski makes the introduction: a handshake and a very cautious glance.

"Pleased to meet you, Cynthia," Özgür says and sits down opposite her, next to Planski, who's both nervous and worked up and probably about to start mumbling to herself.

"You're blue over rain," he tells her with a wink.

"It's what I do best, Turkulese: clear your skies."

Rivka Waters smirks. "How long you guys go back?"

"Long time," he and Planski say at the same time, Planski's eyes going wide, which for her beats a blush. Özgür gets the feeling it didn't go unnoticed by Cynthia, who's vaping again, looking at her phone.

"Is she on the way?" Planski asks, adding something she didn't want to say, reducing it to mumbles, before it gets away.

"She always on the way," Cynthia growls, not looking up, lost under sunglasses, to texts Özgür will never see. "Give me a moment." Cynthia gets up suddenly. Özgür doesn't watch her go. He's seen enough to know he'd linger watching her go.

However long Özgür and Planski have known each other, this is still a first. It's a fact that races his heart.

"She's your CI?"

"When she wants to be."

"Who's on the way?"

"The one who makes this all play," Planski scowls.

"I'll give her this: most just want money," Rivka Waters speaks up. "She really wants to see her sis get treatment."

Everyone has coffee they're not touching. Özgür takes a gulp of Diet Coke. He hates Diet Coke. He flags down a server and orders some crispy avocado tacos for the table.

"It'll be okay," Rivka Waters adds.

"If she comes back," Planski scowls again. "She might not. I can't count how many times I've been through this before." Özgür stands up so Planski can get out and go find her, mumbling louder than she knows, "I'm gonna lose it! Not going through that shit again . . . "

"Jello?" Rivka Waters asks.

"Sure," Özgür rasps back.

It's a good sign that Rivka Waters knows that much.

"Planski tell you?"

Rivka Waters shakes her head. "Just what I heard. Jello was her CI. Cover got blown."

"Some fuck-up there. Planski got the spatter on that one. She was the first to reach him too. Jello Nusian. 5th and Grand. U.S. Bank Tower ∴ Overseas Union Enterprise Ltd. ∴ ∴ *OUE* ∴. Seventy-two stories straight down. She just stood and stared at the mess. Wouldn't walk away. Finally one of the Emergency Response guys asked her what good it did. 'I will never ever fucking forget,' she told him, told all of us. Stayed there until they splashed the sidewalk with Clorox, Windex, whatever they use."

"Jesus."

"Planski's secretive but they're secrets in the right place," Özgür sighs. "She's some police. The garbage she's had to put up with over the years. I thought being a Turk was bad. Her hassles make my post-9/11 years look breezy."

"I didn't figure you for anything breezy," Rivka Waters says, that young-looking grin back in play.

"Not the first time I've been called a windbag," Özgür winks. "You should see me when I have a real drink."

"Sure. Okay. When this is over," Rivka Waters answers. Winks back. Özgür's head spinning over that.

Planski returns. She's still talking to herself. Eyes even wider. "Really am gonna lose it."

"No, you're not," Özgür tells her softly, trying to soothe her, though when has he ever been good at soothing?

"I'm doing my ball sackin' best here."

"Shannon," Rivka Waters says, calm, steady, stepping up. Özgür can't remember the last time he used Planski's first name or even heard it said aloud. "This business we're in is never a smooth road unless it's not true. To my mind all this is a very good sign: it means they understand what's at stake."

Did Rivka Waters really just ask him out for a drink?

Cynthia doesn't disappear.

"She's not coming," she announces, sitting back down, her scowl making Planski's look like rainbows.

Planski starts bobbing her head like she's trying to nod but can't quite get there, her mouth doing its best to murder every rainbow. Eyes narrowing with anger then flying wide for killing. Who knows what she would have yelled next if the tacos hadn't arrived. A modest plate of three but Planski stares at them with such disbelief that Özgür almost laughs.

"Have one," he says instead. At least Planski takes a sip of coffee.

"No thanks," Rivka Waters says politely.

"Am I eating alone?" Özgür asks the sunglasses, but Cynthia just shakes her head, lips pressed together in a smile that's used to saying no. Then thinks twice. Though not about the food.

"She the one wanted a man." She throws a shy glance over to Planski, who's pro enough to calm down fast. "I'm sorry you had to go out of your way for this. For us. Real sorry."

Özgür shrugs. Wants her to see it's no big deal. And it's not a big deal. Özgür's had a lifetime of these misses eating up that life that's supposed to be. It took a while, but he's fine now with living just the life that's gonna be. Getting hammered with Virgil, for one. Waking up somewhere with Elaine, for another. He'll ask for the tacos to go.

"My sister's . . ." Cynthia continues.

"Scared?" Özgür guesses.

But Cynthia snorts. "She a hooker with a heart for gold."

Özgür didn't see that coming. Wonders if her sister is even better-looking than Cynthia. Özgür doesn't see how that's possible.

"What are these?!" cries Cynthia's sister, sliding suddenly into the booth, snug up next to Özgür, already one taco in her mouth, another in her free hand.

She's a child! Maybe twelve. Maybe. And she's covered in freckles. Freckles on freckles. All over her ears, her lips, her eyelids, and skin she's showing and she's showing too much, from her tiny thighs to her tinier wrists.

"You wanna introduce yourself before you eat them all?" snaps big sister.

Little sister doesn't even slow. Might have spit the whole green gob out at her if Özgür hadn't scooted away a little bit to twist back around to better offer his hand.

"Özgür."

"Cricket."

She's an evil little thing. In the best kind of way. Eyes black with spite and will. In another life, she might have become one of those young girls men keep believing is their personal savior, clueless that she's no messiah, but Rome herself, unable to count the souls she will nail to the cross in the name of her empire of adolescence. Instead, this world was nailing her to the cross, and she didn't like it. It was clear she wanted to squirm and tear her way off, eat all the tacos, and with the stakes still in her palms start stabbing hearts.

She has a right to. Özgür's not sure if Cynthia really meant it when she said "hooker," but he can see this child is already out there dancing for a hard time, dirty skirt, dirty button-down shirt, white once, hiked up to expose a belly of freckles with a navel ring, knotted tight across her flat chest. It's not the dirty part that's the trouble but what's under the freckles. You can see the need in the gaunt shadows around her eyes, the white around her lips, haunting her gums. Özgür's spent too much time with addicts to miss that if she isn't already this one's a few weeks from itching to tricking on Seventh Street.

Her getup, though, hints at something else, something familiar, something about two loose braids of black, pink Converse, and what looks like a stuffed animal on her shoulder.

Cynthia notices it too. "What the fuck is that?"

Cricket gives big sister a don't-give-a-fuck sneer, even if she hides the dirty white thing in the lunchbox she's using as a purse, an *Avengers* lunchbox. While she's at it, tosses a handful of chips in there too. Daring big sister to object. Cynthia doesn't.

"You a cop?" Cricket asks.

"Retiring."

"Me too. I like your hat."

"I wore it for you." Özgür tips his hat. Still the black fedora. Giza, his hat girl ∷ TFv2 p. 134 ∷, still hasn't found him another cobalt trilby sweat- and summer-wrecked.

"I bet you say that to all the bitches."

"Just to you."

"I bet you say that too to all the bitches."

"Take the last one."

"These are good!" Grabbing the last taco.

Kid could learn some manners. She could learn a lot of things. Cynthia pockets her e-cigarette and takes off her Wayfarers as if to take in all of her little sister's energies. Özgür isn't prepared for this sight. Should hold up a hand, some smoked glass. Should at least squint. What eyes! Sky blue and bright enough to make every blue a sun. Dark lenses to keep from blinding others. Özgür's sure she's heard that line before. And if she's really close to Téodor Javier de Ignacio Salazar ∴ TFv3 p. 419; TFv4 p. 370 ff. ∴, she knows how to handle all the lines.

She's smiling too, and that's a soft, sad sight. Cynthia just can't hide how happy she is to see her messed-up little sister acting like a kid again, hungry, getting fed, within reach again, for the moment.

Özgür notices something else too, what at other times her beauty, her rack, might have distracted him from seeing, around her neck, on an elegant black band, the figurine he gave Virgil ∴ TFv3 pp. 416–417∴, that he later found Planski wearing ∴ TFv4 p. 98 ∴. Planski must have given Bast to Cynthia.

Then the smile goes as Cricket stands up.

"What?" Cricket snarls. "Can't I piss?"

"I'll go with you," Cynthia answers, quick on her feet, sunglasses back on, now no longer a sun but some creature that wears the sun like a mane.

"Breathe, Shannon," Rivka Waters tells Planski.

"It never stops. One moment fine, next moment *poof.* Don't be surprised if neither comes back." Planski looks at Özgür for the objection she knows he won't give. She looks tired, too tired, but she's also glad to see him. "Thanks."

"She's Teyo's mistress?" Özgür asks.

Planski nods.

"Why's her sister here?" Goodness at stake?

"She's the deal. Rehab starts tonight. Then resettlement. Protection." Bold minds, wide hearts. ∴ TFv2 p. 139 ∵

Rivka Waters takes over. "The agency helped line up a good clinic. But it's all on Cynthia to make sure it sticks. As you know, addictions are tough. One big plus is that Cricket is a minor. We've got more means to keep her in treatment."

"Don't underestimate Cynthia," Planski warns Özgür.

"I wasn't even estimating," Özgür answers, a little thrown by Planski's misread. Digs out some paper. Starts folding.

Katla. Katla.

"She's got an incredible memory and a clear sense of things. Tipped us about Frogtown. The Solder Supply shipment ∴ TFv2 p. 179 ∴. She knows all about the parade. Not just pinks either. She's been to Mexico. She's seen a lab. Says there are black balloons on the way. Pure Synsnap."

"We're not going to get it all at once," Rivka Waters says measuredly.

"I know that," Planski snaps. "I'd just like to see something happen while I'm, you know, still living?"

Katla.

Özgür orders another plate of crispy avocado tacos. Mesquite-smoked pastrami tacos too. He likes the vibe here. Woody wide and high with steel I-beams and low-hanging lights.

Katla-katla. Katla.

Cynthia and Cricket return just as the food arrives, just as Özgür's about to finish his latest.

Katla-katla. Katla-katla.

"I like you!" Cricket coos.

Katla.

Özgür slides the origami her way. Not his best. He hasn't made this one in a while: a blue cat ∷ Hideo Komatsu ∷.

"Ha!" Cricket laughs, spins it between her fingers, lands it on her shoulder before handing it to Cynthia. Then reaches for more food.

"Ask first!" Cynthia snarls, at the same time disappearing Özgür's gift.

"Can I have some?"

"Help yourself," Özgür answers, helpless to stop his laugh, especially as what happens next is exactly what he saw would happen next: a near comedic bit, as the little girl pops the latch and dumps the plate of tacos into her *Avengers* lunchbox.

What he didn't expect dangles around her neck:

Bast.

Now guarding over Cricket.

dot dot dot

I have a glint in my eye.

— *ANOHNI*

jingjing squat sidewalk, shuffle deck more times, draw then, again,

read tombalek cards, lai dat three hours, ai si, mai do'wan to play,

read anything, keep shuffle over-over.

front door stay locked black. what old bag doing in there? mebbe

koon deep macam boh lang ni driver. he koon too, hard one long

one in cab, head back, mouth wide, enuf to bite sky, tapi tonight

dis sky eat him, eat them all.

when just arrive, jingjing was damn sure taxi fly off, off-duty sign

hwuy, there wait ten minute oreddy, ten minute more, but then

instead of cabutting for good, got out and coughed, heaty one,

coughs up rough, ignored jingjing lah, opened trunk then, took out

wood box. stared at it longlong before popped latches.

inside musical instrument.

half sec jingjing thought kum lan one put on concert. jingjing

clamped ears, ready to scream. tapi slaykay lau just clean thing

with cloth, brush, other things. then latched it, hid back in trunk,

him balik back to wheel. little later lai dat did same again.

macam jingjing with cards.

if only jingjing could sleep too, feed self to sky and go.

kia si lang him this! playplay five stones with cards, just chiak

tsua to draw this! mati lah, better die lah. jingjing gawk lost at

these four nightmares, his beh keng, some majing now, suay-suay,

boh beh chow the worst, omens makan omens makan rest, blood,

bones, flesh, whatever jingjing got left, so little left, unless last

card him, super white horse, to his own rescue, how seow, jingjing

sian tao ong but even he can't goreng himself dat much. boh lui

him, poorer, and surrounded by such terrible hunger.

night so nice too, warm, jilo wrong around, tapi jingjing's skin

crawl fierce macam ice, fiercest ice under fiercer ice. what's salah

here? jingjing hong kan liao if he stay! kum pooi! jingjing must

wake driver, speedy gonzales, run off, split, beep! beep!, quick.

of course lor, timing perfect then, door to dirty house swing open,

auntie in frame there calling jingjing in.

back on sofa, auntie kena both parents serve tea for jingjing,

round two, black bean father, chio bu mother, top cups, then leave.

jingjing stomach trampolines too much ai si to take one sip.

auntie sits to his side tapi not close. jaga her now. fresh. macam

just done dreaming hours.

kang kor scrawny thing lepaking in chair now opposite auntie. dis

xanther, she chua one, sweat wet, macam running for hours.

what happened here while jingjing out?

then dawn on him . . .

cat beh with child. not with auntie either.

cat alone, on low table, by tumbled books, dry wax, pomegranates, all candle wicks burning again, white fur cheng glow macam hot ash, if head stay droop, eyes so shut, some kind of stillness on it jingjing never see before. mebbe macam auntie over last months? mebbe animal drool and snore too?

doesn't matter, boh tai ji.

jingjing almost laugh. not at cat. at self, to think child here could ever claim cat! jingjing brave one to admit wrong thought, brave twice to admit right hantam rosak one, if jingjing mong cha cha to find jilo mark on girl's face. osso tian li. jingjing got shame then, swore for sec he peek auntie with scratches across eye, blood deep, now fine, with unblemished cheek.

jingjing shudder.

old bag bo min jingjing when she sent him out, malumalu, to street for long while, with dirty snore driver, until tian li call jingjing back in, offer him seat, tea, macam like he win, pass chia lat trial.

"尔将被召 , 尔将善答。" ⸪ You will be called upon and you will answer well. ⸫

mebbe how jingjing acted he answered well? "纠缠。" now?

"靖靖 , 汝可忆吾之词纠缠？ 汝备之。将面之。" ⸪ Jingjing do you recall how I mentioned the entanglement? Prepare yourself. The entanglement is at hand. ⸫

entanglement!

纠缠！

now!

at last!

jingjing blush.

at last!

jingjing sigh.

at last!

free at last!

saysay dat, yeah, in dis america? jingjing in this america. jingjing

free. done with servitude. done with kao peh kao bu. no guess.

done with smoke. done with yes and bows.

jingjing bow head, grin large, a thousand rooms, chest open big

macam full of ginger, palm tree beach, night blooms.

539

"dear child i deeply regret my rashness. i sought only to serve my mistress and the cat. i sought only to serve that greater cause. will you accept my apologies for my gross actions?" jingjing saysay, blink back surprise over own words, ambush by old paths dis, dat voice, even his? get back! smack that! jingjing hack out gob.

child osso stunned like vegetable, tia boh, mebbe mental case.

great tian li look pleased though. parents too.

"you forgive me, lah?" jingjing saysay again, wrong.

"uh, yeah, sure, of course."

arbo she mental one.

"先于始，尔可有疑？" ∷ *Before we begin is there anything you wish to ask first?* ∷

"不！" ∷ *No!* ∷ jingjing answer, happy like bird.

"靖靖，译之与童。" ∷ *Jingjing, please translate for the child.* ∷

juang lah.

"before i take cat, what?"

scrawny ger snivels, wipe eyes, wipe nose, mebbe sick. parents
at her side, mebbe strike jingjing now, or auntie, jingjing ready
steady, kuat him dis time.

but child object. "mom? dad? i'm, uh, like fine? could i have a few
more minutes? maybe wait in another room? please?"

jingjing expect child get swat then. arbuthen no! parents instead
sulk off to room with piano. sit there in dark.

"与汝诺，吾将问之。" ∴ With your permission then, I'd like to ask you something. ∴

"she ask you now." jingjing try not to spit.

"尔何以火中活之？" ∴ How have you survived the fire? ∴

jingjing sudden blur like sotong. auntie asking jingjing dis? about

smoke? old eye study keen him too. wayang jingjing one still

turning to chao ger.

"why you not dead one?"

"water. now. i guess."

"水，现在。" jingjing translate.

"即？" auntie ask.

"now?"

"cat food? now fresh? uh, like the brand name?" ∴ **Petcurean.** ∴

great tian li beh puas. shake head. mebbe scold kwai lan kia next.

"maybe this?" child say, swoopswoop down on cat. again touches

it! jingjing strike her again!

but old bag mutter: "请，吾欲见之。"

what jingjing won't say. ∴ *Please. I'd like to see.* ∴

awful, argly thing show anyway how she clean ears, clean eyes. cat

sit still, jingjing kena hard time to sit still, watch dis crime.

"it helps," xanther sigh macam siong and hurt.

"我们现在能走了吗？" ∴ we all cabut fast now, auntie, OK? ∴

"其目下清洁，汝可见之？" ∴ *She cleaned beneath the eyes! Did you see that?* ∴

jingjing nod.

"吾从未为之。其耳，是也，然吾未曾洁其目。" ∷ *I never did that. The ears, yes, but I never cleaned his eyes.* ∷

sial lah! auntie shake head macam dirty thoughts, macam ghosts in thoughts, plague her with disbelief.

"时已到。" ∷ *We must proceed.* ∷ old bag shudders, suffers, shivers like she kaykay cold, jingjing oreddy sliding close, to hold her warm.

"靖靖，记之： 事多基于尔与尔择之言。以秋之新修初蕾待之。"
∷ *Remember Jingjing: so much depends on you and the words you choose. Handle each like a new cutting, a last bloom in autumn.* ∷

"aiyah, of course lah!" jingjing answer. "我为你服务。" ∷ i serve you. ∷

auntie suffer again. "非也，靖靖。 尔非侍吾，此晚侍于词。此乃汝

试，汝之挑战。" ∷ *No, Jingjing. You do not serve me, but tonight please serve these*

words. It is your test, your challenge. ∷

jingjing grunt, tu lan one, for damn sure.

"尔须遵二规，成一挑战。" ∷ *Abide two and succeed by one.* ∷ ∷ **Two rules and**

one challenge . . . ∷

"you understand what burden me," jingjing sing, grin, old voice

back in mouth. "i kena arrow by ah mm two task, osso third meh."

"okay," xanther saysay meek, lumplimp in chair, cat on own again,

relief.

"其规一为饲之，" ∷ *The first concerns feeding,* ∷ auntie continue.

"food, first one."

"尔须每晚弃其旧食，而后满其盘。尔勿可失。" ∷ *Every evening you must throw out what remains of the food from the previous feeding and refill the dish to the rim. You must do so without fail.* ∷

"each night, lor, i clean bowl. each night, hor, i refill bowl."

"that makes sense," horrijiber k.l.k. saysay back. "but why are you, or why is she telling me this? i, uh, don't understand?"

"juang lah," jingjing snap. "doesn't matter."

dat stir whispers in piano dark. parents suddenly alert. if not heard words, mebbe catch tone. jingjing better not invite them back in again. stay kay kay soft with smiles from here on out. tries twice. child for sure got no brain. still confused.

auntie catches on though. "其何言？" ∷ *What does she say?* ∷

"她不清楚。" ∷ She not know. ∷

"what kind of food should you feed him?" xanther ask then for some reason.

"我应该喂他什么食物？" ∷ what food i feed him? ∷

"汝定之。" ∷ *That is up to you.* ∷

"dat is up to me," jingjing relays.

"does the time matter? just curious. i mean at night, does that mean anytime at night, or is there a certain time at night?"

jingjing translate. it's good question. auntie osso agree: good question.

"吾不知，汝知。" ∷ *I don't know. You'll know.* ∷

"she say i know," jingjing saysay. ignore toot cartoon look on child face. stare space.

"亦思其食，" ∷ *Also concerning the feeding,* ∷ auntie add, eyeshine jingjing, pat arm too, then point at his neck. "此链橡子内，尔可寻其种。 逢初一晚，置一于食中。至拂晓如未食，种于湿土，避强光，忌极阴。尔勿可失。" ∷ *Within the acorn on this necklace you will find seeds. On the first night of every month, leave one in the food. If by dawn it is left uneaten, plant it in some moist earth — not too sunny, not too dull. You must do so without fail.* ∷

"my dis inside got seeds one," jingjing repeat, hand oreddy to necklace. "start every month, lor, i plant one in bowl. if there by morning, i plant in dirt."

child thing not listening. jingjing beh blame her. no lah, what! why she even here?

548

but jingjing buay loosen hold on wood, acorn tight in fist, warm

too. good. who knew? seeds inside!

"其规二则为削其甲。" ∴ *The second rule concerns cutting.* ∵ auntie move on.

low morale her now, shack lai dat osso. no reason. "每逢黎明，尔

须修其甲。 尔勿可失。" ∴ *Every dawn you must trim each nail on each paw. You*

must do so without fail. ∵

"osso, every morning, i cut nails."

auntie nod head, if look one over him then. jingjing know dat face.

she hear translation a bit the short. juang lah, jingjing just repeat,

lah, repeat twice, satisfy old bag simple.

"okay?" kwai lan kia ask, care jilo, koon if lips don't look kay tight

with enuf pain to chase off sleep, every dream. scratching arms

too macam jingjing know macam own arms scratched.

turn of thought shudder jingjing.

"我们好了吗?" ∷ we done? ∷ jingjing ask auntie.

alamak, tian li have out boh tau bo buay. waving about. black scissors! blades curve macam snakes. how jingjing boh catch sight these before? where got those? and another thing, dis first time: auntie swoop on cat, scoop up, flop on back, cradle between old knees. has jingjing ever see cat kay cham? still won't crack eyes. mebbe really blind this time, real dying.

auntie work each paw, every claw, snipsnip, with strange black blades.

"及。此极利,黎明尤甚。尔得以保命甚久乃奇迹焉!" ∷ *Just in time. These can get very sharp. Especially by dawn. How you survived so long is a blessed mystery!* ∷

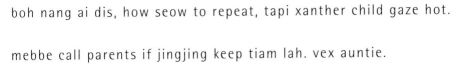

boh nang ai dis, how seow to repeat, tapi xanther child gaze hot.

mebbe call parents if jingjing keep tiam lah. vex auntie.

"aiyah i clip claws every morning."

lai dat child slumps back in chair, eyes close, pain around mouth

leave with boh trace. whole face change. arm scratching cease too.

just smile left. macam mask lifted.

jingjing know dat ka ni na mask. smoke lose it for a while. dead

lose it forever. death and smoke, only two thing jingjing ever see

lift that mask.

mebbe child si liao, loh. dead, heng, ah! jingjing's heart beat, leap,

reach.

then lao chio arrive with tray, more hot water, more tea, more

cakes.

"darling! are you alright? what's the matter?" kay worried. but

what mother not worry when daughter go into coma?

"nothing," scrawny one chirp. "i feel, uh, like, uh, wow, amazing!"

smirks and stretches twisty arms in air, yawns, smirks more.

wah lau, pui chao nuah! enuf! no more of dis place, these people,

dis smirksmirk yawning bodoh. even if great tian li always taught

wait: "尔何以得忍乃为尔之得智之道。" ∷ *How you court patience is how you*

marry wisdom. ∷ jingjing catch patience part tapi kena lost for rest,

because if you marry wisdom you better first kau him? or mebbe

patience and wisdom brothers, woo one for other. jingjing wan'no

marriage. just grab cat, get out, get on with it, be kuat one, damn

powderful.

"此为汝之。" ∷ *These now are yours.* ∷ auntie beam, hold out scissors, by

black blade macam blackest snakes, handle out for grabbing hold,

for jingjing to grab, get on with it, 纠缠!,

and everything changes.

jingjing lurf this place, lurf these people, lurf even smirk chirp-chirp kum gong one. jingjing will slurp all tea, eat all cakes, smile forever for parents. kau patience and wisdom, marry both.

strange scissor tapi wurf all of it. nanny nanny boo boo!

"谢谢，夫人。" ∴ thank you, mistress. ∵

"靖靖，译之，" ∴ Translate, Jingjing, ∵ great tian li declare. "'此为汝之。'" ∴ 'These now are yours.' ∵

"these now mine," jingjing saysay to ger one scrawny, still smiling, kay boh chup, total relief.

jingjing take scissors, watch auntie smile big macam child, bird bright proud.

jingjing cradle strange metal. bow. osso smile big. why not?

then everything changes again.

better if old bag stab blades in chest, carve up jingjing's heart.

"靖靖,将剪刀递于善希。" ∵ *Jingjing, give the scissors to Xanther.* ∵

"for you," jingjing saysay, somehow can submit, mebbe part of test, must pass, must obey. somehow swallow dis.

"uh, okay?" child accept, macam damn cautious one, take black metal macam jingjing huat sio, kena arrow stab her chest, carve out her heart, mebbe sui-sui idea.

scratch, scratch, hum pah lang jingjing have left.

"靖靖?" ∵ *Jingjing?* ∵

"嗯,夫人?" ∵ yes, mistress? ∵

auntie arrow him more task, tapi jingjing catch no ball.

"什么,夫人?" ∵ what, mistress? ∵ jingjing ask again.

"其链亦然。 予之。" ∷ *The necklace too. Give it to her.* ∷

jingjing's hand fly back at neck. "give me acorn," jingjing try tell

girl, to try straighten what oreddy kiam chye.

"huh? you're holding it. how can, uh, i— i don't understand."

"靖靖,予之!" ∷ *Jingjing! Give it to her!* ∷ great tian li command, words

enuf to rip necklace off jingjing, though own hand sabo him fast,

ai si, si beh sick, hand over wood beads, seeds, gone to tum sim

k.l.k.'s grasp! tapi hilang best than what go on next: scrawny gui

hang acorn then around her own neck!

jingjing buay tahan. what more? monster cards? jingjing kill old

bag, kill them all, if dare sapu cards.

"xanther, what's going on?" astair ask, back in room again.

"i'm not sure."

"listen here, i'm her mother," very the smart one mother, if sibeh

pek chek, kiu kiu kio at jingjing direct. "are you attempting some

sort of exchange without my consent? these, whatevers, for my

daughter's pet?"

jingjing lurf ah nia.

"yes! yes! you right! you okay! gifts of thanks! way to say thanks

for keep cat safe. we kay respectful." jingjing yesyes bowbow,

smoke smile, catch auntie do same, smile macam jingjing.

then mistress settle back, sip tea, close eyes. jingjing do same,

forget tea, close eyes on siong mother, so stone child, so mong cha

cha.

shadow open eyes.

"then is he yours?" child ask, necklace, scissors on coffee table,

small pile near cat, refused.

room suddenly dim too, candles dance, for no reason, air chanced

with twists of smoke, light fade, no reason. mother too look for

cause, jaga man anwar enter living room, osso sibeh alert.

macam something going.

something dying.

scared shitless oreddy the whole jin gang tzai si now.

or just jingjing.

auntie cough, eyes wide and ready, alert macam father's eyes,

waiting on jingjing to translate.

"她想知道这只猫是您的吗。" ∴ she wants know if cat is yours. ∴

"非也，未曾属吾。" ∴ *No. Never mine.* ∴ auntie sigh, sian one, and sad.

"no, not hers," jingjing tell child, if knowing too, dis not question she ask.

"then is he mine?" she ask. what just to suggest enrage jingjing again. awful child even swallow hard. macam she has the chance. but question is clear, lor, question is pow ka leow.

"她想知道这是不是她的猫。" ∷ she wants know if cat is hers. ∷ jingjing osso swallow hard.

wah, auntie laugh then, great tian li laugh hard, shake head too, chio kao peng!

"必非之!" ∷ *Absolutely not!* ∷

"absolutely not!" jingjing yip, lose shit, never so happy. slippery meanings sure liao, finally!, finished, at last!

xanther sag. jingjing almost grab cat then.

but scrawny ger, awful pest, don'ch stop asking, leh, what jingjing tak jalan, if mai stop, xanther's look now with only auntie.

"then is the cat his?"

clearest question, biggest question, settle dis once for all, gao ding, done.

"猫是我的 , 然后呢？" ∴ then cat mine? ∵

old bag laugh so hard she spit, saliva up cover jingjing face, gobs direct hit.

"汝之？ 非也！ 汝之药驱汝智。 尔乃一愚童。" ∴ *Yours? Of course not! The drugs you take have taken away your head. You truly are a foolish child.* ∵

"you foolish child," jingjing spit at child, but miss, hit cat, mebbe miss, but close enuf, jingjing tombalek quick.

:: Ah, midnight! ::

:: what midnight matter? ::

cat move then, lai dat stretch long, first, care less for any of dis

how seow, then yawn, then circle to reseat, but don'ch settle, keep

moving around table, past the out candles, past candles still alive

with wild flicker macam flame can fright, wide circle, slow mebbe a

little by auntie, then to jingjing, tan ku ku, thump right by.

step over necklace next, scissors too, then little hop onto ger's lap,

and boh stop there either, keep going, up her arm, to still high, tail

go boa for four paws, little soldier, not bolder, blind by scrawny

get's big ear, on her shoulder, jingjing's worst fear.

:: **Midnight's over.** ::

:: Along with all the claims of midnight anon! ::

"其无主，然今其择汝之。" ∴ *Owned by no one, but for now he chooses you.* ∴

jingjing dot dot dot.

mebbe ready for her sibeh hao lian, tapi xanther not even grin, sink deeper in chair then, face awake now in different way, lagi worse, macam bloom of thorn and flame overtake every escape, picture of horror her, her pain.

"我们如何在忘不了的充实中记得这种空虚？"

∵ How do we remember this emptiness so in fullness we won't forget? ∵

"命中所困将为汝之愉。"

∵ Life's challenges will become your pleasures. ∵

"劳之所获将繁茂，汝将知汝知此始终。"

∵ The rewards of your labors will bloom, and you will know you knew this all along. ∵

jingjing fuck care, wish smash those words fast, break them macam glass, again and again, until returned to sand.

"didn't you say there were like three things?"

kum pooi jingjing translate kan ni na shit now.

but tian li still nod.

"将有人以火焰之睛暗汝目。" ∴ *Soon one will come with eyes of flame to darken your eyes.* ∴

what choice jingjing have?

"someone kill you soon!"

"如尔亡,吾皆亡," ∴ if you die, we all dead, ∴ auntie whine.

"you will die!" jingjing hiss, if mah fan ones not miss it.

"hey, now!" anwar say, with astair one close to add more.

but xanther oreddy warning both, "stop!" heong her no doubt.

"that's it?" she ask.

"她问她是如何存活的?" ∴ she ask how she survive? ∴ jingjing ask, no spee-yak sure, but lagi curious as hell.

"仅有一法," ∴ There is only one way, ∴ tian li softsoft. "欲存己力，尔须缚其攻者。" ∴ In order to survive, you must enslave your assailant. ∴

jingjing sputter something. try twice. no good. jingjing kena qie by what auntie say.

"i'm sorry?" kucing kurap ask, blur with fear, blind animal at ear.

jingjing want kebelakang pusing now, cabut macam yesterday before yesterday, but sapu cat first, like macam cat care who has it? jingjing gasak buta great one now.

macam mebbe dis his test?

"go head, lai dat, slaughter one with eyes of flame!" jingjing at

last manage to say.

"黑暗止于勇者。"

∴ *Darkness braved ceases to be darkness.* ∵

jingjing got licence. *grab cat*.

∴ TFv1 p. 271. ∵

luan luan lai.

[before Anwar can know to run {time does not exist to
run ‹before he can know to fear «time does not exist to
fear (before he can know how to know even this animal
command of instinct ⌈there will never exist the time
necessary to know the order⌋)»›}]

Anwar turns to stone [stone white {stone unheralded ‹stone interred «stone lost ⟨stone⟩»›}] cold. Even as some of him [the sum of him {stone he must have been once ‹stone we must all become›}] recognizes with liberating amusement that he's already tried before to imagine just this [what he didn't {but was reminded of ‹in a different way›} before ∴ TFv1 p. 390 ∵]:

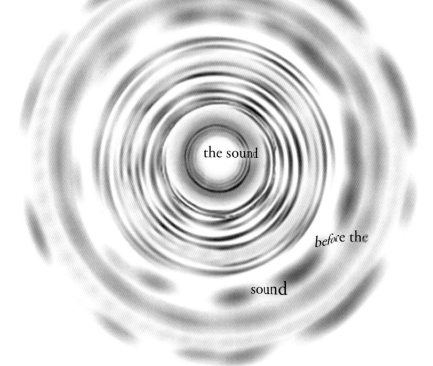

the sound

before the

sound

of the imagination

blowing up

blo w ing   through

blowing away

קוֹל דְּמָמָה דַקָּה

the bomb

the imagination

constructs

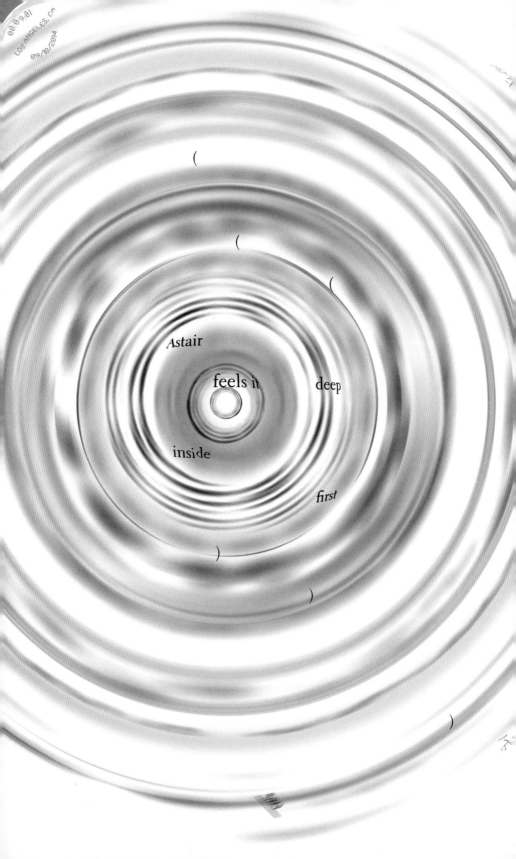

(

(

)

)

(

(

)

)

past her lungs

(

)

through her ribs

(

)

then as a dull *thud*

beneath her   sternum

(

)

before opening up her chest

where (at last (lastly))

she hears it taking

her breath away because it's too loud to hear —

(the problem with knowing just a little is
that you always end up in the same place . . .)

too much to be born of

breath not remembered

but remembering Astair

where knowing oneself known

in (and by) such a blast

bites out the backs of her knees.

Like if sound could see.

Like if hottest stare could
be of coldest flame.

Impossible shape of sense
after sense is burned away.

Not even flame left.

Not even burning left.

Not even Shnorhk left.

Only dream.

Shnorhk trapped in dream.

Shnorhk to claw free of dream.

Except *this* isn't his dream.

Shnorhk dreaming of her. Arms
to make angels on green lawn. Bare
feet to walk on blue sky. Her laughter to outdare impossible.

Worst kind of dream.

Shnorhk saved from this
his first dream in cab.

Roar stabbed both
Shnorhk's ears.

Loud enough for blood.

But too sudden to
check yet for blood.

Too sudden to even blink at.
Blink away that first dream. Blink
away this second dream. Shnorhk
certain he heard once such same
before, if then in such different way,
when pain couldn't be his ∴ **TFv1
p. 413** ∴.

For sure this still too sudden to
blink away what thing now floats
above lawn.

This second dream.

Not a dream.

Not blinking at all.

Just staring back.

Özgür stops short.

Who knows why.

Can't even start to say

what's at the bottom

of this

sudden arrest in direction, still wandering downtown, after another drink, another bar, glad of the absence of company, glad of even Elaine's absence, who's still at work, Özgür's working hard to look like he's still working, when by the end of the week he'll be retired, heading away for fall colors, all the music he wants, Scotch whenever, better thoughts.

Though this thought now is no better thought.

Özgür's guts flip and twist at once, pain matched by the expectation of more pain. He would grab himself — as if palms could calm whatever's stirring within — but there's not yet time for such theatrics, eventually followed by the usual questions of something he ate?, something he drank? Özgür's body hasn't even registered a way to move yet, except with this answering stillness brought on by some latent instinct he's known only a few times before, and chosen by what?, something vaguely familiar but in no way the same thing, when he once had a choice, a chance, recognizable now only in the sound of distant thunder :: TFv1 p. 433 :: , unadvanced by any crash of lightning.

And Özgür's guts keep cinching, until he's buckling over, hands pawing uselessly at his belly, as whatever this portent he's imagining finds answer in the strangest sound:

Özgür bellowing in pain.

Who the fuck knows what for either? A joke? Make em laugh? Maybe make Luther laugh? Like a drained head with mouth still open gonna fill the world with dread.

But sight of it does do just that, these tres pendejos running hard, probably with shit in their pants, as Luther lifts still higher the only thing left of Domingo.

Even as a roar that's nothing to do with Luther or Domingo ∴ **TFv1 p. 354** ∴ teaches Luther how even the dead can still speak.

Las Leonas?

Isandòrno stopped trusting expla-
nations years ago no matter how
easily they arrived.

This one arrives very easily: Las
Leonas must have returned in
some weaponed truck to again
circle The Ranch and deliver
chest-thudding rounds in time to
a stereo blasting out Los Tigres del
Norte.

Isandòrno would have smiled to
see such a sight.

But there is no truck.

There is no exchange of gunfire.

There is no band of killers calling themselves Las Leonas, a strange name as not one woman stands among them except supposedly the memory of two who died before the war.

There *is* only the North.

That this somehow comes from there is somehow even more terrible. ∴ **TFv1 p. 296.** ∵ The rule of something else ∴ **TFv3 pp. 657–658** ∵.

The dogs hear it and

they run from it.

They run past Isandòrno.

Isandòrno doesn't run.

Isandòrno stands to face

the face of

its following silence.

One hand holds Nastasia's gift.
The other hand waits to draw his
gun.

Isandòrno asks only one question: when he fires will he find
recognition?

A Thousand Gates Close

There be no shelter here . . .

— *Rage Against the Machine*

Oh no!

What did she just do?

Xanther feeling rootless, root-broken, in the face of this unleashed shatter, still unleashing, starting to echo even, beyond any face of comprehension, at least in any way Xanther can think about understanding, except that Xanther still isn't really thinking about anything yet, she's still just reacting, animal movements to protect—

∴ Them all! ∵

∴ What's happened, happening, I don't understand, except like I'm deaf, in my right ear for sure, hearing there is definitely going cotton on cotton. ∵

:: **Amazing! Deafness still doesn't shut you up.**

:: Okay, know-it-all, wanna enlighten us? ::

:: Us?! Don't speak on my behalf. ::

:: Oh. You're already enlightened? ::

:: Enlightenment is of no interest to me. ::

∴ **Do** you really think the **munificence** of **the** **multiverse**—∵

∷ *What you'd call reality.* ∵

∴ Thanks. ∵

∴ —comes neatly translatable for **your little** mind? **Have** **you** ever thought **to consider** all that **you miss** whenever **you're shown what is suited to** your seeing? ∵

∷ Actually, uh—.∵

∷ **Has it** ever dawned on **you** that **those** who render **easily surmisable** moments **to** suit the **pitiful coils** in **your** **head** are only **further instituting** the **bars that** cage **your** **awareness?** ∵

:: All the time, I— ::

:: They've enthralled you! And you, in accepting their little screens, their little toys, further enslave yourself! Go ahead! Bow to them! Call yourself by the right name! Call yourself their slave! ::

:: Feisty! Except, uh, wait, no, it's not that simple. ::

:: That's a start. ::

:: Hush. You especially know she's different. ::

:: Different?! You and your satisfactions with little differences. Though to your credit, at least you're not deafened like this one is. So listen! Both of you! Behold what little difference your little differences will make in the face of that! ::

Deaf again! Now in both ears. Deafening too her eyes, with no time left to even shut them, forget rub them, her skin's blinded too, if that makes sense, nothing even to taste, let alone smell, in the wake of this final sensation, not even a sensation, something else, nullifying whatever little differences Xanther's feelings might claim matter.

:: **That last part was a coincidence.** ::

:: *Coincidence! Forever coincidence with you.* ::

:: Uhm, since, well, we're capable of repetition,
are we capable of denial too? ::

:: **Enough.** ::

:: Are we, uh, like, just as susceptible to distortions? ::

:: *Now that's a thought we've never entertained.* ::

A thousand gates close at once, at the same time as the tumblers of a thousand more bolts turn over, as thousands upon thousands of latches and hasps ease shut, and all of it inconsequential before what else also locks . . .

All while the absence left behind in this aftermath keeps tolling the cost of thinking it all might have been otherwise.

:: **TFv1 pp. 470, 486, 490.** ::

No way out.

No way around.

All the keys lost.

The rest preset.

Isn't the end the greatest lock?

The Labyrinth

Knowledge has compassion with the abyss. It is the abyss.

— *Thomas Mann*

Their Clips are going black?

Impossible. But that impossibility was all that mattered to Cas as soon as Alvin departed beyond the dark boughs of the grove, red threats vanishing first, followed by her own protective constellations of green, as she in turn stumbled back to the proximate fire team, uncertain legs evidencing only then the fear Cas had managed to deny.

Getting back to the Mountain House seemed almost worse. Now there was no point in pretending that the laser sights, while no longer visible, had vanished their concomitant weapons. Night-vision scopes were now engaged, covert tactics in action. And there was a lot less champagne.

Bobby helped support her along the path back. He kept reassuring her that friendly snipers would defend them against ambush. Rear guards would defend them against pursuit. But what good were bullets when fear pursued?

At one point Bobby even tried singing to her.

"What are you doing?" Cas snapped.

"Singing with you?"

"*With* me?"

"You weren't singing?"

Cas realized only then that every step she took was landing with a moan. She stopped that. If only to stop Bobby from singing. And then she smiled.

By the time they climbed the steps to the Lake Lounge they were even laughing.

The Carriage Lounge was closed but an obliging server brought Cas a gin gimlet and Bobby a Manhattan. They laughed harder when they saw how badly their hands were shaking. Bobby immediately ordered a second round.

Warlock appeared later with the thick proposition in hand. The first thought had been that it was fitted with mischief.

"Clean," Warlock confirmed. "Weal too."

And if it wasn't real, it demonstrated enormous energies spent counterfeiting intentions: close to nine hundred pages, with DOJ ∵ **United States Department of Justice** ∴ letterheads, assessments — some partially redacted — from department heads at the FBI, NSA, and CIA. Entire chapters were dedicated to clemency plans for their friends. Cas and Bobby would have to agree to complex and intolerable demands, but none were unreasonable.

"We a'e to be comfo'tably employed too with gene-wous vacation days and an admiwable fouw-oh-one k."

"I'm retired," Bobby scoffed.

"Wefusal is not cove'ed in this pwoposition. A cuwious omission."

"An offering without threats?" Cas asked.

"How noble," Bobby snarled, signaling their server for a third round.

"Alvin's religion is appearance," Cas sighed. "This proposition serves as a testament to his good will. He knows that we already know that reprisals will follow if we delay in accepting."

"Did he mention a deadline?" Warlock asked.

Cas shook her head.

"Anothe' cuwious omission."

As they huddled around that small table, surrounded by a scattering of oblivious guests, with their own army manning defenses as near as corner tables to as far as the ridgelines overlooking the resort, Cas kept trying to focus on how Recluse might initiate his attacks.

She knew he knew that Cas and Bobby had fortified the area. He also knew that those acting in her defense were more zealous than the most religious fanatics because Cas did not need to appeal to the unseen. Her premise had never been intellectual. It wasn't even particularly political in the narrow way that politics was now understood as the rhetoric of the promise.

All Cas had to do was show them. It took time but the revelations — however small — were incontrovertible. Recluse knew this too. He was well aware of how her army had grown. The numbers were staggering. She had friends everywhere. But she also had enemies everywhere, people who feared the consequences her truth would have on them. They knew nothing about Alvin or even this engulfing war, but more than a few of them would do anything to see her silenced if just for their own sake. Recluse counted on this.

Cas might be a hard one to attack but she was not invulnerable. The Failed Distribution had proven that, as well as made their entire VEM Identity ∴ **TFv1 p. 642** ∴ vulnerable.

Recluse understood that if he patiently and thoughtfully managed this conflict, he could eventually cage their libertarian vision of a truth set loose and perhaps even succeed in extinguishing forever one historical outcome.

But even thoughts centering on Bobby's, Warlock's, and her own survival could not keep Cas from thoughts far beyond anything she could claim as her own.

The Clips going black? How was that possible? That seemed as unlikely as a change in the laws of thermodynamics. But if Alvin wasn't lying, what kind of world did that describe? Even theoretically, Cas could not fathom the consequences, not to mention the causalities.

If/then: if the algorithms were still the same, then was VEM changing?

Alvin had to be lying. He must be up to some trick to exact the surrender of unanticipated data.

But Clip #1 wasn't a lie. Nor were the rest.

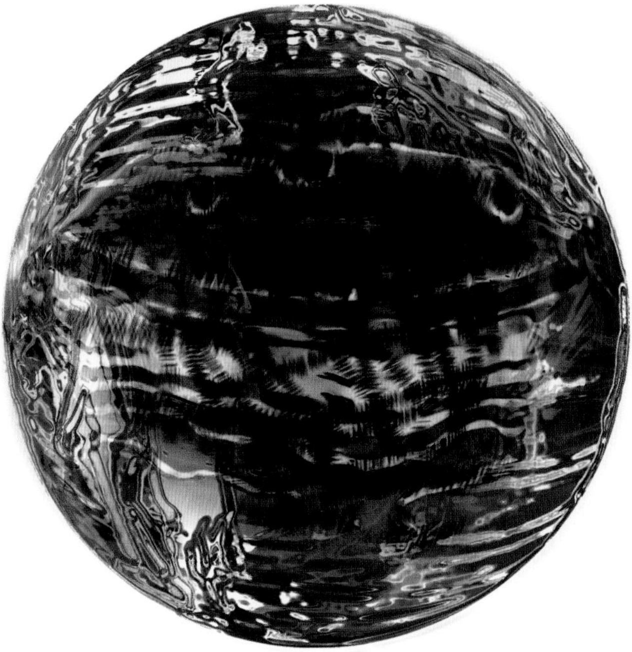

Cas scried every variation too. She blamed the Orb. She shut it down. Reawakened it. Condemned the explosives blackening its blacker heart. Then she cursed Sorcerer's absence. She even cursed Bobby's presence as he tried to pry her away from this latest obsession swiftly consuming her.

"At least in the room," Bobby pleaded, though he knew she knew they would never go to that room. Warlock had already gone off to arrange their departure.

"Not in public!" Bobby also tried, though he knew she knew half the room knew what she was doing — wanted her to do what she was doing — while the other half would consider it a parlor trick.

"Are you a witch?" a blond little pixie, no more than nine years old, interrupted.

Cas nodded. If really a Looking Creature.

"Are you a good witch or a bad witch?"

Even if Cas had said bad, she probably would have earned a giggle. That the question had left her frozen likely played a part in freezing the little boy. Only his apologetic mother could unstick him enough to draw him away.

All the Clips seemed to be closing like an eye swelling shut. Unless it wasn't the Clips at all but rather the Orb itself that was going blind, blinding Cas, blinding all of them. Which was when Cas turned to what apparently still remained hidden in Recluse's blind spot.

Here the clouds had grown thicker, dark swirls
charged with more lightning, as well as thunder even big storms would envy. They
crowded the edges as if to close off every
limit. But there was no sense of shutting
down or closing.

Xanther still held the center.

Only now, the eight-year-old child
seemed on fire with a brightness that
rapidly alternated between a kind of
hyperclarity possessing every surface and
a blindness consuming every surface. Even
in the Orb, Cas could only catch a glimpse
of Xanther before her own eyes clamped shut
against this slowly expanding star.

And then Warlock was back, and despite staff and guest objections, ordering their security details to clear the lounge.

"Whe'e's the child you we'e talking with?"

Cas was already darkening the Orb, reframing her mind as new questions began to surface:

Yes, wasn't it awful late for a child to be up? Wasn't it already after 2 AM?

"I believe his mother took him away," Cas answered.

Cas couldn't even remember the woman's face. Maybe there was an I'm sorry. She had scooped up the boy easily enough, but without commenting on the Orb. Not even a joke or a note of reverence. Not even a look.

As Warlock would say, "A cuwious omission."

Though that's not what he said next.

"Ba'tende' let slip fo' a good tip that the hotel's 'Fall Family Getaway' is exclusively one company: A.L. Chemical."

Cas shook her head.

"I had the same wesponse. But we just hea'd confi'mation that it's owned enti'ewy by Galvadyne." ∷ **TFv3 pp. 352, 706.** ∷

"You mean the guests here are all—?" Cas started to ask, even as both Warlock and Bobby hurried her to her feet.

"It's wo'se. He found ou' London gi'l. The one who taped him in Patek Philippe. They killed he' two flatmates and gwabbed he'."

"When?"

"Maybe an hou' ago."

"Then he'll know our Window Reduction is a sham," Bobby said. ∷ **TFv4 pp. 229, 600–601.** ∷

"He'll know our scrying strengths are the same," Cas groaned.

"But will the pawity of scwying stwength alte' his pwoposition?" Would the darkening Clips stay his hand?

It only took minutes to find out.

Cas was outside, beyond the big building, just past the putting green, and surrounded by a small squad of armed men. The plan was to change the plan and have the convoy pick them up at the Council House up the hill.

Communications still indicated that the Mountain House remained uncompromised but both Warlock and Bobby didn't trust communications.

They were right.

The night sky could only conceal for so long the descending streaks likely authorized and fired while they were still inside.

Night briefly fled before the impact.

Gone, their convoy.

Gone, the Lake Lounge and Lake Porch.

The dock as well threw up a tower of flaming splinters.

It got worse. Red streaks ∴ **30-06 M16 Tracers** ∵ emerged from multiple windows of the main building facing the lake. From up the hill by the Pavilion, green rounds ∴ **XM778 Tracers** ∵ answered back.

By the time they reached Lake Shore Path, the green rounds had stopped. Now the only gunfire was red ∴ **.50 M17 Tracers** ∵, blindly burning up the roads and trails ∴ **.50 BMGs** ∵, in search of a lucky hit.

Cas clutched the Orb as Warlock and Bobby helped her forward, sharp pains in her knees, ankles, worsening with every step.

Their accompanying fireteam of three kept night scopes trained behind them but fired no weapons. The frequent turns in the path helped to cover their escape.

Across the lake more explosions sounded ∴ **M196 Tracers** ∵ ∴ **M195 Grenades** ∵. The smell of burning gasoline slunk through the woods. The smoke of burning wood followed.

"I thought Mohonk was secured!" Bobby panted at their first pause.

"The guests. It's confi'med," Warlock said, the coil in his ear alive with updates.

"How many?" Bobby asked, though the tracer rounds made it obvious.

"All."

Cas shuddered. Had Recluse in the name of this deceit risked families? Children?

"There's a fo'ce ahead," Warlock alerted them next. "We have no one close enough to inte'cept."

"Can we go back?" Cas asked.

Warlock shook his head. "Another squad of thei's is wacing this way."

"Then we fight here," Bobby grunted.

The fireteam at once began improvising tree and low-earth defenses near the shore while laying out lines of fire to defend the path in both directions. Warlock muttered pleas on the radio for reinforcements.

Bobby just stared at the lake, as if staring could materialize a boat or make swimming in such cold water an option. Maybe drowning was the best option.

Which was when Cas heard what no one else noticed, echoing through her, as a thing once so familiar ∷ T ᵣv1 ⱨ 153 ∷ and yet in that remembrance transfigured again as something much stranger and even more terrifying.

"Not here," Cas urges them now, not waiting for an argument, heading off alone, the fireteam scrambling to catch up.

She remembers what Bobby should have remembered, what Alvin would certainly remember if he was here, but he will be nowhere near this pincer move.

The trail is called The Labyrinth — a series of wooden ladders leading up through a series of tight pinches. If they can just make it up and over the cliffs, Skytop Tower is not only near but well defended too, along with the road down, skirting the Mountain House to the west.

In the dark this is no easy trek, especially for Cas. But it's also not obvious. With a little luck, their pursuers will miss the TRAIL CLOSED sign on the first pass and have to double back.

The fireteam must rely on their night scopes to help negotiate the dark cramps of stone while precarious footing further slows everyone down.

The first ladder terrifies Cas. A black vertigo that nearly compels her to fall. But once her hands find the rungs, her feet follow their easy rhythm up.

Bobby carries the Orb in a pack offered by the young woman slinging a rifle thick with additional mysteries ∴ **M4 Carbine with M320 Grenade Launcher Module (GLM)** ∴.

On a slippery trail above, Cas forgives the vertigo on the ladder and even longs for the constancy of another series of rungs.

Halfway up the trail, two of their fireteam
— Cas doesn't even know their names
∴ *Lonnie Gribbs* ∴ ∴ *Jason Boyle* ∴ — set up
weapons to defend their rear. The position is good. They will be hard to defeat.
Warlock orders them to stay for only fifteen minutes and then rejoin them at the
top.

The top comes fast and immediately offers the relief of easier strides. Cas almost feels elated as her breathing relaxes. Even more encouraging, climbing the ladders seems to have somehow quelled the pain in her knees.

When Skytop Tower ∷ **The Albert K. Smiley Memorial** ∷ appears ahead, rising up like something out of Middle-earth, gunfire erupts behind them, followed by two explosions. ∷ *Jason Boyle dead.* ∷ ∷ *Lonnie Gribbs dead.* ∷

Warlock hustles everyone across the road, up a few stone steps, and through a doorway with a lancet arch.

Only a garbage can awaits them inside an otherwise cold room of rock, cement, and barred windows.

Warlock stations the rifleman ∴ *Toni Ho*∴ ∴ **armed with an FN F2000 FCS**∴ at the entrance with orders to wait for the others.

Since Bobby has no weapon, Warlock ∴ **with a Tanfoglio MOSSAD**∴ insists on leading the way up the stairs. Cas goes next.

Behind her, Bobby now and then presses his hand against her back, to support her, urge her on, comfort her, as they tackle together the one hundred steps.

Halfway up, Warlock decides to risk a run to the top. Moments later he yells down that they are alone.

It's good news that Recluse failed to position combatants here. It's bad news that their people aren't everywhere.

Cas has only just reached the small antechamber at the top when machine-gun fire below echoes up the stairs, followed by an obscenely abrupt bang. ∷ *Toni Ho dead.* ∷ Seconds later the ensuing silence is sacrificed to too many boots thudding up the steps.

Cas struggles up the last set of steps, nine in all,
each igniting terrible flares of pain in both knees.

Warlock helps pull her up into the open air,
where Cas flops on her back, heaving hard
to cool the burning in her lungs. But it
is a stunning star-strewn sky that grants
Cas the greatest and most unexpected
moment of relief.

From here on a clear day you can supposedly see six states. But Cas has eyes on
only one thing: a small cupola with green
metal doors rising above a parapet. Cas
starts to crawl toward this final refuge as
Warlock points out a light flying their way.

"Ou' helicopte'."

"Will it arrive in time?"

"Unlikely." But Warlock stills chambers a round as he sets up
to defend the only entrance up there.

Where's Bobby?

Before Cas can reach the steps, she hears him screaming down below in the antechamber: "I have her Orb!"

Warlock tries to block the way but can't deny her the sight of her husband below holding above his head their Great Seeing Eye. Its dark glistens and sparks.

Of course, Bobby knows the security charms.

Cas' mind races ahead to what negotiations he can manage to earn them more time.

She should know better: the future only entertains our plans when it's bored.

And tonight the future is not bored.

Bullets tear into Bobby. Cas keeps seeing them tear into him as Warlock throws her down onto the cement. The impact blackens her eyes. If only consciousness would blacken too.

Cas hears too clearly the sharp clink of the Orb hitting the floor as more boots fill the antechamber.

The explosion thuds beneath her, followed by the awful consequences of hurled pieces no sky will ever put back together again.

"You seen my boy?"

We fight to control territory that isn't ours to begin with.

— Alex Cisernos

"Chingado was gonna score his package here?" Juarez snorts.

Luther laughs. Tweetie laughs so hard gotta hold off more gulps of margarita.

"What the pocket said," Piña shrugs.

Luther nods. After Piña's dice magic, he pulled the address hisself from Domingo's pocket.

Big neon sign, orange and blue, on a bigger wall soaked in black. Club was just off Cesar Chavez, a hundred feet grosso modo. North side. Windows bricked up — for noise ordinances or nosy neighbors.

Mostly well tequila. Cheap beer. Pop shit thumping up the place. Not even the dark booths were safe. Pitbull. Shakira. Piso 21. Strobes and automated spots color up the main floor, empty, except for two couples too drunk to move, moviéndose igual no matter the song.

Luther throws back another shot, swigs his Dos Equis, watches the first couple leave, the second couple lasting only a little longer. Now just the lights dance out there. Not a dance. Just how machines show they can't feel.

"Wednesday nights are always dead," cashier warned them at the door. "Come on the weekend. It's good then. Real good."

Juarez for no fucking reason even los dioses could give suddenly shrieked in kid's face, somewhere between a laugh and a scream, his mouth so wide jaw shoulda broke, kid's expression sure shoulda broke, at least for the rot Luther's perro loco's got, jammed between his teeth, ese tufo has gotta be historical.

But kid didn't flinch.

"Simón ése. Couldn't agree with you more."

Juarez grinned, como Juarez was in love, even patted the kid's shoulder while Tweetie paid the covers, and on Luther's nod threw in an extra twenty, Luther glad to see the kid was it as far as security, no metal detectors, nada de manoseadas. They were loaded too with no plans to loosen and lighten, not now, whole night one long advertencia to keep shit tight.

Pero la facilidad with which they got in, and with so many weapons, should have been Luther's biggest warning, though just moving through the dark velvet curtains made everything he did next seem too late, especially in that place of hard walls, hard shadows, echoes harder than hammers, under a ceiling denso de piñatas, which Luther realized only later, after they had found their dark booth, ordered drinks, started laughing about stupid shit they could say anything about, or serious shit they couldn't put a word to, long after he'd stopped paying attention to the ceiling, or the weirder feeling, almost a ghostly sense muy claro, demasiado claro, that this hollow nowhere was really packed to capacity, barely room to move, less and less room to breathe, only then understanding that they weren't piñatas but balloons, spots and strobes changing their color, because all of them were clear.

Like raindrops falling the wrong way, or tears, if Piña stood on her head and let the inky memories de su cara y cuerpo stream off her feet. Like wet smoke. When the sun weeps. Weird twists of thoughts that kept coming, como si his crew was the clouds, Luther the storm, then up to what world was that flood falling?

Otherwise, the club was a decepción: bored bartenders on a shit night happy to get pestered by bored valets coming inside for shots of vodka in their Cokes. Waitresses looked as miserable as old strippers counting seconds on a Sunday brunch shift. The couples that drifted on and off the dance floor looked like they thought they were somewhere else, some other place, some other state.

"Éstas son mamadas," Juarez barks now, can't relax, won't relax for days. "Let's roll." Like that's gonna take him away from what's pumping his legs, twitching his hands. This place because it's not their kinda place donde es easy poner tacha.

"Only play he had," Tweetie sugiere.

Luther nods, swigs away the rest of his Dos Equis, what their server pronounced Dos Seki. Wants otra, y otro trago también.

"Let's go back after those armos," Juarez grins.

A smile breaks up Piña's face. "Órale vato, they didn't expect that shit!"

"Luther, you terrorized them!" Victor agrees.

"We didn't make midnight," Luther grumbles, only interested in the weird way this place keeps telling him something's about to change.

"You think here was different at midnight?" Tweetie asks.

"No," Luther answers, relaxes. "And even if here was real, it's not like we gonna know whoever was looking for him ∴ **Domingo** ∴, or like whoever knows him is gonna know us."

"Bang!" Juarez giggles.

Piña's smile breaks into a laugh.

"Bang!" Victor says too.

They all laugh. Except Luther, just a smile, y una muy fría, caught up, again?, in that empty dance floor, the way the colored lights keep lightening the rain above, did all the balloons just get smaller?, or did the ceiling get higher?, even the way the spots and strobes seem to move differently, like they're aware, aware that Luther's there, like they were even expecting him there, like now they're dancing for him.

Domingo sure as fuck wasn't expecting his end. The look on his face, that some deal gonna save his ass, was still on his face when Piña sawed off his head.

Juarez got to hack off the hands and feet with his machete. Shit was sharp. One cut. Not even bone argued. Juarez was happy.

They oil-drummed the body next, Victor mixing up his Devil Lye pozole. Pounds of it. Not to hide shit but let it message a cualquier otro pendejo who wants to meterse with the parade.

Maybe for a joke, Piña went off in white then, sprayed MS-13, Loco 18, La eMe, 14 too. Juarez cracked crazy, grabbed the can to add AVES, AMV, White Fence, CxP, ETG, and NLR. Teyo would approve the angle. Let CSI chotas stress the tangle. No prints, no angels. Con safos.

But Tweetie had the last word, tagged the barrel in big bright red letters.

What Luther remembers is how the chemicals and shit, whatever had gotten on the outside, started to bubble the paint, some of it running, the rest of it eaten.

Luther wanted to ask Tweetie to explain, forgot to ask, remembered again, then didn't care.

Storm drains and dumpsters got the heels and palms. A different barrio for each toss. The last one in an alley off Western, north of Fountain.

Piña hopped out the van with the last bag.

Luther is still wondering what those clowns had in their heads? That she was alone? Just left the van idling? Couldn't they tell with a blink that homegirl wasn't someone to get dumb with?

"Baby, you lost? Let's be friends." ∴ **TFv3 p. 231.** ∴

Three armos, verdaderos valemadres, come out of the shadows then, not like shadows can really hide faces that white, so white fear's just beggin to break in, fuck things up, like fuck up their designer jeans, their dumb faces, the dumbest one already talking too much, show-ing a cuete, but like what the fuck for? Stuck big and useless behind his belt buckle. Might as well flash a limp dick.

Though flashing any kind of dick at Piña es una gran pendejada.

Piña stopped. Real casual though. Maybe her eyes narrowed a little. Her smile didn't change.

Another big fucking warning.

Pero estos suatos caught none of it, lit up in the van's headlights like they center stage, squinting Piña into some weak thing she wasn't.

Piña just set the bag at her feet and waited. Good old Piña. Nothing but calm. Takes more than three Armenian fucks to escamar someone who just spent the last hour driving around the city dumping body parts.

"You a long way from home, Señorita," the talker yapped.

"Home's where you make it," she smiled back.

"How's that work?" The one squat like a trash can, round as the lid, joined in. The thinnest one never said a word.

"With this," she said, holding up her knife like a magician that just made a deck of cards appear.

The three smirked. Swaggered closer.

"And this," Tweetie growled, stepping out of the van.

"This too, amigos," Juarez yipped.

"You dumb motherfuckers," Victor howled.

Luther didn't even need to draw. At least the one with the useless fucking gun stuffed behind his belt left it there. Froze too like the rest of his homies, just staring at all that firepower emptying out of the van como pesadillas when there's a fever in your head. Solo miraron espantados: Tweetie with his cannon, Victor steady ready, Piña set to quarter and dice. Juarez was the only one Luther had to check, dog so relaxed Luther knew he was ready to do all three before Tweetie even missed the first shot.

Luther walked over to Piña, squatted down, and opened the bag. Not sure why he did it either. Though this surprise got Juarez's attention. That was worth something. No longer giving those jodidos deadly consideration, looking joyful, might as well have wagged his tail, if he had one, ready for a treat.

Even then Luther could see it was a dumb thing to do. The feeling, though, that took control was old, terriblemente viejo, Luther felt almost humbled before it, como si no pudiera escoger, because this here was what he walked the earth for, had walked it in lives before, and would walk it again in lives later, Luther lifting it out of the bag, to a roar he couldn't hear, or place, except inside hisself, his hand in the coils of the cold black hair, raising up high Domingo's drained head.

The armed one ran first. The other two didn't stick around long enough to como para ver que más hacer.

"Bang!" Juarez screamed, and the slowest one, that looked like a trash can, actually went down, with this big arch, bien dramático, grabbing his back.

"Bang," Tweetie whispers now, coreando a los demás, chuckling too, paying their bill.

Luther's never seen Juarez so happy about not shooting his gun.

"Anyone still jumpy from that bump?" Luther asks as they get up to leave. Nadie is. Maybe Luther isn't either, but something don't square. Luther still wants another shot, but booze isn't smoothing out these clashing edges.

Luther feels wide awake if soñando despierto too, sharp to everything but anxious to keep it that way, like it might get even sharper, y eso no estaría bien. Also the music's changed. Pop shit's gone. The mixes getting weirder, like a mash-up of bachata hip-hop, cumbia electrónica, and merengue house, and even those giving way to a rising grind of massive industrial gears refusing oil, refusing to stop.

It's kind of this no-man's-music, one second familiar without meaning shit, the next strange enough to mean everything, too divided for Luther to ever get, even if — and this is the weirdest part, the part Luther does get — it is relevant only to him.

There's a feeling attached too: like seasick without having to throw up, passing out without falling down, hallucinating without having to see anything made-up.

Luther's step drags. Maybe he'll hit the bar fast. Grab that shot. Only the bar is now crowded. When did that happen? De hecho, the whole place is packed. No more valets topping off Cokes. Most of the men are short too, afeitados o con bigote, none built, slim shoulders, sunken chests, las camisas abotonadas al cuello, some with bolo ties, a few with suspenders, most with hats, alas grandes, hiding their faces con más velos de sombras, and though no one makes eye contact, Luther feels watched, especially from those places too dark to peer into.

A mix of some narco-corrido starts playing. Maybe it's been playing for a while. But whatever this one's about — cartel assassinations, revenge, the getaway — that's not the song Luther suddenly se muere por oír, the real song beneath this night, all nights, terrifying enough to scare away even the bravest ghosts.

"No ladies," Piña notices, like she's catching these other changes too. Her words come out like a sigh.

A man in a white hat and a white suit with lo que parece un gato rosa en su hombro pasa bailando by them.

669

"¿Estamos en un club gay?" Tweetie asks.

Maybe. But if Domingo was a faggot and this was his place, no men take the dance floor. No one even crosses it. Like it's there only for the lights, and those have gotten darker, violets, black light, an ugly glitter trazando un marco Luther would also think twice about entering.

At the exit, the cashier won't even look at them.

"What the fuck's with you?" Juarez snaps.

But the kid still won't look up. Asustado for sure pero not of them.

Outside, the Los Angeles air rights Luther. No doubt now that if they'd made earlier, made midnight, whatever Domingo had set up would never have come their way. No doubt either that Domingo was in on something.

Driving away Luther notices the neon sign has changed:

After the Armos had pissed themselves and run off, and Luther had dumpstered Domingo's head, se fueron directo to Nacho's.

"¿Oye, compa, qué pues?" the old pimp had grinned, wandering out onto the front steps in a dirty salmon bathrobe, fingering the hole in his teeth. "¡Cómo no! Cricket's back."

Just not right then. Out con un cliente. Dark cats? ∵ *TFv5 p. 520.* ∵ Luther almost set about waiting for her. Fuck Domingo's tip. But Nueve Globos won his curiosity.

Now Luther considers returning to Nacho's again. But they're all drunk and loaded with guns, and morning is the better call.

Solo pa' estar seguro, Luther calls Nacho.

"Still not here," the old man mumbles like he sleep-talking. "She goes like that all the time. ¿Quieres que te llame cuando regrese?"

"Ain't no big deal," Luther says. "Just wanted to make sure you all one happy family."

"Te doy todas las gracias," Nacho says, awake now. Means it. "You're a good man, Luther. Un buen hombre."

That's when Tweetie runs over the old woman.

She comes out of nowhere. Just walks off a curb into their swerve. Tweetie stopped fast as he could, just not enough to keep from knocking her down and driving over her.

Luther swears to the bump. Dos brincos. One for each axle.

But as they sit there wondering what the fuck comes next, she pops up, no puede ser, levantando la cabeza like that, and coming around the van to ask if they okay. How fucked is that?! Won't stop saying sorry either.

And it turns out she isn't old. Just worn, muy jodida.

She sure freaked out Juarez. He can't believe she's alive. Goes bug-eyed. Hooting, whistling. Like she La Llorona. Scrambles fast into the back of the van.

Luther peels off some bills and tells Tweetie to give it to her.

"God bless you," she slurs. "Donde sea que he's hiding, God bless, sí, I'll keep looking."

"God?" Tweetie laughs. "God don't hang in this neighborhood."

Not like she hears that, too stuck on the cash, grabbing at it, like kids grab candy, kids Luther remembers now, cuando estaba chamaco though he wasn't grabbing candy. He was the one with the bat, beat that Felix piñata until legs and body flew across the yard, head just dangling there, smiling over its missing parts, heart raining candy down onto those gimme hands. Luther would any day take something to hit over something sweet in shiny silver.

Luther catches a flash too of tonight's transparent balloons on the ceiling.

"I'm not looking for balloons," the woman coughs, Luther realizing he's just lost some of the conversation she and Tweetie are having.

"Get out of here, you crack-ass ho," Victor snarls from the back.

"What's that you just said?" Luther asks her direct.

"I'm looking for my boy s'all. You seen my boy?"

"I ain't see your boy."

"I hear him around but he never stays. Now he's out late. Too late. He leaves me no more flowers. No more flowers. No more blossoms."

Piña's the only one not laughing as they drive off, watching the woman cross the street, wobbling back and forth there, lost again, no clue where next, su senda, every direction, una calle de la muerte.

"You know her?" Luther asks.

"She Hopi's mom."

"Huh," Tweetie grunts. "Ran over her, like all the way, and she's up with not even a scratch."

"Not even a scratch," Victor echoes.

It was fuckin crazy. What were the chances? Coming across her, that kid's mom, and then running her over, and doing no harm?

"You can't hurt her no more," Piña answers. "That's all."

"What the fuck's that supposed to mean?" Juarez growls, gateando para enfrente, mad he got freaked and they all saw. "If they breathing, I can hurt them."

"I think she means you can't hurt no mother worse than by taking away her child," Victor explains. "Just sayin."

"Bullshit," Juarez scowls, still angry.

"It don't matter," Victor placates their mad dog.

"Yeah, it don't matter," Luther speaks up, changing his mind again too. "Back to Nacho's."

Better find out who that little puta knows so high up to make a piece of shit like Domingo worth something a shot caller like Teyo would sick a dawg like Luther on. Domingo gone is one thing, but bringing Teyo algo muy bueno, like *who* blew up Frogstown and cost them all the pinks, now that would earn Luther more than money, like a trip back to Hawaii, and this time forget those Hula Hoop witches, upgrade to that creature in the lobby, tell Teyo he's ready for something real fine, with a long naked back, lipstick on her pearls ∴ **TFv2 p. 757** ∴.

Porque de eso se trata todo: Luther's ready to upgrade, bigger garage for all his cars, better women to put away the hard tomorrows, a lifestyle that's done with this shit, like hacking off heads and running over a childless mother.

"Look what I found," Juarez says, as Tweetie turns the van around and heads for the freeway. "In my pocket the whole time. Sneakin in a seam and shit. That's it, right? What you asked for?" ∴ **TFv1 p. 605.** ∴

676

Luther's fuckin elated. Aunque ni sabe por qué. Doesn't even get it. What the fuck is this shit? Here isn't First Class or Amex black. Probably stupid to even keep. Especially now.

But Luther takes the little nub like it's the fucking Hope Diamond, turns it over too, like if he turned it over just right, and looked at it just right, Hopi's little blue pencil might tell him todos los secretos del tiempo.

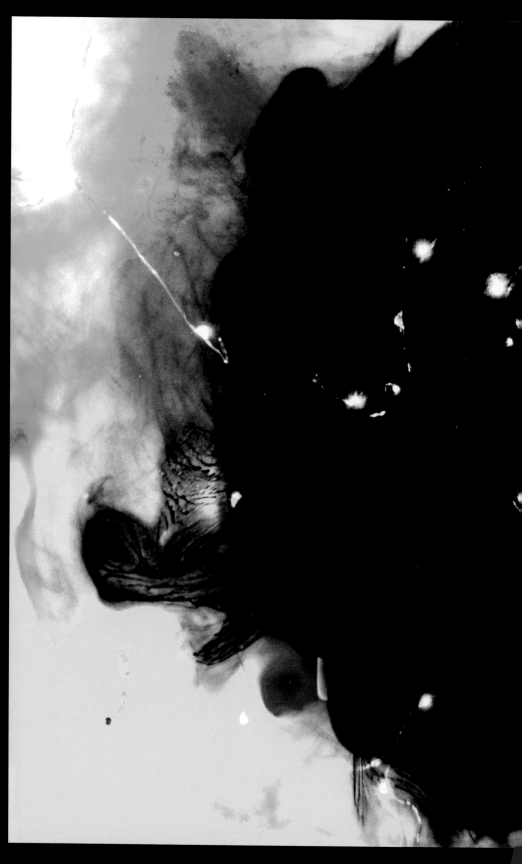

Into hell

Give content to these words . . .

— *Ernst Friedrich*

To recognize. This act and feeling ambushed Shnorhk first.

Shnorhk used to strangers in cab. Used to those he drive before too. Maybe know them at once or know them by look they give when they know him. But that feeling is small. At most find nod or wave back. Never this feeling of attack. Feeling of ambush by ghost.

And worse than ghost had stood in doorway. Terrible shadow. Shnorhk thought midnight thing hovering on lawn had been terrible enough, what dragged him from dream into worse dream. Shnorhk had almost left right then. Had all reasons to leave. Had got rest. No care about money. Phone alive with texts from friends. They started late. Playing not even hour. Six reasons to drive away. Only Ancient Beauty inside give reason to stay.

And Shnorhk had found Ancient Beauty enough reason to delay little more.

Until little more became later more, until Shnorhk made up mind to go. Would knock on door, do right thing, make sure Ancient Beauty okay, make clear exit plan.

Then front door open.

First out, Ferret Man.

Shnorhk almost screech off.

But then couple come out: black man, white woman, both good-looking, tall, both bending their heights around Ancient Beauty, helping her to car.

Ferret Man scurry ahead to yank door open.

"We go now! We go!" Biting at words, if bite now had no teeth.

Something had changed, got lost, a nakedness averting Shnorhk's eyes, as if Shnorhk ashamed for Ferret Man, ashamed too for calling him that, no longer Ferret Man.

Young Man, now bewildered by some shock, sliding in first to help Ancient Beauty inside, help with seat belt, while strange American couple stood back, waved goodbye, also looked bewildered, in shock, if like movie stars, or leads in some TV show Shnorhk would never have watched but what she would have made him watch with her.

Shnorhk turned car around, even raised hand, not sure why, to wave goodbye. Couple in same spot but gone.

All Shnorhk could see.

Her!

How this "to recognize" happening and feeling had attacked.
Feeling so terrible. Attack ongoing.
Until Shnorhk's old head settled
sight.

Another her. Older her.

Or about her age if.

The child didn't disappear from
doorway either, daring Shnorhk
from a silhouette to keep up awful
mistake. Maybe Shnorhk wanted
mistake. He kept staring for possibility of face that never came, if
Shnorhk swore she gazed his way
in familiar way, maybe Shnorhk
making that part up, like everything
afterwards, like a flicker there of
something human eyes can't do, as
if there was not how when Shnorhk
cry at stars, stars won't cry back,
but how when Shnorhk stare at
darkness to see despair, there was
such darkness staring back.

The pyramid of shadow on her shoulder was too unfamiliar to stand, disturbing enough to make this "to recognize" feeling-attack finally stop, even as that thing glittered there like strange something Shnorhk seen once before ∴ **TFv3 pp. 500–501** ∴ ∴ *No. Something else.* ∴, before even it too was gone, Young Man tapping Shnorhk to drive, the couple walking back up pathway to their home, their child retreating inside, if for flash black pyramid on her shoulder had suddenly become pyre, burning so bright, so hot, no color, especially white, survived.

But "to recognize" had two sides to attack: to mistake strange girl in doorway, for one; and two, to mistake that stranger at motel door for Ancient Beauty.

Shnorhk had almost screamed.

So surprised even if for whole drive something had already felt different, from both of them in backseat, so silent, heads bowed, so still, like not even there. Even taxi felt lighter than empty.

Then at motel, Shnorhk had helped Young Man help Ancient Beauty out.

By doorway, her face, like strange child in Echo Park doorway, had also been lost to shadow, maybe same shadow.

Even as Young Man fiddled with key card, failed, swiped again, the shadow had stayed.

"Kay tired," Young Man had muttered.

"What happened back there?" Shnorhk asked at last.

"Sian," Young Man repeated, again red light for swipe, maybe bad light problem, though bad light not tremble his hands.

Shnorhk had seized key card then. Let Young Man hold up Ancient Beauty. She already felt too light to live. Like she never lived. If Young Man held her up like she weighed whole world. Isn't that how love feels when it tests you?

Shnorhk swiped key card then, green light, no problem, motel door swung open, Shnorhk stepped aside.

"What happened?" Shnorhk asked second time. Maybe would have asked third time, if Young Man hadn't flicked on light.

Shnorhk almost screamed.

Almost because Shnorhk too stunned to scream. Too shocked to take step back.

Ancient Beauty gone.

You?

You are not you!

You are not!

Young Man also flinched at what blade of light expose, but hustled her inside, not even slam door. Bigger surprise: return moment later with money for fare.

Shnorhk not even look at cash.

"You need help?"

"We fine."

"I take her to hospital. No charge."

"Take damn money char tau one!"

But Shnorhk waved hands by waist like baseball safe what still felt like surrender.

"No charge."

Young Man looked confused.

"What happened?" Shnorhk asked for last time, even if his confusion transform no one, especially Young Man, still rude man, still Ferret Man.

Cracked lips curled to nasty smile, hateful smile, as Ferret Man buried cash back in pocket, then slammed door, slammed hard, though not before he spat:

"I lost cat."

Shnorhk wished he had spat back, tried to spit on door, but mouth too dry, coughed instead, clamped hand over mouth to keep from coughing more, as he stumbled back to car.

Better to get to Mnatsagan's. There was still time. Shnorhk even answer texts, finally, that he on way. This time with no stops.

Shnorhk drove fast too. Very fast at that hour. City transparent. And Shnorhk very good driver. Bonus: good driving mean focusing on only driving.

By highway Shnorhk forget everything else.

But then Shnorhk exited high-way, slowed down, and lost focus. Could barely see cars ahead let alone traffic lights.

Saw only face of what Ancient Beauty had become: skin sheeted over with ninefold creases, eyes glazed over blue, ash for hair, what any second could blow away, and that nothing compared to hands that rose to hide herself away: like twisted roots of dead tree.

Nothing familiar here anymore.

Only thoughts of seeing Mnat-sagan, seeing lads, warmed ice thing beating in Shnorhk's chest, even if arriving too late to play. Still time for jokes, maybe drink together tea, drink together something stronger, maybe even tell this strange story.

Shnorhk kept mind on reunion and slowly chest relaxed. Thoughts of lads playing and Mnatsagan's violin warmed away ice.

Shnorhk smiled. Maybe even laughed. ։։ Բարձրաձայն ծիծաղեց։ ։։ ։։ *Grace has such a beautiful laugh.* ։։

And when Shnorhk turned up Mariposa, with old professor's house not even block away, Shnorhk was so warmed by finally arriving, that whole street looked warm too, was too, glowing in orange, beautiful orange, more than orange.

Except—

Wait—

This warm not good.

Flashing lights everywhere.
Yellow police tape everywhere.

Then smell hits Shnorhk.

Shnorhk should drive away.
Plenty of excuses. No parking. But
Shnorhk not care about no parking.

Shnorhk just jumps out.

Leaves car in middle of street.

Shnorhk runs.

Or what is falling when falling is
just catching yourself before falling
all over again.

Shnorhk realize he also holding something. Shnorhk didn't just
jump out of cab and start running.
Shnorhk jumped out of cab, raced
to trunk, grabbed blond box, and
then started running.

Police cars are everywhere. Fire
trucks too. Everywhere smoke. Or
what smoke leave behind when
it starts to go: dullness. Specks
of dullness everywhere. Smell of
everything dulled.

Ahead, police marching his way, trying to clear more of block.

"I go to house there," Shnorhk pant.

"Sir, is it your house?" Oriental cop demand.

"My friend live there."

"Then you'll need to turn around. We're securing the area. This street is closed."

"I know my rights," Shnorhk yell. "I go to house there!"

"TURN AROUND!" Oriental cop yells even louder, hand lowering to gun.

"What's your name?" Shnorhk not back down. "I know my rights."

"Officer," someone behind him say softly. "Officer, he's with us."

Is Alonzo. Is all of them. Tzadik and Haruki.

Shnorhk insist Dimi just sweating, insist it just raining, insist if not rain just water from firehoses. Can't insist long. Dimi sobbing. Until he see Shnorhk, see Shnorhk with blond box, then sob harder.

"Oh man, of all nights," Dimi cries, face streaked too, giving Shnorhk hug.

Shnorhk see more police then, surrounding them whole time, pulling his friends aside again, with more questions, more taking notes.

Wait.

"Where Kindo?" Shnorhk blurts.

Big Dimi hears blurt, shoos aside his little cop, moves to Shnorhk.

"Kindo, he was shot."

"How mean shot?"

"Got him good. But only good in side of leg. EMTs got to him in time. He'll live. He's fine."

Shnorhk picture Kindo in back of ambulance smiling, maybe even still with sticks, playing gurney sides, IV bag for tom, getting medics snapping fingers, everyone clapping, smiling.

Except Dimi. Dimi not smiling.

And it's his big no-smile that give Shnorhk the will to look for first time past trucks and hoses, past all firemen, past flashing lights and dull commotion that comes with marking things and measuring things and asking questions and taking down notes about things.

Shnorhk heave in one big painful breath to face big picture: up
street, still out of sight. Shnorhk not
need sight to know place.

"Where's Mnatsagan?"

Dimi no answer, big Russian
chin just start to shake again, face
crumbling like fallen hillside, lost to
sobs again.

Shnorhk running again.

"Hey!" Someone shout from behind. No question cop. Probably Oriental cop. "Hey you!"

Shnorhk hear footsteps too, getting faster if not breaking into run, like fast walk can catch Shnorhk's fast run. Fast walk easily catches Shnorhk's fastest run.

Not Oriental cop. Someone new. Olive skin. Olive suit. Badge around neck like suit just won medal. Black hat with scarlet band like wants medal.

"Detective Özgür Talat."

Talat!? Offers hand too! As if such a hand could want just a hand.

Asks then for Shnorhk's name as if just a name could satisfy a Turk. Such a Turk as this wants whatever Shnorhk have.

Shnorhk start moving away again, moving still closer to house.

"I'm sorry, sir. You can't go up there. It's a crime scene."

"It's my friend."

"I understand."

"You don't understand! My friend live there. I bring duduk. I play with my friend."

"Sir, you need to stop."

Shnorhk stop. Though cop not stop Shnorhk. Shnorhk stop Shnorhk, from going farther, breathing harder, too hard to run now, to walk, to even breathe.

"Stop for who?" Shnorhk heave. "For you? For you I don't stop! I know rights! I have lawyer! I sue you!"

"Shnorhk," Alonzo says, catching up, hand on Shnorhk's poor shoulder, Dimi's too, big hand, on Shnorhk's other poor shoulder, both shoulders shaking.

"I'm sorry, man," Alonzo barely squeaks out. "There's nothing left."

Shnorhk shake them all off. Shnorhk will run again. But Shnorhk take only one step. Finds too soon what gap lies ahead. Between houses. Shape of things charred. Smoke rising into shape too familiar, what needs no shape ⁛ *the way we see within the dream ending* ⁛ ⁛ the gaze closing ⁛ ⁛ **the gaze beyond all dreaming** ⁛, cursing them all.

Only it's not just bones of burned house or house made no more of smoke wavering Shnorhk.

Something really is there.

Shnorhk see it. For a second. For sure.

⁛ What was it, Shnorhk? ⁛
⁛ *You can almost tell.* ⁛

But it's gone if still reminding him of something. If possible to be reminded of something you fail to recognize.

For a moment, Shnorhk thinks again of strange girl in doorway, stupid!, already not thinking of that her, stupid!, but, worse!, the her Mnatsagan knew so well.

"Arshalous say—" Shnorhk cough out, "—so long as daddy play everything okay. Oh."

Shnorhk's chest really clench then. Hard too. Hold on to all costs. ∴ *TFv1 p. 399.* ∴ Breath gone for good. What good? No sense anymore except what this clench grab is cut through with rage, fear, and pain.

Shnorhk can't move. Can't breathe. No more air out. No more air in. Goodbye speech.

Everything seized.

"He went back inside," Dimi
explain to Turk.

"It was a furnace," Alonzo add.
"But he rushed back in."

"A pyre," Tzadik confirm.

"It was hell." Haruki also saw old saint turn around and hurry back into flames.

"But what inside was so important," Turk ask, "that your friend would walk into hell for it?"

Genocide

"*Nobody cares.*"

— The Long Goodbye

"Lisssssssts," the old man ∴ *Shnorhk Zildjian* ∴ saws out of himself, still clutching that wooden box like a little kid can clutch an empty lunchbox like it's Mommy herself. And then he just drops. Just like that. To his knees first, then with a weird sigh flopping over on his side, but somehow twisting enough to still take the last hit on his face.

Good thing there are plenty of medics. Enough milling around that locals start treating the place like some clinic. When Özgür first arrived, an elderly woman had flagged an RA ∴ **Rescue Ambulance** ∴ with gripes about an ingrown toenail. This, though, is no ingrown nail.

Within minutes, two paramedics are hard at work. Good news is that it's no heart attack. Pulse is fine. Breathing's the problem. Maybe asthma-related. Probably from all the smoke, what's been slipping into the weave of Özgür's jacket for hours now, into his hat, be there for weeks, if he can't get it cleaned right. But who cleans a fedora? Maybe the rain. No rain.

Anyway, by minute three, this lucky son of a bitch is masked in oxygen, strapped down, and carted away.

Good riddance.

Hostile from the outset. Özgür knows the type all too well: primed with accusations, pointing fingers before they've heard a single fact, scribbling down names, threatening lawsuits, shouting every chance they get about the ACLU. He's the guy age has finally bested. Forget notions of wisdom, he doesn't have a clue, just getting in the way, turning up to demand sense and just making a mess.

"Know him?" a P-II ∴ P-two ∴ working the perimeter smirks. He's all my-job-is-done and now he's just waiting out a long night. Clean-shaven. Looks like he *just* shaved. And slapped on shiny aftershave too, on that big American jaw ∴ *Grady Vennerød* ∴ **TFv1 pp. 227, 235** ∴. "He's a cabbie. T-boned my car a few months ago. Ran the red and tried to lie his way out. Judge saw straight through that shit. Fucking Armenians. They lie every time. Every time. You know that."

"Do I look like someone you can talk to?" Özgür yawns.

P-II burps up a curse but gets back to the tape.

What's Özgür even doing here? This isn't even a case he'd want to work. He looks around for Detective Perry or funny guy Carter while thinking up the excuse he'll need to leave. Their absence, though, is probably why Özgür got the call. Definitely not on Cardinal's order. With Özgür's retirement papers all ready-set-go short of submission, it's not hard to imagine Cardinal holding off the D-III on the Homicide Table with a grumble: "Let that sleeping dog die." Özgür still could have protested. But he didn't.

Özgür still has no idea why he drove to the address.

Maybe he just wanted one last taste of the scene before he got back to all the shipping and storage boxes multiplying in his apartment, devouring the stacks of LPs of who he once was and might not become again. Or maybe Özgür just wanted to flash his shield one more time. Watch some P-II Dogs moving aside, which they did, even if it didn't mean much, certainly not enough to answer why Özgür had really chosen here over sleeping next to Elaine.

Özgür adjusts his hat, two thumbs restraightening a brim warping from too much sun and sweat. What a mob tonight. Plenty of patrol cars and bikes, with enough collar bars to keep the P-Is jumpy. PeSTs ∴ TFv1 p. 164 ∴ and press are a step behind, but they'll be here soon enough to witness the usual gripes.

"Get on the RTO ∴ Radio Transmission Officer ∴. We don't need Gangs and Narcotics. I don't care what anyone at Northeast is saying. I'm telling you they didn't say it. The last thing they want to do now is come for this Little Armenia fire sale."

Or:

"H2's not your average hooptie which makes this at least a G-ride."

Or:

"SID ∴ Scientific Investigation Division ∴ just arrived. We're calling this arson, right?"

Or:

"Fucked. This is fucked. This is— Sir! Sorry, sir."

Or:

"Whinningham?"

A transient even made it past the tape to beg Özgür for some change: "I promise, man. I'll fax you back."

And on top of it: LAFD ∷ Los Angeles Fire Department∴ is everywhere. Trucks parked up on sidewalks, hydrants tapped, hoses running all over the place like the surfacing roots of a tree so high Özgür will never know its branches as anything but sky, the night sky, still sticky with bad smoke.

Özgür spots Photos going over the scene. Still no sign of a news crew or a KTAL bird hovering overhead.

If power draws a crowd, this isn't much of anything.

Maybe some celebrity-driven drama is going on elsewhere, drawing media and PeSTs away. But if Özgür's theory is right, that the number of people at an event indexes the level of power, then some reality star's escape from rehab exceeds in influence commonplace violence like this, meaning in the future some Twitter star could end up president. Özgür shudders, because if that's right then these kinds of tragedy are slowly being rendered invisible.

Özgür considers heading over for a closer inspection of what's left of the house, encompassed by puddles and plenty of fire-retardant foam oozing over sidewalk and curb.

The trouble is that the victim's friends, with the exception of that raving lunatic who just got hauled off to some hospital, are so nice. Musicians too. Good enough to earn their neighbors' praise. That's pretty rare. They play late too and rarely get a complaint. Mellow stuff but still.

They call themselves These Affictions.

There's Dimitri, or Dimi. Big Russian guy with a forehead broad enough to compete with his immensely broad shoulders. Would belong on the gridiron if it weren't for his fingers: long and as faint as a pencil sketch with hard lead. Balalaika player.

The one named Haruki isn't anything faint: short and focused. All his movements seem a choice. Maybe he plays the biwa that way. Or maybe his playing's just the opposite.

Özgür didn't meet Kindo. They all swear he's the cool one, cracking jokes even with a round in his thigh. He could make you laugh with just the right rhythm of his palms on a stack of collapsed pizza boxes, though he preferred the marimba. His beautiful set of rosewood bars, handcrafted in El Salvador, was another casualty of the fire.

Tzadik plays keyboards. Blue-eyed, raven-haired, and affable through and through. Soft-spoken. Soft too in the way he looked. Soft even in the way he listened. That all-around kind of soft that in the wrong crowd gets hurt but in the right group keeps the night light and easy and moving along just so.

Alonzo looks and is L.A.-born, but nowhere near the east side. He grew up in Huntington Beach and Culver City. No tattoos. Went to Berklee College of Music in Boston and was now studying at USC, where he met the victim. Özgür wouldn't have pegged him with ambitions to join an orchestra someday. His bassoon, sadly, was also consumed by the fire.

"I left it behind when we carried Kindo out. All of us were just trying to get everyone out."

In fact, not one of their instruments survived.

Haruki describes how first something like a rock smashed through the living room window. They were all playing. Dimi and Tzadik confirm that the shots happened about the same time. Only Kindo was hit. Alonzo and Dimi heard the second explosion later.

"The water heater," Dimi grumbles.

"Or the furnace," Haruki speculates.

"The water heater," the big Russian insists.

Haruki stops speculating.

Özgür keeps taking notes about the crime, but what he really wants to know — what seems an equally important mystery — is how these guys found one another. It's like that quip about The Beatles: "The really amazing thing about that band is that those two guys met." Özgür wants to know what kept them playing together for so many years in the small home of an old fiddle player. He's touched by their care for one another. Özgür wants to be in the room when they play. He'd even pay. Though no amount of money now is going to make that happen.

How is it then that flame and gunfire visited a "jam session of despairing tones," as one cranky neighbor described their music earlier?

Only the bassoonist seems to have the through line for the night and even got eyes the perps. Should get him with an SID sketch artist while his memory's still sharp.

"Parking's tough in this neighborhood," Alonzo says, starting again from the beginning. Like his gestures, his talk is just as quick, but not in a nervous way, more alert and nimble, with each syllable — even if he's stammering or looking for the right word — finding the right note. "Tonight I got a space just a few blocks away. Fountain's fine but I didn't walk there. Lot of traffic. So I dipped south and, okay, just walking, me and my case, when I hear the turn, too sharp, tires squealing, acceleration then, and, okay, loud and getting louder. Too loud and too aggressive to not wanna look." Alonzo takes a deep breath, something getting in the way of where he's got to go next. "It's a Hummer. H2 I think. Show me a pic, okay, and I can identify it positive. Bright yellow. Not gonna forget that. Got two antennas with two flags, both the same: red on top, then blue, orange on the bottom. The guys inside are white. All with black hair. I saw three for sure. Two in front. One in back. The guy in the passenger seat up front was in a brown t-shirt and the only one wearing glasses, sunglasses. He was the one who started yelling at me. The one in the backseat was yelling too, but the glass was up and I remember thinking that's pretty dumb. Whatever he had to say, okay, was muffled. Probably the same as the guy up front. Mexican stuff. Typical racist slurs. You know what I mean. All that bullshit."

Özgür stops him. Asks him again about the Hummer, the flags, the sunglasses, patiently reviewing every detail.

"Bey, you one curious motherfucker," Hattaway would say when Özgür got like this with him, putting down his trumpet, if still all grins. "That's why you get this music, man. Can't have jazz if you can't ask. Listen to Charlie Parker, and I mean really listen, that cat is always asking. Question marks all over the place but played in that way that knows you gotta know that no one knows when we're really gonna get going. And that's the only way you get to the joy of going, where we all been going to since time began, before time began, and with jazz, long after time ends."

After which Hattaway had demonstrated how a downbeat on the one can ask. How a rising trumpet line can ask. How a pause can ask what hurts the most.

"Though not all silences be the same," Hattaway warned. "You know that. There are those that open you up. And those that shut you down. They say some can even kill you. But I don't believe that unless you're willing to give that some silences can make you live again."

At some point Özgür finds the right pause and Alonzo catches it right and opens up. With a long sigh.

"Man, it was like fucking middle school again. They're throwing out, I mean you know, like 'Hey beaner!' 'Hey wet-vac!' 'Anchor baby!' 'Field rat!' But I mind my business, walking straight ahead. I'm done looking up, until the guy starts asking where I'm from. That's it. I just take off. Sprinting. But got a good look first. Glad I did. Man, they were angry. One had a gun. Maybe the others too. I don't know. I'm running. Looking for an intersection, a busier street, praying for some traffic. I don't think they expected me to run. Not that fast. I'm pretty fast too. Even with my case. Man, my bassoon." Alonzo shakes his head, the memory eating up his breath. "They followed. Anger like that always follows. I heard the engine roar, heard the acceleration, okay, but then they did something unexpected: they slammed on the brakes. And that's when I heard how they were thinking, and you know this was bad. Doors opening then slamming fast. I didn't have to look. I could hear their shouts. And then I heard their footsteps, them trying to run me down, or I don't know, get within range to gun me down. I was shitting myself. Should have probably dropped my case, but I was too scared to do anything, okay, but hold on tight, man, and run."

Özgür nods, glancing at Alonzo's feet, like he just might run again, because he sure isn't keeping still now, going up and down on his toes. If feet could tell the tale of a thought, these would already be taking off.

"Okay, so I jam it across some yard, bounce over a fence, another fence, dogs barking like crazy, lights popping on. I know I was flying because my legs are torn up now. Must have pulled my groin muscle or something. Left arch still feels funny like I broke something in there if you can break an arch.

"Behind me, I hear people coming out of their homes, to check on their dogs, all the commotion. Maybe someone saw the guys chasing after me. I'd check that out for sure."

Özgür writes down the name of the streets and the descriptions of the yards. When a community alert and plea for witnesses go out, he'll make sure to get some volunteers and extra cadets to canvass those buildings in particular.

"Lots of shouts, lots of barking, but I could hear they were still after me, hitting the same fences, crossing the same yards. And I couldn't help but think: seriously?! You're gonna work this hard?! What for?! What did I do?!

"I looked back then, okay, just to make sure. It was the one in the passenger seat. The one with the gun, in a brown t-shirt, designer jeans. I could tell that, okay, because — and I remember this clearly — they had all this white stitching over it, easy to see. I didn't see the gun though. That's not saying he didn't have it. Man, he was so mad. I remember that too clearly. Like I killed his mother or something.

"He didn't let up until he got to that corner right there. By then I was already at Mnatsagan's front door. My buddies were coming out. Someone called the cops. He ran off fast. No sign of the Hummer then.

"The cops came pretty quick and I gave them this same description. You can check that report, right?"

"I will," Özgür says easily. "Do you remember the officers' names?"

"Maybe Gimenos? I forget."

Özgür waves off the question. The report won't be hard to find. "How long until they came back?"

"A while. We were playing by then. We almost didn't at

all. I was still pretty shook up. We just started trying things like we weren't going to play for real. We were also waiting for our friend Shnorhk to show up. You met him."

"The one they just took away on oxygen?" Özgür asks, vaguely pointing in the direction of where the wheezing guy had face-clocked himself on the blacktop, clutching that wooden box, hauled off by the second ambulance. There used to be three. Now there's only one. Özgür would be happy to see it leave empty. Knows it won't. He knows who comes last. Unfair to even call it an ambulance now.

"Shnorhk's not so bad, okay?" Alonzo adds quietly. "In fact, we gotta get after him. His wife will be worried. Do you know which hospital they took him to?"

"I'll find out for you," Özgür answers, trying to smile. No doubt some tone in Özgür's voice or even in his silence had betrayed his irritation with the cab driver. Özgür has to remember that Alonzo has ears. Good ones. What would Hattaway have said about bassoon players?

"I did overhear that he's fine," Özgür adds. "Recovered in the ambulance. Wanted the ambulance to drive him back."

Alonzo relaxes again. "Sounds like Shnorhk."

"Also a musician?" Özgür asks, as gently as possible.

"Duduk player. Phenomenal player. I mean, we're talking Armen Grigoryan, Djivan Gasparyan. Maybe, okay, not that level, but they're who come to mind when you hear him play. Ask Shnorhk though, he'll say he's a better driver. Tell you he used to race cars, cars that were falling apart, that's how you can tell a great driver, by how well they race what's falling apart. He always makes us laugh." Alonzo trails off then to someplace sad and beyond recovery.

"I'm sorry," Özgür offers.

"This was going to be his first time playing in a long while."

"Why a while?"

"He lost his daughter five or so years ago. He and his wife still haven't recovered. Shnorhk hasn't played since."

And with that, Alonzo's closing up. They got too personal too fast. Özgür kicks himself. Another reason to retire. Another reason to kick this over to Carter or Perry. What's at stake is fast but not personal. Özgür's job is only to find out the who in the what happened here when a little house went up in flames.

"Were you playing when they threw the Molotov cocktail?"

"Yeah. As Haruki said, it was like a rock crashed through the window. Then the living room corner was just . . . fire. I was by the other window because, okay, I was still afraid they would come back and then I saw the Hummer. Like it was all I could see. Big and yellow with flashes coming from the passenger window and they were gone and everything was burning.

"Kindo was already down. His leg bloody. Then the ceiling was on fire too. Dimi was screaming that they were shooting. Tzadik was yelling to get down. Mnatsagan got to Kindo first. Maybe we hesitated. Thinking of carrying him into the backyard but that was farther and by then the fire was on all the walls and had eaten through the ceiling. Place seemed made of paper. All we could do was rush through the front door, crouching like we could get shot at again, but the Hummer hadn't come back, and people were out, calling 911, smoke everywhere. I started counting heads. That's when I realized he wasn't with us anymore. At first that was okay. He was old. I didn't expect him to carry our wounded buddy. But then I couldn't find him nearby. I sure wasn't looking for him back there. But he wasn't anywhere else either. The house was the only place left to look, and that's when I saw him running back inside. A moment later there was that second blast and then more smoke and it seemed a lot more flame." Alonzo drops his face into his hands. "There was no going in after him."

"Was he looking for his violin?" Özgür asks.

"He was working on a book."

Alonzo catches something in Özgür's silence.

"Are we done? I'd like to find my friend Shnorhk."

Özgür asks if he wouldn't mind meeting with a sketch artist. Then someone's shouting Özgür's name. Özgür needs some paper to fold. Something to *katla* into a new existence. But he has no paper on him. And however many reams it takes to write a book is all ash now.

"Oz, they found the last one." It's Detective Carter. Özgür's glad to see him. He needs a joke, even one that doesn't get him all the way to a laugh. A smile will do.

"When did you get here?"

"Captain found out you were running the show and fucked up my date."

"Glad to see this barbecue is in good hands."

More yellow tape cordons off the burn zone, where firemen still mill around, by the hoses, by their trucks, some still catching their breaths, others emerging from what's left of the house, where Özgür and Detective Carter head now, Alonzo starting to tag along.

"Are you sure?" Özgür stops to ask.

Alonzo stops too, hesitates.

"Only if you're sure," Özgür advises, leaving Alonzo to hesitate some more, before returning to his friends.

Carter has been grinning since he saw Özgür, but the grin goes as they approach the gurney topped with a bloom of black plastic cradling charred meat. The body is actually steaming. Özgür's seen plenty of mean stuff but never a smoking corpse.

Fingers and face seem to have hardened into a black glaze, but the cavity of the body has split open, oozing viscera with deep striations of cooked blood.

"It's official: hello, homicide," Detective Carter musters. "And right on cue: the news."

Özgür looks up to find not one but three helicopters circling above, including a KTAL bird with one bright spot searing down through haze. News vans have also started to arrive, including one from KTAL. Özgür wonders if he'll see his friend Gael ∷ TFv1 p. 429 ∷. Plenty of reporters and PeSTs are now at the tape. The P-II with the big American jaw suddenly has work to do, though the way he moves and grins makes him look like he's auditioning for movie work. Like he thinks he'll get cast in a show or at the very least end up in tomorrow morning's *L.A. Times*, front page, above the fold too, if the paper hasn't folded altogether by then.

"Guy must have been someone."

"A professor," Özgür answers. "He wrote books."

"About what?"

The gurney disappears behind closing doors turning the last ambulance into a hearse. Özgür leaves Carter and goes off to find Alonzo again.

"The duduk player mentioned 'lists.' Any idea what he was talking about?"

"Mnatsagan's research would be my guess," Alonzo answers.

"Genocide," Haruki throws in.

"Genocide?"

"He collected oral testimonies of survivors," Dimi adds.

"The Armenian Genocide," Haruki clarifies.

No stopping the awful shudder that tears through Özgür then, like he just swallowed broken glass, shredding up his guts along with everything else, though it's his guts that keep announcing the pain. What an announcement too. Second time that night, and bad enough Özgür has to excuse himself to try to walk it off, circling the remains of the professor's house, as if smoke might say more, or ashes could end pain.

"Detective Yıldırım!" It's the P-I from the K-Mark murders ∴ Stan Gebbis ∷ ∷ **TFv1 pp. 163–164** ∴.

"You're working this?" Özgür thought the kid was Southwest.

"No. I heard *you* were working this. I really would love to buy you lunch and, you know, pick your brain a little."

"Here I thought you were gonna ask for an autograph."

"At lunch."

"Talat."

"Huh?"

"It's Detective Talat. Yıldırım is my middle name. Start there."

"Fuck. Uh. How about if I just call you Oz?" Stan yells after Özgür, who's already moving away as fast as he can.

"How about I pick your brain with a fork?" Özgür yells back.

It goes then from that bad to so much worse.

"Good to see you, Oz," Balascoe says.

"You and I have to stop meeting like this. Your partner will get jealous."

"That boot's not with me. I'm RHD now." ∷ Robbery-Homicide Division. ∵

"Congrats," Özgür says, nodding, clearly not doing a good job concealing his surprise over the promotion. How the hell did that happen?

At least Balascoe's enjoying himself: "We got this now. LT got the three fourteen. Enjoy your liberty."

So as it turns out, so much worse isn't too bad. Özgür's glad to be rid of the case. He wishes Balascoe good luck and means it. Balascoe fucked-up with the K-Mark murders, but who doesn't fuck up? He's good police and the work is hard and the pay isn't enough for what every good cop has to lose.

Özgür tells Balascoe that he'll have the IR ∷ Investigative Report∵ ready by morning and goes off to give Carter that assignment.

But the smoldering ruins check his roll. Özgür even squats down close to the melted porch furniture. The fire really took it all. Even the copper pipes melted in the blaze. They'll have to haul it all away to some landfill and bulldoze the lot. Not even ashes anymore. Just garbage.

By a pile of debris built by axes, Özgür finds something that's not garbage: the wooden box the taxi driver was holding. Özgür doesn't need to look inside to know what a few flips of a few latches will reveal. He tucks it under his arm. Alonzo will get it to his friend. It doesn't weigh much but still feels heavy, the way a coffin might, especially if it's too little.

Something else feels heavy too. Heavier. Özgür senses it briefly beyond the smoldering mounds where the back of the house collapsed in on itself. Maybe on a fence or leaping down to the lower limbs of a scathed tree. The glimpse is fast — an unblemished blur of brightness.

Özgür's first thought is fire. The fire isn't out. The fire has come back. Then thinks it's just window light from an adjacent apartment complex, flicked on by a beautiful hand. But the windows are dark and the fire is out and whatever it is isn't there anymore.

:: But you know what you saw, Özgür, don't you? ::

:: Moving along that charred branch of a coral tree. ::

:: Even worse: you saw how it saw you. ::

:: **The careless flick of a tail reminding you . . .** ::

:: Gazing down at you with those familiar eyes . . . ::

:: **Accusing you . . .** ::

:: As if to say, here I am too, again . . . ::

:: **Beyond remorse . . .** ::

:: Beyond music? ::

:: Beyond reason . . . ::

:: **Just.** ::

// or: bomb?

A theory that fits all the facts is bound to be wrong, as some of the facts will be wrong.

— *Francis Crick*

Bomb!

// or: bomb?

// which seems unnecessary to question

// let alone

// to comment out what seemed so amply

// evident

No doubt that instant could [for Anwar] **have** described anything but his centrality in the event demolishing his home and all lives within [his sweet twins {his inspiring wife ‹the life of his beautiful daughter «even these strangers ⟨. . .⟩»›}].

Anwar's mind had even raced ahead of grief to marvel at the experience of observing [however briefly] this disclosing of a massive explosion [not to mention the marvel that his mind could process so quickly everything {making any slo-mo feature on any phone seem as rapid and cranky as those old flicker tapes at the turn of the twentieth century ‹Anwar even wondering «in tandem with this overriding wonder» another big if: if his mind could work still faster ⟨?⟩ could he ostensibly slow time down to a standstill «and thereby live forever ⟨in the heart of the blast?⟩»›}] with this onstage center seat revealing every brilliant contour of a death continuing to unfold yet never arriving?

Anwar suddenly became a child again!

Not in shape or by the diminishment of grey [unless you included some {miraculous ‹rapid›} aggregation of grey in his frontal cortex {which could not be included ‹because there was no way that was«n't» happening›}].

Rather some access to his blissful discovery of paradoxes [in the way that simple equations suddenly brought Zeno's arrow to a standstill {and not just the numbers ‹because back then the numbers were less real than the arrow «golden for some reason ⟨and floating⟩» **befo**re Anwar's eyes «bullets too ⟨and detonatio**ns**⟩»›}].

Fatima!

Shenouda!

Is this what you experienced too?

Their appearance in his thoughts unanticipated
and yet not unexpected.

Mother!

Father!

يا ترى اولادك لسه بيحبكم اد ايه!

Even as their appearance demands an admission of
a fiction.

Even as shattering glass confirms the creation.
Upholds the declaration. Defends the conclusion.

And it keeps shattering in some awful loop.

Worse than any frozen arrow.

A frozen rain of glittering blades flying sideways.

How else to imagine such a possible impossibility [caught between breaths {within one breath ‹still held «until it serves as neither a breath nor a non-breath ⟨a place ⌈no longer alive⌋ ⌈no longer dead⌋ set as ever on reinforming itself⟩»›}]?

In the face of this impossible ignition.

In the face of the inevitable shock waves.

Gone progenitors. Gone progeny.

By a kiss of a fuse. With the flash of a mistake. Must be a mistake. Round two[!{?}].

Anwar's last gasp of thought [there in his living room {watching the one ‹who had attacked her once already› attack her again ‹or was it *was* attacked«?» plus thrown back«?»?›}] was to throw himself back to another long distant yesterday that never was

// Anwar assembling newspaper clippings

// in a fever trying [over and over] to reconstruct the stories of the past in such a way that the past could not have happened [or must have happened along an alternate path]

// Anwar's collage of longing

// The '80s [1984] were still the art of scissors and glue sticks on an American wall

// Both of them had returned from Beirut [escaped {the employment ‹Shenouda had found there «rebuilding in the coming ⟨ongoing⟩ undoing of Lebanon»›}]

// Back in Cairo. Just in time.
// Cairo was fine.

even as Anwar is also midway through a step [toward Xanther {toward the attacke‹«r»d›}{where else would he go?}] and yet not in either step [at that moment a staggering misplacement {or displacement} of both heaviness and buoyancy {between the determinacy of direction ‹interliminal «in both his physical arrangement and mental derangement»›}] which further fragments himself into even more trees [forest{s‹!›}] of alternate outcomes.

Years later [when {one night} Anwar had recounted his parents' deaths {or more so the break their deaths had visited upon him the following year while he remained in New York}] Mefisto had introduced him to Nufro ∴ *Salbatore Nufro Orejón* ∴ [and his seminal paper 'The Physics of Ero' {written in 1978 ‹republished as *Particle Alternatives* «in 1988 ⦅'. . . how a particle's "choice of path" actually determined "the property of the destination" despite classical expectations when taking into account decoherence and path integrals.' [I. Maldonado]⦆»›}]. Or [in Mefisto's words] 'the extraordinary Chilean physicist who maybe was' ['the great Chilean musician who maybe was' {'the finest composer of "What if . . ."' ‹'the grandest numeric interlocutor of "Or this . . ."'›}] whose work still stands against the unbearable and the inexcusable [continuing to pose in formulae the means to revise whimsical alternatives to all our nows].

Anwar was dancing again with Nufro . . .

Even as he was also seeing again [what he never saw firsthand] the oily plumes of smoke and broken walls tossed aside in the still-raining-down particulates of departure [what offers no hope of reassembly let alone return {to where Anwar still returns ‹via what newspaper clippings reported «or friends and family told him over the phone ⦅or via his actual return to Egypt later ⟦finding their building rebuilt ⟦and the broken glass at his feet '⟦'حاجة تانية ' 'مش من دا'⟧'⟧⦆»» even revisiting the call he had cut short ‹with a joke at the behest of an overdue assignment› the night before they both dissolved the following morning into the scintillae of their story's terminus ‹as if a different shape to that conversation

735

«longer or shorter ‹or just different›» might have made a Nufro difference› while wondering all the while what he would never know: how their near-perfect disappearance had changed Anwar ‹his thoughts «his loves ‹his fatherings of futures›»›}].

Shattered glass was everywhere then and now as the inarticulate explosion continued to perplex the Ibrahims' living room.

Nufro departs and Vladimir Arnold appears [always reappearing {thanks to استاذ Latif Abdelghani ∴ **and Taher Elgamal** ∴}]. One Anosov map [on a manifold M {mapping M ‹from M to itself›}] keeping cool pace with these wild imbrications [of {broken} shards {under ‹re›view ‹if never under «Anwar's ‹literal›» foot›}]: one three decades old and the other underway.

قنبله اسراءيليه! ' ∴ 'Israeli bomb!' ∴ 'عصفور إسرائيلي! ' ∴ 'Israeli bird!' ∴ locals claimed for weeks.

The floor had vanished. Dangling pipes and sheared I-beams could no longer testify on behalf of solidity. The ceiling had also evaporated. Wires melted away like hair recoiling as it burns. And [two or three] storeys down was writ the burr of black char where the blast had preformed its primary vanishing act [{never neat ∴ *TFv2 p. 123* ∴} Fatima and Shenouda were not the only parents disappeared that morning].

Anwar had stared the photographs into a secondary act of oblivion: over-substantiating the explosive radius in order to forget the furniture forget the photo albums forget the records forget the bound bundles of treasured letters generations old forget the carpets forget the rack

of spices forget the cupboard of flour forget the book-
cases forget a tiny glass bottle with a tinier ship inside
forget the toothbrushes always two just two side by
side forget their soft vulnerable feet with their bending
toes readjusting as they stood side by side carrying out
their routine of toothpaste and flossing and rinsing and
mouthwash and amusement over this dull and necessary
routine they had dedicated themselves to ' لده ۳۰ سنه '
:: *for thirty years* :: ' ۳۰ سنه مَش صالحين ' :: *thirty imperfect years* ::
' ۳۰ سنه مش حاستسلم لأي حاجه ' :: *thirty years I wouldn't give up for
anything* :: ' لأي حاجه ' :: *for anything* :: ' جنب باباك ' :: *beside your
father.* :: ' جنب مامتك ' :: *beside your mother.* :: ' احنا كنا مش زي بعض '
:: *We were so unalike.* :: ' احنا كنا مختلفين ' :: *We were so different.* ::
' لكن من خلالك أنور بقينا حاجه واحده ' :: *But through you, Anwar, we
became one.* :: and at least they were still one when they
left side by side before the apartment vanished blowing
loose a chunk of building which in addition to killing
six residents also killed one taxi driver parked on the
street and two pedestrians passing by.

And still in that abattoir of domesticity [as Anwar
discovered firsthand {when he ‹finally› got back to
Cairo}] there was one miracle. Local residents were still
amazed. Jaded soldiers [who arrived after the detonation {whom Anwar had spoken with directly}] were
equally amazed.

Something had survived.

People had spotted it from the street. Neighbors had spotted it from their windows. Firefighters and police and soldiers had spotted it when they ascended the ruins of the structure.

It had sat for hours on one I-beam between where there was no more ceiling and no more floor. In fact in the same place everyone swore had to have been his parents' bathroom:

// what Anwar could never forget

// though until now [how?] had

// his mind

// fixed itself against

// remembering even that

// [?]

one tiny white cat.

Which Anwar had replaced conveniently enough with Vladimir Arnold's more hopeful elocution:

$$\Gamma\left(\begin{bmatrix} x \\ y \end{bmatrix}\right) = \begin{bmatrix} 2 & 1 \\ 1 & 1 \end{bmatrix} \begin{bmatrix} x \\ y \end{bmatrix} \bmod 1 = \begin{bmatrix} 1 & 1 \\ 0 & 1 \end{bmatrix} \begin{bmatrix} 1 & 0 \\ 1 & 1 \end{bmatrix} \begin{bmatrix} x \\ y \end{bmatrix} \bmod 1.$$

But Anwar was wrong [as he had been so many times before {so many ‹many› years ago}]: despite the momentary [if absolute {time-banishing}] certitude that [exactly {in the manner} as each of their respective parent{s} had vanished] both he and Xanther were also to be consigned to fire

. . . they were not.

This was no bomb.

Anwar even spent some time [afterwards] looking after their guests. He [finally] learned their names. He also apologized to Tian Li for relaying the wrong address [forgetting to ask how they had known the correct address {did it matter at that point?}]. He assisted Jingjing with getting her into the taxi [still there waiting {now that was a small miracle ‹they must have paid him a lot «was the old lady rich?»›}].

Both Tian Li and Jingjing looked gaunt and subdued and [in the end] they disappeared as abruptly as they had arrived [leaving behind an impossible confusion were it not for Xanther's indisputable radiance {intact ‹with her «now indisputable (?)» cat›}].

Anwar somehow even forgot the slap.

The twins [though] had awoken with screams and crying [requiring immediate attention]. Anwar did his best to walk back their fear [and panic] to annoyance [and consternation]. Astair came in next to resettle them in a place open to sleep [hard {because Les Parents ‹as Xanther would call them› couldn't offer a satisfying explanation of what exactly had occurred downstairs}].

First Astair read them *Nanette the Hungry Pelican* and then [even if the twins didn't understand it] *The Little Blue Kite* [which seemed the right amount of soothing {Anwar could see Astair was soothed}].

Anwar recalled a moment in their recent visit to the Natural History Museum when Astair had warned the girls to step back:

'Don't touch that. It's real.'

That's when Jingjing's strike returned. And again when Anwar went to find Xanther [still not in her room {now downstairs in the piano room}]. The hit had been too real. A violation [an awful act of violence {in their home!}] that seemed as terrible as it was untouchable.

Xanther's face bore no mark.

Also: how had she risen like that in the face of her father's charge to stop him with just a hand [Xanther {stronger than he's ever beheld her before ‹had he ever seen her move like that «so smoothly»?›}]?
[in the end] It was Tian Li whose face seemed to bubble and bleed [enough so that Anwar's thoughts had {instinctively} raced to getting ice and antiseptics {except that this ‹blemished?› vision also vanished ‹the testifying sound of the hit gone too «leaving Jingjing ⟨of all people⟩ wailing on the couch»›}].

Anwar's memory still protested.

He had seen Xanther attacked. He had seen her knocked down.

His mind was still hunting for local minima or maxima to render the event sensible.

And the sight continued to sear through him [long after the strangers were gone]. Even if Anwar had also observed Xanther and Astair and Tian Li practicing Tai Chi a little later. Even if he had witnessed some strange ritual officially bestowing upon Xanther the cat.

The whole thing was just too fucking weird.

'How is my daughter doing?' Anwar asked Xanther in the piano room [at that moment {‹though› shouldn't this be the other way around?} experiencing another kind of weirdness {that his own daughter was reminding him of someone else ‹a stranger› whom he saw earlier that day while driving ‹a girl «in a hijab» with black braids still poking out and pink everywhere and something «what though ⟨!!!⟩?» stuck on her shoulder›}].

'Pretty, uh, fricking weird, all of it, huh?' ∴ !!! ∴ Xanther responded [standing by the piano {studying the keys ‹like she might start plunking out a tune›}].

'Time to sleep?' Anwar asked gently.

'Oh yeah.'

She looked exhausted [but not to the point of depletion {while the little beast seemed more . . . ‹what? «vital?»›}].

'Daughter,' Anwar asked from the shadows [to the shadows] 'do you have any notion what that was about or even who those people were?'

If she had shrugged he would have apologized for letting them get even near her. Xanther didn't shrug.

'Tian Li and . . . ' [what did she say? { شجرة م د }] 'have been friends for a long time. She needed to say goodbye and I needed her help.'

[{and except for the fact that these words seemed to placate Xanther ‹entirely›} to Anwar's mind] This was an absolutely nonsensical thing to say. Was Xanther lying? Had all this been some kind of strange rendezvous arranged online? Should he press her harder?

'I like that' was what Anwar finally mumbled.

Anwar sure didn't like what he saw in the mirror [a little later] while getting ready for bed. He looked gaunt. Deep lines stabbed at his eyes. His hair seemed to loop with more grey [{who was he kidding?} white!]. [near his hairline] Black dots on dark seemed larger [moles {Anwar must get to a dermatologist ‹just moles «if they still made him antsy ⟨why did too many ordinary moments present the penultimate moment?⟩»›}].

He fell asleep at once but seemed to awake at once too. Astair was cupping his jaw with her hands [like a gentle nest {‹guarding him› the gentlest parentheses}].

'You were grinding,' she whispered.

'Imperative dreaming,' he whispered back.

It was his phrase for dreams that [regardless of their content] seemed charged with a compunction to act [whether reformatting a hard drive or raking up leaves {a sculpture of Dionysus with a panther ‹seen once in the Prado ∴ **TFv2 p. 613** ∴› had been tonight's ‹though how that required action «what the dream still seemed so charged with» eluded Anwar›}].

Though also hanging on to his thoughts [{an additional‹?› juxtaposition ‹what Astair would call parataxis «this memory»›} not a sculpture but a painting of Muhammad on the Venice boardwalk] was an argument [so sparked] that to see the depiction admits to the tyranny of the eye [confesses that the mind has not yet found its way to experience more subtle senses {which ‹if nurtured and strengthened› would still view the depiction but view it insubstantially}]. Therefore those who take great umbrage over such a caricature are not only admitting that they are in the thrall of vision's tyranny but are also idolaters of the eye's attachments.

Anwar sits up now. No need to turn on the light.

'Where are you going?' Astair murmurs.

'I clearly remember hearing glass breaking but I never saw any.'

[so {in the dark}] Anwar makes his way down the stairs. [in the piano room] He finally turns on the lights. Nothing's out of place.

He pulls back the drapes over the French doors. The glass is intact. [however] On closer inspection several panes closest to the floor have hairline cracks challenging the corners.

The lights in the living room go on. Astair has come down too. She's in tiny panties and wearing one of his shirts [Anwar never tires of this appropriation {nor of seeing her in tiny panties ‹she has deliciously long legs›}].

'There are cracks here,' he says. 'But I have no idea how long they've been here.'

'I remember breaking glass too. I was sure one of us dropped some wine glasses or something.'

Glasses is right [like a whole rack of them].

This is the first moment they've had alone [to confront what had happened {their shared experience}] but [suddenly] all Anwar really wants to do is lead Astair back to their bedroom [or take her right there on the couch {let pleasure further distance themselves from what had conjured in him an expectation of death ‹is that why he's suddenly so aroused «some survival instinct kicking in ⟨. . .⟩ or just tiny panties?»?›}].

'What the fuck was all that?' she asks.

Anwar remembers Tian Li saying that the cat had chosen Xanther [when the cat {sitting in the middle of the coffee table ‹in the middle of all of them›} had walked past all of them before {quite deliberately} climbing up Xanther's arm and taking a seat on her shoulder {right next to her ear ‹tail wrapped around his paws «probably purring»›}].

And then not too long after that Jingjing was saying someone would kill Xanther.

Anwar had come in then but again Xanther had warned him away [this time with just a word {'Stop!'}].

Tian Li was speaking rapidly then [in Chinese {if that was what it was}] and Jingjing seemed to have stopped translating until [after Xanther had said something {in effect voicing her lack of comprehension ‹her frustration?›}] he had also said something about slaughtering someone with eyes of flame [which sounded pretty manic {if not drug-induced}].

The part that mattered [though] came next.

Jingjing lunged at Xanther. Or rather at the cat. His arms outstretched [fingers spread wide {eyes fixed on the blind animal}].

This time Xanther was not caught off guard.

She didn't really move though.

She didn't have to.

What happened next happened after Anwar had dropped his eyes to the floor [as if fearfully anticipating {somehow alerted to} what was about to take place].

Anwar never wanted to be one of those weak people who needs to find some alternate mystery to the matter-of-fact grandness of life in order to secure a hope that there was still power left for him to enable his future.

But alternate mysteries are what keep recurring in this memory.

A bomb not a bomb. An explosion not an explosion. More like a jet engine [directed {‹terribly› controlled}]. Loud enough to pop both his ears. Hurt them even. Were they still hurting [no]? Still ringing [yes]? From that storm. That fury. Spitting fury.

Spit?

Every bone of the house was shaking.

Something questioned.

Shattering.

Doors slamming?

'Maybe it was all outside?' Astair asks now [kicking off her slippers {climbing up onto the couch}].

'The oddest part—' Anwar confesses '—in the middle of it, I suddenly remembered that in the aftermath of my parents' death, soldiers reported seeing in the ruins a small cat.'

'You've told me that before.' Astair pauses [one hand on her hip {the other about to draw the curtains back}].

'That it was white?'

'Huh. I think that part's new. Is it true?'

'Fair question.'

'Could you have reconceived it because of Xanther's cat?'

'Maybe!' Anwar laughs. 'Most likely Xanther's cat has provoked over the past few months an association with that particular aspect of my parental legacy that I've repressed.'

'The connection too painful to bring to light? After all these years?'

'It would explain why I would so assiduously urge and guide Xanther to find the original owners.'

'The due-diligence stuff?'

'All that,' Anwar nods. 'Find a way to get rid of the cat in order to avoid so visceral a connection.'

'Or find your parents again.'

And then [as Astair turns away {pulling aside the curtains}] Anwar can't help but appreciate her ass. Is that what blinds him from seeing the windows? He only sees Astair jerk back [nearly falling off the couch {at least Anwar moved quickly this time ‹unhindered as if there for her all the time «*is* there for her all the time ⟨catching Astair in his arms⟩»›}].

Her clenched cry is the only thing resonating in his ear now:

'Jesus Christ!'

(devastation's gaze)

The Dialectical Spirit of History would be an extravagant redundancy even if one could imagine what sort of animal it was supposed to be . . .

— *Tom Stoppard*

Astair (stepping up (on their sofa) barefoot (in a thong)) wasn't oblivious to the desire Anwar was registering in his gaze (also in his speech (however distant from the subject of something still closer (something (still) unhurried))).

It had been there in their waking too (despite the urgency of his mission (she had felt his need (as it moved through exhaustion (through a doze (through a dream))) transformed (finally) into desire (their bodies (like old friends (they were old friends) lying so close the whole time communicating this blossoming want)))).

When she followed him downstairs her own (bodily) ache for him was as much in charge as her curiosity about the question of glass.

How had they forgotten that centrality in mystery without investigating more before they retired?

(though the living room windows (hidden behind a wall of curtains) were still secondary to letting Anwar gaze at her long nude legs (he loves her legs almost more than he loves her ass (though he loves her ass plenty))) Astair had grabbed hold of the curtain (but hesitated there (like her husband might choose that moment to seize her (have her on the sofa (until she turned and buried him (beneath her (the illicitness of the living room's openness turning her on more (children suddenly transformed into taboo-inflicting figures of sleeping parents))))))).

Astair even spread her legs a little more.
And bent over.

She was sure Anwar's breath caught as hers caught too ((as she was sure of her absolute attractiveness at the moment (as she was sure of his absolute desire for her in that moment)) the two of them caught (delivered!) into this early hour (where they would neither have to disentangle themselves from the stickiness of the previous day or call it morning and so submit to the requirements of the coming dozen hours) where they could in a non-hour find the time to be kids be lovers be lustful make love fuck fulfill themselves in a different way a different place an unusual position) for as long as they could hold on to want (so long as she didn't pull back those curtains).

Astair was a little surprised by this show she was putting on (by how wet she was (ambushed by lust)).

Then again she was surprised by so much of what had happened that night.

She had raced (from Hatterly's) straight at the intruders (expecting a fight (spoiling for a fight (she'd fight Anwar too for letting them in))) and then the old woman (Tian Li) had clasped her hands.

There was nothing magical about those hands. (like her face) They were just old. They were dry. They were tiny. They were empty. Except for the fact that they now held Astair's (as if in their own lightness they conjured up (welcomed! (gave a place for!)) Astair's fullness).

If hands can blush Astair's hands had blushed. Because it was more than a touch.

The gaze (too) was so delighted to see Astair that it shocked Astair with a vision (understanding?) of herself she had never experienced before.

Social media had given everyone a taste of fame (the old Warholian adage "Everyone will have fifteen minutes of fame" transformed into "Everyone will be famous for fifteen people" ∴ *Momus* ∴) but what of the (singular) look that beatifies you with thanks (because you have somehow become the bestower of blessings (how often does that happen?)?)?

The reason wasn't so much Astair either (except that she was the mother) but Xanther.

How humbled the old woman had become before her daughter (she had wailed at her first appearance (Xanther rushing to her (like they had known each other their whole lives (and could offer the comfort of lifetimes)))).

(later) Astair had spied the two practicing Tai Chi?! Tai Chi! (Xanther (now and then) answering Chinese(?) with her usual "Uhs" (("Huh?") and even "My mom!"))!! Until Astair was invited to join in (hesitant at first (skeptical (that went with observing close up the old woman's fluidity (experiencing her light touches (tiny adjustments that seemed to open in Astair a way to fuller movements)))))).

Xanther's progress was even more baffling (Tian Li settled her in a way that Astair would have not thought possible (those bubble-headed knees (suddenly) in fixed communion with the whole of her (an unfolding (that recalled (with breath-biting immediacy) how Xanther had already once before unfolded herself (and stopped Anwar's charge)))))).

Maybe that (the freshness of that memory (combined with the revisiting understanding that there was now here (in the center of their living room) a stranger)) had caused Astair to challenge the old woman (even if Tian Li had already invited Astair (with gestures) to push her (maybe already sensing (in Astair) aggression (that combative heat rising)?)).

Astair had placed one palm on the woman's forearm and the other on her shoulder (trying to disregard the blissful look on Tian Li's face (as if thrilled to have this moment (enjoying every bit of it)?)).

Astair (though) was determined not to be disarmed by old age or some show of smiles. Nothing too severe but still a good stern shove. Show her who's boss.

Tian Li and Xanther were both laughing.

Astair had somehow ended up on the other side of the old woman (like Tian Li had become a door and then a doorway and then the nothing Astair fell through). Astair had to catch her balance. Tian Li looked like she hadn't moved. Not even Lambkin could demonstrate that kind of emptiness (so void Astair was convinced the stumble had been her fault (as if Tian Li had not participated at all)).

Xanther spoke up then: "She, uhm, says: don't help the river; it flows without you."

"You speak Chinese?" Astair blurted (confused (was this something taught at Thomas Star Kane?)).

"Uh, huh, she, like, speaks some English?"

Tian Li then invited Xanther to push her and the two barely moved (Astair blushed (ashamed (really) to behold her daughter display greater sensitivity before (clearly) a great master of the art form)). Xanther applied a little pressure (what appeared as a tiny sway) but (before getting sucked into the void) swayed back (resettling again).

When did that happen?

How did that happen?

Astair had been studying with Lambkin pretty much since they moved to California (Xanther for mere months (and under Astair's inexperienced tutelage too)).

Astair's conclusion fell on the cat. At that point it had been on Tian Li's shoulder (and like it belonged there too). (obvious to a mother) Xanther was (herself like a mother) constantly checking in with the creature removed from her yet still right before her. Why push it away or rush past it? Closeness to the little animal invited Xanther to find her root (which she did (magnificently)).

That was the other surprise: tonight (Astair had believed) had been all about claiming the cat (isn't that what the young man had said (isn't that what he (Jingjing) believed?)?) only to turn out to be about the cat (under the guidance of this (magnificent) stranger) claiming Xanther.

Xanther had even named it!

And what a gorgeous name she had picked!

So evocative!

Mythic even in its reality. Cloaked in sea mist. Crowned in clouds. With roots so wide to encircle the world (hold it (while the world too held up this spectacular rise of green needles and rutilant bark)).

Astair even recalled that such magnificent sentinels were so tall they supported (in their tops) entire ecosystems (never needing to descend to the forest floor (angels free of the earth free to fathom the sky)).

(and then (when the little creature had ignored Tian Li and Jingjing (disregarding even the strange little gifts bestowed upon Xanther (black scissors? (an acorn necklace?))) and hopped up her arm (already demonstrating more life than Astair had seen before!) to settle on Xanther's shoulder)) He somehow seemed as permanent and looming as those ambassadors of a deeper time offering their own brightness and shadow ∷ *Ah, Steinbeck!* ∷.

Even if the name (also) seemed familiar (in that way that jangles the mind and heart with (uneasy) premonition). If Astair still couldn't place the association (remember the connection).

∷ **Oh, she'll remember.** ∷

∷ I can (almost) remember. ∷

∷ *She must remember.* ∷

758

So many welcome surprises had followed that they (nearly) drowned out what should have prevailed as the dominant experience of those hours.

The attack.

For starters.

What had risen before Astair as cause for murder (had mobilized her to such action (at once)).

Anwar too.

(Had Astair even seen (ever!) such a display of fury in her husband?)

That young man had beat their daughter down!

But Xanther had stopped both of them (with that uncanny fluidity (and poise (and disregard (for whatever they thought they saw (on display not even the slightest trace of such a vicious blow (her face unscathed (her balance uncompromised (her smile bold and assured enough to make Astair doubt what she'd just seen (it sure stopped Anwar)))))))))).

How often does a parent's overreaction amplify a child's minor reaction? Though tonight what would not even count as a minor reaction had reduced to nil two parents' over(?)reaction.

But what then to make of what finished (answered?) this night?

The grab.

For enders.

When Jingjing had suddenly lunged forward (and though at Xanther (long dirty nails (once again!) daggering in the direction of her sweet face)) Astair understood that (this time) he was after the cat.

Maybe over a year of Tai Chi had taught Astair something (because she seemed to sense the arrival of something her whole body already knew to fear (all of her (this time) trying to get away)).

Not that Astair can remember what she saw (either omen or fear (or the sound!) had banged her eyes shut!).

It couldn't have been more than a blink either (a few blinks (at most)) but Astair's returning focus revealed Jingjing (sobbing) in a heap at Xanther's feet. (unaffected by whatever had just sheared through the room (the whole house! (what also helped further diminish one (already) departing reality))) Tian Li was helping the young man to his feet (!) who was (in the next moment) turning to help the old woman retreat to their ride waiting outside.

(after they were gone) Astair and Anwar had immediately set their attention on the twins (raised from their dreams by the terrifying sound that had inhabited their home (though what else had ((also) briefly) filled the living room? (Astair sensing in her momentary blindness more than just the shadow of a blink (rather a much darker and deeper shadow filling every corner (but cast by what? (or whom? (if not by Xanther herself?)))) a shadow persisting as Astair tried to amuse and soothe Freya (the most disturbed) and Shasti (disturbed the most by Freya)))).

To calm them Astair held up her hands (cupped like blooms ("Smell the flowers!")) and then spread her fingers out like they were commemorating a birthday cake ("Blow out the candles!"). They tried to smell. They tried to blow. She did it over and over again. Until they were breathing in (deeply) and exhaling (completely) and (finally) relaxing.

((though) even while reading aloud to them ("'Good heavens, what *is* it?'" (and later "After all, a little blue kite is just a little blue kite. Where is the fear in that?"))) Astair could not shake the (debilitating (exhilarating)) feeling that she had (all of them had) barely survived something.

Her hands jittered as she turned the pages ((the first book making the point that (in a work for children) illustrations make the point)(the second making the point that (in a work for all ages) the point makes the illustrations)).

Xanther was fine.

Astair (though (when she had (at last) crawled into bed)) was shaking (only exhaustion (and a pounce of deep (and immediate) sleep) stopping that (though it couldn't stop the dreams (half-remembered snippets (one by Sandra Dee Taylor (if she even said it): "The truth isn't something we see, hear, feel, read, or even know. The truth is what we move through." (but that's not true!))) or speculations (it's not that we use only a small portion of our brain (we use almost all of it) it's that the way an individual maps her hundred billion neurons is not even a tiny (tiny) percentage of 100,000,000,000! (even a factorial of ten percent (10,000,000,000!) would be enormous (and hardly diminished if identity resides in a still smaller batch of synaptic connections)) meaning one person's identity is almost zero percent of the possible (collective) personality of their mind) Astair feeling like she was dreaming like Anwar) feeling him sleeping beside her (seizing him (ah her man (her Anwar)))) before finally falling asleep beside her beautiful husband.

If only they had stayed in that clutch.

Or awoken to passion's clutch.

Or if only he had just seized her on the couch.

"Jesus Christ!" Astair grunts (falling back (but Anwar's there (if not to hold her up in time (then still catching her in the nick of time)))).

"إن شاء الله" Anwar grunts too (when he sees what curtains have kept hidden).

Their curtains are made of heavy fabric ((stiff) brocatelle (with bishop sleeves) with additional cotton layers (backed too with blackout to reduce the sound of outside traffic (not to mention dim the eyes of prying neighbors))).

They are (also) rarely ever opened (hardly touched (not even cleaned (not since the Ibrahims have lived there))).

Astair's first touch set a universe loose (lint drift and countless motes and (other) spectral mites suddenly rising (and spiraling (like tiny galaxies)) into the room). But what they announced was worse (as both she and Anwar together pull back these crimson and amber folds hiding their two big windows).

The windows stare back at them like two black (dreadful) pupils (with only the hint of irises (made of (color-drifting) spears of glass (those that still remain ((with muntins dismissed) jutting out of the stiles)))).

Even stepping back into the middle of the room fails to distance either Astair or Anwar from the terrible sight (though it's unclear if Astair's ██████ is the horror of seeing or the horror of being seen by such bright awful (shifting (even pleochroic!)) eyes (devastation's gaze)).

Anwar (dear (dear) Anwar) just laughs.

"Sonic boom! That's it! Oh, no doubt. No doubt either that we're not the only ones. Some jet, some military exercise, breaking the speed limit where it shouldn't."

"Anwar—"

"I'll handle the inquiries. Don't fret. I'll make the calls. If the whole block can get together and coordinate, we will likely get the repair costs covered and perhaps a little more. Though maybe it's best if you call Hatterly. You know him better than I do."

"Anwar—"

"I would have loved to have seen it blast by," Anwar chuckles (genuinely pleased (relaxed (by the only thing about this whole (bizarre) night that makes sense (to him)))). "Must have been some kind of flying machine. Must have come in low, too. To break all this glass. Wow!"

"Anwar!"

"Yes, love?"

"The glass, love. Look at the glass."

Once again Anwar is unsettled (how Astair hates to unsettle him).

"I'm looking. It's gone. Except on the edges there."

"None of it's in the curtains," Astair says quietly. "None of it's on the floor behind the couch."

Anwar steps forward then (close enough to look through one of these terrible eyes (to take in their front lawn ((under streetlamps (and moonlight)) alive with the glitter and razored glints of comminuted glass))).

"Oh," he groans.

"The glass is all outside."

Cold Milk and Figs

> *But I have a family.*
>
> — *Victim #18*

Isandòrno wakes with the dawn. He watches the changing light change nothing.

—Something has happened there that cannot happen again, The Mayor had said ∴ **TFv4 p. 646** ∴.

Later, The Mayor clarified his instructions: —Close The Ranch.

—If there are animals? was Isandòrno's only question.

—I don't care about animals.

First, Isandòrno shoots Maria in her bed. He is surprised Juan is not with her but surprise cannot stop the bullet from pancaking inside her head and soaking her pillow with the spill of dead thoughts.

Juan comes out of the bathroom and Isandòrno shoots him next. He shoots him in the chest. Juan struggles for a moment and probably lives long enough to make out Isandòrno entering the room of his children.

Nastasia dies from a bullet through her throat. Estella escapes down the hallway. He cannot go after her until he has first dealt with the men outside. They will bring rifles and likely an automatic.

Isandòrno stumbles through the front door and falls onto the porch. He clutches his left shoulder.

—In the kitchen. On the floor. I don't know who he is but I wounded him.

Adon and Santiago creep past him. They carry only rifles. What if they had found a Las Leonas warrior in there? Isandòrno shoots them both in the back.

While they die Isandòrno reloads
his pistol. Then he takes one of the
rifles and goes after the boys.

Chavez and Garcia are already running. And maybe because they know Isandòrno won't cross the border, they flee north. The border, however, lies miles and miles away. Still, Isandòrno agrees with their choice: north is their only chance.

It takes Isandòrno a moment
to aim but he only fires twice.
Chavez paints the air with a puff
of cherry before he falls. Garcia
clutches his neck where the round
has likely torn through his jugular
and carotid.

Isandòrno strides the 100 meters amazed by the force of the dawn. It vibrates with colors he knows are there but will never see. Reds and greens if they could wed and not find brown. Blues and yellows if they could wed and not find green. Combinations impossible for his eye. Impossible for any eye.

Cane bluestem pushing toward
the blueing sky caresses his boots.

Isandòrno remembers once sleeping all day in a hammock. He woke to find cold milk and figs. He thought he heard waves but it was only the wind. The sea could never have existed in that place.

The boys are both dead by the time he reaches them.

Squat cacti sharp with violet
bursts and filaments of web catch
Isandòrno's eye. He does not stop.
Spider bones and ocean fossils
remarry dust with every step.

But plenty here can never be crushed, no matter the size of the heel.

The desert always delights Isandòrno. Its clemency is eternal. Its perdition permanent. Isandòrno welcomes its judgment even if the desert does not judge. It does not need to.

On the way back to The Ranch house, a shot rings overhead. After a few more strides, a second shot dares the day. The third round doesn't come until Isandòrno is much closer.

Estella's hand shakes after each
pull of the trigger.

She doesn't know. She's too young. What does young know how to do anyway except point?

Isandòrno's mother told him once that no one with a gun would ever kill him. What did she know? She was wrong about so many things.

Isandòrno taps nine on fingertips and tugs both earlobes.

By the time he is twenty feet from
her, Estella has shot twice more.

One round remains.

—Why? she pants.

Isandòrno only nods and waits.
The last shot comes the closest,
kissing the dirt at his feet.

Estella throws the gun in defiance. She won't nod or have time to wait. Isandòrno fires into her belly.

She is still alive when he climbs into Juan's dusty Bronco.

He had gone inside to look for cold milk and figs but found only some hard cheese in the kitchen, which he did not eat but decided to take with him along with a bottle of water.

Isandòrno rolls down the window and watches her. He had dropped next to her the wooden jaguar head her sister had given him. It waits beside her now doing nothing.

Estella kicks the earth until the earth takes her. Isandòrno starts the truck.

Next to him, in the passenger seat, sits the bowling bag filled with U.S. dollars.

Isandòrno has a few hours' drive. He will go to the address Juan gave him and find the mother of Garcia and Chavez and tell her what befell them. Maite will not believe him. She will offer to pay him back. He will tell her again what happened to Garcia and Chavez. He will keep telling her until she believes him. Eventually she will choke on her sobs. Eventually she will choke on her promises to pay him back. Then she will tell him about her daughter Luna. She will scream. She will collapse. She will fight back. She will keep promising to pay him back.

And maybe Isandòrno will listen.
Or maybe he will just shoot her in
the face. What she knows makes
no difference to Isandòrno.

He knows everything he will ever
need to know.

Isandòrno will live forever. He won't live out this day.

It's the same either way.

Bury the Heavens

My Name is in him.

— Exodus 23:21

In bed, still night, at least darkwise, even if night's almost over, Xanther needs her friends. But it's way too early, and anyway she doesn't want to just text them, she wants to see them, like this past weekend, hanging out with Cogs, Mayumi, and Josh. Kle had been finishing his latest *Enlightenment* called *Satori Tomy Whack #5*. This one asked if meditation, like, that, controls your breathing and slows your heart might really be performing a microlobotomy. Kle visualizes how not enough oxygen detaches synapses until the one doing it feels detached from the hurting reality requires. "Buddha Bob feels super, though the feeling has no bearing on the reality of life. It's just a life hack." The sting part, because Kle's stuff usually has a sting, is that getting all peaceful like that actually doesn't lead to some balanced civilization. The world dies in the last frame.

"So if all that mindfulness stuff isn't the way, what is?" Mayumi asked.

"There isn't a way," Kle shrugged.

That got Josh giggling. Xanther joined in though she wasn't sure why, except that Josh's giggling was pretty infectious.

"Spoken like a true Zen master," Cogs nodded, which maybe said what giggles couldn't.

Would they giggle too about Xanther's latest dawn apprehension? And like, really, that's the scariest thing she can imagine right now, and she doesn't even have to imagine it, since light's already starting to filter in, or Astronomical Dawn is, which Anwar taught her about once ∷ Nope ∷, or maybe not, what Xanther doesn't even have to see, already feeling it seep through the walls.

Probably it had something to do with what Tian Li had shared with her, in the moments that followed when she confessed to Xanther that the name she had known the cat by was lost, stuff involving Xanther too, somehow, with these odd stories, some concerning dawns, how most will be an irresolute gray, but forty green dawns in a row ends all suffering, though Tian Li had only known five green dawns and never consecutively. Red dawns though, those were bad news, just three in a row meant The End, Xanther all the while understanding too that the greens and reds Tian Li meant had nothing to do with colors Les Parents or her friends see, but only those that the forest offers.

Tian Li talked about that forest too. *You can never find the blue flame. You can never go through the forest. You can never behold the Great* . . .

"Stare a thing in the eye," Dov had ordered ∷ **TFv3 p. 519**∷. "Soft eyes," Mom had counseled ∷ **TFv3 p. 838**∷. Either way, Xanther knew what she had to do.

Has Xanther ever wished so hard that Astair would already be awake?, boiling tea, cursing a crossword, because like what if this is already the third dawn?, and it's sopping red?, bleeding out?, and they're all too late?, and this is it?, only just enough time to step outside and watch everything die, Xanther's heart already racing hard, way ahead of thinking, because only a heart knows what lies beyond a thought.

But no one's up.

She can already sense that.

Not even dangerous little one has stirred. Maybe that's a good sign? He's deep in a curl of slumber. Xanther buries him under a fold of blanket, then throws on some sweats and, willing herself downstairs, tiptoes, bare toes, to the foyer, where she suddenly freezes, unable to do more than nervously unwrap a stick of Cedar's Sugar-Free, like chomping gum could resolve, or at least answer, why she's so afraid of what lies beyond the front door, paralyzed by an anxiety she keeps calling stupid, but still can't explain.

She doesn't even believe that dawn stuff, which she probably just misunderstood anyway, right?

:: You tell me. ::

:: *Yes. Tell us.* ::

:: **She can't hear you. She mustn't.** ::

:: *Would the world end?* ::

:: Don't tell me! ::

The necklace with the wooden acorn is still on the coffee table as are those strange scissors with curvy black blades. Xanther remembers how Tian Li demonstrated the way to trim the claws and how with each snip Xanther felt waves of relief, the terrible blue bite of flame inside her not just dimming, but going out completely, extinguished, disappearing, lost in that immense forest, taking with it those searing waves of heat that had threatened to burn through her skin like paper set on a stove, immolating Xanther's every perimeter and limit, suddenly buried beneath fields of midnight snows.

Had Xanther ever felt so good? So strong even?

Then why wasn't she still in bed, sleeping as late as she could?

Tian Li said, or did Jingjing?, that she would have to slaughter someone. There was that. Slaughter?!

And something else too.

He is very hungry.

Tian Li's voice echoes through Xanther as she pads across the foyer. Should she return to check on him? She forgot to check his teeth. But Xanther just stops before the door, transfixed by what she fears most, even as oodles of whys keep mocking her, because what does she really expect to find? Some rip in the sky? Does Xanther really believe that something out there could be so altered?

Xanther is really grinding down now, trying to chomp back an even worse Question Song, trying to understand what has really changed, as if anything could change, did something change?, the gum in her mouth hardly standing a chance, tearing apart in fact, into these gray, tasteless, rubbery strands.

Because what if really, what this is, is just Xanther finally becoming one of those people who is afraid of everything, whether it's going outside, or staying put, or closing a door, from here on out always finding a new thing to fear, afraid period.

Xanther bites down hard. She's no Fraidy K.

She unbolts the deadlock. Then flips the lock above the knob. Presto. The door swings open.

That easy.

And sure enough, here it is, the rising dawn, already heading into, what's it called?, Nautical Dawn?, ∴ *Yes.* ∴ ∴ I don't know how she knows that either. She doesn't know that. ∴ ∴ **She knows more than you.** ∴ ∴ I'm her. She's me. I don't get how that's true but I get that that's true. ∴ ∴ **You're allways and only a subset.** ∴ ∴ Oh, how sweet. ∴ yes, 12° below the horizon, the sky not bloody, but an unremarkable battleship gray, streaked maybe with a little gold and fingers of flame, and sure some pink in there but not much, and slate blue too, maybe shifting toward something like chrysocolla ∴ What? ∴, or not, but overall the sky is just fine.

Encouraged, Xanther slips out onto the front stoop.

There's nothing she can do about the security announcement, though that's weirdly absent, or just really late, and anyway the door is closed again.

Oh, there it goes.

The voice is the same. The languages familiar too. But their meanings have changed, or at least the first one has, in English.

Alert: door closed!
¡Aviso: puerta cerrada!
Hadhari: bab mughlaqan!
Jǐnggào: mén guānle!
Alerte : porte fermée !
Uyarı: kapı kapalı!
Ushadrut'yun: durry p'ak e!
Vnimaniye: dver' zak'ryta!
Achtung: Tür geschlossen!

Xanther recalls then the sensation of things closing, more than a sensation, what she felt happening throughout the house, beyond the house, as if everywhere locks, latches, and bolts were forbidding entrance, and not just entrance, forbidding exit too.

Wait!

Xanther stops chewing. Stops walking. Their whole front lawn is glittering with pieces of broken glass! Talk about, like, the best reason to stop walking, especially since she's barefoot. Xanther even gasps a little as she takes in the two gaping windows. Except for the lack of fire or any sign of smoke, they look as if a bomb went off inside.

The little blue fire is back on too, never failing to pop to life as soon as Xanther crosses the threshold, though it's not nearly as bad as usual, and anyway, neither it nor the slivered glass in the grass is why she's stopped chewing.

Which is what really matters.

It's tasteless.

Really? Already? That's, uhm, very weird.

Xanther at once reaches into her sweatshirt pocket and pulls out the pack of gum. She unwraps a fresh stick and puts the old piece in the foil. The new one is just as void of flavor. None of the juicy delight each chew usually rewards her with.

Xanther stands there going through every stick. Not stale either. Tasteless! It takes an empty pack and a lot of round balls of foil before she remembers how when Jingjing slapped her and she fell down, she hadn't felt anything, or at least before the pain should have seized her, it was seized away by something else, someone else, Xanther discovering then the old woman bearing all the signs of that strike: scratched, bleeding, and bruising, hurt far worse than Xanther too, if she had suffered it all without assistance, is that what had happened?, Tian Li had somehow assisted her?, leaving at least one thing clear: Tian Li centered in those magnificent blooms of Cedar's Sugar-Free Bubble Gum, which without a second thought Xanther had devoured, all of it, gone-gone, like way gone.

Oh.

Is this the price of such flowers?

What other price will Xanther be obliged to pay?

She had sure felt the gravest obligation weigh upon her when she was the most confused, at that point assuming from what Jingjing kept telling her, that in exchange for scissors and a necklace, he was taking back the cat, he even called her a "foolish child" like a curse, spit flying with his pronouncement, except in the face of the pronouncement, little one had suddenly stretched, yawned, and then climbed up onto Xanther's shoulder, where he stayed while Tian Li whispered a lot of things and Jingjing kept spitting more things, until he was more spit than words, until he was instructing Xanther to slaughter someone with eyes of flame, whatever that meant, which was when, when Xanther was puzzling over how to respond, Jingjing suddenly lunged.

No confusion about that. Xanther knew exactly who he was after ∴ Excatly! ∵ ∴ *Really?* ∵ ∴ Back off ∵.

It even felt like she knew it before Jingjing even knew he would lunge.

It rose through her feet first, like Xanther was plugged deep into the earth, into a current that's always available, but for a switch, what she hadn't flicked, wouldn't even know how to flick, what Jingjing had though, probably without knowing it either, the creature on her shoulder, his alertness, being the switch, clicked on by an observance so sensitive it seemed a premonition, closing the circuit, granting entrance, somehow, to the power suddenly rising through Xanther's feet, all around her really, rooting her as it supported her too for what came next . . .

Dwarfing the power of the earth.

Dwarfing the power of the sky.

And, really, Xanther just wanted to warn him.

But Jingjing's hands were already snatching at the cat.

And all the candles went out.

Pomegranates on the table and floor burst open.

Something horrible already there and everywhere.

And far, far away and right next to her ear too. Even as it grew at once too distant to understand and at the same time so loud, and wow!, did it get loud, terrifying ripples rippling outward, abandoning any center, where Xanther remained rooted, the only safe place?, or sorta safe?, maybe?, as everything surrounding her seemed to shatter at once, beyond splintering wolves, the banished pack, oh no!, what had she done?, Xanther already blaming herself, uprooted and useless in this upheaval shivering her senses, before rendering them nil, as the terrifying roar continued to batter the room.

For a moment, Xanther thought the walls would fail, the ceiling fall in, the chimney bricks surrender to a down-ward spiral of undoing.

None of which mattered compared to what else sharp-ened its purpose in the escalation of that warning . . .

What streaked before Xanther's eyes . . .

Slashing toward Jingjing's face...

Xanther somehow managed to reroot herself :. So _extraordinary!_ :. :. **I concur.** :: :: I, uh, me? :: in the only ground left: herself,

throwing her shoulders

away,

a deep arch nearly drawing her scoliotic spine straight, straighter than ever before, as she continued to bend like she'd never known herself to bend before, maybe not like Neo bending backwards, not that far. After all, she wasn't dodging bullets, though she was dodging on behalf of Jingjing, what he couldn't anticipate, what she was originating, the air around her materializing into an impossible accuracy,

claws

not from her hand,

no Wolverine her, but lashing from off her shoulder, off-center, as if, yes,

a monstrous paw

was unleashing a swipe of bone-crushing force,

wielding

seven scythes of glimmer,

far exceeding the trivial hardness of metal, with points too sharp to believe, this one slash promising only one thing:

murder!

:. What!? How? ::

:: **From where else?** ::

:: _You both continually underestimate her._ ::

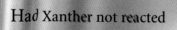

Had Xanther not reacted

so quickly,

The swipe just missing Jingjing, who never had time to minimize himself with even a head twist, forget falling back or reversing his lunge.

He only just managed to stop short, dropping an instant later to his hands and knees, patting his face then, examining both palms, sobbing too, because there was no blood, sobbing more because the wetness was only tears, what Xanther would not call tears, but something else, the water of survival, the water of fear.

Before Tian Li left, she stopped and turned to Xanther in the foyer. Something was already ravaging her features, but it didn't compare to the terror focusing beneath the stones. Tian Li didn't need to ask. The way she opened her face was enough.

Xanther expected her efforts to only materialize more density in those shadows, as they always did, for everyone, her sisters, strangers, and even Tian Li.

But she was wrong.

The stones at once began to lighten, as easily as they do for those nameless specters streaming endlessly through her snowburdened woods.

Only a thought now could flick them aside.

But it was a thought that caused Xanther to pause, because what if she discovered eyes of flame?, was Xanther supposed to slaughter this old lady in her home?, like Xanther would ever do that?, or much worse, what if Tian Li's eyes offered that peculiar bruised granate, what consequences would ensue then?

Xanther, though, understood that Tian Li needed this, and on her behalf, Xanther, without a second thought, easily discarded the stones.

Tian Li's eyes were neither wild with flames nor doomed by red, nor were they even that ever prevalent turquoise.

"You are the forest!" Xanther smiled.

Tian Li also smiled. *No, young lady, now you are the forest!*

Know this too, in the end I visited a wealthy man's home. His son was very sick. Before meeting the son, I wandered through the elaborate rooms. Never have I been so scared. Never had I been so close. We had been there before, stalking together the same hallways.

Xanther understood that "we."

Many will call you blessed but you must always remember this: I have beheld weakness and seen through the eyes of power, but I have never seen through the eyes of weakness and beheld power. Weakness you can command. Power you cannot. Protect yourself and never treat lightly the true nature of your burden: we are weak and we are cursed.

Beside Xanther's bare feet lies a card. An umbrella washed in old rain ∷ *El Paraguas* ∷ ∷ **no. 5** ∷. Xanther turns back to her home.

She thinks of little one wrapped in blankets on her bed and knows he's not there. Already she can feel his and her own revival from their latest feast.

The forest itself seems differently awake now too, in a way that Xanther can't place, alive and familiar, and yet also changing with every moment, like a great storm suddenly liberated of its rain, except without downpour, rather these strange woods serving as storm clouds, releasing a different kind of rain, as if sleet were to suddenly abandon the earth, determined to bury the heavens above.

Except this is not sleet . . .

Everywhere those anonymous specters twinkle nakedly, like possible rivers and streams, with now and then the wink of something green, if not as bright as Tian Li then still ablaze with promise, and more significantly, out of the billions and billions of flickering turquoise, those few ∴ **TFv2 p. 588; TFv3 p. 539** ∴, brighter than garnet ∴ *No!* ∴, taste thicker than cherry ∴ No!! ∴, dark as long-ago read satisfaction ∴ *But—* ∴ ∴ **NO!!!** ∴ their forever fare, now exposed.

. . . as the stones upon their eyes fly to the sky . . .

Xanther raises her eyes to her own sky, where only birds and planes fly, and Civil Dawn reigns, mere minutes from abdicating its rule to the sun.

∷ **How The Verse speaks through us . . .** ∷

∷ *Voice is never enough.* ∷

∷ . . . ∷

∷ *Step into the sadness.* ∷

She already feels the entwining so innately that the need to say the name seems beside the point, but Xanther whispers it anyway.

∷ **We tried to describe a world.** ∷

∷ *Therein lay our vanity.* ∷

∷ But I never tried to circumscribe a world. ∷

∷ *Therein lay your salvation.* ∷

Even if he's already there, like the other side of a dream, on her shoulder first, a new star, a tiny cloud of softest white, and hardly still, or even just purring, but already hopping with a delighted squeak along her already outstretched arm, her left palm turned up for him, where he stops, lightly wheeling around to face her, smelling of smoke.

Has Xanther ever seen him like this, so spunky?, licking a paw, cleaning his nose, his brittle little whiskers, rubbing away something on his jaws, before, with a chirp, lifting his head to yawn. A big yawn too. All teeth accounted for, especially the canines, though their brightness and sharpness are nothing compared to what happens next, as the dark angular lines al*l*ways marking his blind eyes suddenly start to open, and whatever Xanther expected, what she easily could have described as thick forests overwhelming ruins, or black oceans galed in gray clouds, or waves of blue flame dying stars surrender when constellations change,

Xanther doesn't even think of color.

She just stares back into those burning eyes, burning with all the light that ever was, long after all the light that ever could be passed into absence, knowing she's too late, much too late ∴ *we were all allways too late if still somehow there to begin with* ∴, and there's no more chance to turn away, as at last this creature sees her, knows her ∴ as at last this creature knows me ∴ ∴ **knows you** ∴, as at last out of the absence of Xanther's fate . . .

Redwood awakes.

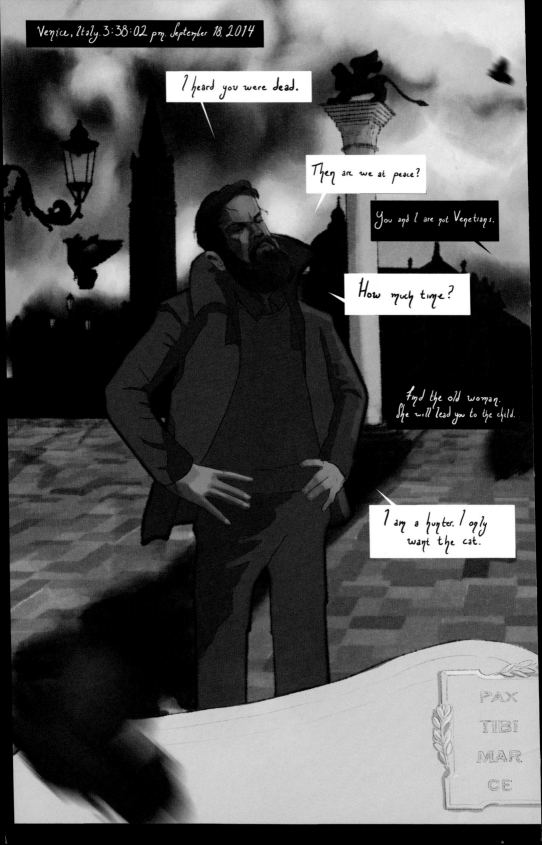

Only marked. A reprieve it seems. The book is still open.
Quil, you surprise me. They are entwined now. Part of the same diabolical mechanism. The only way to kill the cat...
... is to kill the child.
EVAN GELI STA MEUS

THE FAMILIAR

VOLUME 5

THIS IS A WORK OF FICTION. NAMES, CHARACTERS, PLACES, AND INCIDENTS ARE EITHER THE PRODUCT OF MULTIVERSAL ALTERATIONS TOO INFINITESIMAL AND COSTLY TO CREDIBLY ACCOUNT FOR HERE OR THE RESULT OF THE AUTHOR'S IMAGINATION AND SO USED FICTITIOUSLY. BECAUSE FICTION'S PROVINCE IS THE IMAGINATION AND THUS CONCERNED WITH THE ARGUMENT OF EMPATHY OVER REPRESENTATION, ANY RESEMBLANCE TO ACTUAL PERSONS, LIVING OR DEAD, EVENTS, OR LOCALES, NO MATTER HOW FAMILIAR, SHOULD BE CONSIDERED COINCIDENCES BORN OUT OF THE READERS' VERY KEEN AND ORIGINAL MIND.

Permissions information for images and illustrations can be found on pages 836 & 837.

Library of Congress Cataloging-in-Publication Data

Danielewski, Mark Z.
The Familiar, Volume 5: "Redwood"/ Mark Z. Danielewski
p. cm.
ISBN 978-0-375-71502-0 (softcover: acid-free paper).
ISBN 978-0-375-71503-7 (ebook).
I. Title.
PS3554.A5596F36 2015   813'.54—dc23   2014028320

Jacket Design by Atelier Z.

Author Drawings by Carole Anne Pecchia.

Printed in China

First Edition
2 4 6 8 9 7 5 3 1

www.markzdanielewski.com
www.pantheonbooks.com

FONTS

Xanther .... Minion
Astair .... Electra LH
Anwar .... Adobe Garamond
Luther .... **Imperial BT**
Özgür .... **Baskerville**
Shnorhk .... Promemoria
jingjing .... rotis semi sans
Isandòrno .... Visage
The Wizard .... Apolline

TF-Narcon 27 .... **Arial MT**
TF-Narcon 9 .... MetaPlus-
TF-Narcon 3 .... Manticore

MORE FONTS

TITLE .... DANTE MT

Preview #1 .... ᕙ(ㆆᴗㆆ)ᕗ & MetaPlus-
Preview #2 .... *Palace Script* & *Tiffany*
Preview #3 .... Nimrod MT

G.C. .... MetaPlus-

TIMESTAMPS .... **SYNCHRO LET**
Epigraphs .... *Transitional 511 BT*
Copyright .... Apollo
CREDITS & ATTRIBUTIONS .... GILGAMESH
Dedication .... *Legacy*

T.M.D. .... *Minion Italic*

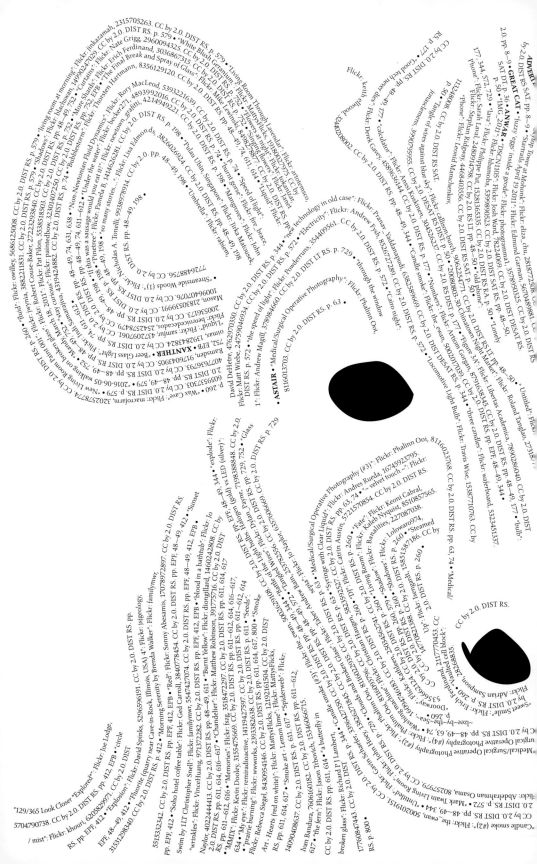

THANK YOUS

Caterina Lazzara

Jesse Stark Damiani

Edward Kastenmeier

Sandi Tan

Lloyd Tullues

Scott Milton Brazee

Detective John Motto and
Lieutenant Wes Buhrmester

Rita Raley

TRANSLATIONS

Arabic .... Yousef Hilmy
Armenian .... Niree Perian
Hebrew .... David Duvshani
Mandarin/Cantonese .... Jinghan Wu
Russian .... Anna Loginova
Spanish .... Juan Valencia
Spanish .... René López Villamar
Turkish .... Gökhan Sarı

MORE THANK YOUS

ADDITIONAL RESEARCH

Claire Anderson-Ramos
and Chris Kokosenski

GRAPHICS

Carole Anne Pecchia, Steven Smith, Mariana Marangoni,
Magdalena Panas, and piesdegallo

GOOD SENSE

Mark Birkey, Lydia Buechler, Michiko Clark, Catherine
Courtade, Dan Frank, Garth Graeper, Andy Hughes, Altie
Karper, Shona McCarthy, James Nash, Jennifer Olsen,
Austin O'Malley, Jordan Rodman, Anne-Lise Spitzer,
Stella Tan, and Dany Wolf

Atelier Z

Regina Gonzales

Michele Reverte

Noam Assayag-Bernot

A CIRCLE ROUND A STONE

PRODUCTION

COMING SOON . . .

THE

FAMILIAR

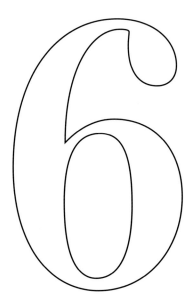

SEASON TWO

SUMMER 2018

Anna

the Hyena

ran.

She ran from the hyenas, from the nasty nipping ones not hers.

Hers were dead.

Many of the nasty nipping ones were dead too.

The breeze still held their dead smells.

The breeze still held the lion smell too.

But lions were the least of Anna's worries.

Like everything else now, they would also run.

Just like the buffalo already galloped away.
Or the bat-eared
foxes scrambled into their holes.
Or the vultures flapped
away.

Those who had a place beneath the ground fled
beneath
the ground.
Those who had a sky flew to the sky.

Anna the Hyena ran with the buffalo.

She ran for the deeper grass.

           She ran for the line of
deeper trees beyond the deeper grass.

      But most of all she ran from the sharp smell.

The sharp smell was a hot smell

         that was also a killing smell
   that was mixed throughout

        with the smell of men who
     made it sharp with

       their fire and their burning.

The sharp smell kept getting stronger

          until it seemed to
  Anna the Hyena that no breeze or wind

         would ever be strong
    enough to lift it from the world.

         Anna the Hyena also heard
the men's

        Woooooooooooooooooooots!
and **Haaaaaaaaaaaaaaaaaaas!**

The cries made her run harder but she

        jerked and jagged
when she heard the snaps and cracks

       and thuds which turned
 the air to a thing

     that could knock down buffalo and tear
  hyenas apart and

     send vultures screaming for clouds they
  would never reach.

Not far behind,
       another thud pursued her.

Dry grass and slab rock
                let go of the earth and flew to
     the sun.
           Brush in big clumps let go of the earth too
and covered the sun.

Anna the Hyena wanted to fly.
                  She even tried, hopping once,
hopping twice,
        but no wind lifted the wings she'd never have.

    So she just ran and ran
              with the buffalo until she couldn't
     keep up anymore.

               Anyway, the buffalo ran for an
      elsewhere that
         Anna the Hyena had no interest in. She
understood
       that their direction,
            like the direction of the
vultures and the clouds,
       was not for her.

    She had only herself
           and whatever strength she alone could
     summon.
          So she ran for the deeper grass.
She ran for the line of
      deeper trees beyond the deeper grass.

    She ran alone.

Until the clods of dirt and
heavy slabs of rock flew back
to the earth in front of her.
Brush too flew back
to the earth
trailing tall branches of angry smoke.

Anna the Hyena leapt over
the fallen earth and veered
around the burning brush and
paid no mind to the falling
pebbles
still falling around her.

And though her legs ached and bit,

and something in her left hind leg bit
harder
with each lunge,
and though her ribs heaved
and hurt
and her jaw hung slack
to chunk down more air,

which never seemed enough air,

her tongue dangling to the side,

tasting the lion smell, the sharp smell, the fear smell,

Anna the Hyena ran still harder.

The thuds behind helped to urge her on.

So did the snaps and cracks.

　　　　　　　　　　　　　　The flashes too.

　　　　But fear, most of all,

　　　　　　　　kept her going.

And then something else

　　　　　　　　　　　　washed down her throat,

　　　　rushing all around her,

　　　　　　　　　　　from somewhere up ahead,

　　a cool taste,

　　　　　　blackgreen and watery

　　　　　　　　　　　　　like quenching whirls

　　　　that keep black stones slippery.

In the wide churn of the day's

　　　　　　　　　　　burning and panic, it was

only a thin ribbon,

　　　　　　　　but it was an unbroken ribbon,

and it grew stronger

　　　　　　　with every surge forward.

　　　　This kept Anna the Hyena going.

This thin ribbon of air promising throat-quenching.

This thin ribbon of air promising coolness.

This thin ribbon of air promising shelter.

And the more she ran

                               the wider that ribbon grew

       and the wider it grew

                     the more it promised peace.

But Anna the Hyena was

                             not blinded by her nose

            and dangling tongue.

                      She did not forget the snaps behind her.

She obeyed the thuds

                falling all around her as well as the ache

and heave

                in her chest. She heeded all the warnings

        and world

              blurs racing after her.

    Loud and fast.

            And unflagging.

                    Sturdy men perched

  atop black spinning eyes which

                    paid the ground no mind and

only seemed to move faster.

              And though the jeep with its five

     sturdy men was still far

              away, soon enough it would cut off

Anna the Hyena from

             the deep line of trees offering that

  ribbon of

        peace-promising cool air.

                    Some of the sturdy men

pointed spindly sticks against the day

                    and they flashed like

fallen stars and cracked like falling trees.

                 And the closer they

got, the brighter their teeth flashed

and the louder their

Haaaaaaaaaaaaaaaaaaas!

and **Wooooooooooooooooooots!**

grew.

One sturdy man

released a part of himself

that was round and small

against the blue sky and

Anna the Hyena watched

how this round

and small and spinning thing flew ahead

until it disappeared

in the tall grass, where, with a terrible

flash, the tall grass

surrendered itself to the sky, which refused

the tall grass and

sent it back to the earth, twisting and

burning

with black, clawing smoke.

The rib-thumping thud followed after.

It knocked Anna the Hyena to the side,

and knocked her

head, and worst of all knocked away

the cool ribbon of air,

leaving behind only the sharp smell

and the man smell and

the killing smell, and Anna

the Hyena was lost.

She didn't stop but she did

slow, her hind leg biting more,

her poor chest heaving more,

even as she swiveled her head

from side to side,

        this time spotting a second jeep

coming from the opposite

        direction, packed with still more

men

    and their spindly star sticks

        and white-bright teeth.

That was when he overtook her.

        Anna the Hyena had not

   seen him or heard him

      or caught his smell on the air.

He looked like

      one of the nasty nipping hyenas.

Strong and very fast.

      He was twice as fast as Anna the Hyena,

and as he matched

    her he did not slow, or look, or even

  grabble at her

    as he passed by, determined to outrace

those spindly men

    with their cracks, snaps, and flashes borne

  along upon

    their accelerating jeeps, determined to

cut him off,

   cut her off,

     cut off everything.

The nasty nipping hyena

     did not slow or change course.

  Why should he?

       He was so fast

and so strong.

  He did not smell of panic or fear.

He left behind a wake of that smell
that speaks of power and
dominance. And blood too.
Not his own blood either.
Anna the Hyena was not that strong,
and while she didn't
know her own smell, she knew
she did not reek of power
and dominance, and the blood
she smelled was her own
blood coming from her flayed
flank and biting hind paw.
And maybe a nasty nipping
hyena who was not so fast
might have pushed
Anna the Hyena to run a little faster, but
this one was so fast,
Anna the Hyena just snorted, slowed,
and, finally,
where the nearby grass stood tallest and stillest,
she stopped
completely and there
dropped her head.
No more nasty nipping hyenas shot by.
No more buffalo.
Not even vultures flapped overhead.
Only men, with stars
falling by their hands, forests falling
by their teeth, roared
closer and closer. Anna the Hyena
just lowered her head
still more. Because for Anna the Hyena
there was nowhere left
beneath the cloudscraped sky to go.
She dropped her haunches.

Tall grass … Tall grass … Tall grass … Tall grass … Tall grass … Tall grass …

She dropped her belly. She
dropped her head until it
rested on the ground, amid the tall,
still grass where she panted
and finally just waited. Afraid.
But before the jeeps
could reach her, a bat-eared fox
sprinted by. Anna the Hyena
surprised the little fox but
she did not frighten him. The way
she had pressed the whole
of herself against the ground
showed submission and defeat.
He probably smelled
her fatigue and her wounds.
So he didn't
change direction or even jump aside.
The little bat-eared fox
just disappeared into a very large hole.
This was the first time
Anna the Hyena had noticed this hole.
Probably because,
unlike other hyenas, Anna did not like holes.
She preferred
the open, or any place that was wide to wind
and rain and sun
and moon and traveling smells.
Anna the Hyena had always
been a little different from others.
Now though, with sturdy
men drawing closer and closer in
their swift jeeps, Anna
the Hyena forced herself to approach
the dark gap in the earth.
Fox smell here. Old-bone smell too.
And something else.

Inside, Anna the Hyena found two

　　　　　　　　　　　　　old moons waiting for her,
　　　guarding his old-bone smelly hole.

　　　　The fox growled at her too but

　　　　　　　　　　　　Anna the Hyena
still shoved herself forward.

　　　　　　　　　　She had no choice.

She had nowhere else to go.

　　　　　　　　　The roaring jeeps kept growing
louder and louder with more

　　　　　　　Wooooooooooooooooooots!
and **Haaaaaaaaaaaaaaaaaaas!**

　　　　　　　　　　　and more cracks,
snaps, and thuds, getting closer and closer,

　　　　　　　　　　　　until it seemed like
a strange sky screature was striding across the land,

　　　weighing too much for any land or sky to bear.

Anna the Hyena kept scrambling forward

　　　　　　　　　　　and the two old moons
kept retreating backwards too,

　　　　　　　　　though never so far as to
disappear. Anywhere else,

　　　　　　　Anna the Hyena with one belly
grunt and snap would have

　　　　　　　　　jaw-crunched down in one gulp
this petulant creature,

　　　　　　　but down here, these narrows
robbed her of breath as the earth pressed

　　　　　　　　　into her sides, clamping down
　　around her, harder and harder,

　　　　　　　the farther along she
　　　　crawled, until

Anna the Hyena
              could crawl no more, wedged
          in by clay and root,
              whimpering.

The two old moons drew closer then.
                        Angry over her intrusion,
    her weakness, and something else.

    After all,
                there was something back there all this time,
a stir of darkness,
                movement beyond the darkness, which
    the little fox refused
                to let her know, which Anna the Hyena
suddenly knew in her
                own wounded deep, what she could
    never call her own.

All of which she forgot when the great sky screature above took
another terrible step
                        closer.
                        Much closer.

The jeeps so much nearer.
                Almost on top of them.

Anna the Hyena yelped and shoved herself as deep as she could
            into that old-bone smelly hole. So deep her nose
almost touched the little fox's nose.
                Two old moons neither
    yelped nor moved.
                Instead, the little fox curled up its lip
to reveal its long teeth.

Anna the Hyena curled her lip
to reveal her longer teeth.

Then neither moved.

Curled lip to curled lip.

Sharp teeth to sharp teeth.

All while the jeeps raced overhead and jeering men lobbed
wounds of themselves to turn the earth overhead.

That's when the sky screature seemed to
                              come down all around
Anna the Hyena.

And the earth darkened

as the earth heaved

and Anna the Hyena cowered
                              within the darkenings and
heaving
                  as her ears heard a falling too much for
any ear to hear.

The little fox heard it too and also heard no more.

But still neither retreated.

          There was nowhere else to go.

Lip to lip.

Tooth to tooth.

Still.

Until the sky screature moved on.

And the jeeps drove on.

Until whatever snaps, cracks,
          and thuds they conjured
seemed like an ebbing memory.

          Anna the Hyena
   shook her head then
          to shake off the memory

and tried to back out of the hole.

          But the earth refused her.

Jaws of rock, root, and clay had clamped

down on her ribs

and would not let her go.

On top of it, those somethings

began to stir behind the little fox.

And the little fox with eyes

old as moons obeyed his kits.

He did not uncurl his lip

or try to retreat. Instead

he lunged forward and sank his

teeth deep into the nose

of Anna the Hyena.

The bite hurt more than the bite of the earth.

It surprised Anna the Hyena too!

She squealed at once

and clawed and snapped,

scrambling back against the trap

until rock and root

and all that comes of the earth's

long hold on life

and on all that life becomes after life's done

had no choice but

to let go.

Unmake her grave

for the old fox with two eyes

old as moons

guarding over all he had left.

For them too.

Out in the day, Anna the Hyena shook herself off,

                                         jumped

once,

            circled twice,

                    before limping off.

      No more little foxes.

                      No more jeeps with sturdy men.

No more buffalo smells

                or vultures stilled against a wind.

Only twists of smoke rose to reach

                    what Anna the Hyena

would have to dream about to touch.

                      And silence held.

But it did not hold forever.

                  And as her hearing returned,

    Anna the Hyena discovered the thuds and cracks,

growls and screeches were gone.

                    Only the wind

whippered of unplaceable devastations.

        Then familiar smells regathered to warn her:

sweat-damp dirt was cloaking her shoulders,

                  blood was

leaking from her flank and hind leg.

Though mostly the blood she smelled,

       she tasted, inhaled in
bubbles, swallowed in drips,

     from the little fox's bite.
And not only blood.

     Anna the Hyena inhaled hurt and
swallowed that too.

    Or tried.

There was too much hurt to swallow it all.

       Not just her snout.
 Her lungs and sides splintered

     every time she breathed.
Her shoulders and hips

    shrieked every time she turned.
 Most of all,

   her back paw sliced and dulled and sliced again
and sometimes

   vanished altogether whenever she took a step.

     And that wasn't all.

Something inside her was wrong.

 As if something deep, deep inside her was lost.

     Anna the Hyena stopped.

 Here was lost too.

    Here lay the nasty nipping hyena.

                                        The strong and fast one.

    Who once smelled of

                power and dominance and blood.

He still smelled of blood.

        Though now the blood was his own.

    Now he was nothing of anything else.

    Now he was not even himself.

    Now he was just meat.

Most of his head was torn off,

                his shoulders mutilated by

    the departure,

            ribs crisscrossed and splintered,

coils of his belly

      steaming on the grass.

                    Flies

  covered his carcass.

         Any other time, Anna the Hyena

would have nuzzled

              the guts and ground down

  the bones with her back teeth

             gulping down shreds of flesh.

She would have eaten and eaten

               until the only thing left to

   eat already filled her belly:

              hunger's slumber.

    She would have enjoyed herself.

Cawing branches. Arched roots. Green leaf lifted flutter. *(repeated in a swirling, spiraling pattern across the page)*

But something was different now.

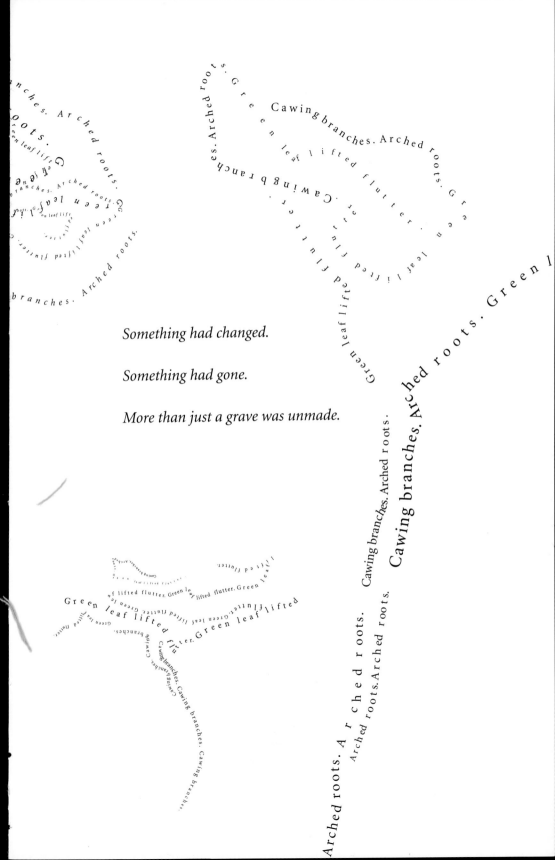

Cawing branches. Arched roots. Green leaf lifted flutter. Green leaf lifted flutter. Cawing branches. Arched roots. Green leaf lifted flutter. Green leaf lifted flutter. Cawing branches. Arched roots. Green l

Something had changed.

Something had gone.

More than just a grave was unmade.

Cawing branches. Arched roots. Cawing branches. Arched roots. Cawing branches. Arched roots. Green leaf lifted flutter. Green leaf lifted flutter. Green leaf lifted flutter. Green leaf lifted flutter. Green leaf lifted. Arched roots. Arched roots. Arched roots. Cawing branches. Cawing branches. Cawing branches.

And all Anna the Hyena could do was limp on.

Then as sound kept returning, so again did smell.

Beyond blood smells,
she again
 found the sharp smell
  and the killing smell
and the hot smells, and then she found
  again
the cool ribbon of air
 which had grown wider and stronger.

Now it was no longer a ribbon
 but a river
flowing beyond this deep grass
 past the line of deeper trees.

To where Anna the Hyena limped and loped.

To where Anna the Hyena loped and trotted.

To where Anna the Hyena stumbled,

 sometimes yipping
with pain,
 as she finally crawled in the shadows of trees,
and slid down under the crouching brush,
 and without a yip or
yelp sprawled at the bottom,
 where she pulled herself along
a sandy way
 beneath clawing branches and arched roots.

whirls keeping black stones slippery . . . a cool taste . . . blackgreen . . . whirls keeping black stones slippery . . . a cool taste . . . blackgreen . . . whirls keeping black green . . . whirls keeping black stones slippery . . .

. . . a cool taste . . . blackgreen . . . whirls keeping black stones slippery . . . a cool taste . . . blackgreen . . . whirls keeping black stones slippery . . . a co

. . . a cool taste . . . blackgreen . . . whirls keeping black stones slippery . . .

. . . a cool taste . . . b l a c k g r e e n

Until the crouching brush thinned and the branches lifted.

Until the ground softened.

Until the cooler smell was all around.

. . . a cool taste . . . blackgreen . . . whirls keeping black stones slippery . . .

. . . a cool taste . . . blackgreen . . . whirls keeping black st

. . . a cool taste . . . b l a c k g r e e n . . . whirls keeping black stones slippery . . .

pery . . . a cool taste . . . blackgreen . . . whirls keeping black stones slippery . . . a cool taste . . . blackgreen . . . whirls keeping black stones slippery . . . a cool taste . .

hirls keeping black stones slippery . . .

. . . a cool taste . . . b l a c k g r e e n . . . whirls keeping black stones slippery . . .
tones slippery . . . a cool taste . . . blackgreen . . . whirls keeping black stones slippery . . .
taste . . . blackgreen . . . whirls keeping black stones slippery . . . a cool taste . . . blackgreen . . . whirls keeping black stones slippery . . . a cool taste . . . blackgreen . .
. . . whirls keeping black stones slippery . . .

No more sharp smell. No more killing smell.

There was even the giggle of ripples.

What not even the taste of her own blood could drown out.

ones slippery . . . a cool taste . . . blackgreen . . . whirls keeping black stones slippery . . . a cool taste . . . blackgreen . . . whirls keeping black stones slippery . . . a co
. . . a cool taste . . . blackgreen . . . whirls keeping black stones slippery . . .
blackgreen . . . whirls keeping black stones slippery . . .

. . . whirls keeping black stones slippery . . . a cool taste . . . blackgreen . . . whirls keeping black stones slippery . . . a cool taste . . . blackgr

reen . . . whirls keeping black stones slippery . . .

And so with great relief,

                Anna the Hyena approached the edge

of blackgreen water with

              the quenching whirls that keep

black stones slippery,

            and she sunk her muzzle into

      the gentle wash

                  and she drank

         and drank.

. . . a cool taste . . . b

And though the fox's bite

              flared and hurt more

when the water touched it,

           the pleasure the water gave

      in return

           when it touched her throat

outmeasured the pain.

. . . a cool tas t e . . . b l a c k g r e e n . . . whir

whirls keeping black stones slippery . . . a coo

whirls keeping black stones slippery . . . a cool taste . . . blackgreen . . . whirls keeping black stones slippery . . . a cool taste . . . blackgreen . . .

stones slippery . . . a cool taste . . . blackgreen . . .

. . . whirls keeping black stones slippery . . . a cool taste . . . blackgreen . . . whirls keeping black stones slippery . . .

. . . a cool taste . . . blackgreen . . . whirls keeping black stones slippery . . .

. . . a cool taste . . . blackgreen . . . whirls keeping black stones slippery . . . a cool taste . . . blackgreen . . . whirls keeping black sto

. . . a cool taste . . . blackgreen . .

kgreen . . . whirls keeping black stones slippery . . . a cool taste . . . blackgreen . . . whirls keeping black stones slippery . . . a cool taste . . . blackgreen . . . whirls keep

whirls keeping black stones slippery . . . a cool taste . . . blackgreen . . .

. . . a cool taste . . . blackgreen . . . whirls keeping black stones slippery . . .

keeping black stones slippery . . .

taste . . . blackgreen . . . whirls keeping black stones slippery . . .

Here at last was safety.

Here at last was peace.

Anna the Hyena kept drinking and drinking
until she could
fill herself no more
with coolness and safety and peace.

Only then, when she stopped lapping,
did Anna the Hyena
realize the lapping had not stopped.

This thin ribbon of throat-quenching. This thin ribbon of coolness. This thin ribbon of shelter.

What had her nose failed to find?

What had her ears failed to catch?

What had her eyes failed to glimpse?

This thin ribbon of coolness. This thin ribbon of throat-quenching. This thin ribbon of shelter. This thin ribbon of throat-quenching. This thin ribbon of coolness. This thin ribbon of shelter. This thin ribbon of coolness. This thin ribbon of throat-quenching. This thin ribbon of shelter. This thin ribbon of coolness. This thin ribbon of throat-quenching. This thin ribbon of coolness. This thin ribbon of shelter. This thin ribbon of throat-quenching. This thin ribbon of coolness. This thin ribbon of shelter. This thin ribbon of throat-quenching. This thin ri

There!

Across from her

        also drank a swirl of
speed and might.

        Gold and violent.

The brutal limits of what

        Anna the Hyena could never
overpower.

    Never outrace.

So Anna the Hyena never even thought to try to escape.

Anna the Hyena sighed instead

                                   and then settled back

   on her hind haunches.

Which was when the lion looked up.

For Regina Marie Gonzales